The Cavendon Luck

BOOKS BY BARBARA TAYLOR BRADFORD

Series

THE CAVENDON CHRONICLES
Cavendon Hall
The Cavendon Women
The Cavendon Luck

THE EMMA HARTE SAGA
A Woman of Substance
Hold the Dream
To Be the Best
Emma's Secret
Unexpected Blessings
Just Rewards
Breaking the Rules

THE RAVENSCAR TRILOGY
The Ravenscar Dynasty
The Heir
Being Elizabeth

Others

Voice of the Heart
Act of Will
The Women in His Life
Remember
Angel
Everything to Gain
Dangerous to Know
Love in Another Town
Her Own Rules
A Secret Affair
Power of a Woman
A Sudden Change of Heart
Where You Belong
The Triumph of Katie Byrne
Three Weeks in Paris
Playing the Game
Letter from a Stranger
Secrets from the Past

The Cavendon Luck

BARBARA TAYLOR BRADFORD

ST. MARTIN'S PRESS
New York

Doubleday Large Print Home Library Edition

THE CAVENDON LUCK.
Copyright © 2016 by Beaji Enterprises, Inc.
All rights reserved.
Printed in the United States of America.

For information, address St. Martin's Press, 175 Fifth Avenue, New York, N.Y. 10010.

ISBN 978-1-68331-043-3

For Bob, with all my love always

The Cavendon Luck

CONTENTS

PART ONE:
The Inghams & The Swanns: 1938

PART TWO:
Women & War: 1939–1945

Part One

The Inghams & The Swanns
1938

Predictions

Tinker, tailor,
Soldier, sailor,
Rich man, poor man,
Beggar man, thief.

—an old English nursery rhyme

One

Cecily Swann Ingham stood on the outside steps of the office annex at Cavendon Hall, glancing around. What a change in the weather, she thought. From a gloomy, overcast morning it has become a radiant afternoon.

Blue sky. No clouds. Brilliant sunlight filtering through the leafy trees. A perfect day in late July. A smile of pleasure touched her face fleetingly.

Walking down the steps and crossing the stable yard, she headed for the dirt path through Cavendon Park which led to Little Skell village.

Cecily thought suddenly of her son's birthday earlier in the month as she strode ahead. It had poured with rain that day and spoiled their plans for the garden party. The celebration was held indoors in the end. She couldn't help wishing it had been a glorious day like this. On the other hand, David hadn't minded about the weather. It was his ninth birthday and he had enjoyed every moment, as had his brother, seven-year-old Walter, and their sister Venetia, who was five. It had been a happy time for the family, and that was what counted most, their enjoyment derived from the festivities, and what Miles always called the "gathering of the clan."

Later that night when they were in bed, Miles had drawn her closer to him, and had wondered out loud where all the years had gone. She had said she didn't know and had reminded him that time always flew when they were together.

He had laughed and pulled her even closer, stroking her hair. After a moment, she had added that they had been busy raising three children, going about their own business and keeping Cavendon safe.

She recalled how he had murmured his thanks for all that, had wrapped his arms around her, then slipped on top of her, kissing her, touching her tenderly. Within seconds they were making love to each other with the same excitement and joyousness they had always known.

Suddenly, remembering that night so clearly, she couldn't help wondering if he had made her pregnant on their son's ninth birthday? They had both been so eager for each other, and intense. It had been a passionate night.

The idea of pregnancy lingered. She was thirty-seven. If she **was** pregnant, then so be it. I must think of another child as a gift, because soon my childbearing years will be over. But having a child with war coming? This thought troubled her. She pushed it away, and hurried on toward the village. And her mind turned to the huge amount of work she and Miles had done to make Cavendon Hall and the family safe. Her brother Harry had plunged in too, as well as her four sisters-in-law. They had been hard years in so many ways.

Each of them had made all sorts of sacrifices, and had frequently used their own money to keep everything afloat.

But they had done it.

The Inghams and the Swanns, pulling together, had accomplished miracles. Cavendon was now set on the right course. And it was safe.

Yet even now, today, there was that awful little knot in her stomach. Earlier, Cecily had put this down to her worry about Harry plus her concern for Greta, her personal assistant, but she knew instinctively that neither were the real reason for her anxiety.

It was something entirely different, and it troubled her constantly, nagged at her, gave her sleepless nights.

Germany's menacing Third Reich was casting a giant shadow across Britain, as it had done for the longest time over Central Europe. And that was causing her tension. The Reich was sinister and dangerous, and the threat of war hovered. Cavendon would be at risk if there was an invasion…the whole country would be at risk. And Europe, too. The whole world, actually. She understood that only too well.

When Cecily came to the walled rose garden she paused, then pushed open the heavy oak door and went down the steps. The fragrance of late-blooming summer roses enveloped her instantly. She breathed deeply and sat down on an iron garden seat. Leaning back, she closed her eyes, endeavored to relax for a few moments.

This lovely old garden had not changed for centuries and it was a tranquil refuge for her, as it always had been since she was a child. She sat in here almost every day if only for a few minutes. She loved the scent of the roses, the peacefulness behind the high brick walls. This place soothed her troubled senses, helped her to clear her mind, sort out her worries.

Her thoughts went to her mother. Cecily knew she was busy with preparations for war, working with the women in the three villages who were members of the Women's Institute. It was run by Charlotte, who was the president. They were quite an amazing collection of village women, and had come up with solutions to make life easier if war did come to their shores.

Of course it will come, Cecily muttered to herself. The prime minister, Neville Chamberlain, believed he could appease Adolf Hitler, who had already annexed Austria and was eyeing Sudetenland in Czechoslovakia.

On the other hand, Winston Churchill understood the futility and terrible danger of appeasement, and kept on warning the government that war was imminent. Churchill was right, she was certain of that. Horrific as that thought was.

The drone of a low-flying aircraft cut off Cecily's thoughts, and she jumped up, lifted her head to the blue sky, and that first flash of fear dissipated at once.

The small plane did not bear the emblem of Nazi Germany, the swastika. It belonged to Noel Jollion, the nineteen-year-old son of Commander Edgar Jollion of the Royal Navy, who lived on the other side of Mowbray village, near High Clough. The commander had built an airstrip in a long field on his land at Burnside Manor because his son loved flying.

Returning to the garden seat, Cecily sat down, and tried to throw off her concern about the war. But she was finding it difficult this afternoon. It was on her mind.

Last week Hanson had taken her and Miles down into the vast cellars of Cavendon, where he showed them the preparations he had begun to make for war.

The cellars were always crisply clean, with whitewashed walls and well-swept floors. Hanson had pointed out a stack of cots which he had brought out of storage.

There were sofas, armchairs, and small tables, all of which had been brought out of storage in the attics. The earl had told him to make the cellars as comfortable as possible, in case they had to live in them. Also all of the paintings and objects of art would be placed in the lower vaults as soon as there was a declaration of war between Britain and Germany, he had told them.

It seemed to her that Hanson, as usual, had been his efficient self. There was even a refrigerator which had been purchased at Harrods and delivered by a Harrods van. What would they do without Hanson? He was supposed to retire in December. He was seventy-six and had been in service at Cavendon for fifty years. She for one hoped that wouldn't happen. He looked as fit as a fiddle and they needed him.

Reluctantly, Cecily left her sanctuary, and continued on her way to her parents' house in the village. But first she must stop at the Romany wagon where Genevra lived. She needed to talk to her.

Two

When Cecily turned the bend in the dirt path she immediately saw Genevra, who was sitting on the steps of the wagon, waiting for her. As usual, she was wearing an old Cecily Swann frock, given to her by Cecily's mother. It was red-and-white-striped cotton, a summer frock, and it suited her.

The Gypsy raised her hand and waved.

Cecily waved back, smiling. She noticed that there was a wooden chair waiting for her. This thoughtfulness pleased her.

Genevra had an excited expression on her face, an expectancy about her. She was thirty-nine, the same age as Miles, though she did not look her age, appeared to be much younger. She was still a good-looking woman, dark, exotic, and her abundant hair was as raven black as it had been in her youth.

When they had moved their wagons to the lower field, five years ago, Genevra had invited

Cecily into her wagon for the first time for a glass of mint tea. Not wishing to hurt her, feeling bound to accept this invitation, Cecily had gone inside and had discovered, to her enormous surprise, a treasure trove.

Genevra was an artist, and a talented one at that. The paintings on the walls of the extremely neat living area had astonished Cecily. They were landscapes of Cavendon for the most part, and executed in brilliant, vivid colors. Later, DeLacy had told her they would be categorized as being in the naïve school of painting.

Yet they had a style, a genuinely unique style of their own. Genevra's style, Cecily called it. The paintings were bold, commanding, caught the eye at once. But it was the shimmering look of the bright colors, the odd sheen on the canvas that captivated everyone, and at once.

Cecily had soon found out that Genevra had been painting since her childhood. Gervaise had encouraged her, and when she was older he had bought her canvases and oil paints when he could afford them. She was totally self-taught, a natural and gifted artist.

Cecily had instantly asked if she could buy one of them. Genevra had refused that day. Instead she had offered her a painting as a gift. In the end, Cecily had chosen one that was evocative, and very meaningful to her. The painting showed a corner of the high wall in the rose garden, and a profusion of late-blooming roses…a fusion of many different pinks and faded reds against a portion of the gray stone wall.

Genevra came down the steps to greet Cecily, and as always she did a little bob, a sort of curtsy, as she took Cecily's outstretched hand in hers.

"I put out a chair, Mrs. Miles," Genevra said, indicating the wooden chair.

"Thank you," Cecily murmured, and sat down.

Genevra returned to her place on the steps.

Cecily stared at Genevra, frowning. She thought she looked a bit pinched, tired. "You haven't been sick again, have you?" she asked worriedly. She had not seen her for ten days.

Genevra smiled faintly. "No. Not sick. **Good**."

"You look a bit peaked to me."

"I'm not sick, liddle Ceci," Genevra muttered, eyeing her knowingly. "I'll be first ter knows that. Then I'll tell yer, and yer'll be the second ter knows. Not dying. Not yet."

"Don't be cross, I care for you, Genevra."

"Aye, I knows that, Mrs. Miles."

"I'm going away on Monday with Miles. We're going to visit Lady Daphne and Mr. Hugo in Zurich. If you need anything while I'm gone, my mother will help you." She smiled at her. "You just have to go and see her."

Genevra nodded. "Yer going on holiday.

Mrs. Alice tell me that."

"Just for two weeks. Miles needs a rest..." Cecily's voice trailed off. She had suddenly noticed a strange look on Genevra's face. "What is it? Is there something wrong?"

"The sight. It just comes over me. Yer knows that."

Cecily nodded, remained quiet. After all these years, she knew she had to be still. And mute.

"Yer'll have ter be brave, liddle Ceci, as yer've allus been. There'll be deaths. War is coming. Big war. Bad times. Terrible things coming." The Romany woman halted, closed her eyes. After a moment she opened them, added, "Yer'll rule at Cavendon. I've allus knowed that."

"Why now?" Cecily asked, a frown settling on her face.

"What do yer mean?" Genevra sat staring at Cecily.

"Why are you telling me this **now**? Usually you're somewhat secretive, not always so open."

"'Cos I knows yer believes me, tek me predictions as truth...understand 'em."

"I do, yes, that's true, Genevra."

"The future. Yer'll have that, Ceci. And yer **will** rule."

"With Miles?"

Genevra did not answer, staring up at Cavendon Hall towering on the hill high above them. The golden house, shimmering in the sunshine. A blessed house.

"When you sound strange like this I don't really understand what you mean," Cecily protested, returning Genevra's hard stare.

"Bad times are coming."

"Do you mean the war?"

Genevra inclined her head. "**Life.** Hard times. Bad times. Death, destruction, sorrow, pain. Much suffering. All coming."

Turning her head, Genevra looked at Cavendon once more. Unexpectedly, tears filled her eyes. The golden sheen which usually gilded the walls had vanished. It was no longer golden. It was doomed. The great stately home was covered in shadows...shadows growing darker and darker. In her mind's eye she saw huge black clouds floating around its rooftop. She heard thunder; there were streaks of white lightning.

After a while, Genevra finally opened her eyes, said in a low tone, **"Turmoil. Chaos."** She shook her head, became silent, and wiped the tears from her face with her fingertips.

There was a long silence.

Cecily said, "Cavendon has been lucky over the past few years. The luck will last, won't it? Nothing will change, will it?"

"It allus does. Good luck. Bad luck." Genevra shook her head, and leaned forward, her gaze penetrating. "It comes. It goes. Nobody knows …Luck belongs ter nobody…luck belongs ter life. Nowt yer can do about it, liddle Ceci. Do yer understand me?"

"I do, Genevra, and I thank you."

Three

When the front door suddenly flew open, Alice sat up with a start, and then instantly jumped to her feet as Cecily walked in, a huge smile on her face. Hurrying forward, Cecily took hold of her mother and kissed her, hugged her close.

"Sorry I'm late, Mam," she said, and then turned and closed the door behind her.

"I was just doing paperwork, no problem, Ceci," Alice murmured, and mother and daughter walked into the room together. They sat down in two armchairs facing each other, and Alice said, "You look bonny today, love, but pale pink has always suited you."

"I know, and thanks. You look pretty good yourself, Mam."

"Of course I do, I'm wearing a dress my daughter made for me. I like it, and it's comfortable and cool on a hot day like this."

"I've made another version of it, also in cotton," Cecily confided. "It's a sort of wrap dress, almost like a robe, and it ties at one side. I'm doing the same style for the winter collection made of light cashmere. I'll bring you several when they're ready."

"Thank you, love, you're always so thoughtful."

"Don't be silly, you're my mother, you can have anything you want from me. Anyway, when we spoke on the phone yesterday you said you were making a plan. But for what?"

"I came up with an idea. Creating a communal allotment for the village. I went straight to Charlotte and asked her for a field. And she asked the earl, and he agreed it was a wonderful idea, very practical, and he immediately gave me a field."

Alice nodded as she finished her sentence, looked a little pleased with herself. "That's how it came about and it was as simple as that... just asking."

Alice stood up, and beckoned to Cecily. "Come over to my desk, and pull up a chair. I want to show you my plan."

Within seconds the two of them were sitting side by side at Alice's desk, where her Women's Institute papers were spread out, along with the detailed plan of the field which was going to be the communal allotment. This would be planted and tended to by the women who wished to do this work.

Turning to Alice, Cecily said, "It **is** a practical

idea. Food will be a problem if war comes."

"**When** it comes," Alice corrected.

"Too true," Cecily agreed, and then said in a slightly odd tone, "You could just as easily have asked Miles for a field, or even your son. Harry does run the estate with Miles, you know."

"You're right, I could have done that, Ceci. But I don't think that would have been the correct thing. The sixth earl is still the sixth earl; he's not dead yet, and it is his land. I thought it only proper to approach him, via Charlotte."

"I understand now, Mam," Cecily answered, offering Alice a warm smile.

Looking down at the large sheet of paper, she saw how cleverly the field had been designed to work as an allotment.

Each square patch was marked, and the name of the vegetable to be grown there written in. "Potatoes, carrots, parsnips," Cecily read out. "Onions, sprouts, cabbage, cauliflower..." She stopped, suddenly laughing, and shook her head. "You're a master planner, Mother! Harry must get his talent for gardening and landscaping from you."

"Goodness me, he's much cleverer than I am," Alice murmured, and turned in her chair. She gave her daughter a knowing look. "Did you manage to speak to Harry? You know...about that...person."

Shaking her head, Cecily replied in a low voice,

"No, I didn't. We were supposed to have a chat earlier this afternoon."

"His affair with that scandalous woman has started to leak out!" Alice exclaimed, her tone suddenly turning angry. "He thinks it's a big secret, but it isn't, and your father now knows about it. He's furious. You know how much his lordship abhors scandal. And scandal is about to flare around your brother."

"I agree with everything you're saying, Mother, but he is a grown man. Forty years old to be exact. He'll tell me it's none of my business."

"But you will speak to him?" Alice sounded anxious, and there was a concerned look in her eyes.

"I will, I promise. I'll do it tomorrow morning," Cecily reassured her mother.

Alice nodded, and pursed her lips. Her voice was more even and steady when she said, "He ought to know better than to get involved with her. Pauline Mallard is a married woman. Furthermore, she's an American heiress, a socialite, living the high life in London and New York. And now in Harrogate. But I suppose you know all this."

"Well, yes, I do, Mam."

"In the end she'll make a fool of him, you'll see. And not only that, she's a lot older than he is."

"But rather beautiful, I hear. A stunning

redhead," Cecily interjected.

"And somewhat promiscuous…that's what I hear," Alice shot back, obviously wanting to have the last word.

"Genevra said something rather odd right out of the blue. She told me not to say anything to Harry about **the woman.** I was really taken aback. Genevra then added that **she** would drop him, that **she** was not his destiny, some other woman was."

Alice stared at her. "How could Genevra know about Pauline Mallard? Do you think he brought her here to his house? And that Genevra saw them together?"

"No, I'm sure not. However, I was struck by the way she said it, so sure of her **sight,** as she calls it, her visions of the future. And then there was her use of the word 'destiny.'" Cecily's voice was puzzled.

She cleared her throat, and went on slowly. "Genevra has her own particular speech pattern, Mam. It's jerky, rather staccato, and mostly her sentences are composed of small words. So I found it curious that she even knew a word like 'destiny,' since she doesn't read."

"Oh but she does!" Alice exclaimed.

"Are you sure?"

"Of course. I taught her."

Cecily was so surprised she gaped at Alice. "When did you do that and why didn't you ever tell me?"

"It never occurred to me. It was just sort of… happenstance. After you'd gone off to live with Aunt Dorothy and Uncle Howard in London, I'd dropped off some of your old dresses for her. She came over to thank me, and asked about you. She was very intense, and it struck me then that she had a strong connection to you, Ceci, and was concerned about you and your well-being. I showed her some of those first little stories about your designs in the fashion magazines. That's when she confessed she couldn't read. I taught her. She learned to read at my knee."

"How lovely of you to do that." Cecily was impressed and it showed on her face.

"She was very appreciative." Alice hesitated for a few moments before finally asking, "Did you ever feel there was this…**connection** between you, Cecily?"

"I did. I still do. She told me twenty-five years ago that Swann will rule. So yes, there is this connection between us."

"What did she actually say twenty-five years ago?" Alice asked, filled with curiosity.

"It wasn't actually what she **said**…I ran into her one day on the dirt road. She took a long twig and drew a square with a bird perched on top of it in the dirt. I asked her what it meant, and she wouldn't tell me. Then she said it was

nowt, nothing, and skipped off."

"And today she told you what it meant?"

"No, she didn't. I sort of figured it out years ago. The square represented Cavendon Hall and the bird a swan. What she was saying in the drawing was that the Swanns and the Inghams would link up."

Alice did not respond for a moment and then murmured quietly, "She couldn't have known then that your life would turn out the way it did, and that you, a Swann, would marry the son of an earl. So there must be something to her claim to have the sight, to have the ability to foresee the future. You believe her predictions, don't you?"

"Yes. I have always believed them, and I always will." Cecily took hold of her mother's hand. "She's proved it to me. She gave us a piece of paper at our wedding. **Swann Rules,** it said, with the drawing next to it."

After Cecily left, Alice went out to the garden, carrying her watering can. As she moved around the beds, giving the flowers water, her thoughts remained on the Swanns and the Inghams.

Blood. It was her three grandchildren who had the mixed blood: Ingham and Swann. Like Cecily, she sometimes wondered if there really had been other members of the two families who had produced an offspring. Or maybe two.

She had no idea.

Only Charlotte Swann Ingham would know that. She had the record books that dated back for centuries, locked up in a safe, a safe now at Cavendon Hall. It was in her dressing room. After telling her this, Charlotte had handed her a sealed envelope, and told her the new code for the safe was inside. "Please give it to Cecily and tell her to lock it up," Charlotte had then instructed, and this Alice had done.

Putting the watering can down, lowering herself onto the garden seat, Alice sat for a moment or two looking out toward the moors. It was the end of July on Sunday, the first day of August on Monday. That was when the heather would start to bloom and within a week the moors would look like a rolling sea of lavender.

David, Cecily's first son, had eyes the color of the moors, the lavender eyes so unique to the Swanns. Otherwise, he was the spitting image of his father, Miles, with his features. Walter had them too, but he had also inherited Cecily's coloring and her chiseled features. As for five-year-old Venetia, she was a true Ingham through and through with her golden hair and bright blue eyes. Alice smiled to herself, thinking how much Venetia resembled Lady Dulcie when she had been the same age.

Grandchildren. They were very precious, and she would love to have more. Harry wanted a family. He had said that a few months ago. He would like to be married, he had confided, so he could have a child, several children, in fact.

He had the makings of a good father; there was no doubt in her mind about that. But Pauline Mallard, believed to be forty-eight, was certainly past the childbearing age. A spurt of anger erupted in Alice. Instantly, she pushed it away. She wasn't going to dwell on that woman.

Within a few seconds her natural compassion overcame her anxiety about Harry, and her annoyance with him. She suddenly felt a rush of sympathy for her son.

Four

Greta Chalmers put the receiver down and let her hand rest on it for a moment. She felt as if she had a tight band around her chest and tears brimmed in her green eyes. She swallowed them back and blinked a few times.

She had never heard her father sounding so despairing and morose, and she knew the reason why. He saw no way out of his predicament, no solution to his dilemma. At the end of their conversation he said, "I'm trapped. We're trapped. There's nothing anybody can do, **liebling.**" After telling her he loved her, that they all loved her, he had hung up.

And she loved **them:** her father, her stepmother, Heddy, her half sister, Elise, and half brother, Kurt. They lived in Berlin but being Jewish they had now come to realize that they must leave as soon as possible, escape the dangers of the monstrous Third Reich. They wanted to come to England; they knew they had a home with her until they found a place of their own. They had passports but no visas, no travel papers. They were stuck, as her father had just said.

Greta's mind raced. So many ideas were jostling around for prominence. She glanced at her watch. It was now almost three-thirty and Cecily would be coming back into the office at any moment. Taking control of herself as best she could, Greta let go of the phone, sat up straighter, arranged the collar of her cotton dress, and smoothed one hand over her dark brown hair.

Reaching for the last letter she had typed she put it in the folder, reminded herself that she must be composed when Cecily arrived. She knew that Cecily worried about her, and her father's problems. But so far she had not come up with a solution. No one she knew had, and she did have a number of good friends in London. Her employer had also turned out to be a true friend who had her best interests at heart.

The moment they met Greta and Cecily had "clicked," as Cecily termed it. They had taken to each other at once and had been on an even keel ever since. Never a cross word, never a step out of place on both their parts.

Cecily often joked about their compatibility, the way they were frequently thinking the same thing at the same time. "May babies, that's why," Cecily had said after their first year of working together. They were both born in the first week of May, but Cecily was six years older than Greta.

She loved her job as Cecily Swann's personal assistant, and even though there was a lot of work, her boss worked just as hard as she did. They found satisfaction in their careers, and sometimes Greta shuddered when she remembered how she almost hadn't gone for the interview at the shop in the Burlington Arcade. Cold feet, timidity perhaps, or even her lack of experience had got in the way for a while. But in the end she had gathered up her courage and gone to meet the famous designer. And she got the job. She had started working at Cecily Swann Couture the next day.

Following Cecily's earlier advice, Greta took her small notebook out of her handbag and picked up a pencil. She would make a list, as Cecily had suggested, writing down everything she had to do to make her house ready for her family.

Yesterday, when she had arrived at Cavendon, Cecily had told her to be positive about the future, reassuring her that her family would make it out of Nazi Germany eventually, that she would have to take them in. Greta wanted to do that, and to cherish them.

Many times in the last few years, Greta had wished her husband, Roy, were still alive. He would have taken care of this situation in no time at all, made short shrift of it. But he was dead and gone. Five years ago now, and he had been far too young to die.

Bending her head, Greta began to make a list of extra things she would have to buy to make her house in Phene Street more comfortable—

"Here I am!" Cecily cried, hurrying into Greta's office. "Sorry I'm late when you've got your train to catch."

"I've plenty of time. Goff said we should leave at four-thirty for me to get the six o'clock to King's Cross."

"So we can relax for a moment, and have a chat. I'll sign my letters and go over my appointments with you. What do I have in London on Monday?"

"There aren't too many," Greta answered. "I kept the day light since you're leaving for Zurich on Tuesday."

After signing her letters Cecily looked across at her assistant and said carefully, "Did you manage to get hold of your father?"

"I did, and he sounded a bit down in the dumps, to be honest." Greta was surprised her voice was so steady.

Cecily nodded. "Of course he did, he's troubled and frustrated. But look, I'm going to try to help you solve this. And you know what I'm like when I get my teeth into something."

Despite her worries, Greta laughed. "A dog with a bone."

"That's true," Cecily answered. "When there's a problem I have to solve it, and quickly, before it gets out of hand. I need help regarding this matter, Greta. I'm sure you realize that. I do have someone I can talk to, who might be able to guide me in the right direction."

Greta simply nodded. She had total faith in her, knew that if anyone could help it was Cecily—this beautiful and talented woman whom she trusted totally.

Cecily was crossing the grand entrance hall at Cavendon a little later when she heard the sound of music. Instantly she stopped, stood still for a moment listening intently.

The magical sounds were coming from the yellow drawing room and the piano, a recent addition, was being played by Daphne's daughter Annabel. No one else could conjure up such miraculous music on the ivory keys the way she did.

The fourteen-year-old had been playing since her childhood. It was her passion and she was superb. Cecily was forever telling Daphne how gifted she was. And good enough to be a concert pianist one day, she always insisted.

Daphne merely smiled serenely, no doubt because she believed the same thing yet did not want to admit it. The lovely Daphne, to whom Cecily was devoted, was far too refined to push her children forward for accolades. But the five of them were talented and very clever. Alicia wanted to be an actress, Charlie a journalist, and the twins intended to join Hugo in the world of finance.

Continuing across the hall, knowing she was yet again running late for afternoon tea, Cecily headed for the drawing room. She opened the door and stood on the threshold, peering in.

She let out a small sigh of relief when she realized she was not the last after all. For once. Aunt Charlotte and the earl were already there, and so was Lady Gwendolyn. Annabel, of course, was still sitting at the piano, starting a new piece. It was Beethoven's **Moonlight** Sonata. Obviously Diedre had arrived from London earlier than usual. She sat between Lady Gwen and her son, Robin, who was eleven, and was busy chattering to her, filling her in. As he usually did, he was spending the summer at Cavendon with his cousins.

Her own brood, David, Walter, and Venetia, were at the children's table on the other side of the drawing room. This was an innovation of Charlotte's, who believed they would enjoy afternoon tea better if they had their own private table. The children had jumped at the idea. There were two empty chairs, obviously for Robin and Annabel.

As she stepped forward Cecily heard a little shriek of delight. Venetia had spotted her. A small bundle of joy composed of an angelic face, blond curls, and bright blue eyes hurtled toward her, her face wreathed in smiles.

Crouching down, Cecily caught her five-year-old daughter in her arms and hugged her. She whispered, "You see, I kept my promise. I'm not the last today."

Venetia's blue eyes sparkled with laughter and her face was filling with dimples. She whispered back, "Daddy will be last, Mummy. LAST!"

Suppressing her own laughter, Cecily looked at her and shook her head. "Maybe not, darling. Where's Aunt DeLacy? Is she hiding somewhere in the room, do you think?"

Giggling, shaking her head, Venetia whispered, "She'll be the last?"

"I think so," Cecily answered. This was a little game between them. Cecily was generally always the last to arrive for tea, and Miles teased her about it. Her little daughter would protest about his teasing and now Venetia was obviously thrilled to bits that her mother had arrived before her father this afternoon.

Taking hold of Venetia's hand, Cecily led her

into the room, smiling at everyone and greeting them affectionately. Walking over to the children's table she kissed her sons, David and Walter, who were grinning at her and nodding their heads. They were also pleased she had made it before Miles; that was quite clear and very obvious. Cecily was highly amused.

Robin stood up and went to kiss her, then hurried over to the children's table, followed by Annabel. She bent over and kissed Lady Gwendolyn, and said, "How beautiful you look in your purple frock, Great-Aunt. It still suits you."

"Thank you, Cecily, and I must tell you, it's several years old. But then you know that." Lady Gwendolyn chuckled, went on. "I'm very thrifty, and I keep all of the clothes you make for me. It's a good thing your other clients don't, or you'd be out of business in no time at all."

Nodding her agreement, Cecily sat down between Lady Gwen and Diedre. She turned to Diedre, said sotto voce, "Can I speak to you later? A work thing."

Diedre merely nodded her agreement.

Looking across the room at her, the earl said warmly, "Thank you, Ceci, for allowing Greta to do those few letters for me this morning. It was a great help."

"It wasn't a problem, and she was happy to help out."

Charles Ingham gazed at his daughter-in-law, a loving expression in his eyes. He treated her like one of his own daughters these days, and he admired her tremendously. "I feel sorry for Greta. She worries so much about her family, and feels helpless to do anything. Has she heard from her father lately?"

"As a matter of fact she spoke to him today. Professor Steinbrenner believes they are stuck in Berlin for the moment."

The earl's face was serious when he began, "Things are bad in Europe. And we—"

Charlotte interrupted him swiftly. In a low voice, she murmured, "Let's not discuss Europe and what's going on...in front of the children." She had just noticed that David and Robin were listening intently to their grandfather's conversation. "Little pigs have big ears," she finished in a low tone.

Before Charles could make a response, the door flew open and DeLacy came into the room in a rush, looking flushed and out of breath.

"Hello, everyone!" she exclaimed, and went immediately to her father and Charlotte, kissing them both. Gliding across the floor she went over to Lady Gwendolyn, and sitting down next to her, DeLacy squeezed her hand, leaned in, kissed her cheek. "You asked me for news of Dulcie and James when you phoned me at the gallery the other day. I'm happy to tell you I received a letter from Dulcie this morning—"

"Sorry, Charlotte, sorry, Papa, for being late. Couldn't avoid it. I had to take an important phone call," Miles announced, entering the room on the heels of DeLacy.

"It's not a problem, Miles," the earl said.

"You're forgiven," Charlotte added, her voice warm and welcoming. He had always been a favorite of hers.

"You're late, you're late, you're late," sang a chorus of young voices all sounding very gleeful indeed.

Venetia began to giggle, and so did Cecily, and just at that moment the door opened and Hanson strode in, looking purposeful.

Focusing on Lord Mowbray, he asked, "Shall we serve tea, my lord?"

"Yes, please do so, Hanson. Now that everyone has arrived."

Inclining his head, Hanson turned on his heel, beckoned Gordon Lane, the underbutler, to come in with the largest tea trolley filled with a silver tea service, cups, saucers, and plates. Gordon was followed by two of the maids, also pushing trolleys laden with tea sandwiches, scones, strawberry jam, and Cornish cream. There was a cream cake and a variety of delectable pastries.

Cups were filled, plates of sandwiches were passed around, and once again afternoon tea was served in the same way it had been for years. It was a ritual everyone enjoyed.

Once the staff had moved the trolleys to the back of the yellow drawing room, and everyone had settled, Lady Gwendolyn spoke out. "Now come along, DeLacy, do give us the news from Hollywood, U.S.A."

"I will indeed," DeLacy answered, putting her cup in its saucer. "Dulcie and James are well, as are the twins, Rosalind and Juliet, and little Henry. In fact, the children are flourishing. James is halfway through his new movie and enjoying working at Metro-Goldwyn-Mayer. However, Dulcie and James want to come back to England." DeLacy paused and gave Great-Aunt Gwendolyn a pointed look. Her eyes went to her father, Charlotte, and her sister Diedre.

Lady Gwendolyn said, "I believe we know the reason. A true-blue Englishman like James must feel it's his duty to be on these shores at this particular and dangerous moment in history. And knowing Dulcie I'm quite certain she feels exactly the same way."

"Oh, no question about that," Charles said, then glancing at Charlotte he asked, "Don't you agree?"

"I do indeed. And you know that Dulcie's an Englishwoman down to her toes."

Miles, jumping into the conversation,

exclaimed, "I suppose they'll leave California when he finishes the picture."

"Hopefully, yes," DeLacy answered her brother. "However, according to Dulcie there might be a problem. James has a big contract with MGM. Apparently Louis B. Mayer, who runs the company, is a great fan of his and signing James was a coup for him. Dulcie thinks he might not want to release James from the contract."

"Because he has other films to make, I suspect," Diedre asserted. "A signed contract is very binding as you well know. Not only that, James is a big money earner for MGM. Of course they won't want to let him go."

Cecily interjected, "But everything's negotiable. I'm sure there is a way around the problem, should one develop." Glancing at DeLacy, she smiled at her dearest friend. "What about Felix and Constance? I thought they were in America at the moment, DeLacy."

"Yes, in New York. They'll be going out to Los Angeles next week. Dulcie's praying Felix will be able to handle Mr. Louis B. Mayer."

Staring at DeLacy curiously, Miles asked, "Why do you refer to him by his full name? It sounds so odd."

DeLacy laughed. "It does, doesn't it? But that's how Dulcie refers to him in her letters, and I guess I just picked up on it, repeated her words."

"I am perfectly certain Felix Lambert is a great agent and quite a crafty fox and Constance as well," Diedre said. "Leave it to them. They'll come up with something. After all, they are professionals. I've discovered it's always a good idea to leave it to the pros."

Cecily nodded. "I couldn't agree more. And from my experience with him, Felix is bound to pull something out of the hat."

DeLacy nodded. She then addressed her father. "You'll be very pleased to know Dulcie is thrilled with the way I've been running her art gallery. Especially since we've been making huge profits, and especially this year. It should make you happy as well, Papa. You'll be getting quite a large check from the gallery for the Cavendon Restoration Fund."

"I am delighted, DeLacy. Well done, darling," her father said.

"I say, that's great news, old thing," Miles exclaimed. Rising, he went over to his sister, leaned over and hugged her. "And it's true, you have been doing a fabulous job."

DeLacy smiled up at him. "Thanks to you. You're the one who has trained me how to run a business. And so has Ceci."

Miles half smiled, and went over to the children's table. Before he could say a word, a little chant started. "Late, late, late. Late, late,

late."

He ruffled the hair of Walter, who was the leader of this choir. "You're all little rascals. Very naughty boys, don't you know?"

"Am I a naughty girl?" Venetia asked, staring at her father, her eyes dancing.

Walking around the table, standing next to her chair, he said softly, "I suppose you are. But that doesn't mean I don't love you, Venetia." He smoothed his hand over her white-blond hair. "And you are definitely my favorite daughter."

"Oh, Daddy, don't be silly. There's only me."

"I sometimes feel there are quite a few of you lurking around."

Five

The arrangement they had made was to meet in the conservatory just before dinner, but Diedre was not there when Cecily arrived. Walking across the terra-cotta floor, she went over to the French doors, stood looking out at the moors rolling toward the North Sea, admiring the view. It was familiar but never failed to please her.

Twilight had descended and the sky was already growing darker. It was a deeper blue and the far horizon was streaked with a mixture of colors...lavender and apricot, and a deep pink bleeding into red.

Red sky at night, shepherd's delight, red sky at morning, shepherd's warning. These words ran through her head as she remembered how often her mother had said them to her when she was a child.

Turning away from the window, Cecily strolled over to the desk, ran one hand across the mellow old wood, and lovingly so. How often she had stood here, talking to Daphne, who had made it her desk, having commandeered it when she was seventeen and facing terrible problems in her young life.

The conservatory had soon become Daphne's private place, her haven. None of the family ever used it, and so she had taken it for herself.

From here she had planned her marriage to Hugo, a joyful event, and later it had become her command post.

This was when her mother, Felicity, had run off to join Lawrence Pierce in London, leaving the entire family shocked, her husband stunned, and her children shaken up. And she had never come back.

Daphne had had no alternative but to take over the running of Cavendon Hall for her father; she had done an excellent job until Charlotte became chatelaine once she was married to the earl.

After a moment longer, lingering near the desk, Cecily walked across to a wicker chair, part of a grouping, and sat down. Her thoughts turned to Diedre. Cecily knew that the best person to talk to about Greta's family and their predicament was Diedre. In 1914 she had gone to work at the War Office and had remained there after the Great War had ended. Only when she became engaged to Paul Drummond did she resign.

Cecily knew how grief-stricken she was when Paul had unexpectedly, and very suddenly, died; she had helped her as best she could through that devastating first year of widowhood. One day, quite unexpectedly, Diedre had confided she was returning to her old position at the War Office. She had explained that work would ease her grief and loneliness. Also, she had explained, there was going to be a war, a very bad war, and she would be needed.

Although Diedre had never discussed her job at the War Office, Cecily was quite positive she worked in intelligence, and Miles agreed with her. Therefore, if anyone knew how to extract someone from a foreign country, she was sure it was Diedre.

Cecily's thoughts now turned to Greta. She had grown very attached to her and cared about her, worried about her well-being. Her assistant was extremely sincere, had enormous integrity, and was a hard worker; certainly Cecily had grown to depend on her. She had great insight into people, especially those who were meaningful to her; Cecily knew how much Greta was suffering because of the situation that existed in Berlin.

Greta's father was a well-known professor of philosophy. He had studied Greats at Oxford years ago, and become an expert on Plato. In fact, he ranked as one of the greatest professors in his field. Greta adored him. She was fond of her stepmother, Heddy. As for her two half siblings, Kurt and Elise, they were almost like her own children, and she worried about them constantly. Cecily hated to see her suffer and was mortified that she herself could do nothing to help. Leaning back in the wicker chair, Cecily closed her eyes, her mind whirling with all manner of wild ideas about rescuing them.

The sharp click of high heels on stone brought Cecily up sharply in her chair when Diedre strode into the conservatory, looking elegant in a navy-blue silk dress which Cecily had made for her.

It was cut on the bias and made Diedre look taller and even svelter than ever. But then Diedre had long been known for her chic fashion sense, spending much of her time in London.

"You always make my clothes look so much better," Cecily exclaimed, her face filled with smiles.

Diedre laughed. "Thank you for the lovely compliment, but it **is** the dress, you know that. And it's become my favorite." Diedre sat down in a chair, and said, "You sounded anxious earlier. So let's talk. What's wrong?" Like Great-Aunt Gwendolyn, Diedre got straight to the point.

"Greta's family is Jewish. They need to get out of Germany. I would like to help her if I can.

But I need advice. Your advice, actually."

When she heard these words Diedre stiffened in the chair. She shook her head vehemently. "That's a tough one. Hard. And there's no advice I can give you, Ceci."

"Her father, stepmother, and their two children don't have the proper travel documents apparently. They're at their wit's end," Cecily said, and fell silent when she became aware of the look of dismay on Diedre's face, the fear in her eyes.

Diedre, who was acutely observant, understood people, knew what made them tick, was aware Cecily was being genuine and sincere about wanting to help Greta. Yet Cecily was unaware how hard a task that would be. Not wishing to be too quickly dismissive, Diedre now said, "You told me a bit about Greta, when she first came to work for you. Please fill me in again. I've forgotten most of what you told me."

"Greta is German by birth, like her father. But her mother, who died when she was a child, was English. Her name was Antonia Nolan. After her mother's untimely death, her father sent her to live with her grandmother, Catherine Nolan, who's still alive, by the way, and lives in Hampstead. It was she who brought Greta up."

"Now it's all coming back to me," Diedre murmured. "She went to Oxford, didn't she?"

"Yes, following in her father's footsteps.

Eventually, her father remarried, but Greta stayed on in London, preferring her life here."

Diedre nodded. "And I remember something else. Greta married an Englishman, an architect."

"That's right, Roy Chalmers. Sadly he died of leukemia about six years ago now."

"Just out of curiosity, is Greta a British citizen? It occurs to me that with an English mother and an English husband, she must have become one. Didn't she?"

"Yes, and she has a British passport."

"I'm glad to hear it, and that passport is important here, a necessity in wartime. It won't help her family in any way, but I'm relieved to know she can't be interned, anything like that."

"She could be if she were a German? Is that what you're saying, Diedre?"

"I am."

"Well, she's all right, protected by her English nationality. Still, she has been talking about going to Berlin to check up on her father, assess the situation," Cecily murmured.

"She mustn't go! No, no, that's dangerous."

"Perhaps I could go instead. What do you think?"

"Absolutely not. I won't let you. There's something else...her father might well be under scrutiny. He's a famous man, could easily be on a list of troublemakers, so-called. Being watched and not knowing it."

"She'll be very upset if that's true," Cecily exclaimed.

"Don't tell her what I said. She must not know. And she certainly cannot go to Berlin." Diedre sounded stern as she continued. "Look, I'm sorry to be negative, but the situation in Berlin is worse than you can possibly know, or even imagine. It's dangerous, full of thugs, foreigners, and Nazis, a sinister city. No one is safe."

Cecily nodded. "I understand. And I do make a point of listening to you. You're the one who knows what's going on there better than anyone else I know."

"A few months ago a new rule was made. Jews were forced to go and have their passports stamped with the letter **J** for Jew." Diedre said this quietly.

Cecily gaped at her, aghast. "What a hideous rule!"

"Yes, it is. Everything they do is hideous. No, horrific." Diedre leaned forward, coming closer to her sister-in-law, went on in a lower voice, "Hitler was made chancellor of Germany in January of 1933, and only months later he built the first concentration camp. It was opened in March of 1933. It's called Dachau."

"Jews are interned in the camp. Is that its purpose?"

"That's right, it is. And so are others... Catholics, and dissident politicians, and **anyone** who doesn't agree with the Nazi credo. Anti-Semitism is rife. Hatreds fester. Violence is paramount. And people are arrested for no reason at all." Diedre gave Cecily a long hard stare. "Hitler became a virtual dictator in January of 1933 and he means to swallow up as much of Central Europe as he can."

"Why? Power? Does he want to rule the world?"

"Yes. But he also wants land, the blessed **space,** to breed his perfect race of Aryans. **Lebensraum**...that's what he calls it...this dream of land, on which to create a master race."

Cecily was pale, and her eyes were fastened on Diedre. "I don't frighten easily but what you're telling me does make me worried," Cecily confided softly.

"Worry if you want, Cecily, but don't be afraid. We must all be brave and strong. And we must make sure not to have our necks under the German jackboot. That would be disastrous."

Diedre paused. "Look, Ceci, please don't repeat any of this to the family. I shouldn't really have told you. I trust in your confidentiality and your loyalty to me."

"You know you can trust me. But could I tell Miles?"

"Yes, you can. However, he must be discreet as well. No chitchatting with Charlotte and Papa. You must insist on that."

"I will." There was a slight hesitation before Cecily went on, "Yours **is** an office job, isn't it? I mean, you're not out there, are you? Out there doing…**things**?"

"No, I'm not. I'm…well, let's say I'm in management. Nevertheless, I have my own rules and I do not forget them."

"What are they? Can you tell me, Diedre?"

"Believe no one. Tell no one. Remember everything. Walk alone."

Six

Instinctively Harry Swann knew that something was wrong. Pauline had not been herself since his arrival at four o'clock, ostensibly for tea. They actually did have tea in her elegant drawing room. But it was swift. She was anxious always to retreat to her bedroom for several hours of intimacy and extraordinary passion.

Now as he lay next to her in bed, their sexual appetite for each other sated, he endeavored to figure out why she had been so strange. Not remote, not distant, as she often was, rather she had been distracted. Or perhaps preoccupied was a better word. Certainly he had picked up on it the moment he had entered her house and when she had greeted him coolly in the entrance foyer.

Even when they first began to make love she had been less fervent than usual; but once he had begun to arouse her in the way she liked she had become more focused. She was a voluptuous woman, extremely erotic and sensuous, eager for sex, hungry for it, and she oozed feminine lust. Her craving for him was enormous and endless; she gave herself willingly to him, did anything he wanted. It had been this way since the beginning of their affair and they never failed to give each other enormous sexual pleasure.

They had done that this afternoon, but instead of lingering in his arms, touching him, stroking him, murmuring loving words, she had moved onto her side at once, her back to him.

Puzzled and slightly hurt, he finally spoke. "What's wrong, darling? You've turned away from me, and you're very silent. Usually you're full of love for me...after we've devoured each other. And we certainly did that a short while ago."

There was a moment of silence before she said, "I've misled you...and I'm feeling guilty."

Pushing himself up on one elbow, Harry brought her face around and looked down at her. "Guilty in what way?"

"I let you think Sheldon was coming home tomorrow. He phoned at lunchtime today. He said he'd be here for dinner tonight. You've got to leave, you can't linger as you generally do."

Genuinely taken aback, Harry gaped at her for a split second, then got up and hurried across the room, making for the chair where his clothes were laid.

Pauline leaped off the bed and rushed after him, put her arms around him and pressed herself close to his body. "I can't bear for you to leave like this. We always make love again before you leave. Always. Let's do it now, here, standing up. Come on, I'll lean against the door." She reached up, pulled his face down to hers and kissed him passionately. He responded; he never failed to do so with her. He felt himself growing hard, and just as he was about to succumb to her red-hot desire for him, his common sense kicked in.

"No, no, we can't. It's too risky," he said firmly, glancing at his watch. "It's almost six-fifteen. Sheldon could be here any moment and we'd be caught red-handed."

Pauline shook her head. "No, he won't make it before seven, I'm certain of that." She leaned against the door, staring at him, her desire running high. She was hot with longing for him, had never wanted anyone like this, never loved any other man before him. And she knew she could not have him. Unexpected tears welled and she moved back and into his arms so he would not see them.

But he had. He held her tightly, stroked her long auburn hair. "Why are you crying?"

"Because you're angry with me...because I didn't tell you he was coming home tonight," she lied. "Say you forgive me, Harry. **Please**."

He looked down at her and smiled, touched her face with tenderness. "There's nothing to forgive, my Pauline, my dearest love. I was startled that's all, not angry, never with you."

Reaching for his clothes Harry rushed over to her bathroom.

Pauline stood watching him moving across the bedroom, struck yet again by the beauty of his lithe body, and the tears came back, rolled down her cheeks. Slipping into her dressing room, she closed the door, stood for a moment wiping away her tears. Then she picked up a towel, placed it on the padded stool before sitting down.

They had made love several times this afternoon and she was full of him. He might have made her pregnant. She hoped so. But she was forty-eight. Too late, wasn't it? She breathed deeply. The scent of his cologne, Jicky, and the smell of him was all over her.

She reached for a bottle of perfume, was about to spray herself, but changed her mind. She wanted his smell on her. There was a knock on the door and she went to open it.

Harry stood there, gazing at her. A slow smile slid across his face. "You look beautiful." He took hold of her arm, tightened his grip and brought her closer. "You'd better get dressed," he said, and asked, "Will you be alone next week?"

"I suppose so." She touched his face gently. "I'll phone you as soon as I can."

Harry nodded, and let go of her arm. And he was gone.

Pauline turned away from the door, dressed swiftly, attended to her hair and makeup. Usually she bathed after their lovemaking but not today. She wanted his seed in her, wanted his baby, yearned to have part of him for the rest of her life. A son or a daughter. It didn't matter as long as it was **his.**

Pauline Mallard went downstairs to wait for Sheldon Faircross, her husband, knowing he would be arriving shortly. Crossing the floor of the library, she went to the drinks table and filled a glass with sherry. She stood for a moment, staring down into the pale liquid, her mind still on Harry Swann.

In some ways she regretted meeting him and having an affair with him, because he had, in a sense, ruined her life. She had fallen in love for the first time. That was **verboten**. And now she knew she would have to let him go. A divorce and remarriage was not in the cards. Harry could never be hers. She was in a trap.

When she had married Sheldon fifteen years ago she had agreed to play by his rules. He would sort out the mess of her finances, created by her first two husbands. Both of them had spent a great deal of her inheritance from her father, the late Allan Mallard, one of America's greatest tycoons.

With Sheldon's help, her financial affairs were in better order, but she was not quite the great heiress she had once been. Nevertheless, she was by no means poor. And neither was Sheldon; he was a millionaire many times over.

Sheldon's rules were very simple. A self-made man, he wanted the prestige of her name, her beauty and elegance on his arm and at the head of his dinner table. He also demanded her total loyalty.

However, because he had no interest in her sexually, preferring young men, he had told her she could have her love affairs as long as she was discreet. Also he had made her swear she would never reveal his own sexual predilection.

She had willingly agreed at the time. Not only did she have her own money intact again, she had the legitimacy of marriage to a well-known tycoon, a wonder on Wall Street, but also Sheldon's great fortune to spend as she wished. And permission to have as many affairs as she wanted. Sheldon had made it clear that her dalliances with other men must be only sexual. No emotional entanglements, he had insisted. And until Harry it had all worked. Now she wanted to marry Harry, be his wife, have his baby. And have Harry all to herself. He was the best lover she had ever had. And a lovely man.

Still staring into the sherry, she thought: I could walk away from Sheldon. He manages my money and has control of it. But money doesn't matter to me. Harry will look after me.

Bringing the glass to her mouth, she swigged some of the sherry, and reminded herself that the money did matter to her. She had been born into it, enjoyed spending it, and she would miss it. If she was honest she would also miss her life on the international scene. Harry would never enjoy that life; he might well be genuinely besotted with her, but he was devoted to Cavendon and the Inghams.

No way out, she thought, I'm stuck. And then she swung around as Sheldon said, "Good evening, Pauline. I see you're alone."

"Hello, Sheldon, and naturally I'm alone."

"Harry's just left, though. I'm certain of that."

Pauline merely nodded and walked over to the fireplace. Sheldon joined her, kissed her cheek. He went and poured himself a single malt and strolled across the room.

"The affair must have run its course by now," Sheldon said, joining her on the sofa.

"I suppose…" was all she could say.

"Harry has no doubt fallen in love with you. They all do, actually. But how do you feel about Harry?"

"He's been gentlemanly, caring. He's a nice man."

"And great in the sack, I've no doubt. He wouldn't have lasted this long with you if he hadn't been hot to trot whenever you beckoned." Sheldon laughed.

Pauline was silent. She hated Sheldon's weird outbursts of vulgarity and discussions about her affairs. She had frequently thought that he might get some sort of kick out of discussing them. In the way some men enjoy voyeurism.

When there was no response, Sheldon said, "I spoke to our friend Tiger this morning. She's invited us to stay with her at the château in Versailles. She's giving a big summer party. We're invited. And I accepted for us both."

Pauline was momentarily startled, then said swiftly, "That's great, Sheldon. She's such a marvelous hostess."

"And she has great taste. In other guests. There'll be a lovely group of delectable men and women staying for the long weekend."

"I see," Pauline murmured, realizing what he was getting at. After a brief pause, she asked, "How's your Italian lover?"

Sheldon grinned at her. "He's run his course. I've sent him back to Italy. I'm fancy-free, my darling, just like you."

"Am I fancy-free?" Pauline raised a brow quizzically.

"Of course. Harry has to go now, Pauline. It's been too long, this affair, and it's becoming serious. Remember, we have a deal, you'll always be married to me, and I'll safeguard your money, and you can have as many men as you want. Just think, Tiger is bound to have someone delicious lined up for you."

Swallowing back incipient tears, Pauline said, "When is this party in Versailles? And are we going to Paris first?"

"We're leaving Harrogate on Sunday. We'll go back to London for a few days. Paris next weekend, then on to Versailles."

"Good heavens, Sheldon, I can't leave on Sunday. You're only giving me tomorrow to pack!"

"All you need is your jewelery and a few clothes, Mrs. Heath will send on everything else. It doesn't matter, really, because I intend to take you shopping at Chanel and Schiaparelli. I also have in mind a few new pieces of jewelry from Cartier."

She nodded, forced a smile. "What great ideas you have, Sheldon," Pauline remarked, understanding that he was taking her away from Harrogate before she could see Harry again. Today was the end of their affair. Sheldon had just made sure of that.

As she sat there, listening to him talking about their Paris trip, she suddenly heard another voice at the back of her head. It was her late father, Allan Mallard, explaining that he never did anything without a lawyer at his side. A bevy of lawyers, if need be. He had said that so many times. Warning her, she supposed.

I need a lawyer, maybe a bevy of lawyers, she thought. High-powered, Manhattan lawyers with clout. They will help me to take back control of my life. My inheritance. A divorce from Sheldon. Then I can go to Harry. We can be married. The mere idea of this made her smile.

Sheldon, as usual scrutinizing her intently, said, "You look happy all of a sudden, Pauline. Why the smile?"

"I was just thinking about the future..." She let the sentence go unfinished, leaning back against the cushions.

"Ah, yes. Our trip to Versailles will be part of that, and lots of fun."

Pauline nodded, her mind racing, making plans to go to New York. She would not allow Sheldon to thwart her. He was about to get the shock of his life. Yet another happy smile spread across her face as she thought of Harry Swann and **their** future together.

Seven

Harry had left Harrogate behind and was driving north heading for Cavendon, filled with relief that Pauline had revealed why she had acted so oddly this afternoon.

He chuckled to himself. How well she knew him after only a few months. If she had told him when he had arrived this afternoon that her husband was on his way back to Yorkshire he would have left immediately. She had not wanted to forgo their tryst and so had kept it from him.

Pauline Mallard. What a unique woman she was. Stunningly beautiful with her luxuriant dark auburn hair, pure white skin, and amber-colored eyes. She had a flair for clothes, and the money to buy the best, and consequently everyone stared at her wherever she went. She caused quite a stir. Women envied her looks; men undoubtedly lusted after her.

He loved her, was devoted to her, and if she finally agreed to divorce Sheldon Faircross he would marry her at once. Not only were they well matched sexually, he enjoyed her company, found her extremely intelligent. Also she was filled with knowledge about so many things, she made a wonderful companion. And she made him laugh with her quirky sense of humor.

As he drove on he thought of a conversation he had had with his mother recently. To his surprise he had found himself confessing that he wanted to get married because he wanted children. Not one, or two, but lots.

How he envied Miles and Cecily with their little brood, and Daphne and Hugo with their five marvelous offspring.

That's what life was all about, wasn't it? Marrying a special woman and creating a wonderful family, a family to love and protect and cherish.

He winced as he remembered his mother's comment after he had confided his wish for children. She had told him in a cold voice that his current lady love was far too old for childbearing; she had added that his secret love affair was about to go public.

When he had tried to explain his feelings for Pauline, his mother had shushed him up, and terminated their conversation.

But he was well aware why Cecily wanted to talk to him. She was going to chastise him and tell him to end his relationship with a woman who was married. His sister disapproved, and there was no doubt his mother had egged Cecily on to have a confrontation with him.

Pauline must leave her husband, that's the only way to go, Harry decided, as he turned off the main road and onto Cavendon land.

And as always when he came back here, even after only a few hours, he felt a rush of happiness, contentment, and a sense of belonging. This land was home...this land he tended and protected with love in his heart. This was where he belonged.

He never saw the girl on the bicycle who was racing down the lane on the left side of Cavendon Road which led into Little Skell village. He was only aware he had hit her when there was a crunching sound, a high-pitched scream, a pair of bare legs in the air, and then a thud.

Pulling on the brake at once, Harry jumped out of the car filled with alarm. He saw the bent front wheel of the bicycle on the ground but there was no sight of the girl. He looked to his left, then his right and was baffled.

A moment later, a girl's voice cried, "I'm here in the ditch. Can you help me, please?" He ran across the road and up onto the grass verge as a mop of curly red hair appeared on the edge of the ditch. The girl was pulling herself up, holding on to tufts of grass and weeds.

Thank God she's not dead, Harry thought. He knelt down on the grass, offered his outstretched hands. She took hold of one of them, and then the other. He pulled her up and a moment later she was crouching next to him, panting heavily.

Harry looked at her, his eyes scanning her swiftly. "Are you injured? Does anything hurt?" he asked worriedly, concerned about her.

"I don't think anything is broken," she answered, frowning. "I do feel a bit shaken up, though."

"I'm not surprised," he answered. "I'm so sorry I hit you. I didn't see you coming down the side lane, I'm afraid. Perhaps I ought to drive you to the hospital in Harrogate, and have you checked for injuries."

The girl shook her head vehemently. "No, no, I'm perfectly all right, but thank you."

Harry said somewhat insistently, "I do think you should see a doctor. You could have internal injuries. Yes, I'd better get you to a doctor."

The girl burst out laughing, and shook her head again. "I'd know if something was damaged. Honestly I would. My brothers say I'm a tough bit of stuff." She half smiled, and went on, "I must apologize. I was riding my bike far too fast. So sorry about that."

Harry nodded, and said, "If you're certain you're all right, I won't insist on a trip to the hospital."

"I am sure." The girl straightened her colorful floral frock, pulled up her white socks, then brushed her hands over the cotton frock. "Not even the dress is damaged," she announced, her eyes twinkling. Thrusting out her right hand, she said, "Thank you for hauling me out of the ditch. I'm Phoebe Bellamy, by the way."

"Harry Swann," he answered, smiling at her, taken with her girlishness, her friendly manner. She had a pretty face covered with freckles and hazel eyes. He thought she was about twelve, and he had no idea who she was. He wondered why she was on Cavendon land.

Giving him a surprised stare, Phoebe cried excitedly, "Are you one of the famous Swanns of Cavendon? You're not related to Cecily Swann, the Fashion Queen of the World, are you?"

Chuckling at this description of Cecily, he answered, "She's my sister."

"Oh gosh! Oh wow! Oh my goodness me! What an honor to meet you, Mr. Swann."

Harry was amused by her undisguised enthusiasm. He said, "And so you are Phoebe Bellamy. Nice to meet you, and I'm truly sorry it was in such an unfortunate way. Now, where does Miss Phoebe Bellamy live? It must be somewhere close."

"It is, Mr. Swann. I'm staying with my uncle,

Commander Jollion."

"I know him well, and his son, Noel, who must be your cousin."

"He is. We're all staying with Uncle Edgar for the whole summer."

Harry got up off the grass and offered Phoebe his hand, pulled her to her feet. "Let's see how well you can walk, and let's hope all is in order. If nothing's hurting I shall drive you back to Burnside Manor."

Together Harry and Phoebe crossed the road to the car. He eyed her carefully as they walked and saw that she seemed perfectly normal.

They both stopped when they came to the broken bicycle. Looking down at it, Phoebe said, "Oh gosh! What shall I do with the bike?"

"I'll put it on the grass verge over there," Harry replied. Picking it up he did so. "I'll send someone for it tomorrow morning. Perhaps we can repair it for you. We have a workshop."

"Oh how nice of you. Thank you, Mr. Swann. I'm so sorry I'm causing you so much trouble. Listen, I'm fine. I can walk back to Mowbray."

"No, you're not going to do that. I shall drive you to the manor and explain to Commander Jollion exactly what happened."

"That's not really necessary, the telling part," Phoebe protested, sounding alarmed.

"I shall take the blame. Now, please get into the car, Phoebe."

Eight

Diedre had not slept well. She had spent a restless night, her mind working overtime, so many thoughts spinning around in her head.

For once she had not been worrying about her father and his health. For the last few weekends he had been almost like his old self, much more vigorous, in good form, with his humor restored. She was aware that she shouldn't ever worry about him. Charlotte loved him and looked after him with great care and diligence. They all owed her a lot.

It had been the favor for Cecily that had occupied her thoughts most of the night, and Greta Chalmers, in particular Greta's predicament.

With her years of experience in British intelligence, Diedre knew there were many different ways to get visas and travel documents, and other means by which to extract people from Germany. The problem with the

Steinbrenners was that hideous **J** for Jew stamped on their passports. Four brand-new passports would be difficult to obtain. It was the same with visas and travel documents. Four were just too many; even two would be hard to come by. Acquiring **one** might be impossible, in fact.

She had two contacts who might be able to help. The one she had asked several favors from was the most powerful. He was in the High Command of the Third Reich, and she knew he would do anything for her, if it was at all possible. Yet she was reluctant to ask him. They had been friends for years; she admired and respected him as a dear friend. She did not want to go to him yet again. And so soon.

Sitting up in bed, blinking in the pale dawn light coming in through the draperies, Diedre bunched the pillows up behind her head, lay back and concentrated on her other contact.

The second one she had to dismiss immediately as well because he was linked to her first contact. He was also in a powerful position in the High Command, and might easily bring his superior down if caught. She dismissed him as well. Also, he would be more useful in other areas.

It struck her that her own man in Berlin was the best to use. He was young but thought fast on his feet, and had a lot of experience.

Also she could telephone him with a degree of impunity.

That was one of her main considerations these days. She had known for several years that telephones were monitored in Germany, and especially foreign phone calls. Undoubtedly the British embassy in Berlin was not immune; she believed the Gestapo listened in, but she and her man there had their own language, which would be Double Dutch to anyone else.

Glancing at the clock she saw it was almost six. The household was still sleeping. Jumping out of bed, Diedre went into her bathroom, washed her hands and face, brushed her teeth, and combed her hair. Back in her bedroom, she slipped on a silk dressing gown, stepped into her slippers, and went downstairs.

Silence reigned. No one was moving about, nothing stirred. No sound except for the ticking of the hall clock. It was just a little too early for Hanson, the footmen, and the maids. But in half an hour, the housekeeper would be on duty, and they would all be bustling around preparing for breakfast, and Cook would be in the kitchen, getting an early start.

It was cool and quiet in the library. Diedre sat down at her father's desk, and leaned back in his big leather chair, thinking for a few minutes. His desk calendar was right in front of her. She stared at it. Oh God, it's **Saturday,** she muttered under her breath. **Saturday the thirtieth of July.** Damn, she thought, then making a swift decision, she picked up the receiver and dialed the overseas operator and gave her the number in Berlin she wanted.

"Hallo?" a man's voice answered gruffly on the fourth ring.

"Is Toby Jung still staying there?"

"Is this his Daffy Dilly?"

"Yes, it is."

"What a pleasure to hear your voice, Daffy. What's up?"

"I left a suitcase with you the last time I visited, Toby. I wondered if you knew anyone who might be coming this way and would bring it for me. I'd pay them."

"I'll ask around. What else is new?"

"Not a lot. How is it in Berlin? I have a friend who might be visiting, she's asked me about the weather."

"Hot as hell. Not a breath of fresh air. The city stinks. We're all sweating. We need a good wind blowing through."

"Weather changes all the time, Toby."

"I know that, angel face. About the suitcase. Is it heavy?"

"I'm afraid so."

"Could one person carry it?"

"I don't think so. It needs another person, maybe two more. But they have porters at railway stations, you know, and I'll provide the gratuities."

"I'll see what I can do. Where are you right now?"

"Looking at the heather."

"For how long?"

"Two days. Why?"

"Just needed to know. I'll get back to you. Next week. At the old place? Will you be there?"

"I will. Thanks, Toby."

"Big kiss, angel face," he said and hung up.

Diedre put the receiver back in the cradle and leaned back in the chair. If someone had been listening in they wouldn't have understood much. But Toby now knew she wanted to get people out. They always spoke in their own code. His message to her had been about conditions in Berlin, relayed through comments about the weather. All she had to do now was wait and see what he could do, if anything.

Hearing her name being called, Cecily turned her head to the left and saw her brother waving to her. He was walking down the stable block, wearing his riding clothes. He always did on Saturdays because he rode around the estate checking everything out on the Ingham land.

She smiled when he came to a standstill next to her, kissed her on her cheek. "You look positively radiant this morning, Ceci," he said.

"Flattery will get you everywhere, as you well know, Harry," she answered with a slight laugh, and added, "And you don't look half bad yourself. Have you done your rounds yet?"

"No. I wanted to see you first. Let's go down to the gazebo where it's cool, shall we?"

"And also very private," Cecily pointed out, falling in step with him.

He glanced at her. "True. Point well taken. But my office was rather warm this morning... it's all this July sun."

"I'm not going to chastise you or anything like that, you know. You're a grown man and have every right to lead your life as you see fit. I just wanted to have a little chat, mostly because of Mam."

Harry exclaimed, "She's not ill, is she?"

"No, of course not, but she is concerned about you."

"I know" was all he said.

They walked on in silence, lost in their own thoughts. After a while it was Cecily who spoke first. "I want to thank you for helping Walter with his riding, Harry. He's always been a bit frightened of horses, as you well know, and you've managed to banish that fear, and he loves his riding lessons with you."

"And the horse I bought him. She's a gentle little filly and he's making wonderful progress. I'm rather proud of him."

"He told me yesterday that he's catching up with David, and that soon he'll ride better than his big brother."

Harry chuckled. "I think he's on the right track. By the way, I had a weird experience last night, I knocked a girl off her bicycle."

Startled, Cecily stared up at him, frowning. "A bicycle? Where? Not here on the estate, surely?"

"Yes, it was. She came hurtling down the main Cavendon Road leading into the village. I didn't see her." He told Cecily the story without any embellishment, and finished, "She turned out to be Phoebe Bellamy, the niece of Commander Jollion, and when she found out I was a Swann she wanted to know if I was related to Cecily Swann, the Fashion Queen of the World."

Cecily burst out laughing, then shook her head, highly amused. "I've never met Phoebe, but her mother is Commander Jollion's sister, Adrianna. She has quite a big family. About seven children."

"My goodness, that's quite a brood. But she only mentioned two brothers," Harry said as they went into the gazebo. They sat down opposite each other, and Cecily explained, "Mam's not angry with you, Harry, just concerned—"

"About the possibility of gossip," he cut in, his

face gloomy.

"I suppose that does worry her a bit, because of your position here. But she's more concerned that you're **on a road to nowhere,** as she put it. You told her you want children and very much so, and she thinks that's not going to happen because Pauline Mallard is too old."

Harry nodded and now a reflective expression slid onto his face. "Mam's right, Pauline is forty-eight, and she herself thinks the same thing. Her childbearing days are more than likely over. At least that's what Pauline believes."

"She doesn't look forty-eight, so much younger."

"That's what I said when she told me her age. She's been very honest and open with me, Ceci. Pauline's a good woman."

"A married woman," Cecily said very softly, reaching out, taking hold of Harry's hand on the table. Holding it tightly, she said, "Listen to me, I'm your sister and I know you better than anybody. Therefore, I know you must be madly in love with her to keep this affair going." Cecily paused, shook her head slowly, finished, "But it's going nowhere."

When Harry remained silent, Cecily murmured, "I suppose she has an unhappy marriage, right?"

"Yes, she does. Sheldon travels a lot, and, well, it's not an intimate relationship, from what she's told me."

Cecily couldn't help sighing. "Oh Harry, Harry, that's what they all say, be it a man or a woman who is committing adultery. It's the same old story, and has been for centuries. Forever, I suppose."

"In Pauline's case I think it's true. He has other interests…in a different direction."

"What do you mean?" She lowered her voice when she asked in a cautious tone, "Do you mean he's a homosexual?"

"She never said that, just that it was not intimate," Harry answered sotto voce. "And he had different tastes."

"I'm not surprised she didn't say anything else. He could be sent to jail."

He nodded. "I believe her, Ceci, and that's that. I do know it would be hard for me to leave her."

"Has she ever mentioned getting a divorce?" Cecily asked, her eyes focused on Harry.

"She says he'll never agree to a divorce, and that we have to make the best of it."

"I don't think you should make the best of it, as Pauline calls it! You're stuck with a woman too old to have your children, and one who obviously won't get a divorce for some reason."

Leaning forward Cecily said emphatically, "Harry, please be sensible, think of yourself. And your future. You're forty years old. Get out now and go your own way. You will meet someone, I just know you will."

"That's very funny talk coming from you. I can remember your litany...you always said you could never love anybody else but Miles. And that's how I feel about Pauline."

"It's hard, I do know that, I really do. Mam thought it might be a good idea if you could get away for a while, take a holiday. Actually, I wish you could come with us now...to Zurich."

Harry half smiled. "I run this estate with Miles, and when he's away I have to be here. That doesn't mean I wouldn't enjoy a holiday with you both in Zurich. I love being with you and Miles. The thing is, though, you take your problems with you, wherever you go. And before you naysay me, those are words **you** once said to **me** about your feelings for Miles."

Cecily nodded, filled with love for her brother, and also understanding his situation, his emotions. He was in love with a woman he couldn't marry, one who most likely couldn't bear his children. Cecily didn't want to chastise him, or question him, only to comfort him. And encourage him to move on. She wished she could introduce him to someone special, but she did not have anyone in mind at the moment. Anyway, he would resent her interference.

Rising, Cecily said, "I'm here for you whenever you need me, Harry, and so is Miles."

Harry also jumped to his feet, and he took hold of her arm affectionately. "I know that, and thank you for caring."

They went up the path together without speaking, holding hands. He broke away when they arrived at the stable block. After kissing her cheek, Harry murmured, "I'll look after David and Walter while you're gone, Ceci. I love them, you know."

She nodded. "You're the perfect uncle," she responded.

He smiled at her and walked off.

She watched him go, thinking what a good-looking man he was, and how kind and caring. And he did love her children. That was only too apparent in the way he spent time with the boys, and taught them so much. What a wonderful father he would make and certainly a good husband.

Walking toward the terrace she could not help thinking what a sad life her brother had. He loved Cavendon and his job. He and Miles were the closest of friends and worked well together. He was popular with everyone, and much admired and surrounded by loved ones here.

But he was alone, living in the house Great-Aunt Charlotte had given him. **All alone.** He must be filled with hollowness inside. He cooked his own meals. Or he went across the village street to their parents' house, or ate at the village pub, Little Skell Arms. He was not a social animal and was mostly on his own.

It's not fair, Cecily suddenly thought, with a rush of anger. That woman is using him. I wish I could find a way to break them up. My brother deserves better. And I'm going to make sure he gets it.

Ten minutes later there was a knock on Cecily's bedroom door, and Diedre was saying, "Can I come in?"

"Yes, of course," Cecily called out, and went over to the door as Diedre walked in, smiling, and holding a dress. It was one she had recently purchased from the Burlington Arcade shop.

"Is there something wrong with it?" Cecily asked, eyeing the dress.

Diedre glanced around. "Well, I'm not sure about the pleating on the side. I hope I'm not disturbing you and Miles? Is he in your sitting room?"

Cecily shook her head. "No. He's out in the garden with the boys, and Venetia is helping Nanny to cut some flowers for me. You want to speak to me alone, is that it?" she asked, her mouth puckering into a smile.

"That's right." Diedre put the dress over a chair. "As usual it fits me perfectly. It was just a ploy, a reason to come and see you."

"Let's sit here. If Miles comes back sooner than I expect, he'll make for the sitting room. He always does."

Diedre sat on the sofa next to Cecily. "I don't want to get your hopes up high, but I did speak to a contact of mine. This morning. In Berlin. He's going to see if there's any way he can help Greta's family."

"Oh how wonderful!" Cecily exclaimed, her face lighting up.

"Don't get excited, Ceci. And don't say a word to Greta. Or anyone else for that matter. Not even Miles. There is a huge problem for the Steinbrenners, and that is their passports. They need brand-new ones, as I told you yesterday. Too many to get at one time, in my opinion. The family may have to be extracted one at a time, over many months."

"Oh no, that would be so difficult for them," Cecily protested. "Greta will be upset."

Diedre gave Cecily a hard stare, and her face was grave. She said, "You must understand that this is the hardest thing to do. Virtually impossible now. Greta won't have a say in it. If I can get just one person out I'll be lucky. And so will that person. Who would the family member be? What do you think?"

"I have no idea. From what I know about the professor, I am sure he would want his children to leave first. If it's only one then I think he would pick Elise, his daughter. But I can ask Greta and—"

"You cannot speak of this to Greta!" Diedre cried sharply. "I just told you that, Cecily! **No one can know.** The choice will have to be made at the last moment. Please say you understand what a tough thing this is to do. And dangerous."

"Yes, I do, I'm sorry, Diedre, if I'm sounding stupid."

"You're not, and I know you don't realize what the situation is like in Berlin. The Gestapo are everywhere, and the SS, and everyone is under suspicion. I'm sorry I snapped at you but someone will have to do this for me, and it could cost them their lives if they are caught."

Cecily had turned pale. She nodded. "I wasn't making light of it. I realize what a serious matter this is."

Diedre reached out and squeezed her arm. "Secrecy is imperative. Nothing can be said to Daphne or anyone else when you get to Zurich. You do know that?"

"I do. It's between the two of us. I will never betray you." Cecily clenched her fist and stretched out her arm. "Loyalty binds me," she said.

Diedre did the same, and put her clenched hand on top of Cecily's. "Loyalty binds me," she answered, repeating the Ingham family motto.

Foreign Intrigue

Jack be nimble, Jack be quick,
Jack jump over the candlestick.

—an old English nursery rhyme

Nine

Daphne fell in love with the Villa Fleurir on Lake Zurich the first time she saw it just over twenty-four years ago. Hugo had taken her to Paris for their honeymoon and then they had traveled on to Switzerland where they had stayed for some time.

The villa was spacious, with large rooms flowing into each other, and all of the colors used were soft, muted: cream and white, pale pink and peach, and the lightest of blues.

It was an airy and welcoming place and there was a certain informality about the house and its furnishings which Daphne had never changed, loving its sense of ease and comfort.

Mellow antiques were placed here and there in most of the rooms, intermingled with large, comfortable sofas and chairs covered in lovely fabrics, and there were beautiful paintings on the walls. All these furnishings enhanced the rooms, gave them a certain familiar look, but the villa was by no means decorated in a full-blown traditional style, which frequently looked far too stiff to Daphne.

Its informality had led her to create a more casual way of living over the years, especially after more of their children were born, and everyone loved staying at the villa, be it summer or winter, because of this. Cavendon was their home, but with a great house came responsibilities, expectations of certain standards. Over the years the villa had become the holiday home for Daphne and Hugo and their children, and other members of the family as well. Daphne's father, the sixth earl, and Charlotte Swann had spent their honeymoon here and had been captivated by its beauty and tranquility.

The main reception rooms opened onto a large garden which swept down to the lake, and the views were spectacular. Hugo, who had bought the villa long before his marriage to Daphne, had never wanted to sell it, and had hung on to it even when financial problems loomed. He had always understood that Villa Fleurir was a wonderful place to escape to and relax in, and also to enjoy the natural beauty surrounding the house and the ancient town of Zurich, which had great charm.

The one room Daphne had changed was a small sitting room which opened off the library. She had eventually taken this for herself. By adding a desk she had instantly made it into an office. As long as she had a safe place for her papers and a spot in which to work she was happy.

On this sunny morning in the first week of August, she sat at the desk, going over the household books. Having run Cavendon for years for her father, she had become accustomed to checking everything, including the money spent at the villa. Satisfied she was within her budget, she closed the last book, and sat back in her chair.

When she had first married Hugo, Hans and Hilde Bauer had run the house with great efficiency, and kept everything shipshape and running well. Their son Bruno, his wife, Anna, and two maids who came in daily had taken over after Hans had retired. If anything, the son was better than the father, but Daphne always kept that thought to herself. And Anna was the best cook, but Hilde had equaled her. They were lucky to have the Bauers to take care of them.

Getting up from the desk, she walked out into the foyer and hurried through the drawing room, making for the door leading to the garden. She stood on the threshold of the French doors, shading her eyes in the bright sunlight, spotted her daughter Alicia sitting in the gazebo at the end of the lawn. Glancing around she realized the house was still, very quiet for once. Everyone had disappeared except for Alicia.

Daphne walked down to the gazebo, admiring the grounds as she moved toward the lake ahead of her. The flowers were magnificent, making the garden breathtaking this year. Everything had bloomed so well, and fortunately at the right time.

Alicia looked up when she saw her mother standing next to her and smiled at Daphne.

Her mother bent down and kissed her cheek, and sat next to her. "Where is everyone, darling? Have they all gone out?"

"No, not at all. Cecily is upstairs in their bedroom. She told me she has work to do. And some telephoning, checking her business, I've no doubt. Charlie is in his room writing. My father went to a meeting and took Miles with him. He said they would be back in time for lunch, and not to worry about them being late."

Daphne laughed. "Your father's hardly ever late, bless him."

"I'm glad Cecily and Miles are here, Mummy," Alicia said. "I thought she looked tired. They both did. But Cecily seemed tenser."

"I know what you mean. I noticed that myself when they arrived on Tuesday night. But a few days here and she seems to be more at ease, don't you think?"

"It's the house, you know, everyone sort of collapses here. And they become soft and unworried and genial. I guess I'm right about that."

Daphne laughed. "I know you are. They let go, actually. So, have you made a decision, Alicia? Are you going to join your brothers at the Bowens' in the south of France or not?"

Alicia shook her head. "No, I'm not, Mummy. I'm going to go home to Cavendon next Monday, actually. I want to prepare for work, for September, which is when Felix and Constance will be back. I had a note from him yesterday, and he says they will take me on as a client."

"I'm so glad, darling!" Daphne exclaimed. "They're the best, they will do well for you. And it won't do you any harm as an actress being the niece of one of England's greatest actors."

There was a sudden commotion, laughter and masculine voices echoing in the air. Daphne stopped talking and glanced behind her. So did Alicia, who exclaimed, "It's Papa, Miles, and Charlie. But what on earth are they doing?"

Daphne shook her head. "I've no idea, however, I do see a pair of ladies' shoes peeping out from behind their collective trouser legs."

"Oh, it's Cecily, obviously! They must be teasing her about something," Alicia volunteered. "They're certainly joking around a lot."

It was Charlie, Daphne's eldest son, who began to march down the garden path, raising his arms, moving his hands gracefully, like a conductor commanding a huge orchestra. He sang out, "Ta-da! Ta-da! Ta-da!"

At that moment Cecily appeared on the scene. She came through the French doors and onto the terrace, walking over to the men.

Alicia said, "Oh they must be hiding someone else, Mummy. Whoever could it be?"

"I don't have a clue," Daphne answered and stood up, moved out of the gazebo, staring at the terrace. Instantly she knew who it was and her heart lifted with a flare of happiness. There was only one person in the world who had those gorgeous legs, now fully visible in very high heels.

"Hey there! Don't hide behind those silly men!" she called out. "I know it's you because of your legs and your shoes, Diedre."

Hugo, who was well aware that very little ever surprised his darling wife, stepped to one side, and so did Miles, allowing Diedre to run down the path and into Daphne's outstretched arms.

Cecily, who stood next to Miles, was wondering why Diedre was in Zurich. Was she here with news for her? Cecily dismissed that idea at once. It was far too soon for news. It was only last Friday, just a week ago today, that she had first spoken to Diedre about Greta's problem. Maybe Diedre had just wanted a chance to relax for a few days away from Cavendon, needed new scenery, a little respite from the family.

Cecily knew how hard she worked, and how involved she was with her job at the War Office. Not that she ever said a word. She could not, presumably because she was bound by the secrecy laws of the country. If she **was** working in intelligence. None of them knew a thing about her job; she had never been talkative about her life in London before her marriage to Paul. Nor after she returned to work in 1935.

The two sisters clung to each other for a moment or two. They had become closer than ever over the last nine years, working together through the family troubles and travails and especially after Paul had died so suddenly. Diedre was felled by the most terrible grief, had relied on her, Cecily, and DeLacy. They had each helped as much as they could, been there for her when sorrow threatened to overcome her.

Finally stepping apart, they grinned at each other. "You're a sight for sore eyes," Daphne said. "Welcome, Diedre darling. I'm so happy to see you."

Before Diedre could respond, Hugo cut in, "I couldn't believe it when we arrived back at the villa and Miles was shouting, 'Look what the wind's blown in,' and there was Diedre standing just in front of us, paying off a taxi."

Diedre turned to her sister, and said, "The

thing is this, Daphne. I had to go to Geneva on Wednesday night. I was surprised at how well it all went on Thursday, and it struck me how close I was to Zurich. And I suddenly wanted to be with all of you, spend a few days here. And I decided just to come and surprise you without even phoning."

"And we're glad you did," Miles said. "You're a **wonderful** surprise."

"It's lovely to have you, Diedre," Cecily murmured warmly, and went to kiss her sister-in-law on the cheek.

Diedre gave Cecily a very direct look. Their eyes locked and the knowing glance they exchanged said everything. **Say nothing.**

Daphne slipped her arm through Hugo's. "Let's go to the terrace and have cold drinks before lunch. It's getting quite hot out here." Glancing at him, she added, "Anna and Bruno know Diedre is here, don't they?"

"Oh yes. Bruno took Diedre's suitcase up to her room, and he said he would tell Anna to set another place at the table."

Daphne nodded and started up along the path with her husband, the others following behind.

The long terrace at the back of the villa, facing the lake and the mountains, was actually a roofed gallery in the form of a loggia, the roof offering shade and protection, and the open ends allowing air to flow freely. It was usually cool even on the warmest of days, and the family always ate lunch here in the summer, and often dinner as well.

The seven of them sat down in white basket-weave armchairs which surrounded a glass-and-iron table. As they were settling themselves, Bruno arrived with a tray of glasses and a large crystal jug of lemonade. After serving them, he turned to Daphne and murmured, "When would you like luncheon to be served, my lady?"

"In about half an hour, Bruno, thank you."

He nodded and took his leave.

Charlie said, "Do you often get to Geneva, Aunt Diedre?"

"Only occasionally, Charlie. Why do you ask?"

"I was just curious. Also, I thought you should consider dropping in more often, don't you agree, Mama?"

"I do indeed, but your aunt has Robin to think of, you know, and he spends the summers at Cavendon, which is where we'll usually find Diedre. At his side, being a good mother."

"Maybe I'll bring him over here again for a few days," Diedre interjected. "He's always enjoyed himself when we stayed, and especially with you, Charlie. Thank you for spending time with him and making him feel special, and most importantly, grown-up."

"He's a fabulous boy. When I talk to him and listen to his answers to my questions, and look into his eyes, I can't help thinking he's been here before, that he's an old soul."

Diedre nodded. "I think he is." She paused for a moment. "He misses his father, and you've sort of filled the breach during the holidays. He adores you, Charlie, and you've given him the writing bug. He told me last weekend that he wants to be a journalist, like you're going to be after Oxford."

"I did encourage him. I hope you're not upset."

"No, not at all."

Changing the subject and looking across at Miles, Charlie now said, "Talking of journalism, I've noticed the British newspapers have been full of stuff about Edward and his lady love. Our former king seems to have really embraced Hitler and the Nazis. There was a quote in one of the papers the other day...apparently he told someone that he was entirely of German blood. I think he said it to Joachim von Ribbentrop when he was the German ambassador in London, but I'm—"

"I read that, too," Miles cut in. "And he actually said it to Diana Mosley, not Ribbentrop." Miles shook his head. "I'm sure she was thrilled to hear that, given Sir Oswald's admiration of Hitler. She and Mosley are in Berlin constantly and so is her sister Unity, who's obsessed with Hitler."

"Those Mitford sisters take the cake!" Hugo

exclaimed. "Worshipping at the shrine of the Führer, and Unity fawning all over him. He's very flattered by all the attention he gets from certain members of the British aristocracy. Fools, the lot of them. No wonder Churchill sits fuming, I would, too. In fact, I do fume, in sympathy with him."

"I know what you mean," Daphne interjected. "I've noticed a lot of the establishment feels the same way, though; they think Hitler's a great leader. They're afraid of Communism, that's why."

Alicia gave Miles her attention, when she said, "But our royal family **is** rather German, isn't it, Uncle Miles?"

"Indeed. Our ex-king spoke the truth about his German blood. Let's not forget that his great-grandmother, Queen Victoria, was German through her forebears, the Hanoverian kings, and her mother was German. Victoria married a German, her cousin Prince Albert of Saxe-Coburg und Gotha. That was the name of our royal family for years and years. King George V, Edward's father, changed it in the Great War, thinking it was too German, perhaps. That is when the family took the surname of Windsor."

"And their cousins the Battenbergs became the Mountbattens for the same reason," Hugo remarked. "Mind you, I think George V did the right thing, and I do rather admire Louis

Mountbatten. He's a good man."

Miles cleared his throat and was about to speak when Daphne exclaimed, "I see Bruno hovering, so let us go and have lunch. And please, Miles, no history lessons. I grew up listening to them at every meal."

Her brother had the good grace to laugh, and Cecily exclaimed, "I loved his history lessons, and still do. Miles has a fantastic memory for such marvelous historical details."

As she rose Daphne threw Cecily a warm look and teased, "Of course you love his history lessons. You love everything he does. You worship the ground he walks on."

Grinning at Daphne, Cecily shot back, "That's true, I do, and I don't care who knows it."

"We've all known it since you were about twelve," Hugo murmured, squeezing Cecily's arm as he walked past. Leaning over her shoulder, he whispered in her ear, "And I for one love you for the way you love him."

Ten

Diedre, naturally observant, had had this particular trait underscored by years of training at the War Office, and she thought watching people was a fascinating occupation even when it was her own family under her scrutiny.

And so, as they all sat at the other end of the loggia enjoying lunch, she was able to indulge herself. Saying hardly anything at all, she made a show of savoring the food but kept her ears wide open.

During the first course, a cold vichyssoise soup scattered on the top with chives, her family talked about Wallis Simpson, the American divorcée for whom Edward VIII had given up the throne so that he could marry her.

Diedre was not especially interested, and only listened with half an ear, her thoughts focused at this moment on her immediate boss, William Lawson. He had joined "the firm," as he called it, several years before she had returned in 1935, a year after Paul's sudden and tragic death. He had welcomed her warmly, and with enthusiasm, and made no bones about his admiration for her and her many talents. In consequence, he had given her a lot of leeway in the three years she had worked closely with him, and he listened to her ideas.

She focused on that now, knowing that if she asked for a few extra days off, he would agree. Certainly he had had no qualms about her coming to Zurich today, to spend the weekend with her sister and other family members. She might phone Will later and ask for this favor.

Diedre had relaxed for the first time in months when she had arrived at the villa only several hours ago. Much of that had to do with Daphne, who had always shown love and understanding to everyone. And Diedre was no exception to that rule.

Surreptitiously, she looked down the long table at her sister and couldn't help feeling a great sense of pride. Daphne was now forty-two, but did not look it. She was still the great beauty of the family, the gorgeous peaches-and-cream blonde she had always been. She **had** put on a little bit of extra weight, but not much, and there was a lovely aura around her. It's goodness, sincerity, and devotion, Diedre decided, knowing how much of herself Daphne gave to others.

Hugo, too, helped to make Diedre feel better, perhaps because he had such a gift with people, knew how to make them welcome. Also, he had been close to her Paul, her husband's business partner and best friend. So many of her happiest memories were associated with her sister and brother-in-law, and these memories warmed her, took away some of the pain inside.

Diedre was brought out of her reverie when Bruno placed the main course in front of her, and Hugo said, "Anna makes the best branzino in the world, as you know."

Smiling at him, she said, "I do remember. And Daphne always creates the greatest menus."

"Mama is the best," Charlie announced. "The magical mother. Who does everything perfectly."

Hugo grinned and Alicia agreed, as did Miles and Cecily. It was Diedre who added, "And without a doubt the best sister that ever was."

A slight blush crept up Daphne's neck to her cheeks, and tears glistened in her eyes, but they all knew they were tears of happiness. She sat there smiling at them, obviously pleased.

Diedre let go of her people-watching habit and concentrated on her plate of food. The branzino had been grilled and there was a lemon sauce with tiny segments of lemon mixed with capers in it, and small new potatoes.

"It's delicious," Diedre said to Hugo, and

added, "Are you going to be here next week, Hugo? Or will you be in Geneva?"

"Oh, here, of course, Diedre. No business next week. We just want to enjoy the Villa Fleurir for a couple of weeks longer. Then it's back to Cavendon."

"I thought I might go to Berlin next week," Charlie said, looking from his mother to his father, a brow lifting quizzically.

"Berlin!" Daphne exclaimed, staring at her son in astonishment. "Whatever for?"

"To see it. Get a feel about it. I've read so much about all these little men prancing around in ridiculous operetta-style uniforms—"

"Which would only be funny if these little men, as you call them, weren't a bunch of dangerous gangsters," Diedre interrupted, her tone serious, her face grimly set as she looked at her nephew. "Make no mistake, they are tyrants and will stop at nothing to attain their aims. Be assured of that, Charlie."

"I've no intention of allowing you to go to Berlin," Hugo said in a firm voice. "And what would be gained by it, I ask you?"

"This is a particular time in history," Charlie said in a mild, steady voice, not wanting to alienate his parents, who always stood together on all things. "As a budding journalist, I want to see what's happening, take photographs with my Kodak camera, do a general walk-around. I hear the Unter den Linden looks amazing…Nazi flags, great German eagles atop high columns, searchlights beaming. Very colorful."

"No," Diedre said in a harsh tone. "They've ruined that beautiful avenue with their theatrical trimmings. Anyway, no one should go to Berlin alone, Charlie, and especially a twenty-year-old."

"I'll soon be twenty-one," he interjected, still speaking in the mildest voice.

"I'd go with you," Alicia said. "But I'm off to Cavendon on Monday." Wanting to avert a quarrelsome scene between her brother and her parents, she hurried on, "I had a letter today from Felix, who's in Los Angeles with Dulcie and James. He and Constance have agreed to represent me, and be my managers. I want to make films, you see, not tread the boards."

"What? You? A film star!" Charlie cried, shaking his head, chuckling. "You're the ugly duckling of the Inghams."

"No she's not," Cecily said. "She's a graceful and elegant swan, if you'll excuse the use of my name."

Charlie grinned at his aunt, and said, "I'm only teasing the beautiful Alicia and every one of you knows that."

"Yes, we do, darling," Daphne said. "And you've taken lovely pictures of Alicia on your Kodak. But it's still **no** to Berlin."

Cecily looked at Diedre, and said hesitantly,

"Maybe we all ought to go with Charlie...what do you think, Diedre?" She sat waiting for an answer, quaking inside, hoping Diedre wouldn't be angry with her.

Diedre didn't respond immediately, not particularly surprised by Cecily's suggestion. She always said what was on her mind. Her sister-in-law had never shown fear in her life. And, as a matter of fact, she had voiced what Diedre had herself been thinking at that moment. It would be a way for her to speak to Toby Jung in person, and plan the extraction, if there was going to be one. But how to pull it off? Finally she spoke.

"What do I think...? Well, I believe a family like ours would be perfectly safe in Berlin. Particularly if we were invited to a reception at the British embassy by Sir Nevile Henderson, the ambassador—"

"Gosh, Aunt Diedre, could you arrange that?" Charlie asked, cutting in, awe echoing in his voice.

"Oh no, Charlie, I don't have that kind of clout, but I know my superior's had wind of the annual reception being given sometime soon. For important visitors to Berlin. I could investigate, find out if that's true."

"Hitler loves the British aristocracy. We all know that, and yes, of course, **we** would be safe," Miles said in a positive manner. "And I see what you're getting at, Diedre. Being feted at the British embassy would give us the stamp of approval."

"Oh, surely we have that already," Daphne exclaimed. "We're the Clan Ingham. Everybody's heard of us. We're sort of, well, famous in our own way."

"We're certainly blond enough," Charlie added. "And we all have blue eyes. Well, almost. One of us does not."

Cecily cut in through her laughter. "I know I'm not a blue-eyed blonde. However, I am quite famous, too. Several German princesses are my clients."

"There, you see, we're in!" Charlie exclaimed. "Oh, Papa, do let's go. I'm sure it would be quite an interesting experience."

Hugo stared at Daphne, who looked troubled, and said very slowly, "Let's talk about it, Hugo. Weigh the odds." Turning to Charlie, she added, "We'll let you know tomorrow."

"I don't know why you always do it!" Alicia exclaimed, sitting down next to her brother on the edge of the swimming pool. This was located on the far side of the gazebo, at the edge of the lake.

Glancing at her quickly, he asked, "Do what?" His blond brow drew together in a furrow.

"Announce something that's really provocative

and bound to cause trouble when we're at lunch or dinner. Thank God you don't do it at breakfast or tea."

"I don't think what I said at lunch was provocative at all," Charlie protested. "You're always exaggerating, and you're very bossy."

"I'm neither. And you **were** provocative because you mentioned something that was bound to upset Beauty," she shot back, using the nickname they'd had for their mother since childhood.

"Suggesting I was going to Berlin doesn't seem provocative to me. I was only telling her, **them,** my travel plans. Actually, I thought it showed initiative on my part. As a future journalist I am naturally curious, focused on the news. And Germany's certainly in the news these days. This happens to be an extraordinary time in history. The world is changing even as we speak."

"They won't let you go," Alicia asserted. "Remember, they always stand together. Knight and Beauty are on the same page."

"Oh for heaven's sake, I know that, and why are you going on about it? They weren't as bothered as you're making out." He was obviously exasperated with his older sister.

"Oh yes they were! I could see another unpleasant scene developing. That's why I saved your bacon by changing the subject, spoke about Felix."

"You enjoy talking about yourself, Miss Alicia Ingham Stanton. You're all puffed up about your looks and your elegant figure. **And your career**."

"No I'm not. But I am serious about my acting and getting my career off the ground."

"That's the way I feel about working as a newspaperman. I've definitely settled on being a war correspondent. There's bound to be a war, and I want to be right in the center of it all, writing about it."

"Oh my God, don't tell **them**. Beauty will have a fit and the Knight in Shining Armor will put his foot down. Hard. Forget about Berlin. It'll never happen."

"Guess what, Miss Know-it-all, I bet you five bob we'll go to Berlin. Aunt Cecily gave me the solution."

"I'm sure you don't have five bob to make a bet," Alicia muttered, eyeing him sourly.

"Yes I do. And going en masse to Berlin **will** work. Pity you won't be coming. You're off to start your brilliant career as a film star. Ta-da! Ta-da!"

"Oh do stop saying that, you sound utterly inane, and it's irritating." She glowered at him yet again and he in return smiled at her, put his arm around her, and pulled her close. "Don't be like this...you know you're my best friend and true companion. I don't know what I'd do without you. Thank you for averting what might have turned into an angry confrontation with **them,** and he is always on her side, you're right about that."

"Mummy worries about you a lot…about all of her children, Charlie. That's why she does seem a bit restrictive at times. Listen, she's very smart and clever, that's why I listen to her. **Always.** She just makes perfect sense. You, however, seem to flout her wishes and go out of your way to make dumb choices."

"None of that's true. **I do not.** And in case you've forgotten, I'm a man and I can certainly look after myself."

"So can I."

"Mmmmm." He shook his head. "Not true. Sadly it's a man's world, Ally."

"Don't call me that! Mummy doesn't like it and neither do I."

"Let's not quarrel."

"We're not quarreling," she answered, her voice changing, becoming softer.

"We **are** bickering, though," Charlie shot back.

"I just feel very protective of you, brother of mine. I don't want you to get hurt in any way, shape, or form, and you can be a bit rash, reckless even, at times."

"I know." He laughed, took hold of her hand. "Guilty as charged, old thing. I'll try to mend my ways just for you. To please you."

When she was silent, he added, "You can't be that mad at me. You came down to have a swim, as I asked you to earlier."

"No, I came down to tell you off."

"Liar." He chuckled, his eyes holding hers.

Alicia leaned closer, kissed his cheek, then hugged him to her. She had mothered him since the day he was born, and still did. They were extremely close and had been hand-in-glove since their childhood. In a certain sense, they were more like twins than their siblings Thomas and Andrew, who **were** twins.

After a few moments of silence, Alicia murmured, "You win, Charlie, I did come down to swim with you. At the same time, I wanted to talk to you…to ask you to stop saying things that alarm our mother. She's anxious enough. Remember, Uncle Guy died in the Great War."

"I will, I promise. I know I sort of blurt things out, spontaneously shoot before thinking. I'm sorry, I'll do better."

"Just edit yourself a bit more, that's all." She jumped up, and he followed suit. They looked at each other, smiled knowingly, and dived into the pool in perfect synchronization.

Eleven

Whenever she came to stay with Daphne and Hugo at Villa Fleurir, Daphne always told her she could use the small office just off the library. And Diedre did so now. Everyone had scattered, gone off to do things, and she did have a need to do some thinking and make several phone calls.

Sitting down at the desk, Diedre glanced around, noting how much this room reflected Daphne and her taste. It had apricot-colored walls and matching silk draperies, and the comfortable sofa and armchairs were covered in an apricot cotton fabric. The room came alive with the vivid colors in the paintings hanging on the walls, and the cushions on the sofa.

Diedre sniffed and smiled to herself. The room was redolent of Daphne's favorite perfume, lilies-of-the-valley, which had been created especially for her by Cecily.

A deep sigh escaped Diedre, and she focused

on Cecily and her suggestion about Berlin. It would be a clever solution, please Charlie, and it would certainly suit her to go along with the family group, if Daphne and Hugo agreed. However, she would have to tell William Lawson, her immediate superior. She could see no reason why he would object; also, being in the middle of the Ingham family group was the perfect cover for her. Diedre had no intention of mentioning a possible extraction to Will. There was no need for him to know. Anyway, it was unlikely to happen quickly, if at all.

Diedre placed the call through the overseas operator, using Will's private number. He answered immediately, was obviously glad to hear from her. Once she had explained about the family trip, he had agreed she should go. "It might prove useful," he said. "It's the annual shindig next week. I'll make sure you're all invited. By the boss himself."

"That would be wonderful." She noted how careful Will was even though he was on a safe phone. "I thought I might see the sights…if you get my drift."

"Your sister would enjoy it, too, if you get **my** drift."

"I do. Solo out."

"Correct. Don't neglect me."

"I won't."

They hung up. His last words had meant that

she must call him every day. That was mandatory when she was in a foreign country.

Her next phone call, via the international operator, was to Berlin.

"May I speak to Toby Jung, please?"

"This is he, Daffy."

"I'm checking in as you asked."

"In the same place as yesterday, are you? Or did you do a bunk, follow your heart?"

"How did you guess?" She smiled to herself. How well he knew her.

"You sounded so serious, very intent. Nobody could've stopped you."

"True." Diedre settled back in the chair, staring at the painting of the autumn woods at Cavendon, painted by Genevra some years ago. Its russets and golds were perfect for this room. Her eyes remained on the painting as she went on. "No progress, I presume?"

"Nothing's changed, Daffy. Everyone's on the move, on holiday, going back home. And some are simply flying their own kites."

"So your usual helpers have dwindled?" she asked.

"I'd say that."

"Perhaps I should leave the suitcase with you, Toby. Just forget it."

"You might have to, Daffy Dilly."

"Thanks for keeping it for me. How's the weather?"

"Boiling hot. Beastly, in fact."

"I don't like hot weather." Diedre added, "I grew up in the north."

"Are you thinking of making a trip here?"

"That's a possibility," she answered in a quiet voice.

"Daffy Dilly, that would be a treat for me!"

"And me, too. And perhaps I can just get rid of the suitcase."

Ignoring the mention of the suitcase, he asked, "When?"

"Don't know yet."

"I'm free as a bird—" He cut himself off, and then after a moment he continued in a low tone. "There **is** a person who could no doubt get the suitcase to you. But you yourself would have to ask."

"No. It's not possible!" she exclaimed. "I cannot. I should say I will not. In fact, it's out of the question. I must not involve him."

"I understand. Please come, Daffy. We might even have a bit of fun."

"We might. So long." Diedre hung up the phone, leaned back in the chair, and closed her eyes. Her thoughts were whirling, and she asked herself if she should go to Berlin or not.

Diedre sat in the small office for another twenty minutes, running everything through her mind. Her main focus was on the trip to Berlin. It would work only if they went as a group, and it would be quite a large group. Six of them altogether, because Alicia would not be going. A group was not easy to miss so they would stand out. But they were the Inghams of Cavendon, therefore protected by their nationality and their famous name.

What Miles had said earlier was true. Adolf Hitler did have a fondness for the British aristocracy, and the two Mitford sisters were a prime example of his preferences. Diedre was also well aware that a number of highborn men in the establishment and certain politicians were admiring of a man she truly believed would become the dictator of Central Europe and in no time at all.

She could not understand why they didn't see through him, see him for what he was. A man of evil who wanted world domination. Part of their problem was the fear they all had of Russia. They saw Communism as a greater threat than Fascism. Diedre let out a sigh. She held the view that they were facing a grim future and a worse horror than in the Great War.

There was a light knock on the door and Daphne looked into the room. "Are you busy? Can we talk for a moment?"

"Of course, Daphers." Diedre rose and moved away from the desk, went and sat down on the sofa.

Daphne took the chair opposite her. "Hugo and I have just been talking about this idea Charlie has of going to Berlin. We don't want him to travel alone; on the other hand we do understand why he's interested. So what is your opinion?"

"I agree with you and Hugo, he shouldn't go alone," Diedre said. "I think any person without a companion in that city is very vulnerable at this particular time."

Daphne nodded. "I realize you know Germany better than any of us. You've studied the country for years and you speak German." Daphne suddenly smiled, then went on, "Not to digress, but I recall when you went off on a trip with your friends Maxine and Laura in 1914. Just before the Great War. And you came back full of warnings about the Germans rearming. You were very het up."

"Gosh, what a good memory you have. Yes, it was a very revealing trip, indeed. I sensed they were readying themselves for war, and I was right."

"And now they're doing it again. Only twenty years later," Daphne murmured, her expression grave.

Diedre nodded. "People in Britain remember the horror of it, the death, the destruction, and that's why there's all this talk of appeasement. But it won't work."

"Why not?" Daphne asked, leaning forward, paying attention to her sister.

"Because Adolf Hitler wants the war, although not necessarily with Britain involved. That's why he, too, is encouraging the British to come forward with the idea of appeasement."

"I understand. Getting back to Charlie, why can't he go alone **actually**? I need to give him reasons."

"Because Berlin is the most dangerous city in the world today. It's militaristic, in a certain sense, filled with thousands of men in uniforms …the SS, the SD, the Stormtroopers. And the Gestapo. There is unrest, bigotry, anti-Semitism, and very loutish behavior on the part of many people. Not only German thugs, but vagabonds. Hundreds of Poles, Czechs, Hungarians, Serbs, you name it, have flooded in and Berlin has become a cosmopolitan melting pot."

Diedre paused, letting all this sink in. After a moment, she said, "Here's a scenario. A young man on his own, minding his own business, goes into a bar or a beer hall for a drink. He jostles somebody or something like that, and a split second later he could easily be in a fight, getting beaten up. People are tense, volatile, very taut. And that's why anyone on his or her own is vulnerable."

"I understand, Diedre, you have explained it

well. Hugo and I want him to be independent, to fly, to be himself, but since it is unwise for him to travel alone, do you think this idea of going as a family would work?"

"If you wish to please Charlie, which obviously you do, I can make it work if we go as a family. I've spoken to my office and I can have next week off. And I would come with you."

"That would be simply marvelous, Diedre. Actually, I honestly don't believe we would go if you weren't able to accompany us."

"I'll make all the arrangements. We'll stay at the Adlon Hotel. I know it, and it's the best. All we have to do is decide when we should go."

"I'll talk to Hugo, and we'll settle on a date. Have you any thoughts?" Daphne asked.

"Tuesday of next week, actually. That's when we should travel to Berlin," Diedre answered.

Twelve

Much later, as she was dressing for dinner, Diedre's thoughts went back to the two telephone calls she had made earlier.

William Lawson had been his usual cordial self, greeting her warmly, agreeing she could take the week off. Now two things stood out in her mind.

He had suggested the trip to Berlin with her family could be **useful**; he had told her not to go out solo. That had not sounded like a warning, but it was. Saying she might pick up something **useful** was a direct order. He wanted her to snoop wherever she could. Discreetly.

Will had given her permission to do what she had planned to do anyway. Not going out solo might present a problem. On the other hand, she had to listen to him because if anyone knew how dangerous Berlin now was, he certainly did. Will Lawson was much admired by others who were in constant touch with him.

The Secret Intelligence Service, otherwise known as MI6, in particular. This aside, he was her boss and, also, she trusted his judgment.

Toby's contacts had entirely vanished, from what **he** had said on the phone. The fact that he had suggested she speak to her old friend in the German High Command told her he was desperate. His other message to her had been a dire warning. Whenever he said the weather was **hot** she understood that the Gestapo were increasing their surveillance of many people and were all over the city, ready to pounce and arrest. Instinctively, deep within her inner self, she now realized that the professor had left it too late to flee.

Standing back from the cheval mirror, Diedre eyed herself, pleased with the way she looked. She had borrowed a simple chiffon evening dress from Cecily. It was delphinium blue, tailored, as usual, and had full sleeves and a flared skirt. Her only jewelry was her wedding ring, watch, and pearl earrings. Now she pinned Cecily's famous white rose silk brooch on her shoulder as a finishing touch.

When she went downstairs Diedre realized she was the first, and then, as she looked around, she spotted Cecily standing at the bottom of the garden near the water's edge.

"Cooee!" she called out, walked down to join her sister-in-law beside the lake.

"Another early bird," Cecily said, turning around, smiling. "I knew you'd be down at the same time as me."

"Aha! I understand, you want to talk to me." Diedre stood eyeing her, a quizzical expression on her face.

"Just to thank you for agreeing we should accompany Charlie to Berlin. I wasn't sure you would when I suggested that."

"I didn't want to deprive him of the visit since he's so eager and sincere about his career as a journalist. And to be honest, it gives me an opportunity to speak to my contact in person."

"Have you had any news?" Cecily asked, sounding eager, her eyes lighting up.

"Yes. And it's not good. However, he's still trying."

Cecily was silent, a worried expression suddenly crossing her face. "Other people have been able to get out, according to Greta."

"Those extractions were early in the game... several years ago," Diedre explained quietly. "The professor should have left long ago. Things are moving very swiftly in Berlin, from what my contact indicates. Nothing remains the same, everything's constantly changing. Every day." She stopped. She must not appear to know too much.

Cecily nodded, looked out across the lake, her face full of sorrow, her heart aching for Greta.

Diedre put her arm around Cecily's shoulders. "I think it's a good idea to be positive right now. You never know what might happen. Life is funny."

"Thanks for being so helpful, Diedre. I do appreciate it."

"You cannot say a thing to Greta. Or give her the slightest hope. That would be cruel. And you must not visit her father when we're in Berlin. Not under any circumstances. That is absolutely mandatory." Diedre gave Cecily a long, hard stare, her eyes narrowing.

"But she'll know I'm in Berlin, and it's not as if I'm going alone!" Cecily exclaimed, sounding startled. "She'll think it's strange if I don't go and see him."

"I realize that. And it will no doubt be common knowledge soon enough, because of the others going on the trip. They'll talk about it. However, the professor may well be under observation, as are many prominent men in all professions, and especially intellectuals. You can't go near him, you could endanger his life."

"I swore on our ancient oath that I would be loyal to you. That still stands, as you well know. A Swann has never broken an oath made to an Ingham," Cecily snapped.

Diedre nodded her understanding, and relenting slightly, she added in a gentler voice, "I will ask my contact if he can arrange a meeting between you and the professor accidentally, so to speak. I must leave it at that."

"Just out of curiosity, is your contact in the War Office with you?"

"No, and I really can't discuss him. I'm sure you understand why. Let's just say I met him… accidentally. No more questions."

Cecily made a moue. "Sorry. I shouldn't have asked. I was wrong, and I will do exactly as you say. I realize this matter is grave, not to mention dangerous."

"You're smart, Ceci, and I trust you to keep your silence. Do you recall my personal code?"

"Believe no one. Tell no one. Remember everything. Walk alone."

Diedre inclined her head. "And now it is your code, Cecily Swann Ingham. Understand?"

"I do."

At this moment they saw the rest of the family gathering on the loggia, and Diedre took hold of Cecily's arm. She said, sotto voce, "Look surprised when Daphne announces that we're all going to Berlin with Charlie."

"I will." Cecily fell into step with Diedre as they walked up the path. She was now fully aware that she was helpless, just as Diedre was. Aunt Charlotte was right when she had once said that no one was in control of their own life. It is the other way around. Life controls every one of us, she thought.

All evening Diedre kept her face still and said very little. She answered any normal questions about Berlin and the Third Reich, and that was it. Any questions which were extreme, political, or complex she left unanswered. She simply said she didn't have a clue.

Not one person in the world, including every member of her family, knew she was with British intelligence. Even those loved ones who were dead had never known. Great-Aunt Gwendolyn was the only person who had once had the nerve to come out and ask her bluntly. Even then Diedre had not answered her aunt in any specific way, leaving her to speculate, still not sure of the truth. Her cover was intact.

When any of her friends or family broached the subject of her work, she always said exactly the same thing: That she was in administration, doing clerical work like the other women employed there. Diedre always left it at that and they didn't press her. That was the way it must be now. A blank face, empty answers, a posture and attitude that proclaimed lack of knowledge.

Later, when she was alone in her bedroom, she would make her plans for Berlin. And she prayed to God that they would work.

Cecily looked at the clock on the bedside chest. It was well turned midnight and she was still wide awake, her thoughts running on unchecked. It had been a lovely evening, with sumptuous food and the best wines. Of course it had become extremely lively once Hugo had announced they would all accompany Charlie to Berlin.

Charlie's whoops of joy filled the air and even Alicia had wondered out loud if she should join them rather than returning to Cavendon on Monday. It had been an easy evening with everyone on an even keel, and for once no quarrels.

After her conversation with Diedre, earlier in the evening, Cecily truly realized that it would be a wild-goose chase as far as the professor was concerned. Diedre had made no bones about that, and had been extremely negative. Cecily let out a long sigh at the thought of the trip, now no longer meaningful.

Miles touched her arm, and she realized that he was awake. He said softly, "I can almost hear that busy mind of yours turning and turning. What is it, darling?"

"I don't know really, I'm just a bit restless, Miles. Perhaps it's the wine, you know it often keeps me awake. It must somehow fuel my imagination...or something like that."

"The same happens to me," he replied. "I'm just as restless as you. Tell you what, let's go down to the kitchen and forage for—"

"You can't possibly be hungry after that

fantastic dinner," Cecily interrupted, sounding surprised.

Miles laughed. "I was about to say forage for some bananas. Don't you remember how Aunt Charlotte used to tell us to have a banana if we couldn't sleep, when we were children? She said it would do the trick, and it did."

"Of course, so let's go and forage." Slipping out of bed, Cecily put on her robe and slippers, and Miles followed suit.

A few minutes later they were standing in the sparkling kitchen which had been thoroughly cleaned by Anna and Bruno after the lavish dinner. A bowl of fruit stood on the countertop; Miles took two bananas, grabbed Cecily's hand, and led her outside.

"It's such a gorgeous night, let's go and sit by the water," Miles murmured, heading for the lake with her.

Although the sky was a dark midnight blue there were no clouds; the thousands of stars appeared more visible than ever in the pure air. The mountains stood out ruggedly against the sky, their white tips glistening in the moonlight. The lake was placid, like a sheet of silvered glass.

There was a low bench on the edge of the lake and Cecily and Miles sat down on it, the two of them enjoying the magnificence of their surroundings.

"Look at the mountains up there, tipped with snow, and the great arc of the sky glittering with stars…how beautiful it is here, Ceci."

"I know. There's a peacefulness, a serenity." She shook her head. "And not too far away there's madness, chaos, and rumors of an impending war. The earth we live on is staggeringly beautiful, and yet there are those who want to go out and destroy it. Evil men like Hitler, hungry for power and dominance."

Cecily shivered. Instantly Miles put his arm around her. "I know exactly what you mean. The tranquility here is unique and it has kept Hugo sane all through those difficult years. At least that's what I think." There was a pause. Miles looked down at her, tilted her face to his. "Don't you want to go to Berlin, Ceci?"

"Yes and no," she answered truthfully. "I want to see what's going on, and yet I don't want to see anything at all. I suppose because I think I'll be frightened by the ghastliness of the place."

"Nothing will happen to us, darling. We're totally protected as a well-known English family," Miles reassured her, pulling her closer.

"Yes, I know," she muttered.

"Was Diedre able to do anything to help Greta's father?" he suddenly asked.

"I don't believe so," Cecily responded quietly, alarm flaring inside. She must now be very careful what she said. She could not betray Diedre.

"I thought she had a contact?" Miles murmured.

"From what I understand, it's an…**old friend,**" Cecily improvised. "She told me the person couldn't do anything about helping to get travel papers. Seemingly they've become scarce. None available."

Miles nodded. "The professor, like so many other Jews, believed they were German and therefore nothing would happen to them. How mistaken they've been. Tragically, in fact."

Cecily remained silent.

Miles said in a somewhat reflective tone, "Did Diedre say anything to you about visiting Greta's family?"

"Not exactly, Miles. She just made a comment about intellectuals being watched. She said she had read about this development in one of the British papers," Cecily lied.

"I did, too. The Gestapo are a menace…they swoop down on so many people who are perfectly innocent." There was a small silence. Finally Miles added, "Perhaps it would be wiser if we didn't draw attention to the professor by going to see him."

"I agree. We might be doing him a favor if we stayed away." She hesitated, being cautious. "Are you suggesting that the famous Inghams might be under surveillance?"

"There's a strong possibility that we will be, my darling. So what? We're just visitors passing through, so to speak. Diedre's position at the War Office has always been a mystery to me, Ceci. She's never told anybody one single thing, except that she does clerical work. What's your opinion? Is that the truth? Or do you think my sister **is** in intelligence?"

"I'm certain she does clerical work, **is** in administration. Let's face it, Miles, if Diedre **was** in intelligence, she might have had the ways and means to help Greta's father."

"Perhaps. Perhaps not. But I tend to agree with you. Anyway, Diedre's not the type to play cloak-and-dagger, that sort of thing. She's far too staid."

"I agree," Cecily replied assertively, relieved she had managed to throw Miles off the scent.

Thirteen

On their first morning in Berlin, Daphne, Diedre, and Cecily met for breakfast in the dining room of the Adlon Hotel where they were staying. Hugo and Miles had taken Charlie on a sightseeing tour much earlier and would not be back until late afternoon.

"I'm so glad we didn't have to go," Daphne murmured, looking from her sister to Cecily. "First of all, I didn't want to get up at the crack of dawn, and secondly, I don't really have the desire to see too much of this town, especially since there are so many uniforms underfoot."

Diedre laughed. "**Underfoot,** indeed!" she exclaimed. "They're everywhere."

"Have you been out already?" Cecily asked, eyeing Diedre, unable to conceal her curiosity.

"No, I haven't," Diedre replied. "But I noticed when we went for a stroll after dinner last night how many Stormtroopers there were, crowding in among us poor pedestrians. They all looked like bullies to me."

"What **I** noticed last night were how many smart women were dining here. In fact, some of them were extremely chic, very well groomed," Cecily said. Turning to Daphne, she went on, "I'd like to browse around a few of the best shops later. Are you up for it?"

"I'd like that, Ceci, but I'd also love to go to the Tiergarten, either this morning, or this afternoon, if you prefer. Hugo told me that it's a really beautiful spot, rather like an English park. It used to be the private hunting grounds of the Brandenburg princes several hundreds of years ago."

"Let's do that," Cecily agreed.

"You're very welcome to come with us, Diedre," Daphne said. "Unless you've made other plans."

"I have actually. I must make a courtesy call to the British embassy, for one thing."

"So join us for lunch," Daphne suggested.

"I can't. Thanks for wanting to include me, though. I have an old friend who works there and we've made a lunch date. Also, I must see one of the attachés at the embassy, about the reception tomorrow evening. I understand we're on the list."

"I'm glad we're being invited," Cecily said. "I enjoy ogling all the women and their clothes."

"Apparently it **is** black tie," Diedre said. "So

I'm relieved I told you to have the men pack their evening clothes."

"And what shall we wear, Diedre?" Daphne asked, raising a brow. "I suppose we have to get all fancied up?"

"I'll say. We're the famous Inghams after all," Diedre replied with a chuckle. "As far as you're concerned, you can wear an old sack and still look beautiful. No doubt you'll be the belle of the ball tomorrow."

"I'm not so sure about that, but thank you for the compliment. I brought several summer evening frocks."

Standing up, Diedre said, "I must go. I hope to be back by four. Shall we try and have tea together?"

"That's a grand idea," Cecily answered. "Have a nice day."

"I aim to." Diedre smiled and took her leave, hurrying out of the restaurant.

After buttering a piece of toast, Daphne looked at Cecily and said, "I've been wondering if Charlotte has said anything to you about Papa? About his health, I mean."

This question surprised Cecily, and she frowned. "No, she hasn't. But why do you ask? Do you think your father might be ill?"

"Not really. He was very good when we left, but that is several weeks ago now. It was just something Alicia said on Sunday...She really did want to come with us to Berlin, I suppose because Charlie has made it sound so exciting. And those two have always been joined at the hip. I agreed she should come along, but she suddenly said she couldn't let her grandfather down. Then she added that he was longing for her to come back to Cavendon and at his age it was important for her to be there."

"I don't think she was referring to anything to do with his health," Cecily reassured her. "Anyway, if the earl isn't well, Miles would certainly know, and he would have told me." Cecily paused, sipped her tea. "Your father has always adored Alicia, she is his first grandchild after all. He doted on her when she was little and they've been very close. I'm sure he has missed her. Alicia obviously understands this and just wants to keep her promise."

Daphne nodded, a look of relief crossing her face. "I'm sure you're right. I'm just being silly." A smile slid onto her face. "The old man and the young girl have a special bond. I know that for a fact."

"Alicia's a lovely person, very considerate to everyone," Cecily pointed out. "My mother adores her, you know."

"The feeling is mutual, and I also adore Mrs. Alice." Daphne looked off into the distance, as if staring back into the past. She said, after a long moment, "Your mother saved my sanity, saved my life when I was seventeen...well, you know all that."

"I do indeed." Cecily said no more, thinking of that terrible summer when Daphne had been violently assaulted. Only the Swanns had known about it, and Daphne's parents.

As if reading her mind, Daphne said, "I've been terribly afraid of violence ever since. I think that's probably why I'm not particularly happy here in Berlin. I sense an undercurrent of danger, of trouble brewing, then erupting. That's why I'm relieved we're only staying a few days."

"There does seem to be a lot of tension and trouble in the streets. I know exactly what you're referring to, Daphne. There's fear in the air. But look, we'll be back in Zurich on Sunday, and anyway we are perfectly safe."

"Yes, I know, Hugo reassured me of that."

As they finished breakfast a silence fell between them. They were both preoccupied with their thoughts. Cecily was focused on her father-in-law, wondering if Alicia had spotted something she had recently noticed. The earl did not seem as robust, and it had struck her several times lately that his health might be failing. She had not said anything to Miles, or anyone else, but he wasn't the same anymore. Now, unexpectedly she could suddenly pinpoint it. The spirit had gone out of him, and this saddened her. She resolved to keep this insight into her father-in-law to herself. Nobody needed to know for the time being.

Diedre left the Adlon Hotel, stepped out onto the Unter den Linden, and turned right onto the Wilhelmstrasse where the British embassy was located. She thought about Tony Jenkins, whom she was about to see. It was a relief to know that she could talk to him face-to-face in plain language rather than on the phone in code. Even so she was quite certain he would call her Daffy Dilly but she had made up her mind not to address him as Toby.

Here at the embassy he was Tony Jenkins, an attaché. He did not really work for the Foreign Office; he was with British intelligence, working for her, although none of his colleagues knew this. Self-confident, in control, blessed with natural charm, he managed to play the role of an attaché with great élan, and success. Not for a moment was he like an agent.

Diedre came to a stop at number seventy and looked up at the Union Jack on a flagpole above the huge front door of the British embassy. It was flaring out in the light breeze, a dazzle of red, white, and blue, and she felt a little surge of patriotism. To her that flag represented not only her country, but democracy, justice, and freedom.

Glancing up the Wilhelmstrasse she saw the

swastika on the German flag flying above the Reich Chancellery a few doors away. Inside that building sat Hitler and his henchmen, a bunch of gangsters in charge of the German government, plotting their evil schemes and the domination of Central Europe. Hitler's vandalization of democracy was abhorrent to her, and what an irony it was that these two buildings stood on the same street.

Moving swiftly, Diedre went up the steps and into the embassy, her head held high in her pride at being an Englishwoman, and one determined to defend everything her country stood for.

Within minutes of giving her name to the young woman seated at the reception desk, she saw Tony Jenkins hurrying toward her. He had a bright smile on his face, and was obviously happy to see her standing there.

A moment later he was shaking her hand. "Lady Diedre, good morning, and welcome back."

"It's nice to be here, Tony," she said, and allowed herself to be led away, down a short corridor to his office.

Once inside, he gave her a huge bear hug. She hugged him back, and then they stood apart and smiled at each other.

"I can't tell you what a relief it is to see you," he said.

"I know what you mean. I feel the same."

"Let's sit down over there on the sofa, and then I think we should go for a walk." As he spoke he gave her a knowing look.

Diedre nodded. "I think that's a good idea. Why stay cooped up inside when it's such a lovely day?" She swung her head around, her eyes searching the walls and ceiling, and then she stared at Tony, mouthed, "It's not wired, is it?"

He shook his head. "It's better we go out before we get interrupted. Somebody might pop in."

"I understand. What about Sir Nevile? I should pay my respects to the ambassador."

"He asked me to explain that he is unavailable at the moment. But he welcomes you, and is looking forward to seeing you and your family tomorrow evening."

Tony stood, went over to his desk, and picked up some envelopes. "These are your invitations to the reception and dinner, Diedre. I thought of sending them over to the Adlon by messenger, and then decided just to give them to you."

"Thank you," she said, and took them from him. There was one for her, another for Cecily and Miles, and a third for Daphne, Hugo, and Charlie. "We'll all be there with bells on," she said with a chuckle. Opening her handbag, she put the three envelopes inside, and got up. "What are we waiting for? Let's go."

Fourteen

They got out of the taxi on the Tiergartenstrasse, and went straight into the Tiergarten, after Tony had paid off the driver. Diedre knew the park well, having strolled through it in the past, and it was one of the few places in Berlin today where tranquility still reigned.

It was truly beautiful, laid out in the manner of a traditional English park, with large expanses of green lawns, limes and horse chestnut trees and many weeping willows growing everywhere. The abundance of magnificent trees aside, the flowering bushes and flower beds were in full bloom this month, and the air was fragrant with their mingled scents.

Tony and Diedre made their way to a secluded spot near one of the artificial ponds where there was a wrought-iron garden seat.

Once they were seated, she said, "You didn't say much in the taxi, Tony, so do let's talk now. It's so tricky when we speak in code."

"But safe," he said, and smiled at her. "My office isn't wired, I have it checked all the time. Very simply, I didn't want to stay at the embassy because I knew we would be interrupted. People popping in and out. That's the reason for our visit to the Tiergarten."

"It's nice," Diedre answered. "My sister Daphne wants to come here later. But actually she hasn't taken to Berlin. I sense that she's picked up on the free-floating apprehension that's in the air."

"Most people do, Daffy Dilly."

She laughed. "I knew you'd have to call me that once today. But that's it, not again. Understood?"

"Understood." He laughed with her, then said, "I think I might have someone who could handle a suitcase for you."

Diedre sat up straighter on the garden seat and looked at him alertly. "I thought all of your contacts had gone missing."

"They have. This one fell into my lap, so to speak, and quite unexpectedly."

"Who is he?"

"It's a **she.**"

"Tell me about her."

"She's titled, well-known in Berlin, socially acceptable everywhere, young, quick, and clever. And quite by accident I learned that she's associated with one of the secret underground movements, you know, those anti-Nazi groups who help to get people out."

"Have you mentioned anything to her yet?"

"Not exactly. You'll meet her tomorrow. I put her on the invitation list for the reception, and she's accepted. You'll also meet some of her friends, of the same ilk, I suspect, oh, and a lovely Englishwoman who's married to a German prince. Come to think of it, you might know of her. I believe she comes from a family in Yorkshire."

Diedre frowned, her mind racing. And then it came to her in an instant. "Is her name Arabella von Wittingen?"

"Yes, she's married to Prince Rudolf Kurt von Wittingen."

"Her maiden name is Lady Arabella Cunningham, her brother is the Earl of Langley, and he still lives at Langley Castle in North Yorkshire. Daphne knew her slightly when they were young girls. How interesting. Daphne will enjoy talking to her, I'm sure."

"Now that we're in a safe place, tell me about the people you wish to get out," Tony said. "I don't know anything, as you're well aware. It's been so difficult on the phone."

"I will tell you. But there's just one thing…I did wonder if your phone at the flat is safe? Sure nobody's listening in?"

"**It's safe.** I have ways and means of checking.

I've someone clever with that kind of thing. So, how many exit visas are we talking about? That was never very clear."

"Four."

"It's too many, Diedre. There's been such a clampdown lately and people are getting scared!" Tony exclaimed, his smile fading. "They think they'll get arrested."

"I understand. My sister-in-law, Cecily Swann, has a personal assistant by the name of Greta Chalmers, and it's her family who are trapped here. Cecily's trying to help Greta."

"What's their name?" Tony asked, sounding anxious.

"Steinbrenner. Greta's father is a professor of philosophy and—"

"Professor Helmut Steinbrenner, the famous expert on Plato?" Tony interrupted. "My God, this is such a strange coincidence. That's the third time his name has come up in the last few days. It is him, isn't it?"

"I believe so. He is definitely an authority on Plato. Why has his name come up, Tony? That's a bit bothersome, isn't it?"

"No, it's not. We have another important visitor here from London, Diedre, Sir Anthony Parry, the author, journalist, broadcaster, and he's also a professor at Cambridge. Big, big name in academia."

"I know that, I've read some of his columns in

the **Daily Telegraph,**" Diedre said. "Has he mentioned Professor Steinbrenner?"

"Yes, he has. At the beginning of the week he asked me if it was at all possible to invite Professor Steinbrenner to the reception tomorrow. As a personal favor to him. They are old friends. And so I did. I included Mrs. Steinbrenner, and then one of the newspapermen I know from the press corps here was asking about him."

"Has Professor Steinbrenner accepted?" Diedre cut in.

"I'll have to check that out. I didn't pay much attention, mainly because I was just doing a favor for Sir Anthony."

"Do you have any idea why a newspaperman would ask you about Professor Steinbrenner?" Diedre asked, her face thoughtful.

"No. But he's a friendly chap, owes me a few favors, so I can easily find out. But let us get back to that very important point. The exit visas. I'm not exaggerating when I tell you the supply has dried up. You could go to Valiant."

"I will not go to him! Don't mention him!" Diedre exclaimed, cutting across Tony, her voice sharp, angry.

"All right, all right. I won't bring him up again. He's **verboten**."

Diedre took a deep breath, shook her head. "Sorry, Tony. I'm really sorry. I didn't mean to snap. To continue, I'm afraid we have another problem."

"What is it?" He looked at her swiftly, his light gray eyes suddenly turning anxious.

"Their passports have **J** for Jew stamped on them," Diedre said.

"Oh God, no! I can't get new passports. Not anymore." Tony slumped back against the garden seat, looking and feeling defeated.

Diedre took another deep breath and said, "What's the worst scenario? Obviously not getting any exit visas. Could you get one?"

"Probably, if my new contact works out, and helps me."

"Professor Steinbrenner has two children. I'm certain he will want to get one of them out first."

Tony closed his eyes, and let out a deep sigh. Then he sat up and said, "**A child.** How are we going to handle that, Diedre? A child couldn't travel alone. It's too dangerous for one thing. A child is too obvious a target in more ways than one. If you get my drift."

"I do. A target for everyone. But when I say child, I don't mean a young child. From what Cecily told me, I believe Elise, the professor's younger daughter, is about sixteen or seventeen."

"That's better, easier, but it's still a tough one. A young woman traveling alone on a train.

They're full of troops today, Diedre. Troops going on leave, going to other postings. A woman of any age is a bit vulnerable, actually."

"You're right, of course. Look, I did some hard thinking in Zurich, and I came up with a plan, working on the assumption you could only get one exit visa, if that. And—"

"I should never underestimate you, should I, Daffy Dilly?"

"No, you shouldn't, Toby Jung," she shot back through her laughter. "This is what I thought might work. I have a friend in American intelligence, whose former college roommate is an impresario. This man is often in Berlin, visiting the Berlin Philharmonic Orchestra. He'll do occasional favors for his best buddy. I'd put **him** on the train out of Berlin that goes to Paris via Aachen. With the girl. To protect her, so to speak."

"That's the border town before the crossing into Belgium and then France, and what if something goes wrong?" Tony asked. "A civilian wouldn't know what to do."

"I've made that trip, and I realize there are very tough guards at the border. Passengers have to get off the train, show their passports, exit visas, whatever travel documents they have, and the guards do open suitcases. But things don't often go wrong. You'll have to brief this man, the escort, and if he sees something odd, or feels there are suspicions about them, he'll simply get off the train with the girl, and go into the town of Aachen. From there he'll contact you."

"Understood, and I'll have to take it from there…" He let his sentence trail off. They didn't have a safe house in Aachen now.

"It won't go wrong," Diedre assured him.

"What about the passport the girl has? With **J** stamped on it?" Tony suddenly asked.

"If the girl has a return ticket to Berlin, she won't come under any suspicion. She's going on vacation to Paris, returning home to Berlin in two weeks."

"And she's going with a man, is she?" Tony shook his head. "That might look strange to some people, especially if he's older."

"I agree. The alternative is to put the man on the train alone in the same carriage. The girl will be told he's there to watch over her, and therefore he's not a threat. But they'll behave as if they don't know each other, look like total strangers."

Tony nodded his head vehemently. "That's much better. I think that will work. How do you know this fellow will do it?"

"I don't. But it is a workable plan, a good one," Diedre asserted.

"What happens when the girl gets to Paris?"

"He'll take her to the British embassy, where

she'll get an entry visa for Britain. It will be waiting for her. And then they'll take the train to London together, and I'll pick it up from there."

"Do you think Germans who are Jewish and have a **J** stamped on their passports are likely to travel, to go on vacation?" Tony pursed his lips. "I can't help wondering if the guards might not think it odd. And there are often Gestapo on the trains."

"I understand what you're saying, but the **J** is to proclaim they're Jewish. It's not to stop them going anywhere. The passport is **valid.** Look, they have a passport, nobody's taken it away from them."

"Right. I get your point. So the passport with **J** is not really a stumbling block. However, I'll see if I can get a new one. But it won't be easy, and it'll be costly."

"Thank you. And money is no object, Tony. Whatever is needed."

"What happens if I manage to obtain two exit visas? Does that mean Mrs. Steinbrenner will be going, which would make everything easier, don't you think?" Tony cocked his head to one side, eyeing his boss curiously.

"I do indeed, but I believe the professor will want his son to get out. At least that's what Cecily has said to me. That will have to be last-minute planning."

Tony nodded, and then said carefully, "Going

back to problems. Let's say the American gent and the girl jump ship in Aachen. Where will they go? They'll be adrift. We don't have a safe house there anymore."

"We do, actually," Diedre told him. "I'll give you the details later. Now, what is the name of the person I'm going to meet tomorrow, the one who might help with a suitcase?"

"I'll tell you over lunch," he said.

The restaurant was in a narrow alley in the middle of a tangled web of back streets in an unfashionable part of Berlin. But they served the best homemade Bavarian food and it had been Tony's favorite for several years. He was a regular, and because of his inherent charm, good manners, and generous tips he was treated royally by Frau Weber, the proprietor, and the small staff of waiters.

He always had the same table in a corner near the front door with his back to the wall. He could easily see everyone who entered and left, and if necessary, he could be out of there in a flash.

Diedre loved the little restaurant as well, and whenever she was in Berlin, Tony took her there. And that was where they were headed when they left the Tiergarten and hailed a taxi on the Tiergartenstrasse.

After receiving a warm welcome from Frau

Weber they were shown to Tony's usual table, and within minutes tall glasses of lemonade appeared along with the menus. Neither of them drank alcohol when they were working, and so after a few sips of the lemonade, Tony leaned closer to Diedre, and said, "I'd like to tell you about my new contact before we order."

"Yes, yes, do," Diedre said, "I want to know all about her."

"I don't know too much, but certainly enough for you to understand where she's coming from, the background of her rather turbulent life."

"Turbulent?" Diedre raised a brow questioningly, frowning. Turbulent backgrounds alarmed her.

"Yes, I'm afraid so, although she seems intact on the surface, controlled, calm. Anyway, here goes. Her name is Princess Irina Troubetzkoy. Her father, Prince Igor Troubetzkoy, was murdered in 1917, when Irina was about six and her mother, Princess Natalie, in her early twenties. Because of his death and the fall of the Romanov autocracy, they fled Russia. It is my understanding that her mother is a cousin of the late tsar, by the way." Tony paused, took a swallow of lemonade.

Diedre said, "And so they came to Berlin?"

"No, they didn't, at least not at first. They were in various countries, and spent quite some time in Poland where they had close friends in the Polish aristocracy. Ten years ago they came to Berlin and stayed, tired of being refugees apparently and wandering from country to country."

"Did her mother work? Or Irina when she was older? How did they manage to live, do you know?"

Tony shook his head. "I'm not sure. But I don't think Princess Natalie worked, or Irina when she grew up. The person who introduced me to Irina just recently implied that they had managed to escape with a lot of jewelry and some money, and certain Romanov relatives who had also escaped helped them financially."

"It's the same story about many White Russians who fled the revolution. But I will say this, those I've met proved to be very resilient, and commendable."

"Good words to use. I think Princess Irina and her mother must have been extremely resilient indeed over the years. Anyway, the good news is Princess Natalie recently married a Prussian baron, a widower, and at last they have a real home. The Herr Baron has a house on the Lützowufer, and all seems to be well with them, and the marriage is a grand success, so I'm told."

"Happy endings warm the heart," Diedre murmured quietly. "So, what makes you think Princess Irina can help us get an exit visa, or visas?"

"I'm sure it will be only one, Diedre, the way things are at the moment." Tony leaned back in the chair, looking off into the interior of the restaurant. At last he said, sotto voce, "A close friend in my line of work who's at another foreign embassy in Berlin tipped me off that Irina often works with an underground anti-Nazi group. The ones helping Jews, dissidents, and Catholics to leave Germany. He made me swear to keep her secret a secret."

"I fully understand. Your secret is my secret. How old is she?"

"I figured out she must be in her mid-twenties since she was six in 1917. She was probably born in 1911. She's attractive, rather good-looking, in fact, and loaded with charisma. She appears to have led a life of ease and luxury, when that's quite to the contrary. But you'll meet her tomorrow."

"I assume I'm meeting her as an English socialite and not a woman who works at the War Office?"

"Correct, and that's why I'm so pleased you have Lady Daphne and her husband with you, and your brother and his wife...it all plays well for me. You're important British visitors on holiday in Berlin."

Diedre nodded. "I agree, and that means you'll be doing the asking, dealing directly with

Princess Irina?"

"Yes, I will. Don't worry about that. You've got to keep your cover. Obviously. Now, let's order, I don't know about you, but I'm famished."

Diedre smiled at him. "So am I, but I must be careful. This food is so tempting, I always eat everything and then have to starve myself for a week. And I can't put on any weight at the moment. I'm living in borrowed clothes from Daphne and Cecily. I only had a few things with me when I did an errand in Geneva, and then decided to stay in Zurich to be with Daphne and the others."

"And just look where you ended up. With me. And that's been good because we've been able to have a proper talk without fear of eavesdroppers. And we've made a plan."

"Now everything depends on you, Tony." Picking up the menu, Diedre stared at it, but her mind was on the days ahead and what she had to do.

Tony stared at her and said, "Don't forget to tell me about the new safe house in Aachen."

"I won't." Looking up from the menu, she added, "I'm afraid I shall stick with my usual… bockwurst and sauerkraut, with potato pancakes and applesauce first."

He laughed. "I'm having the same, I love their Bavarian white sausage." He frowned, then said, "I would love to have a cold beer but I suppose I can't."

"I'd join you if I could, but we daren't drink, Tony. We've got to be on our toes at all times. Life can change in a split second. You never know what's going to happen. Especially in our business."

"You're right." He signaled to the waiter and ordered the food, and then turned to Diedre. He murmured softly, "I think there might be a time element here, things are changing so swiftly in Berlin. I want to try to get the suitcase out before the end of this month."

Diedre looked at him, her blue eyes searching his face. "Do you know something I don't?"

"No. But I think trouble is brewing. Also, there's a whole new feeling in the air…a sense of expectation…something big is coming. I just don't know what."

"Then you will have to be quick and nimble," Diedre answered. "Now, here's the information you need about the safe house in Aachen."

She spoke and he listened, and memorized the address and other details. A few minutes later, Tony asked, "By the way, what's the name of the impresario, the American gent who's often in Berlin?"

"He's called Alexander Dubé, and he **is** American. Born and brought up there. French father. He's apparently very dignified and elegant in his appearance. Speaks French and

German, and he's clean as a whistle. And he doesn't mind doing a favor for my friend at the American embassy, whom I will fill in when I get back. But you'll have to deal with Alexander Dubé here."

"No problem, boss," he answered, and grinned at her. "Here comes our gourmet lunch, Daffy Dilly."

Fifteen

I'm glad I found you alone," Diedre said, following Cecily into her suite at the Adlon. "Where is everyone?"

"They decided to go to the Tiergarten, because Charlie hadn't seen it, and Daphne went along as well. They were then going to Horcher's for lunch."

"I see. Didn't you want to go, Ceci?"

"Not really, I'm already back in my work mood…" She paused, half smiled. "I'm not very good at holidays, you know that. I needed to speak to Dottie, go over a lot of things. With a war undoubtedly in the wind I have so many plans to make for the business. It's all rather urgent."

"I understand. Did you speak to Greta this morning?"

"No, I didn't really have reason to, and anyway I wanted to avoid it, if the truth be known. Rather cowardly on my part, isn't it?"

Diedre shook her head, and said, "Not at all. I know how you feel. I got a bit of unexpected and interesting news yesterday, only by chance, of course. And I know it's going to please you."

Cecily looked at her sister-in-law, expectancy filling her eyes. "Is it about Professor Steinbrenner?"

"There's no one quite like you, Cecily!" Diedre exclaimed. "Quick as a tick, that you are. And yes it is, but I don't want you to get too excited. Over lunch yesterday, my friend Tony Jenkins from the embassy happened to say that several English people would be at the reception tonight. He mentioned Lady Arabella Cunningham, the daughter of the late Earl of Langley, who is now married to a German prince. Daphne used to know her when they were girls."

"How amazing. And it will make Daphne feel better about going. She really doesn't like being here."

Diedre nodded. "I know. She has a great aversion to Germany, so it seems. Anyway, to continue. Sir Anthony Parry, the famous academic and broadcaster, will be attending, and Lady Parry may even be there. I've met her a number of times and she's a great friend of Great-Aunt Gwendolyn's." Diedre paused. "Sir Anthony is bringing an old friend. **Professor Steinbrenner.**"

"Oh, thank God! I'm going to meet him, and in the most normal way...quite by accident." Cecily was obviously thrilled.

"Yes, you are. However, the professor hasn't yet replied to the invitation."

Cecily's face fell. "I do hope he comes. It would be lovely to go back to London and tell Greta I had talked with her father. I know it would make her feel so much better." Cecily paused, and then asked quietly, "Do **you** think he'll come?"

Diedre shook her head, gave a half shrug. "I just can't answer that. However, I got the impression that Sir Anthony and the professor are very good friends of long standing, so I'm going to hazard a guess and say it's more than likely he'll be there this evening."

"Why didn't you tell me last night?" Cecily asked, frowning.

"There really wasn't a chance, we were sur-rounded by family and Charlie hardly stopped talking. Anyway, I need to speak to you very seriously, that's another reason I waited until this afternoon."

"You sound so grave," Cecily responded, searching Diedre's face. "Go on, tell me. I'm all ears."

"I want to caution you to be extremely careful how you handle the meeting with Professor Steinbrenner. You must watch your words.

There can be no discussion about getting the family out, or anything like that. Talk mostly about Greta, how wonderful she is, how much you rely on her. Be very positive in every way. No woeful commiserations about his predicament." Diedre paused for a moment, then continued, "I've only been to a couple of these receptions over the years, but they are now very crowded, so Tony explained. Everyone comes to the British embassy 'bun fight,' as he calls it. Look, Ceci, all eyes will be on us, because of who we are. And never forget walls have ears."

"Even carpets do," Cecily shot back, and they both laughed, breaking the solemnity of the moment.

Swallowing her laughter, Cecily said, "I promise to be extremely cautious, careful in everything I say and do. I truly understand the situation. You've made it very clear to me. And I know I must keep this bit of information to myself, correct?"

"Yes. It's better you look surprised when Professor Steinbrenner is introduced. So don't tell Miles or anyone else."

"I won't. Are you going to mention Lady Arabella to Daphne?"

"I thought about it long and hard today, and I think it's better if I just leave it alone. She'll meet her in a natural way, be brought over to Daphne, I'll make sure of that." Noticing a look of puzzlement in Cecily's eyes, Diedre went on swiftly, "I want the evening to be casual, very normal. And I want us all to enjoy it. Tony says there'll be lots of interesting people there, and that it will be fun."

Cecily made a face. "Fun, eh? At a time like this, with the world on the edge of a precipice. Sometimes I can't figure it all out...or why people behave the way they do." She shook her head. "To be honest, deep down inside I'm filled with alarm about the future."

"And so am I," Diedre answered quietly. "But not everyone sees things the way we do. They don't understand politics, what's happening around them. And so they live their lives as usual. And **we** have to do that for the moment as well. We must keep a smile on our faces, Ceci, and never show fear."

The two women sat talking for a while, mostly about the impending war and how to keep Cavendon safe. Cecily told Diedre about all of Hanson's plans, and she was pleased to hear about the conversion of the basements.

After a short while, Cecily said, "So you're going to wear my black crepe de chine frock tonight, but you will need some jewels to liven it up."

Diedre laughed. "I didn't take anything like that with me to Geneva last week. I'd gone on an overnight trip. Can you help me out?"

"I certainly can," Cecily exclaimed. "Come with me to the bedroom, I'll show you some of the pieces I brought. They're all fakes, of course, from the Cavendon Collection."

Diedre nodded, and the two of them went into the bedroom. Cecily removed several black velvet bags from a chest of drawers, and emptied the contents onto the bed, sorting through them.

Diedre joined her and couldn't help exclaiming about the beauty of the pieces. "They all look like the real thing," she said, and instantly reached out for the long strand of pearls. "What a fabulous copy of the Marmaduke," she said. "I think I'd like to wear this with the black dress, if you're not choosing it for tonight."

"I'm not, and the pearls will look great with the black dress." She sorted through a selection of ear clips and produced a pair of fake diamond flowers. "These work well with the Marmaduke pearls."

"Hello, ladies," Miles said from the doorway.

He had startled them both, and they swung around in surprise, not having heard him enter the suite.

"Gosh, you made me jump!" Cecily exclaimed, and hurried over to her husband, hugging him tightly. "You're back earlier than expected."

He nodded, smiling at her, and turning to his sister, he said, "You're looking very smart today, Diedre. I like the suit…but it does look a bit familiar." He chuckled as he said this.

"Courtesy of your wife, Miles. How was the trip to the Tiergarten? And where are the others?"

"Gone to their rooms. I said we'd all go down for tea a bit later. Not that I'm hungry. We had quite a lunch at Horcher's."

The three of them went back into the living room, and Diedre, showing him the pearls and ear clips in her hand, said, "I'm staggered by these pieces, Ceci's a wonder."

He grinned at her. "Oh I know that, I've known it since she was five."

"Did Charlie enjoy himself going around the sights this morning?" Diedre asked, sitting down.

Joining her on the sofa, Miles nodded. "He did, and I must say he's really sharp and bright, and has a wonderfully searching, very curious mind. He'll do well as a journalist. He's picked the perfect profession for himself. He wants to know everything…about everything. He's artic- ulate, and has great clarity when he speaks. And what knowledge is stored in that mind of his. I was quite amazed by him, actually."

A smile spread across Diedre's face, and she said, "I'm glad you've seen that, Miles, and I hope Daphne knows it, too."

"I believe she's learned a lot about him while we've been in Berlin."

Cecily interjected, "Daphne worries about him because he can be very impetuous."

"I think adventurous might be a better word," Miles said. "Hugo was certainly impressed by his son today, wanted to know how he knew so much about Hitler and the Third Reich, and what's going on in the world."

"I believe it's because he reads all of the British newspapers," Diedre announced. "As do I. He explained this to me the other day, and he is indeed a mountain of information, as you've just said."

"I think Daphne finally gets it about him," Miles murmured, settling back against the cushions. "She's such a good mother, and not possessive really, but she does fuss about **him.**"

"I know," Diedre agreed. "She loves all of her children, but it's Charlie she seems to focus on. No wonder they have these contentious quarrels at times. He just blurts things out. He doesn't know how to edit himself around his parents."

Miles said, "Look, she's seen him with us today and every evening we've been here, and she's come to understand he's twenty, almost twenty-one. I kept murmuring that to her. I think it's finally sunk in he's a grown man."

"I hope he doesn't do something silly, like trying to become a war correspondent if war breaks out," Cecily cut in.

"**When** it breaks out," Diedre corrected her. "And I agree. But never fear. No newspaper in Fleet Street is going to hire him, just like that. They already have seasoned war correspondents on the staff. And I know he does intend to finish Oxford."

"Fingers crossed," Cecily said softly, knowing how anxious Charlie was to break free, go out into the world.

"I've never seen such a militaristic city," Miles now said, changing the subject. "There are more uniforms here than you can possibly imagine. Horcher's was full of them."

"What sort of uniforms do the Gestapo wear?" Cecily asked.

"They don't. They're in civilian clothes. But they look so sinister in their leather trench coats and snap-brimmed trilbies you can't fail to miss them."

"I'd better go and put the jewelry away," Diedre said, standing up, wanting suddenly to escape. "Are we having tea in their suite or downstairs, Miles?"

"Downstairs, in about an hour, darling."

"See you then," she said, and looking at Cecily she added, "Thank you for putting me properly together for tonight."

Sixteen

Miles couldn't help smiling to himself as the six of them walked through the lobby of the Adlon. Every head turned to stare.

No wonder, he thought, the women look stunning. Cecily was in lavender chiffon with several strands of amethysts around her neck; Daphne wore white silk and her sapphires, while Diedre was in her borrowed black dress and the fake Marmaduke pearls. They were elegant, stylish, and carried themselves well.

Even when he was much younger, just twelve, he had been well aware that the Inghams en masse caused quite a stir, just by their very presence, and he knew the same thing would happen when they arrived at the embassy.

A few seconds later they went through the front door of the hotel and out onto the Unter den Linden. Then they immediately swung right onto the Wilhemstrasse, where the British embassy was located at number seventy. Diedre had mentioned to him earlier that the Reich Chancellery was only a few doors away. Miles suddenly shuddered at the thought of Hitler and those other gangsters sitting plotting their heinous schemes. Ruthlessly, and with enormous German thoroughness, he had no doubt.

Unexpectedly, Diedre fell into step with him, and slipped her arm through his. "I've warned everyone that it's going to be a mixed bunch, and they shouldn't be alarmed by the number of Nazi officers present. They'll be dressed in their best field-gray uniforms, smiling, smartly clicking their heels, bowing and scraping like dummies. To no avail with us, of course. And you'll recognize the Gestapo from their sinister expressions and cheap suits."

Miles couldn't help laughing. "There's no doubt in my mind that Dulcie inherited your colorful use of the language, and that you, in turn, inherited it from Great-Aunt Gwendolyn." He tucked her arm tighter against his. "I can't wait, and neither can young Charlie. Mind you, Daphne's still a reluctant guest, in my opinion. Let's keep an eye on her tonight, shall we?"

"She'll be fine, Miles. Well, here we are at the embassy and about to enter a bit of our own land in a foreign country where we know we are truly safe. And there's the Union Jack fluttering right above us."

Glancing up, Miles nodded, and then smiled

knowingly at his sister; he swung around, beckoned to the rest of the family, indicating he wanted them to hurry.

Together they went into the embassy, and within moments they were being greeted by His Britannic Majesty's ambassador to Berlin, Sir Nevile Henderson.

The ambassador stood on the central landing at the top of the wide staircase. There was a genial smile on his face as he greeted everyone with his usual charm and graciousness.

Diedre ushered Daphne, Hugo, and Charlie toward the ambassador first, and they were followed by Cecily and Miles. She herself finally came to a standstill in front of him as the last member of the family.

After shaking her hand, he spoke to her for a moment, saying quietly that they would speak later and longer at the small dinner after the reception. His expression was welcoming, his voice full of affection for her. She walked on, knowing there were other guests behind her.

Diedre joined the family and led them forward to one of the two reception rooms, where Tony Jenkins was waiting in the entrance. He hurried toward her, a huge smile on his face.

After he kissed Diedre on the cheek, welcoming her, she introduced him to Daphne, and realized at once that he was stunned by her sister's great beauty, actually rendered speechless. It took him a second to greet Daphne.

Immediately taking charge, Diedre introduced Cecily, Miles, her brother-in-law Hugo, and then Charlie.

Once the introductions were over, Tony said, "Let's go in and partake of a glass of champagne. Only the best served in this territory, and then I'll present you to a few interesting people." His smile was wry.

"The world and his wife are here tonight...it's quite a throng," Tony added. "There are a lot of diplomatic parties in Berlin these days, at the different foreign embassies, but everyone says ours are the best. There's even a waiting list now!" He chuckled when he said this, looking rather pleased about the success of their parties.

They stepped inside and stood in the entrance momentarily, surveying the scene. Diedre at once noticed how full the room was, packed with people. The women were elegantly dressed, all rather chic, and the men were in black tie or uniforms.

It was a large space, with windows at one end, and two huge crystal chandeliers dropped from the ceiling. Masses of flowers were placed everywhere, and it struck her that there was a feeling of real glamour here tonight. A quartet played in one corner; white-gloved waiters in tails moved deftly between the guests, their silver trays filled with flutes of champagne and an assortment of canapés.

Swiveling her head, glancing about, Diedre noticed the life-sized portrait in oils of King George VI hanging on one wall. He had stepped into the breach last year, when his brother Edward had abdicated, and was now their king. Thank God Edward was never crowned, she thought. There would have been an even bigger mess.

Instinctively, she felt George VI would be a good king. He was brave, the way he managed and dealt with his speech impediment, that awful stutter. He had a lovely wife, who was now their most graceful queen, and two little girls, Elizabeth and Margaret Rose. He was very much a family man, and always referred to them as "us four," as if they were united against the world. Perhaps they were.

Tony, Miles, and Charlie were taking flutes of champagne from the passing waiters, and handing them around. Once everyone had a glass in their hands the group moved farther into the room.

As usual, there was an instant lessening of the chatter, and the overall noise dropped several octaves as many heads turned to ogle the glamorous, aristocratic Inghams.

Within minutes Charlie and Hugo had wandered

into the middle of the crush, curiosity propelling them forward.

"I wish them lots of luck, plunging into the crowd," Diedre murmured.

Cecily said, "Do you know anyone here, Diedre?"

"No, not really. But I do recognize a couple of faces over there...among that group of men. They're all foreign correspondents, mostly from the British papers, and I think the fellow they're focusing on is William Shirer, an American writer. He's considered to be **the** expert on the Third Reich. He's covered Berlin for years."

Daphne said, "I want you three to know that I'm really rather impressed with Charlie. I've seen his seriousness about going into journalism, and he's certainly very focused and knows a lot. He just sucks up information."

"He really is a gatherer of news," Cecily interjected. "Miles thinks he's got what it takes, don't you, darling?"

"Yes, I do indeed. He's good, Daphers, very committed to his future career. He just needs air, space, the way you've given it to him the last few days," Miles thought to add, not wishing Daphne to say defensively that she didn't stifle her son.

A moment later, Tony was coming back, ushering a handsome couple. Drawing to a stop, he said to Daphne, "This is your old friend

Lady Arabella Cunningham, who is now Princess von Wittingen, and her husband, Prince Kurt."

"Goodness me! Arabella, how lovely to see you," Daphne exclaimed, thrusting out her hand, a huge smile spreading across her face.

The princess smiled back, and said, "It's been years since we've seen each other, but you haven't changed, Daphne. You're still the great beauty."

After shaking hands with the von Wittingens, Diedre, as usual, became the observer, listening to everyone else, enjoying the warm conversation in progress. She thought Arabella and her husband made a handsome couple, and from what she was hearing they were regular visitors to the British embassy, as were several of their friends, whom they were expecting to arrive shortly.

After a few minutes, Hugo returned and was presented to the von Wittingens. After speaking to them cordially, he edged closer to Diedre and Tony. He said in a low voice, "Charlie's having the time of his life, chatting to a beautiful Russian. Another princess, actually."

Tony exclaimed, "That must be Princess Irina Troubetzkoy. I need to speak with her. Excuse me for a moment."

Diedre smiled at him, nodded, and turned to Hugo, "I for one will never really worry about

Charlie ever again. I do think he knows how to take care of himself, and he's deft when it comes to meeting new people. He certainly has the gift of the gab."

Hugo smiled when he said, "Oh yes, he's undoubtedly kissed the Blarney Stone, words just flow out of him." Dropping his voice, he whispered, "What a collection of strange people are gathered here tonight. Somebody on the ambassador's staff must have gone slightly mad. I overheard a man say a few ladies of the night are here…from Madame Kitty's, the best brothel in Berlin."

Diedre burst out laughing. "That's true. Those women down there in the very gaudy clothes and cheap jewels undoubtedly spring from Kitty's. The SS officers with them appear to be entranced, will no doubt be all tucked up with them tonight."

"Lots of luck to them all," Hugo muttered, and swung his head as Tony said, "Hugo, Diedre, I would like you to meet Princess Irina Troubetzkoy."

Diedre found herself looking into a small piquant face filled with laughter. Large blue eyes sparkled, and the princess's burnished brown hair framed a lovely, rather delicate face. There was a carefree air about her, denying the turbulent youth Tony had described.

"I am so pleased to meet you," Irina said to

Hugo, repeated the same words to Diedre, then added, "Tony told me Lady Daphne is an old friend of Arabella's. How nice they have met again after so many years."

"My sister was thrilled, as you can probably tell from the conversation they're having. They haven't stopped talking," Diedre said.

"I do see, yes," Princess Irina answered, her voice light, musical, her slightly accented English perfect in its pronunciation.

Diedre was instantly drawn to her, liked her effervescent personality, her easy open manner. She wore a black lace dress of three-quarter length; her only jewelry were small pearl ear clips and a watch. But she was elegance personified, and had a special aura about her.

Charlie, who had trailed after the princess and Tony, edged into the small group they made, stood next to his father, his admiration for the princess reflected on his young face. He thought she was about twenty-five, but he didn't care. He would like to get to know her better. What a beauty she was.

Tony, giving Diedre a careful glance, murmured, "I wanted you to meet Princess Irina, and now I must take her away. But only for a moment or two. I need a quick private word with her."

"That's fine, Tony," Diedre responded, and then frowned. Her eyes narrowed as she stared at him. "I think Sir Anthony Parry is coming toward us, along with another man."

Following her gaze, Tony nodded emphatically. "Oh gosh, it is him, yes. And I believe that is his old friend Professor Steinbrenner with him."

Moving forward immediately, Tony went to greet the two men.

Within moments Sir Anthony was shaking Diedre's hand before he introduced Professor Steinbrenner to them all. Diedre asked after Lady Parry, told Sir Anthony that Lady Gwendolyn was keeping well, in answer to his question, then addressed the professor. She said, "Your daughter Greta works with my sister-in-law, Cecily, Professor Steinbrenner. She happens to be here tonight. I know she would love to meet you."

Helmut Steinbrenner's face changed instantly when he heard those words. His dark brown eyes so dull and tired a moment ago brightened considerably. They were sparkling and there was a sudden expression of eagerness in them. He broke into smiles. "That would be wonderful, Lady Diedre."

He couldn't help glancing around, asking as he did, "Where **is** the great Cecily Swann my Greta never stops talking about?"

"I'm going to bring her over," Diedre announced, and gave Tony a very pointed look when she left the group.

He understood she wanted him to get the princess alone, in order to ask for her help. He watched Diedre go over to Cecily, who was with the von Wittingens and Daphne. Once they were engaged in conversation, he said to Sir Anthony, "If you would excuse us for a moment, sir, and you too, Professor Steinbrenner, Princess Irina and I must have a quick word with William Shirer. We'll only be gone for a few minutes."

"That's not a problem at all, Jenkins," the academic answered.

"Thank you, Sir Anthony."

Hugo said, "Don't worry, Tony, we'll look after Sir Anthony and Professor Steinbrenner, won't we, Charlie?"

His son nodded, and immediately zeroed in on Sir Anthony, saying in a most reverential manner, "I read your column in the **Daily Telegraph,** sir, and enjoy it very much. I'm hoping to write for newspapers myself one day."

The famous academic smiled indulgently, and the four men were immediately off to a good start on a conversation about the British press. The pros and cons of it, and the sheer delight of it at times.

Diedre led Cecily and Miles to a corner, and explained quietly, "I've just met Professor

Steinbrenner. I told him you are here. So come on, let's go."

A bright smile flew onto Cecily's face, and Miles simply gaped at his sister, taken aback by her announcement. "I say, what good news this is," he managed, surprise echoing in his voice.

"Fabulous news!" Cecily exclaimed. "I wonder why he's here at the embassy reception?"

Diedre answered swiftly, "I understand he's a very close and old friend of Sir Anthony Parry, who's with us tonight. Apparently, Sir Anthony came to Berlin to give a series of lectures on philosophy."

Miles said, "Take us over to them." As he spoke he started to walk across the room, having recognized Sir Anthony with Hugo and Charlie.

Diedre stopped Cecily from rushing after him, grabbed her hand, held her back. "Remember, not a word about anything. And behave naturally. Miles is swift, and he hardly ever takes his eyes off you, Ceci. Be careful what you say."

Cecily nodded. "I'm aware of everything. Please don't worry, Diedre. I'm not dense. I know what's at stake."

"I know you do," Diedre murmured, and followed her sister-in-law, who was now hurrying after Miles.

No introductions were needed when Miles

and Cecily came to a standstill next to Professor Steinbrenner. He stepped forward, grasped hold of her hands, and pulled her closer to him. "What a wonderful surprise to find you here! I never thought I would ever meet you. Thank you, thank you, for being so good to my daughter. Greta never stops talking about you."

"She's a marvel, Professor Steinbrenner, my good right hand. I don't know what I would do without her," Cecily said.

Diedre stepped away, wanting to leave the professor alone with Cecily and Miles. Hugo, Charlie, and Sir Anthony did the same, but remained together, deep in conversation.

Diedre's eyes scanned the room. She needed to get an overall view of the scene in general. The von Wittingens were still with Daphne, and had been joined by another couple she did not know, but decided were German. Tony huddled with Princess Irina in a corner obviously confiding in her. Cecily and Miles were behind her with the professor. She knew exactly where her lot were.

It was when the large crowd in the middle of the room shifted slightly, lessened, that Diedre saw her. **Pauline Mallard.** The woman Harry was involved with. Diedre stared at her again to make sure it really was her. And it was. Diedre could hardly believe her eyes. Mrs. Mallard stood next to an older man and another woman, who seemed oddly familiar to Diedre. And then it clicked in her mind. Pauline Mallard was with Lady Diana Mosley, one of the Mitford sisters, and wife of the British Fascist leader. Well, well, well, she thought, wonders never cease, and she couldn't help speculating about Pauline Mallard's political persuasion. Was she an admirer of Hitler as her companion was?

At this precise moment she saw him walking toward her. **Valiant.** My God, what was he doing here?

Seventeen

You look surprised to see me," Valiant said, drawing to a standstill in front of her.

"I am," Diedre answered. "Flabbergasted would be a better word. You hardly ever socialize, so why show your face at the British embassy, of all places?"

A faint smile flickered. "If you look around, you'll see that I'm not the only German officer present. The room is loaded with us, including Gestapo." Taking a step forward, he took her hand, bent over it, kissed it lightly, his manners as always impeccable.

He went on, "I was invited, and so I came tonight because I heard you would be here. I thought it would be nice to see you, Diedre."

"It is, yes, of course." Lowering her voice, she murmured, "But you know I worry about you."

"I do. And you mustn't. I'm not under suspicion and the High Command are impressed by my career in the Great War. Anyway, here I am. And why are you in Berlin?"

"I came with my family," she began, endeavoring to keep her face straight. As head of the Abwehr, German military intelligence, there wasn't anything he didn't know. He had built an enormous and highly efficient organization over the last three years since his appointment. It was filled with officers mostly of his ilk. All were anti-Nazi and attempting to work against Hitler's deadly regime in secret.

Clearing her throat, Diedre now continued, "My nephew Charlie wanted to visit Berlin and we decided to make it a family affair. That's his mother, my sister Daphne over there, still chatting away to an old friend. One she didn't know she was going to meet."

He followed her glance. "Ah, yes, Princess von Wittingen. The prince is the roving ambassador for the industrialist Krupp..." Valiant stopped, gave Diedre a pointed look. "Someone is heading our way."

"It's my sister-in-law, Cecily Swann, the designer." As she was speaking Diedre saw that Cecily had paused, was hesitating, looking at her questioningly. Diedre knew she had no option but to beckon her to come and join them.

"It's perfectly all right," he said sotto voce as Cecily came closer to them.

"Cecily, I'd like you to meet Admiral Wilhelm Canaris...Admiral, this is my brother's wife,

Cecily Swann Ingham."

"I'm pleased to meet you, Admiral," Cecily said evenly, not showing the surprise she felt, offering him her hand.

"It's my pleasure, Mrs. Ingham," he responded, shaking her hand, inclining his head in a small bow. "I was just telling Diedre how happy I was to run into her. We're very old acquaintances. My family knew Maxine Lowe and her father, who often came to the Ruhr. And seemingly Lady Daphne also met an old friend this evening."

"Yes, she did," Cecily answered, relaxing now that he had explained himself. "It's years since she saw Arabella."

"So Diedre told me."

There was a silence.

Diedre took command swiftly, and said, "Did you want to ask me something, Ceci?"

"I did, yes. Sir Anthony has invited us to lunch tomorrow with the professor. Miles and myself, that is, and I was wondering if that would fit in with the family?"

"Oh dear, I don't know how to answer that. I'm not sure if Daphne is planning a lunch—" She cut herself off, then added, "Now, what was it she said to me earlier?"

The admiral remarked, "Sir Anthony is an enormously talented man. I hear his lectures are already sold out. I should think lunch with him would be most enjoyable." He smiled at Diedre and went on, "I wouldn't mind having lunch with him myself."

"Oh, would you like to join us?" Cecily asked. "I'm sure it would be all right."

"A nice thought, but I am working, I'm afraid."

Instantly understanding that the admiral had seen no objection to the lunch, Diedre now said, "It's all right with me, Ceci, I have other plans tomorrow so why not ask Daphne? I think that would be the best."

"Good idea, I'll go and talk to her. Sorry to have intruded. A pleasure to have met you, Admiral Canaris."

"And likewise, Mrs. Ingham," he replied.

Cecily gave them both a huge smile and slipped away, heading across the room to Daphne.

"Why were you hesitating?" the admiral asked, when they were alone, searching Diedre's face. "About them lunching together?"

"Because the professor's daughter works for Cecily in London, and she's anxious about him being here in Berlin."

In a low tone, Canaris said, "An exit? Is that it?"

"Yes," Diedre murmured, her voice as low as his.

"Why didn't you get in touch? Ask me?" He sounded puzzled.

"Because you've done too much for me

already."

"Haven't you put anything in the works?" He frowned. "That's not like you."

"I have. Tony's dealing. He's over there..." Her voice trailed off. She inclined her head toward Tony and the Russian princess still together in a corner of the room, across from them.

"I see. That's all right. She will come to me. Consider it done." When Diedre remained silent he stared at her. "What is it? What's wrong? You look worried."

"Four exits," she whispered. "Such a lot. Everything new."

He nodded. "Consider it a done deal, Diedre," he repeated quietly in a firm voice.

"Thank you. Thank you so much. I'm so grateful." She shook her head. "I suppose I should have asked you, but I do worry about your safety."

"I told you, you must stop that. I'm not in harm's way. In the meantime, I would like a bit of help from you."

"Anything. You know you just have to ask me."

"Time with you. Tomorrow. Alone. I heard you say to Cecily that you had plans. Do you?"

"No, I don't, but I always try to protect myself in case something comes up. And now it has." A smile surfaced at last.

"I need to give you some information. I want it relayed to William Lawson when you get back to London. Meet me at our usual place at one. Now, let us have a glass of champagne." He turned around, cornered one of the passing waiters, and lifted two flutes off the tray, handed one to Diedre.

They touched glasses, and he said, "After this I must leave."

"I understand," Diedre said. "I will be there tomorrow."

She watched the admiral walking out, confident, sure of himself as he moved through the crowd with ease, stopping to speak to an SS officer, and then a colleague from the High Command. All those who knew him or worked with him cared about Canaris and his welfare. He had enormous integrity and courage; by birth, upbringing, conviction, and instinct Canaris was an anti-Nazi. He had never joined the Nazi party, and last year he had told Diedre that he believed Hitler would be the ruination of Germany, had added that the Führer was leading the fatherland into a hell on earth.

Her eyes followed his black naval uniform until it disappeared from sight, and then she swiveled around, her eyes seeking Cecily. She saw her still standing next to Miles, chatting to Sir Anthony and the professor, and immediately walked over to join them.

When Cecily saw her, she reached out, took hold of her hand, and drew her gently into their circle. In a low voice, she asked, "Where's the admiral? You should have brought him over to meet Sir Anthony."

"He had to leave." Drawing close to Cecily, Diedre murmured, "You'll never believe who's here."

"Who?" Peering at Diedre, frowning, she said, "You sound funny. Who on earth is it?"

"Pauline Mallard."

"**What?** That can't be. It's not possible."

"Well, it is, because she's standing over there, and with Diana Mosley, no less. Take a look. Don't you see the redhead in the purple dress? Do you think it's a matter of birds of a feather flock together?"

"Yes, you're right, it is her. My God, Harry will be shocked when I tell him. I think the older man must be her husband, Sheldon Faircross." A flash of annoyance flickered on Cecily's face when she added, "She's obviously traveling with him and therefore the marriage must work. She's just using Harry."

"I agree. But do you think she's one of the cheering English crowd surrounding Hitler?" Diedre raised a brow quizzically.

Cecily was silent for a moment, and then she said in the same low concerned voice, "I don't know. Perhaps. I am determined to get Harry out of her clutches, that's the one thing I do know."

While they had been speaking quietly together they had edged away from the group, and stood a few feet away. A split second later Miles joined them, and looking from his wife to his sister, he asked, "What are you two whispering about? You look like a couple of conspirators."

Diedre smiled faintly, and said, "Harry's lady friend is over there with her husband. Well, I think he's her husband, and also Lady Mosley."

Miles was as taken aback as Cecily had been, and he glanced around, asked, "Where? Where are they standing?"

"Near those big windows," Cecily replied. "Come on, let's walk down there and stand near them. Let **her** see that **we've** seen her."

Giving Cecily an odd look, Miles said, "As long as you promise you won't verbally attack her, Ceci."

"I promise. I just want to make her feel uncomfortable."

The three of them strolled down the long room and came to a standstill not far from the Pauline Mallard group. Within seconds she noticed them, flushed bright red, and simply turned her back to them.

"It didn't take long for her to blush in embarrassment," Cecily said, her eyes flashing.

Miles grinned at her, amusement flickering in his eyes.

Diedre said softly, to her brother, "She is rather beautiful though, isn't she?"

Cecily threw her a pointed look, and exclaimed, "Never say that to my mother. Her angry retort will be that Mrs. Mallard is also very promiscuous."

"Everyone says that," Miles murmured. "But yes, Pauline Mallard is a stunner, Diedre, and so is Diana Mosley. As are all the Mitford women, in fact. Although not quite as ravishing as the Ingham girls, in my opinion."

"I wish you had warned me Admiral Canaris was coming to the reception," Diedre said, staring across the table at Tony.

"I didn't know he was, and if I had of course I would have told you," he shot back swiftly in a slightly injured tone.

"But you're in charge of the list," Diedre pointed out, and took a sip of cognac.

The two of them were sitting in the small bar in the Adlon Hotel. Her family had all gone to bed after the embassy dinner, but Diedre had stayed up to have a nightcap with Tony, wanting to discuss Princess Irina.

Now he protested, "I'm not in charge of the entire list, only part of it! The diplomatic corps, the press corps, the German princelings and the international lot. The ambassador looks after special guests. He invited Valiant. But the admiral declined, that's why I never even mentioned it to you. When I saw him come in tonight, I was as shocked as you obviously were."

Diedre nodded. "All right. I believe you. So let's get on, talk about Princess Irina. What did she say? What's your assessment of her?"

"I believe she will help, she more or less said as much. She indicated she's part of an underground movement, and by the way she is vehemently anti-Nazi, calls the German government a bunch of thugs and murderers. I explained the number of exit visas needed, gave her all the details, and she didn't seem to be thrown by anything. She said she would get back to me next week. As for my assessment of her, I think she is completely trustworthy, and will do everything possible to help. Her early life taught her a lot. She's compassionate."

"Valiant's going to help her help us," Diedre volunteered.

"So in the end you asked him," Tony said, eyeing her carefully, somewhat surprised by her words.

"Not exactly in the way you think," Diedre answered, leaning back on the banquette, endeavoring to relax. "He thought I was troubled about something, and he sort of dragged it out of me. I told him. When he asked if I had anything in the works, I said I did, that you were hoping Princess Irina would make it happen. His comment was that she would come to him, and that he would do it. He called it a done deal."

Tony was silent for a moment or two, and then he said slowly, "Perhaps they work together on a regular basis. What do you think?"

"I don't know, and I don't want to, Tony. But let's face it, he has managed to get a lot of people out of Berlin, Jews as well as Catholics and dissidents." She fell silent, looked off into the dimness of the bar, before finally saying, "That's why I gave him the code name Valiant. And I suppose that's why I worry about him, his safety. On the other hand, he insists he's not under suspicion, or in harm's way."

"I don't think he is. Nor are any of the others at this moment in time. Actually, I don't know how the generals do it…they play up to Hitler by day, and plot his downfall at night."

Diedre was silent again, knowing Tony spoke the truth. He had his ear to the ground, and he also had unique informants, all sorts of sources passing on information to him.

Misunderstanding her silence, Tony said gently, "Don't worry, we'll get the professor and his family out, and the admiral will be safe, I assure you of that."

She gave him a long, thoughtful look, and said in a voice so low it was hardly audible, "Last year, Valiant said to me that he and his compadres, as he called them, would undoubtedly end up on the gallows. And I haven't forgotten that."

"He was joking," Tony said. "Surely." He laughed as he continued, "Everyone knows Admiral Canaris is revered, and his record is legendary. Why, he made history in the last war, because he's a past master in intelligence. We all know, in our circles, how his ship the **Dresden** eluded the British Royal Navy because of his brilliance. He's a hero in Germany."

"I know," she answered. "He is to me too, but for his other deeds."

Eighteen

The restaurant the admiral regularly frequented was located not far from Abwehr headquarters. In some ways it reminded Diedre of the little restaurant she and Tony used, being also somewhat plain. But this place was better furnished and more sophisticated in style, and in the food it served.

Most importantly, Cafe Baumer, as it was called, was mostly frequented by officers and staff who worked in German military intelligence. In other words, the admiral was always surrounded by his own people; very few passersby stepped inside and stayed, no doubt put off by the plethora of naval uniforms; anyone phoning to make a reservation was firmly told the cafe was fully booked. It was the admiral's domain.

When Diedre arrived on Friday, at one, as arranged with Canaris, she was shown to his preferred table. The waiter poured her a glass of water, and once she was alone, she picked

up the menu and studied it, and she remembered how good the Wiener schnitzel was here.

Letting her eyes roam around the room, she
saw a number of uniformed naval officers, and
a couple of women who were obviously secre-
taries. And then a moment later Major General
Hans Oster was standing next to her table, his
hat in his hand, smiling down at her.

"It's so nice to see you again, Diedre," he said,
and lowered himself into a chair. "He'll be here
momentarily; he's just delayed a few minutes."

Like the admiral, Hans Oster spoke good
English, but not with the perfect Cambridge
accent the admiral had acquired years before,
having been taught by a Cambridge graduate.

"Hans, what a lovely surprise. I saw you in
the distance at the embassy party last night,
but before I could come over you disappeared
into thin air."

He grinned at her. "I'm rather good at that, as
you well know, Diedre."

Suddenly there was a small flurry of activity
near the entrance, and as they both looked
across the room they saw Admiral Canaris
arriving, and being welcomed by the owners,
Alfred Baumer and his wife, Giselle.

"My apologies, Diedre," he said a moment
later as he sat down on the other side of her.
"I was held up in a meeting."

"That's all right, I only just got here," she

replied, and smiled at him. "And before I could even blink, Hans arrived."

The admiral nodded. "Hans is joining us for lunch, just for a while, and then we'll have that time alone I need with you."

"I understand," she answered. The two men had already picked up their menus, and she did the same. Within a few seconds, the admiral beckoned for the waiter, who was by their side in an instant.

The waiter looked at her, and she said, "I'll have the Wiener schnitzel, please. Nothing first."

"Bockwurst sausage and red cabbage," Oster ordered, and added, "I won't have a first course, either."

"Wiener schnitzel," the admiral murmured. "And please pour the water, Gunther."

Once this had been done, and the three of them were alone, the admiral leaned closer to Diedre, and asked, "When are you leaving Berlin?"

"Tomorrow, as planned. We are all returning to Zurich, and on Sunday afternoon I shall leave for London. I need to go back to work."

"Are you returning alone to London? Or is the rest of your family traveling with you?"

Diedre shook her head. "Charlie is coming with me, he wants to prepare to go back to Oxford. Daphne and Hugo will spend another few days in Zurich, and then go home to Cavendon, and so will Cecily and Miles."

"I see. That's good, very good. Things are not going to be so easy on this continent, I'm afraid." He had dropped his voice, and it grew lower still when he added, "I'm afraid for Czechoslovakia. Hitler has his beady eyes on Sudetenland, which can only lead to disastrous events."

Diedre, taken aback, simply gaped at him. Sudetenland had been on everyone's lips. But now? Sooner than they had thought, that was the truth.

Hans Oster's brow drew together in a frown, and he murmured softly, "Surely Britain and France will intervene? Daladier and Chamberlain wouldn't permit it."

Canaris let out a deep sigh. "I'm afraid it is a given."

Leaning in to the admiral, the major general whispered, "Talk to General Keitel. As Hitler's chief of staff, surely he can talk him out of it."

"He can't. He's tried and failed. In fact, it's Keitel who told me to be prepared for the worst. And that was exactly twenty minutes ago. The Führer, seemingly, can't be stopped."

Oster's face settled into hard lines and his eyes blazed with a furious glint. He took a deep breath and clasped his hands together in his lap, obviously striving to keep control of his flaring emotions.

Canaris spoke calmly. "Keep yourself steady, Oster. **Our time will come.** For the moment, we must play his game, while playing a double game. Ours."

"Will he invade Britain?" Diedre asked quietly.

The admiral gave a small shrug. "You know, I honestly believe he doesn't want to, not at all. I think he'd like to avoid it at all cost. He's quite an Anglophile, you know. He loves the British aristocracy, admires the Royal Navy, and wants **me** to create a military intelligence division to rival Britain's, which he considers the best in the world."

"Are you saying he wants appeasement, that he would go along with Chamberlain?" she asked, drawing even nearer to him as she spoke.

"At the moment, yes. However…" The admiral stopped, and shook his head. "I never know what **he's** going to come up with next. And that makes me fearful. Also, I truly believe there's only so far the British government will go."

"I wish to God Churchill were in power now, and not on the back benches," Oster muttered, his face a picture of genuine dismay mingled with frustration.

Forty minutes later Major General Oster said his warm good-byes to Diedre and departed.

Finally she and the admiral were alone. After ordering more coffee for them, he settled back in his chair, and said, "It's a simple message I want you to pass on to William Lawson, Diedre. But it is extremely important."

"You know I will relay it exactly."

"I do indeed."

After the waiter had brought the coffee, Canaris continued to speak in a soft voice. He told her what he wanted her to say to her boss. And he spoke for quite a long time.

Games of Chance

Strong is the soul, and wise, and beautiful;
The seeds of godlike power are in us still;
Gods are we, bards, saints, heroes,
if we will!

—Matthew Arnold,
"Written in Emerson's Essays"

Nineteen

Harry Swann was angry. In fact, he was in a fury, and he had been for days. He now fully understood that Pauline Mallard had dropped him, and he didn't understand why. Except that he really did. She did not love him, or at least not enough, to give up her life of ease, style, and international flitting around.

A deep sigh escaped him as he flipped up the collar of his white shirt, slipped the silk tie around his neck, and made a knot. He stood in front of the cheval mirror in his bedroom, getting dressed to keep an engagement he didn't really need. Or want, for that matter.

But he had accepted the invitation and had left it too late to cancel, so he must go. What he really wanted to do was go out and chop wood to vent his anger. Or find a boxing training gymnasium in Leeds, and hit a punching bag for a couple of hours. Until he was exhausted, his anger spent.

After putting on his jacket, he went and sat down at the desk in front of the window, and looked at his engagement book. Today was Friday, August 12. On Saturday, the second, in the middle of the night, Pauline had telephoned him and explained she was leaving early on Sunday morning for London. She had no choice, she had murmured. Her husband had business in Paris and insisted she accompany him. She had sworn her undying love for him and promised to phone him every day.

An empty promise. He had not heard a word from her since. On Wednesday, Charlotte had asked him to take young Robin, Diedre's son, to the dentist in Harrogate. He had done so. While waiting for Robin to have a tooth removed, he had driven around to Pauline's house near the Stray, the stretch of common green land in the middle of town.

Harry had been flabbergasted to see the FOR SALE sign in front of her house. After parking his car, he had gone up the steps and rung the doorbell, knowing only servants would be there. It was Mrs. Ladlow, the cook, who had opened the door, and smiled broadly at the sight of him.

Cook, a friendly soul, had ushered him inside and confirmed that her employers had indeed left Harrogate. And for good. She confided they were planning to buy a house in Paris.

Keeping tight control of his emotions, Harry

had thanked her, and turned to leave. On the doorstep, Mrs. Ladlow had told him she was looking for a job, should he know of anyone needing an excellent cook. He said he would pass the word along.

Shock and disbelief had turned to anger and today it had become total fury. He shook his head. They had been right, his mother and his sister. Pauline Mallard had been using him. He had been her sex object, her means of slaking her overpowering sexual lust. Miles had suggested she was a nymphomaniac several months ago, and that any man would do for her as long as he was attractive and could get an erection if she merely smiled provocatively.

I've been a fool, he muttered under his breath, and turned the page, noted that Diedre and Charlie were coming back to London in a couple of days, and so were Miles and Cecily; Daphne and Hugo would be home here at Cavendon in time for tea on Sunday, the twenty-first.

Closing the engagement book, he sat back in the chair for a moment, and closed his eyes. How he had missed them—each and every one. They were his family, his world, as was Cavendon. Yes, his whole world, and he knew, suddenly, and with a flash of insight into himself, that this was where he belonged.

He could never leave here, traipse around the hot spots of the world with the likes of Pauline

Mallard. He would be viewed as her gigolo, her plaything. Anyway, he wanted a child. Children. And she was too old. He had always desired a family. A wife and children to love. That was what life was all about, what made it worthwhile.

Downstairs, the grandfather clock struck three, and he realized he must get a move on. He must leave at once. He wanted to walk across to see his mother first before driving to Burnside Manor. He groaned inside. Tea with Commander Jollion was not something he relished, but young Phoebe Bellamy had been very persuasive, and he had finally agreed to drive over to meet her family.

Alice Swann stood in her pantry, gazing at the gleaming jars that lined the shelves, a smile of pleasure flashing across her face. How beautiful they were...her bottled purple plums, snow-white pears, green gooseberries, and pinkish-red rhubarb. And below them, on another shelf, bloodred beets, creamy-brown mushrooms, red cabbage, pickled onions, pickled cucumbers, and her very own special glowing yellow piccalilli.

Nodding to herself, happy with her growing hoard, she turned out the light and went back into the kitchen, glancing at the clock on the mantel shelf as she did.

In fifteen minutes Evelyne Bourne would be

coming to see her for a chat and a cup of tea. Alice was looking forward to seeing her. She had known Evelyne since her birth, and although there was a difference in their ages, almost twenty years, they had become the greatest of friends in the last fifteen years. They had drawn close when Evelyne had joined the Women's Institute in Little Skell village, and had grown to love it as much as Alice did.

Filling the kettle, putting it on the gas ring, Alice thought about their WI and the difference it had made in so many countrywomen's lives. And always for the better, which is why it had been created in the first place. It had first started in Canada in the late 1800s, was introduced in America in the 1900s, and had finally come to England.

In 1915, an English aristocrat, Lady Denman, had started the first WI. How they had spread through all of the villages across the land. The Women's Institute now had many thousands of members, and what a boon these country-women were going to be when the war came. Alice knew deep within herself that they would be the backbone of the country, growing food in the allotments, bottling fruit, making jams, knitting scarves and socks, sewing clothes, making sure the sick were properly looked after, as well as those in need of anything else.

Taking cups and saucers from the cupboard,

Alice placed them on the kitchen table, and then jumped in surprise as the door burst open and Harry marched in looking like thunder.

"Goodness me, Harry, you did give me a start!" Alice cried, staring at her son, wondering what ailed him. "Is something wrong?"

"No, no, not really, Mam." Closing the door more quietly behind him, he walked across the room, brought her into his arms and gave her a hug, holding her tightly. "Sorry about bursting in like that," he said softly against her hair. "I'm actually in a bit of a hurry, that's all."

As he released her, he looked down at her and smiled. "You look bonny, Mam, you really do. Red suits you."

"You're a tease, Harry. Bonny at my age, indeed."

"Well, you are."

"And you're my favorite son."

She had said this to him for years and years, and as usual it made him laugh. "Now you're the tease. Sit down with me for a minute, I have something to tell you, Mother."

"You sound serious. What is it?" she asked, her eyes narrowing, and not leaving his face.

"I'm no longer with Pauline Mallard. It's over. Finished. Gone. Dead as a doornail. And now I'm fancy-free."

Alice said nothing for a moment, simply stared at him, filled with relief at his statement. She had thought she would never hear those words. And now she had at last. Thank God. Finally finding her voice, she asked, "Do you want to talk about it?"

"I don't mind. I think you and Cecily should know anyway, because you've both been so concerned, and for some time."

There was a moment of silence as Harry settled back in the chair, staring into space, a reflective look in his eyes.

"You don't have to tell me now, it must be fresh, and you must be a bit raw," Alice murmured softly, suddenly knowing he was in pain.

"I'll manage." He forced a smile. "I'm a big boy."

"So what happened?" Alice asked carefully, riddled with curiosity, knowing that he had truly been in love, had cared deeply about Pauline Mallard. And that he had been reluctant to end the affair.

Slowly, carefully choosing his words so as not to offend his mother, Harry told her about the last time he had seen Pauline...on that fateful Friday when her husband was suddenly about to arrive unexpectedly and catch them together.

Alice did not interrupt him. She sat listening, her attention focused on him. He then explained about the lack of communication from Pauline, and finally his visit to the house in Harrogate on Wednesday.

"I felt she had dropped me, and suddenly I understood that I **had** been used, as you'd said, Mam. They are not coming back here. They're selling their house, going to live in Paris apparently. Well, according to Mrs. Ladlow, the cook. Even if she phones me now, or gets in touch, I won't have anything to do with her." Standing up, Harry finished in a firmer tone, "And after all, as you so frequently said, she's too old for me. And too old, most certainly, to bear my children."

Jumping to her feet, Alice went over and put her arms around her son. She began to cry, and eventually she murmured against his shoulder, "I'm sorry you've been hurt, Harry. But I'm happy, so very happy for you. Now you can begin a new life. And I know that somewhere, out there, there's a woman who is your true destiny. You'll find her, you'll see, and when you least expect it."

"Perhaps," he answered, and kissed her cheek. "No more tears now, Mam."

"They're tears of happiness," she protested.

"I know that."

Walking over to the front door, he added, "I'm now off to tea with Commander Jollion. When they invited me I attempted to turn the invitation down, but that little Phoebe Bellamy is incorrigible. Once she gets her claws in, she won't let go. She's only twelve, but she's as tenacious as the devil. If she were older I'd think she had designs on me. But of course she doesn't. Don't look at me like that. She **is** only twelve, you know."

"I know that, you silly thing. She's an endearing little girl with lots of persuasive powers. Phoebe's used to getting her own way, and they've spoiled her."

Harry frowned, hesitating in the doorway. "Do you know Phoebe, Mam?"

"No. Her aunt, Mrs. Jollion, the commander's wife, is with our WI, and when Adrianna is up here she comes to the institute with her. That's Phoebe's mother, by the way."

"Who has quite a brood, I hear. Not only Phoebe but several sons."

"Yes, that's correct," Alice answered, and thought: She also has four other daughters, but I'll let you find that out for yourself.

Not long after Harry had left, there was a light knocking on the door. Evelyne pushed it open, put her head inside. "It's me, Alice," she said.

"Hello, love. Come in, come in, don't stand there," Alice answered, smiling warmly, glad to see her friend.

"I've got a pram full of jams and bottled fruit. Is it all right if I bring it in?" Evelyne asked.

"Of course. Let me help you."

Alice walked across the kitchen as Evelyne pushed the pram into the room. "You know we've got a real problem," Evelyne announced, as she began to take the jars out of the pram and handed them one by one to Alice.

After placing them all on the table, Alice swung around, frowning. "What kind of problem?" she asked, puzzlement echoing in her voice.

"I'm afraid we've run out of jars. I've only got about a dozen left. Do you have any?"

"Ten, that's all. And you're right, it is a problem. I wonder where we can get some more? Perhaps ask some of the women in the village?"

"They don't have any, either. Let's face it, we've been quite busy." Evelyne let out a hollow laugh. "We'll have to beg, borrow, or steal some from somewhere, that's all there is to it."

Alice nodded, a thoughtful look settling on her face. Then she exclaimed, "We'll splurge and **buy** some. We've no other choice."

"They're not cheap."

"Yes, I'm aware of that. I'll try and cadge a few from Cook up at the house, but she does a lot of bottling herself these days. I'll get Cecily to buy some in London, she'll be back next week. Somehow we'll manage. Will you help me to put this stuff in the pantry? Then we can sit down for a bit, have a cup of tea and a nice chat."

The two women carried the foodstuffs into the

pantry, and once they had finished Evelyne went over to the stove, turned on the gas; Alice sat down at the table.

"It's boiled once already," Alice explained, "Harry was here and I put the kettle on, but I never made the tea."

"I saw him driving off hell-for-leather," Evelyne said. "In a hurry, he was."

"Late for tea at Commander Jollion's, he told me. Don't you remember, he knocked young Phoebe Bellamy off her bicycle, and one of our boys here repaired it. I think the commander wants to thank him. Well, something like that."

Evelyne nodded. "He's lovely, a nice man, your Harry. I do wish he could find a nice young woman, settle down, have a happy family life."

"I couldn't agree more," Alice murmured, and then said, in an even lower tone, "He is now fancy-free, as he calls it. That messy situation has suddenly evaporated." Alice paused, smiled knowingly at her friend, and finished, "It vanished into thin air."

"I was in Harrogate the other day. I noticed there was a For Sale sign in the front garden of that house. It pleased me, Alice, because I knew it meant they'd gone. Hopefully for good."

"I believe so."

Evelyne poured hot water into the teapot, and carried the tray over to the table. She asked, "Do you know the woman who has become the new president of the WI in Harrogate?"

"No, I don't think so. She has a long name, tell me what it is again, please."

"Margaret Howell Johnson. She and her husband, Stephen, own a high-class jewelry shop on the Parade. Anyway, Clara Turnbull told me the WI in Harrogate has bought a canning machine, and I was thinking that they might lend it to us...it would help with our lack of jars, sort of tide us over."

"You're right, it would. Perhaps my aunt Charlotte knows her. The WI presidents often get together."

"Would you mind asking the countess?" Evelyne picked up the teapot, filled the two cups. "Perhaps your aunt might even go to see Mrs. Johnson, ask her to do us that favor. What do you think?"

"I will certainly mention it to her. I'm seeing her tomorrow. But if she doesn't want to do it, I don't mind making a trip over there. In fact, maybe we should go together."

"That would be nice," Evelyne exclaimed, a sudden sparkle in her eyes. "And we could have lunch at Betty's Cafe. My treat."

"I'd like that, yes," Alice answered, sipping her tea. "I haven't been to Betty's for ages."

Twenty

Burnside Manor was close to High Clough village, and Harry arrived much sooner than he had expected, mainly because there was no traffic. As he drove down the drive and turned into the courtyard of the Elizabethan house he spotted Phoebe sitting on the front steps.

As he came to a stop, she jumped up and ran over to the car. The moment he turned off the ignition key and got out, she was thrusting her hand at him, a huge smile spreading across her freckled face. "Hello, Mr. Swann. I'm so happy you came."

He smiled back, shaking her hand. "I've been looking forward to it, Phoebe," he answered, surprising himself with this white lie. But there was something special about this little girl that gave his spirits a lift. Perhaps it was the many freckles on her face, the spiky auburn hair, the cheeky smile. Whatever it was didn't matter really. Quite simply he found her endearing.

"You'd better take the ignition key," she instructed, giving him a peculiar look.

"Why?" he asked, sounding puzzled.

"Because my twin brothers love cars, and they might just sneak out and go for a joy ride in your jalopy. Don't look like that, Mr. Swann, I speak the truth. They've been known to do it before. Mind you, they've never crashed. **Yet.**"

He began to laugh, opened the car door and pocketed the ignition key. Turning to her, he said, "Does that make you feel better?"

She nodded her head and grinned. "I've lost a tooth." She pointed to the side of her mouth. "I fell and broke it. Sabrina says I should keep my mouth closed, but I can't. Anyway, my mother will take me to the dentist next week. So I'm not worried."

"You shouldn't worry about anything, you're far too young for that."

"I do worry about all sorts of things. Never mind. Let me tell you about my siblings."

"Shouldn't we perhaps go in to tea? It is four o'clock," Harry replied, glancing at his watch.

"Tea is at four-thirty here. The butler rings a ship's bell. My uncle prefers it to the gong. It makes him feel more at home. Like on his ship."

"I see," Harry said, endeavoring to keep a straight face. "So tell me about your siblings, since apparently we have time. I might as well know what's in store for me."

"Oh, they're going to love you, Mr. Swann, that I know. And you'll love them. Well, I'm not sure you will. But think of it this way, you don't have to live with them like I do."

Harry said, "Let's sit on the front steps, shall we? Or do you want to go inside?"

Phoebe shook her head somewhat vehemently. "Better stay outside. Certain people have been known to eavesdrop. Spies, you know."

Once they were seated next to each other on the steps, Phoebe said in a low voice, "Haven't you noticed my hair? I cut it a few days ago."

"It's unusual," he said, giving her an encouraging smile. "Very different," he added, not sure how to praise the jagged spiky cut which did not exactly flatter her.

"Oh thank you so much! I'm glad you like it. Nobody else does. Sabrina told me I have to buy a wig from a theatrical wig shop until it grows again."

"You keep mentioning Sabrina. Shall we start with her?" Harry suggested, enjoying being with this very grown-up twelve-year-old who was hilarious. She reminded him of Dulcie a bit and she also made him laugh.

"Sabrina is fifteen and she believes she has the best taste of anyone in the family. She's always criticizing **me.** And the others, as well. But she is gorgeous. We call her the beauty of the family...like Lady Daphne is the great beauty of the Ingham family. And actually she is my **real** sister."

Harry frowned. "What do you mean by **real**?"

"Oh gosh, you don't know about my mother and all her husbands, do you? Well, Sabrina is my blood sister. We have the same father, Gregory Chancellor Bellamy. And he is the father of the twins, Gregg and Chance. We're all ginger heads like our father. The rest call us Carrot Tops, but we don't care, and we sort of stick together. Especially when we have to defend ourselves."

Harry gave her a long, speculative look. "And why would you have to do that?"

"I have three more sisters. Claudia, she's thirty-one and has never been married, Angelica is twenty-nine and is recently divorced. They are my mother's daughters by Alan Robertson, so they're my half sisters. And they can be bossy. They order us around, like they know what's best for us."

"I understand. But you said you had three more sisters, Phoebe, and you've only mentioned two."

"I always keep Paloma separate from everyone else, because she is very, very **special**. She is also my half sister, but she loves me very much, and I think she's just...wonderful. She's twenty-seven, and she's not been married, either."

"And who is her father?" Harry asked, intrigued by all these sisters, brothers, and their different fathers, not to mention Adrianna, the mother of this brood.

Phoebe leaned closer and said in a whisper, "Edward Glendenning, the actor. My mother says he was the love of her life, and she can't imagine why she ever let him escape."

Harry chuckled. "And where are all of these husbands now?" he asked, riddled with curiosity.

Shrugging, Phoebe murmured, "I don't know. Knocking around somewhere, I suppose. Now we'd better go in; Gaston is about to ring the ship's bell."

Phoebe led Harry into the manor house just as the ship's bell began to ring. They walked together down the gallery, which echoed with the bell's mournful tolling. Phoebe rolled her eyes and Harry laughed at her expression.

The gallery was long and wide, and typically Tudor in design and character; he now recalled how he had always liked this house. He had not visited it very often, but whenever he had come over to see the Jollions he had appreciated its beautiful Elizabethan architecture.

Harry glanced around, liking the profusion of flowers in tall glass vases, the landscape paintings, and the overall decoration in general.

Big sofas and armchairs were covered in pale-colored fabrics, filled with pillows, and they looked comfortable and inviting. Several elegant, antique chests caught his eye, and he thought how perfect the mahogany looked against the pale wood-paneled walls.

Breaking into his thoughts, Phoebe said, "We always have tea in the garden room, and here it is." She indicated a heavy oak door banded in black iron. It stood open and she gave it a push, ushered him inside.

The first thing he noticed when he stepped into the room was the brightness of the light coming in through the mullioned windows. The room had an airy spaciousness to it, and it was filled with potted plants, including an array of different kinds of orchids, some of them exotic and colorful.

Sylvia Jollion, the commander's wife, hurried forward, a smile illuminating her pretty face. Coming to a stop, she said, "Hello, Harry, we're so glad you were able to join us today. We've been looking forward to it."

"Thank you for inviting me," he answered, shaking her hand.

The commander had followed her, and he stepped forward, welcomed Harry warmly. "Good to see you, Swann."

The commander was a typical military man in his bearing, the way he held himself. He was tall, ramrod straight, his head held high. His expression was somewhat stern, yet Harry was aware this belied his true nature. Commander Edgar Jollion, of the Royal Navy, was compassionate, caring, and ready to help anyone in need.

"I'm very happy to see you, Commander," Harry said. "I ran into Noel the other day, and he told me you'll soon be taking over a new battleship. Congratulations, sir."

"Thank you, Swann, and also thank you for looking after young Phoebe here. When she was trespassing on Cavendon land, no less."

"She wasn't really, Commander, and I was careless, not paying attention, in fact."

The commander nodded. "I must also thank you for putting her bike in dry dock. It came back totally shipshape."

"It looks spanking new," a woman's light, slightly amused voice announced.

Both men swung around, and the commander said, "Ah, Adrianna, let me present Harry Swann...this is my sister, Swann, Adrianna Bellamy, and Phoebe's mother."

A hand as white as driven snow, elegant and long fingered, was stretched out to him. Harry took it in his. How cool it was, and her skin felt like silk. "I'm so pleased to meet you, Mrs. Bellamy, Phoebe has told me about you."

"I bet she has!" Adrianna began to laugh, her

pale green eyes twinkling. "I was touched that you took the time and trouble to bring her home the night of the accident, Mr. Swann. Most people wouldn't have bothered. Thank you."

"I certainly wasn't going to let her walk all the way here, and I didn't really know if she'd hurt herself or not. She said not, but I decided I must deliver her safely."

"And you did," Phoebe exclaimed, joining them. "Let's go and sit over there, Mumma, be seated together before the Swarm rushes in."

The commander chuckled. "Good thinking, Phoebe, but then you're always at the top of the ropes, on the lookout for danger."

"Yes, I am, Uncle Edgar, just the way you taught me. I've been a good naval cadet, haven't I?"

"Indeed you have."

There was a sudden burst of laughter among them, and they went and took their seats on two huge sofas and big armchairs grouped together.

Mrs. Jollion said, "As soon as Noel arrives, I'll ring for Gaston. We don't have to wait for the others; they seem to appear at different times these days."

"Good idea, Sylvia," Adrianna murmured. "They've been doing that for years now, and there's no point fretting or even mentioning it. They come and go at will, and now so do I. If they don't care, then neither do I."

The Jollions laughed, and Phoebe winked at him, and he smiled, realizing what a warm and loving family this was. He had liked Adrianna the moment he had laid eyes on her. She was accessible, outgoing, and nice-looking in an understated way. No flash there. Just cool good looks, great bones, lovely skin, and shining honey-colored hair that fell to her waist.

She looked remarkably young, no more than thirty-five perhaps. But he knew she had to be much older, since her first daughter, Claudia, was thirty-one. Could she be close to fifty? No, not possible. But yes, she has to be, he corrected himself.

Adrianna was sitting opposite, and she looked back at him, her eyes narrowing. He half smiled at her and glanced away, realizing he had been staring. She chuckled, and as if she had read his mind, she said, "Yes, I do have a thirty-one-year-old daughter, Mr. Swann. And I'm fifty-one."

Harry felt himself flush, but managed to pull up his most charming smile. "I was just thinking how lovely you look, not wondering how old you are, Mrs. Bellamy."

"Most people do, though. And knowing my Phoebe, who always lets the cat out of the bag, I'm sure she told you a lot about me."

"No, Mumma, no, I didn't!" Phoebe cried,

grabbing her mother's hand. "I just spoke about the others. But not Paloma. She is sacrosanct."

"Indeed she is," Mrs. Jollion said, and glanced at the door when Noel walked in. "Oh there you are, darling," she exclaimed. "Please ring for Gaston. Let's have a nice cup of tea."

Noel Jollion did as his mother asked, and then joined the group, greeting everyone, and sitting down next to Harry on the other sofa. "So, we finally got you here, Harry. Good to see you. How are Miles and Cecily? Are they back yet?"

"No. But they will be soon. They're leaving Berlin tomorrow," Harry explained. "Lady Daphne and Mr. Stanton will return a few days later."

"Been in Berlin, have they?" the commander asked, focusing his attention on Harry. "I hear it's become an extremely militaristic city these days. I can't help wondering how the Imperial German Navy reacts to the Third Reich. Everything the navy stands for is against the Nazis. They modeled themselves on our Royal Navy you know, which is over four hundred years old. We have our code of behavior as gentlemen, and so do they, by the way."

"My sister, Cecily, told me it's a city full of uniforms, and a great deal of theatrical flash," Harry remarked. "And it's become very cosmopolitan."

Before the commander could answer there was a sudden flurry at the door. Gaston, the butler, entered with two maids, all of them bringing in afternoon tea.

There was a large round table near the window next to the seating area. The butler and the maids put everything on the table and began to arrange the food.

As Harry watched them, he couldn't help thinking it was the same array of sandwiches, scones, clotted cream, strawberry jam, and cakes which were served at Cavendon. He supposed an English afternoon tea was usually the same in every stately home.

As a Swann he'd grown up "between stairs": familiar with the rituals of the Inghams, but not part of their social class. Yet not below stairs either—the Swanns' position as retainers was unique.

Phoebe jumped up, and came and sat in the chair next to Harry. "Any minute, the Swarm will arrive, and I want to be next to you. After all, you're **my** friend, not theirs."

"Of course, Phoebe," he answered, realizing that she didn't want to be pushed to one side. He caught Adrianna watching him with curiosity and he smiled, his eyes lingering on her.

She smiled back, and he was suddenly aware that there was enormous charm there and an understanding of people. She knew what made people tick, and especially men. Her soft, under-stated looks were most appealing, accentuated by her peach chiffon dress. It was somewhat long and floating, and very feminine. Allure, he thought. That's what it is. She has enormous allure.

"Tea is ready to be served, madam," the butler announced.

"Thank you, Gaston," Mrs. Jollion answered, and then swung her head around as two red-haired boys came bounding into the room, followed more sedately by a younger girl with the same flame-colored hair.

"These are my brothers and that's my sister, Sabrina," Phoebe told him.

"I see what you mean about Carrot Tops," Harry answered, and patted her hand. "Remain seated. I want you by my side when the Swarm arrives here."

Twenty-one

It had not taken Harry long to understand that he was in the midst of a unique, rather bohemian family, at least as far as Adrianna Bellamy and her tribe of children were concerned.

Aside from bearing a physical resemblance to her brother in her height and fair coloring, Adrianna was quite the opposite in so many other ways, as far as he could tell.

Commander and Mrs. Jollion were normal, down-to-earth people, pleasant, warm, and rather sedate. And yet they appeared to enjoy having Adrianna and her family around them. He understood why. Her lot were a funny, endearing, cheerful group, and they brought a certain élan to this gathering.

Perhaps there was another reason they accepted them, and encouraged the Bellamys to be themselves. The Jollions had lost their first child, Kay, who would have been twenty-two had she lived. She had died at the age of seven, of some rare form of cancer. He knew from his aunt Charlotte that it had been a terrible loss and a great blow to them. Fortunately, they had their son Noel, on whom they both doted.

But Harry had to admit that it was probably Adrianna's children who brought a sense of excitement and fun to their lives, and to Noel's, too. The commander's sister was obviously most welcome here and surely it was for the love and pleasure she and her brood brought to this house.

The afternoon tea was in full swing, and there was a lot of laughter and chatter around him. Everyone seemed to be enjoying themselves, and what he himself felt was a sense of ease being among them, and their acceptance of him unconditionally.

After the arrival of Phoebe's sister, Sabrina, and their two brothers, Gregg and Chance, the three older siblings had come in a few minutes later.

When they entered the garden room together he knew at once who the two eldest were. Claudia and Angelica had a strong look of each other and their mother. They had Adrianna's fair coloring, honey-blond hair, and light green eyes.

The third young woman did not look at all like any of Adrianna's other children. Her father, Edward Glendenning, was a well-known film actor, and Harry certainly saw him reflected in her. She had Edward's black hair and bright blue eyes fringed with black lashes.

Harry was used to the "Ingham blues," as he called them, but Paloma's eyes looked bluer, almost violet. Or perhaps it was her black hair that emphasized their color more. In any event, she was a nice-looking young woman, with high cheekbones and a chiseled nose like her father, but she had inherited Adrianna's height, her willowy bearing.

The thing that struck Harry the most was her tranquility. Like her siblings, she had come to greet him and introduce herself. And then, on Phoebe's insistence, she had seated herself on the sofa opposite him.

It was not long before he became aware of her stillness, a sense of serenity about her. Quite a contrast to her brothers and sisters, which was no doubt why her calm and gentle demeanor stood out so forcibly.

Phoebe interrupted his meandering thoughts, when she asked in a low voice, "What do you think of this gang? Characters, aren't they?"

Harry swallowed the laughter that bubbled up. "And so are you, Miss Phoebe, perhaps the biggest character of all. I must admit, you are special, and they are very nice...easy to like."

Phoebe, who loved flattery and attention, beamed at him. "Aren't you glad you knocked me off my bike? If you hadn't, you wouldn't have met all of us."

"That's absolutely true. And I can't imagine why I haven't met you before, or at least heard of you."

Leaning closer, she said, "My father never wanted to come to Yorkshire, and he didn't want Mumma to bring us without him. So she always invited Aunt Sylvia, Uncle Edgar, and Noel to her house in Kent. My father didn't want to go there either, because it belongs to Mumma, not him. She always said he resented her former husbands and her brother, and it upset her. So they finally got a divorce. Then we started to come to stay here. Only for August, though, because the boys have to go back to Eton."

"So you'll be leaving soon?"

"In two weeks. Perhaps you can come to tea again," Phoebe suggested, and then a sudden thought struck her. "You could come and see us when you're in London. We live in Kensington, and Mumma loves company and cooking for everyone. You could have dinner with us."

"Perhaps," Harry murmured cautiously, aware that Phoebe was only twelve, and should not be inviting him to dinner without her mother's permission.

There was an awkward silence for a moment, and when he saw the odd, disappointed look on Phoebe's face, he asked lightly, with a smile, "Don't tell me you all live together?"

Phoebe made a face. "No, just the Bellamys. Claudia, Angelica, and Paloma have their own flats. But they come to see us a lot." She began to giggle. "They miss us urchins."

Paloma, who had been listening to this conversation, interjected, "I'm sure our mother would invite you, Mr. Swann, and me as well, and my sisters. She's a wonderful cook. She enjoys giving parties." There was a pause, and before she could stop herself, Paloma went on in a rush, "But in the meantime, I wonder if I might invite myself to Cavendon? Or rather, I should say, to see the Cavendon gardens? I'm a photographer. I know my aunt is a friend of the countess, and she could easily arrange it. On the other hand, you're the estate manager and—"

"Mr. Swann created the gardens," Phoebe cut in. "Aunt Sylvia says they are fantastical, magical."

"Did she really?" Harry said, sounding surprised.

"Those are her exact words, Mr. Swann, and she never exaggerates," Paloma interjected, gazing at him, unexpectedly so drawn to him she couldn't look away. Her eyes locked on his.

Harry stared back, mesmerized by those violet eyes holding him. He felt a sudden tightening in his chest, a frisson of excitement. He was struck dumb by this sudden rush of feelings.

Although he had no way of knowing it, Paloma was equally as surprised at herself. Never in her life had she reacted to a man like this, and so suddenly. She felt an overwhelming pull, a need to know him better. Much better indeed. She was floundering…this was not like her.

Phoebe, witness to their reaction to each other, smiled to herself. She didn't want to break the spell they were under, so she remained silent. They were oblivious to everyone else, saw only each other. A moment later Phoebe knew she must intervene. Someone might notice. She said, "Can I come with you, Paloma? Be your assistant? **Please**."

Paloma sat up straighter with a jerk, cleared her throat, and said, "Of course, you can carry the film."

Harry, pulling himself together, said quickly, "You don't have to ask your aunt to ask my aunt, Miss Glendenning. You may photograph the gardens anytime you wish. It will be my pleasure to show you around."

"Can we come tomorrow?" Phoebe asked.

"Sunday would be better. Sunday morning actually, Miss Glendenning," he answered, looking directly at Paloma.

"Thank you. And please call me Paloma, we don't stand on ceremony around here."

Harry could only nod, once more captivated by those violet eyes fixed so intently on him.

"Harry," he managed to say. "Call me Harry."

She smiled at him. He smiled back.

And Phoebe smiled at them both.

Harry drove slowly and carefully back to Cavendon, somewhat befuddled, bewildered, really, by his own behavior. He couldn't believe he had responded so readily and so easily to Paloma's intense and suggestive gaze. And that he had actually returned it, had felt a flush of sudden excitement inside. Was he that shallow?

Only a few hours earlier he had been in a fury about Pauline Mallard's defection, hurt and rejected, and wondering how he would ever get over her, this woman he was in love with.

But was he in love with Pauline? Or had he been in lust, as Miles had often suggested? A huge infatuation, perhaps? Not real love? He didn't know...but what he was certain of was that Paloma had wanted to see him again. Photographing Cavendon gardens was an obvious ploy. The thing was, he had agreed with speed, revealing that he wished the same as her.

As he drove through the village of High Clough, it suddenly struck him that wily, clever Phoebe had been witness to the scene of them gazing at each other in rapt silence. She had broken the mood by speaking to them. Before others noticed? Was that her motive? He wasn't sure...he wasn't sure of anything anymore, not even of himself. Maybe he wasn't the man he thought he was.

By the time he arrived at Little Skell village, the light was draining out of the sky, and after parking by the side of the house, he glanced at his watch. He was amazed to discover it was turning off seven-thirty. He had stayed a long time at Burnside Manor.

He shivered when he went into the house. It felt cold, and there was a dampness in the air. He turned on the hall light and walked into the living room. It was dark, gloomy, and he moved around swiftly, switching on several lamps. They glowed brightly, but it still appeared gloomy to him, and sitting down on the sofa he realized how empty the place was.

He was here alone. As he always was.

A deep sigh trickled through him, and he leaned back against the cushions and closed his eyes, wondering what to do. He didn't feel like making dinner for himself, or even going to the pub for a pint, although that would be more cheerful than being here.

I'm forty. And alone. No woman by my side, no wife, no children. Family, and good friends, yes. But no one to call my own, to share my life with. And I've done it to myself. The odd romantic dalliance. No one ever serious. And then months and months with a married woman who never had any intention of leaving him for me...

There was a knock on the front door, and as it opened he sat up, snapped open his eyes to see his mother coming into the living room. "There you are, Harry," Alice said. "What are you doing? Sitting there like that? All alone. Come on, let's go."

Rising, he walked over to her, gave her a hug. "Where to, Mam?"

"The house where you grew up. Where there's a fire and hot food. A good supper for you." She glanced around the room, and shook her head. "It's miserable here, cold and cheerless."

They went out together and crossed the main street to his parents' house. Harry walked through the front door and felt his spirits lifting as he entered. The fire was burning high in the grate, and delicious smells of food cooking filled the air. In the background, music was playing on the wireless. His parents' home was warm and welcoming as it always was, and he was glad she had come to get him.

After opening the oven door, looking inside, Alice straightened, and said, "Let's go into the front room, Harry, and have a drink, and you can tell me all about your tea party this afternoon. Were you there all this time?"

He nodded, and followed her into the front room, which was actually at the back of the house facing the garden. It was spacious, with large windows; the moors were visible in the distance.

"Sherry or a single malt?" Harry asked, turning to Alice, who was already poking the fire, making flames shoot up the chimney, then dropping on another log. "Sherry, please," she answered.

A moment later, he was sitting in the chair opposite her in front of the fire. After clinking his glass to hers, Harry said, "Can you imagine, I didn't leave there until almost seven."

Alice smiled at him, her eyes twinkling. "Those girls wouldn't let you go! Was that it?"

Frowning at her, he exclaimed, "Did you know Adrianna Bellamy had so many daughters? Why didn't you tell me?"

"What for? You're a grown man, you can take care of yourself." Alice smiled knowingly. "I thought it would be a nice surprise for you. Would cheer you up. So, did you find one you like, pick one out?"

Harry couldn't help it, he burst out laughing, and when he had calmed, he said, "It felt like one of them picked me, actually, Mother."

"Really?" Alice looked at him quizzically, focusing on him intently. "Or are you teasing me, Harry Swann?"

"No, I'm not." He took a sip of the single malt Scotch, then sat staring into the fire for the longest moment. Eventually, he told her exactly what had happened over tea, and Paloma's reaction to him; he told her the truth. Harry had never lied to his mother in his life. She always knew everything about him.

Alice, who had listened intently, said, "Well, she is obviously interested in you. And since you responded so fast, with an invitation to see the gardens, you must be taken with her."

"I suppose I am, but I must admit I've been a bit bewildered ever since. Only this afternoon, before I went over there, I was in a fury about Pauline's behavior, believed I was in love with her, as you well know." He shook his head. "I just don't have a clue...I don't know what to think about myself."

"I know what to think about you, Harry. You've come to your senses, realized that Pauline Mallard isn't the only woman in the world for you. As for being in love with her, I believe perhaps you were, in a certain way. Infatuated with her, taken with her looks, and then there was your sexual attraction to each other. Let me put it this way, you **thought** you were in love, because you had strong feelings. But now, well, you've fallen out of love. And so you should."

Alice paused, then said, "Ceci phoned me this afternoon. She wanted me to know she and Miles will be leaving Zurich for London on Monday. They'll stay in town through Tuesday, so she can go to the shop, then they are coming to Cavendon. They can't wait to see the children."

Harry nodded, and a smile surfaced. "I'm happy they'll soon be back here, I've missed them."

"I know that. So what about this young woman, Paloma?"

"Have you never met her, Mother?"

Alice shook her head. "No. I haven't met any of Adrianna Bellamy's daughters or sons. You see, they've only been coming here for a couple of years, and they don't visit the village. Well, Adrianna has been to the WI with Mrs. Jollion, as I mentioned to you before."

"She's twenty-seven. Young Phoebe told me that," Harry explained. "And she's not like the others, who are either redheaded or blond. Paloma has black hair and bright blue eyes, almost violet in color, and she seems calm, serene, actually."

"So you liked her?"

"I did."

"Who is Paloma's father? Do you know?"

"Of course Phoebe is a mine of information. Paloma's the daughter of Edward Glendenning, the actor."

"Oh goodness, yes, I know who he is. So she takes after him in looks?"

"Yes. I gather she's a professional photographer, and likes taking pictures of nature. Also, according to Phoebe, she has her own flat in London, as do the other two older girls. And that's it. I did enjoy meeting them. The whole family is nice. But they are rather bohemian, I think."

"Aunt Charlotte has indicated that. She's friendly with Mrs. Jollion, who likes her sister-in-law, Adrianna, apparently, and enjoys having the whole brood to stay."

"They were very warm, Mother, and I must say the younger ones, the Bellamy children, are well behaved, polite, and I found them all easy to be with. One thing struck me very forcibly, Commander and Mrs. Jollion really do adore them."

"They bring a lot of joy into that house," Alice murmured. "And I'm not surprised they are well brought up, the Jollions are an aristocratic family, famous in Yorkshire. You may not know this, but only Jollions have lived in Burnside Manor since it was built in Elizabethan times."

"I didn't know, I've only been inside a couple of times when Mrs. Jollion has wanted some gardening advice."

"I realize that. Oh, and there's another thing, Harry, Adrianna's first husband is titled. He is Sir Alan Robertson, so you know manners abound, if nothing else."

"Oh there's much more than manners, I think. Much more."

Harry Swann felt full of vitality as he walked through Cavendon Park on Saturday morning.

He was wearing his riding togs, as he always did on Saturday when he toured the estate. He was looking forward to riding, and his spirits were high; he was in a good mood.

Approaching the gazebo, he was surprised to see a woman hurrying down from Cavendon Hall. As he drew closer, he realized it was Paloma Glendenning. She saw him, and waved, then increased her pace, started running toward him.

Wondering why she was there, he began to run himself, and they literally bumped into each other and came to a stop. She almost fell; he grabbed her arms tightly and kept her upright. She clung to him, steadying herself. "Are you all right, Paloma?"

She nodded. "Thank you for keeping me upright. We don't need another bad fall in the family."

"What do you mean?"

"That's why I'm here, to tell you about my father's fall. Off a horse. He insists on doing his own riding in films. My mother got a phone call last night. He's in the hospital in London. He has a broken shoulder."

"I'm very sorry to hear it, Paloma. A broken shoulder is a nasty injury, very painful. How can I help you?"

"You can't. But I wanted to tell you myself that I can't come to photograph the gardens tomorrow. I have to go to London with my mother."

He was disappointed, but said, "I understand. Could we meet when I'm in London? I would like to see you again."

"I think that would be lovely," she answered.

"I'm due for a few days off next week. How do I find you, Miss Glendenning?"

"I've written my phone number down for you." She reached into the pocket of her jacket, took out a piece of paper and gave it to him.

"Thank you," he said, and put it safely away in his inside breast pocket. "I might be in town next week. How does that sound?"

"It has a happy ring to it. I've got to go drive back to Burnside, I have to pack."

She had moved away from him, cried in a light, happy voice, "Be careful of horses, Harry!" With a wave she was gone, running back the way she had come.

What an extraordinary young woman, he thought, and took the piece of paper out of his pocket. Underneath the phone number was written **P.T.O.** He turned the paper over. There was a message: **Please don't lose this. Paloma.**

He smiled to himself, put the paper back in his pocket for safekeeping, and walked on up to his office, thinking of Paloma.

Twenty-two

It was a brilliantly sunny morning when Diedre arrived at the War Office building in Whitehall. She pushed open the heavy wood door and decided to walk up the stairs. She liked the exercise, and also never grew tired of admiring the architecture in this mellow old building as seen from the wide stairs.

Miles and miles of corridors on seven floors housed a thousand offices dealing with the management and running of the British army. She had nothing to do with that at all. In fact, she did not work for the War Office. This was cover for a special group which she was part of, and had also worked with during the Great War.

The group had been founded in 1907 by a brilliant young colonel in military intelligence, and gone from strength to strength over the years. The young colonel had finally retired in the 1920s after an extraordinary career, and building this special intelligence crew into a great unit.

Small, clandestine, the unit was now run by William Lawson, who was answerable only to the prime minister. That was the way it had originally been set up, and it was so top secret only a very few people knew of its existence, including the head of the Secret Intelligence Service, known as MI6.

The small clutch of offices was on the fifth floor, at one end of a long corridor. The small brass plate on the door was engraved with a meaningless name: Administration Bureau. Its door was always locked. Its real name was Special Secret Undercover Unit. Those who worked in its ranks simply called it Sue, which served as a clever code name.

When she arrived at the door, Diedre unlocked it and went inside, locking it behind her. It was mandatory that the inside front door be locked at all times even when people were there.

Snapping on the light in the entrance foyer, she went down a short hallway to her own office, unlocked it, and went over to her desk. She had only just seated herself when the phone began to ring.

Lifting it immediately, she said, "Hello? Who is this?"

"Is that Daffy Dilly?"

"Yes, Toby. Where are you?" she asked,

pleased to hear his voice.

"At work. Best to speak our speak. If you get my drift."

"I do. Equipment uncertain? Is that it?"

"Not sure. I wanted to tell you about a great caviar."

"I'd love to hear," Diedre answered, knowing he was referring to Princess Irina, to whom they had given the code name of Caviar. Valiant had been code-named Source. For this situation.

"The caviar lived up to your expectations. You will want to try it again, once you've tasted it. And the source is good."

"All this is nice to know, Toby. I wish I were there in Berlin."

"I do too, because I'm going to be partaking of the caviar next week."

"I don't think I can make it. So sorry," Diedre said.

"By the way, on the matter of that suitcase, no problems. It can be handled very nicely and quite quickly. What shall I do?"

"How wonderful and the quicker the better. Process it fast, that's what you should do."

There was a moment or two of silence, a hesitation on the Berlin end of the phone.

"Toby, are you there?" Diedre asked urgently.

"Very quickly," he agreed. "I am here. Somebody just put their head around my door, that's all. I waved them away. Proceed."

"I understand. So, all is well in general then?"

"Not exactly," Toby replied quietly, sighing for emphasis.

"What does that mean?" she asked, her voice rising.

"An unfortunate development," Toby said.

Diedre clutched the receiver tighter. "What's wrong, Toby? I know there's a problem. I can hear trouble in your voice!"

"I think we have to buy a pair of bed socks... to put on someone who needs them."

"Who?" Diedre asked tersely, understanding that one of the Steinbrenners had cold feet about the exit. They had been using this speaking code for several years and she and Tony were accustomed to it by now and very adept.

"Pink," Toby finally said. "Pink bed socks would be best."

"Very well, that's what I'll buy. Small, medium, or large?"

"Large, I'm afraid."

"Anyone else on the in?"

"Moi. Only **moi.** And that's the way it must be. Agreed? No tittle-tattle."

"I agree with that. So, what can I do to help you? It's you who's in Berlin...with the suitcase, I mean. And the problems."

"Nothing for the moment. I believe Daddy Bear will make some good moves," he replied quietly.

"**That must happen.** And very fast. We cannot leave the caviar out, by the way, it could be bad, which would be a shame. Also, it might, no, would upset the source."

"Spot-on. Where will you be visiting at the weekend? No doubt where the heather blooms and the robin sings."

"Exactly. I need to hear the robin sing, as you can well imagine. Shall I give you a tinkle?"

"Yes, please. Usual day and time, usual place."

"It's a done deal."

"All the deals will be done by next week."

I hope to God you're right, Diedre thought but said, "Let's keep it all under a cat's hat."

"Sure will, Daffy Dilly."

Diedre sat back in her chair, glancing at the clock on the desk as she did. It was exactly eight o'clock, the usual time she came in, and as always she was the first to arrive. She thought about Cecily, knowing she must speak to her as soon as possible, but then decided to leave it for a little longer.

Staring into space, she went through Tony's words again. Princess Irina was obviously true to her word. Valiant had come through with the necessary documents. But now Mrs. Steinbrenner was having cold feet about leaving Berlin. Probably because of fear they would be caught fleeing and instantly killed.

But then they would die anyway if they remained in Nazi Germany. So many people were being targeted and shot in cold blood. Or they just disappeared, never to be seen again. Thousands were herded into the concentration camps, or sent to slave camps.

Why were they called concentration camps? The proper name for those hideous places was **death** camps. Death stole them immediately.

Tony had told her last week that there was a terrible system in use. People were told they were going for showers, made to undress, and then ushered into the shower stalls. But water did not flow. Gas did. And they died. And those barbaric guards pried out their teeth for the gold, and stole their wedding rings and watches. And what other few possessions they had brought with them.

A shudder swept through her at the mere thought of these heinous crimes being committed in a so-called civilized country. Monsters had taken over. No wonder Valiant was disgusted and furious and anti-Nazi at this foul brutality...and that's why he did what he could to fight against the regime, and save people. And why he had joined the generals who wanted to overthrow Adolf Hitler.

The telephone shrilled again, and Diedre reached for it. "Hello? Who is this?"

"Hello, Diedre darling, it's me," Cecily said.

"When your phone didn't answer at home, I knew I'd find you at work. Which is exactly where I am right now."

Diedre laughed. "And I suppose you've been there for at least two hours."

"No, I haven't. Anyway, I need your advice. I didn't want to say anything at all to Greta, not without first talking to you. I know the professor told her we met at the embassy, because he explained that he had when we had lunch last Friday...I don't want to make any mistakes."

"You can tell her everything that happened when you were at the embassy, and at your lunch, because I'm sure he's filled her in. But you can't give her any hope that they will ever get out. You just mustn't."

"I understand," Cecily replied in a more subdued voice. "I had hoped against hope that something might happen when you were in Berlin, but it didn't, did it?"

"I'm so very sorry, Ceci, but no, I wasn't able to get help for them. Tony said he was glad we were leaving, actually, because things were getting more fraught in Berlin. And who knew what would happen. He said that he'd heard Hitler was on some sort of rampage, throwing tantrums in the Reich Chancellery and shouting about a world war."

"Oh God, that sounds so awful! The poor Steinbrenners."

Diedre exclaimed swiftly, "Don't tell her what Tony told me, it will only frighten her, Ceci."

"I won't, I promise. It would frighten anybody with a family unable to get out of there most especially. If she asks me anything, like were we able to find anyone to help, what shall I say?"

"Do you think she will?" Diedre wondered out loud. "I'm not so sure of that. But should she bring it up, say that you'd heard from me, who'd heard from an attaché at the British embassy, that all the exit visas have dried up and no one is able to get out anymore. Which is the truth."

There was a small silence, and then Cecily said in a sorrowful voice, "I wonder how she will ever bear this? In a certain way, she was always sure they would somehow make it."

"She is close to you, and you will be able to help her, Cecily. And I will too, if you need me. I'll do whatever I can," Diedre said in a low tone. "You know that. You only have to ask me."

"Oh, I do know, Diedre. And I'm aware what a good person you are. Anyway, I've got to buck up and get on with it. I've a busy day. Are you coming to Cavendon for the weekend?"

"You can be certain of that. I can't wait to see my Robin."

Twenty-three

After hanging up on Diedre, Cecily turned her attention to the papers spread out on her desk. Mostly they were lists of the factories they used, and also those women who sewed the haute couture Cecily Swann clothes by hand.

She sat back in her chair, her mind working rapidly, knowing that a whole lot of new plans about manufacturing and the creation of clothes would have to be made. As she sat writing notes she began to feel overly warm on this August morning, and stood up, went to open a window.

The noises of Piccadilly came flowing in, reminding her that a new working day was starting in this city she loved so much. She glanced down into the street and saw Aunt Dorothy walking toward this building, where her new offices were located. Cecily had bought it in 1934, and it had been an excellent investment. As the business had rapidly expanded, there was plenty of space to hold the growing staff, and a whole floor had been converted into several rooms where certain accessories were made by hand, such as fabric flowers and the silk scarves.

Within a few minutes, Dottie was hurrying into Cecily's office, exclaiming, "Good morning, Ceci, sorry I'm late."

Cecily laughed. "Good morning, Dottie, and you're not late, you're early. It's not even nine."

"Lots of traffic," Dorothy Pinkerton murmured, as she walked across the floor and sat down in the chair on the other side of Cecily's desk.

Although she was now fifty-five, Dorothy was still a good-looking woman, with a trim figure, who looked easily fifteen years younger.

She continued to manage Cecily Swann Couture, and had retained her office in the Burlington Arcade shop, just as Cecily continued to use her design studio over there, as well as this office in Grafton Street.

Grafton Street was close to the arcade, and the distance between the two buildings was only a few minutes, and it was easy to move from one to the other.

Cecily said, "To get to the crux of the matter, I think we're going to have to find new factories in Leeds to make our ready-to-wear items, and some of the accessories."

"I'd already guessed that," Dottie said, and

reached out her hand to Cecily, who was holding a sheaf of papers.

Handing them to her aunt, Cecily said, "The government will soon requisition those factories of ours in Leeds. They'll need them to make army, navy, and air force uniforms." Cecily sighed. "I said that to Mike Leigh yesterday, and he sort of pooh-poohed the idea. He won't accept there's going to be a war. He dismisses every-thing I say. He's got his head in the sand."

"What do you expect? He's gormless in many ways, even if he is a good production manager. And anyway, you're cleverer than anyone I know, yards ahead of all of us. No one can keep up with **your** thought processes, and certainly no one has your vision."

Cecily smiled, shook her head. "Oh come on, Aunt Dottie, you're just prejudiced. My mother says I'm too clever for my own good and I should keep my mouth shut, because that's much safer."

Dorothy nodded. "Alice is partially right, of course. But please don't keep your mouth shut, we need to hear what you have to say."

Dorothy now dropped her eyes and scanned the two sheets of paper. "I agree with you, these factories **will** be taken over by the govern-ment. Howard says it's going to be a big war. Actually, he foresees a world war, with huge armies involved."

A grave look spread across Cecily's face, and she said quietly, "I tend to agree. After being in Berlin for only a few days, I quickly got the picture. There were soldiers everywhere, and from what I heard, Germany has rearmed to its teeth. They've been making guns, munitions, and battleships in secret for years. And planes, as well."

"Howard says their army and air force are huge, much bigger than ours. He thinks the Luftwaffe could flatten London in a day, dropping their bombs."

"I won't argue. I was told they have enormous supplies. A war **is** coming imminently; I explained to Mike that factories will have to be passed over to the government to make uniforms, but he wouldn't accept that."

It was obvious to Cecily that Dorothy was genuinely annoyed, and she squeezed her arm, and said, "Don't be angry or worried. I didn't pay attention to anything he said. I have a plan."

Looking somewhat relieved, Dorothy asked swiftly, "What kind of plan, Ceci?"

"I am going to create my own new factories."

Dorothy stared at her in surprise. "How? Where?"

"In Leeds. And on the outskirts of the city, in some of the outlying areas...Upper Armley, Kirstall, Stanningley, Hunslet, and down by the river Aire in Leeds, and also near the canals.

I've already got someone working on this, and he's found some empty warehouses and old mills that are available. To rent or buy. I shall buy them so they are in my control."

"You're going to redo them? Turn them into manufacturing factories to make clothes?" Dorothy asked, her eyes riveted on Cecily.

"Two of them for clothes. The other three will be revamped as well. I'll install cutting tables, sewing machines, all of the usual things, then offer them to the government, and I will offer to make uniforms for the armed services. They'll accept, I can assure you of that, and they'll agree that I can make ready-made jackets and skirts in the smaller two. Trust me."

Dorothy began to laugh. "Haven't I always trusted you on everything?"

"You have, and you've been wonderful. I couldn't have created all this without you, Aunt Dottie. And Aunt Charlotte as well."

Leaving her office, after she and Dorothy had gone over several other urgent matters, Cecily walked across the hallway to talk to Greta.

The door was slightly ajar. Cecily pushed it open, and said from the entrance, "Here I am, safe and well and all in one piece."

A wide smile settled on Greta's face and she jumped up, came around the desk to greet her employer. "Welcome back!" she exclaimed.

Cecily hugged her, and then said, "I know you're aware I saw your father...and the whole family."

Greta nodded, her smile intact. "He told me everything. I was thrilled you met him like that and so accidentally. I was taken aback when he told me."

"Fate, I suspect," Cecily responded. She sat down in a chair, and Greta returned to the one behind her desk.

"Whatever it was, being with you certainly cheered him up. All of them, actually. My father had been longing to meet you, he'd heard so much about you from me. And unexpectedly, he got his wish."

Cecily grinned. "So he said. I thought Elise and Kurt were attractive, so pleasant and out-going, and your stepmother was lovely. She seemed like a very nice woman."

There was a moment of silence, before Greta said slowly, "Yes, she is, although she has a rather nervous disposition. She's so easily upset, rattled, if you know what I mean."

Cecily was not at all surprised by this comment. She had detected a jitteriness in Heddy, even a deep-rooted nervousness. Without mentioning this, Cecily went on, "We had such a nice lunch the next day, and Miles and I had hoped to see them again before we left, but your father was tied up with Sir Anthony Parry.

What good friends they are."

Greta nodded, and leaning across the desk, she said in a low tone, "I know you haven't been able to help them to leave; my father had assumed it would be impossible. But Sir Anthony hopes to do something, to pull some strings." Greta forced a smile. "I'm very hopeful that he will."

"I think you should be...surprising things can happen," Cecily said. "Anyway, I thought they looked in good health and your father was cheerful, optimistic, and naturally having his old pal in Berlin was a great boost, gave him pleasure."

"They've always been very close. For years. And thank you, Cecily, for being so kind to my family. I'm really appreciative. And now perhaps we should get down to work."

Cecily nodded. "I do have a few things I'd like you to follow up on." She handed Greta a sheet of paper, and continued, "This is a list of the women who do hand sewing for us. Some of them work on the top floor here, others at home."

"Yes, the ones who make the haute couture clothes."

"As you know, haute couture has to be made by hand; otherwise, it can't be called couture."

"That is the law in France, you told me that," Greta murmured.

"It is, and it's a sort of unwritten law here, too.

Couture must be hand-sewn. I'd like you and Dorothy to talk to the women upstairs, and Dorothy can also visit those who work at home. I would like to know if they are going to continue working for me? Or whether the younger ones are thinking about going to work in one of the munitions factories, out of patriotism?" Rising, Cecily walked toward the door, and paused, turned around. "I'm going to go over to the Burlington Arcade shop in about half an hour, Greta."

Greta nodded, half smiled. "I can run over there if you need me."

Cecily left, and Greta sat staring at the door vacantly, thinking about her father and her family. He had been so optimistic about Sir Anthony solving their problem, she had had to take a positive attitude with him. And yet she had become pensive and concerned late last night; the worry had returned this morning.

If Cecily had been unable to help them through Diedre, who worked at the War Office, then what kind of chance did Sir Anthony have? He was an academic. She had begged her father to leave Germany several years ago, and he had not. Now they were stuck there.

Greta pushed back tears, and put her head down on her desk. She said a prayer, and kept repeating it like a mantra for ten minutes. Most people did not believe in prayers, but she did. Prayers could work miracles.

"What a beautiful day it is, Charlotte," the earl said, looking at his wife. "I hope the weather lasts for the weekend, when all the family is together again."

She smiled at him, squeezed his hand. "I'm as glad as you are that everyone is coming, it will be like old times."

"Except that Dulcie and James won't be here," he murmured, a hint of sadness in his voice. "What have we heard lately, darling?"

"That Felix is now in Los Angeles. In fact, he and Constance are there together, and are staying at the house in Bel-Air with Dulcie and James. I think meetings are about to start with MGM about James being released from his contract. The minute he is, they will go to New York, spend a couple of nights there and then take a ship to England. Probably the **Queen Elizabeth**."

"It will be a relief to have them back **now.** I hate to think of them traveling in the middle of the war, which is inevitable. The Atlantic will be rife with German battleships, and dangerous."

He sounded suddenly nervous, and troubled, and Charlotte took hold of his hand. "It's going to be all right, Charlie, I promise. And just think, we'll be together to celebrate Christmas."

Charles Ingham, the Sixth Earl of Mowbray,

couldn't help laughing. "It's still only August," he spluttered, amused by her.

"Well, at least I made you laugh," she shot back and laughed herself.

"And you make me happy, so very happy, Charlotte. And where is it you said you're going this morning?"

"I have to go to Harrogate, to see a woman called Margaret Howell Johnson. She's the president of the WI there, as I am here. Alice wants me to go over to see her because apparently the Harrogate branch has a canning machine, and our WI would like to borrow it."

"You will be back in time for lunch, won't you?"

"Of course I will. It's only ten-thirty. Half an hour there, half hour back, and maybe fifteen minutes talking to her," Charlotte assured him, then asked, "Do you need anything from Harrogate?"

"No, only you to come back quickly," he answered and winked at her. She laughed, got up from the sofa, and he asked, "Goff is driving you, I hope?"

"Yes, he is. Please don't worry so, Charles, I won't be long, and anyway Alicia is coming in to talk to you in a while, so you'll have some good company."

"You know I've lots of post to go through," he muttered. He, too, rose, and followed her across the library, sat down at his desk.

"I believe she wants to discuss her acting career..." He paused, his blue eyes warm and loving. "And Annabel confided she wants to be a concert pianist. It looks like we're becoming a family of entertainers."

Charlotte blew him a kiss and left the library.

About forty minutes later Charlotte Swann, the Countess of Mowbray, was walking down the row of shops known as the Parade. Charlotte had always loved Harrogate, with its stately homes, elegant restaurants and hotels, and the Stray, that long piece of common green lawn in the town center which was covered with hundreds of daffodils in the spring.

In the Victorian and Edwardian eras, Harrogate had been a true spa town, with visitors from all over the world coming to take the waters from the underground sulfur springs. In Edwardian times, most especially, it had been a favorite of royalty, the aristocracy, and stars of the theater, hence the elegance of the houses and hotels, and, of course, the beautiful baths where the waters were enjoyed.

She finally came to a stop outside the jewelry shop owned by the Johnsons, and stood for a moment looking in one of the two windows on either side of the front door. They had some very beautiful pieces artfully displayed, and she could tell that the jewels were of the best quality. It was Harrogate's finest jewelry shop and quite renowned.

After staring in the other window, and admiring a lovely old cameo, Charlotte finally opened the door and went inside.

It was a large shop, and there were several glass cases containing jewels, and, to the right, a small mahogany table with two matching chairs. One of the two young saleswomen came forward, a smile on her face. "Good morning, madam," she said. "May I be of help to you?"

"I telephoned earlier and made an appointment to see Mrs. Johnson, but I think I'm a little early."

"You must be Lady Mowbray from Cavendon... you are, aren't you?" the woman asked.

"Yes, I am."

"Please, my lady, be seated here, and I shall go and fetch Mrs. Johnson immediately. She's waiting for you."

Several seconds later a tall, slender woman was walking toward her. She was elegantly dressed, and wore her blond hair swept back from her face and turned under in pageboy style. As she drew closer, Charlotte felt a sudden flash of recognition, thinking she had met her before, and she stood up, smiling.

A split second later, Margaret Howell Johnson was offering her hand to Charlotte and saying,

"Good morning, Lady Mowbray, I'm very happy to meet you. And most especially since we are both so involved with the Women's Institute."

Charlotte was stunned.

That flash of recognition was not because they had met before. It was because this woman, whose hand she was still holding, was the spitting image of a slightly older Diedre, and she had those peculiar smoke-gray lavender eyes she knew so well. They were her own eyes. Swann eyes. Oh my God, she thought. **Oh my God.**

Slipping her hand out of Mrs. Johnson's grip, Charlotte steadied herself against the back of a wing chair, and swallowed. She said, "I'm terribly sorry, Mrs. Johnson. I suddenly feel a little faint. Could I sit down for a moment, please?"

"Of course, Lady Mowbray, come with me." Holding her by the elbow, Mrs. Johnson led her to a far corner of the shop, and helped her to sit down in a comfortable chair. Leaning toward Charlotte, she asked, "Can I get you a glass of water? Or perhaps smelling salts?"

"I would appreciate both, please," Charlotte answered, amazed that her voice was so steady.

"Please excuse me for a moment," Mrs. Johnson said. As she walked away, Charlotte's eyes remained glued to her.

Twenty-four

Charlotte had always exercised great control over herself, and she could keep her face neutral, showing no emotion whatsoever. A long time ago, the Fifth Earl of Mowbray, David Ingham, had told her never to display weakness, never show face, and she had listened to him, and did as he said as usual. It was a stance she had adopted and never given up.

Now she knew she must not show any unusual interest in Margaret Johnson, nor should she stare at her. A moment later Mrs. Johnson returned to Charlotte's side, with a glass of water on a small tray and a bottle of smelling salts as well.

At once, Charlotte took the latter, unscrewed the top, and sniffed. The smell of ammonia in the salts was so potent, she drew back, gasping, her eyes watering.

"They're very powerful, aren't they?" Mrs. Johnson asserted. "I'll take them from you, please, m'lady, and do take a sip or two of the water. It will help you."

Charlotte did as she was asked, and drank half the glass and placed it on the tray. "Thank you so much, Mrs. Johnson. I don't know what came over me. I thought I was going to faint."

After handing the tray to one of the sales-women, Mrs. Johnson said, "Why don't we go into my office, m'lady? It's quiet in there, and we won't be disturbed if any customers come into the shop, which is likely."

"I think that's a good idea," Charlotte responded, stood up, and followed Mrs. Johnson across the floor.

Once they were settled in two comfortable wing chairs in front of the fireplace, Charlotte said, "I came to see you to ask a favor, Mrs. Johnson. Two of my WI ladies heard you had a canning machine at the Harrogate WI, and we were wondering if you would possibly lend it to us. Apparently, we've run out of jam jars."

Mrs. Johnson was nodding her head, and smiling. "The machine does solve that problem, Lady Mowbray, but one of our ladies will have to show your members how to use it." Quite unexpectedly, she let out a loud guffaw, and laughed for a few seconds.

Charlotte had stiffened. Margaret Howell Johnson had the same hearty laugh as Lady

Gwendolyn. As Mrs. Johnson endeavored to stifle her merriment, Charlotte glanced at her surreptitiously and noticed that she had a broad brow and an aquiline nose, as did Diedre. Is it my imagination? Charlotte glanced away, afraid that this rather nice woman would notice her fixed scrutiny.

Finally, Mrs. Johnson calmed herself, and said, by way of explanation, "I burst into laughter when I suddenly remembered that a can exploded last week, and we were all covered in strawberry jam. What a mess we were in. Obviously the machines do need careful handling. But of course we would be happy to lend ours to you, no problem at all."

They spoke for a while about how wonderful the Women's Institutes were for country-women, and how useful they were going to be during the coming conflict. And they made an appointment for the canning machine to be picked up from the jewelry shop next week.

On the drive back to Cavendon Hall, Charlotte sat in the backseat, pondering this extraordinary resemblance Margaret Johnson had to Diedre. Her hair was not quite as golden as Diedre's, but she was tall like Diedre, and had her finely chiseled nose and broad brow, very obvious because of the way her hair was swept back.

Years before, Lady Gwendolyn had confided

a secret to Charlotte, a secret no other soul knew.

The problem was, Charlotte knew she had no one to talk to, no one to confide in, except for Lady Gwendolyn herself. But at this stage she didn't like the idea of doing that. Why get an old lady worked up about a child she has thought about every day since she had given her away? And what if I'm mistaken? Charlotte thought. She couldn't bear to think how disappointed Lady Gwen would be.

I wish I could confide in Cecily, Charlotte thought as she went upstairs to her boudoir, to take off her coat and hat, and freshen up for lunch. But I dare not. No one can know about Lady Gwen's love affair with Mark Swann. Cecily? Her name hovered in her mind. No. Not possible.

But she's your heir, Charlotte reminded herself, and one day she will be the keeper of the record books. And the matriarch of the Swann clan. And anyway Ceci made the oath when she was twelve. The oath to protect the Inghams with her life. So she would be silent, would never reveal anything to a soul.

Knowing she must now go downstairs to join Charles and the grandchildren for lunch, Charlotte pushed this matter to the back of her mind. For the moment.

"I hope I'm not bothering you, Diedre," Cecily

said, gripping the telephone tightly. "But Greta told me something earlier today, and I thought I ought to tell you."

"What did she say?" Diedre asked, her ears pricking up. Anything to do with Greta Chalmers and the Steinbrenners interested her no end at the moment.

"Greta told me that she understood why you hadn't been able to help her family, because you had no real contacts in Berlin now. Then she went on to add that Sir Anthony Parry was going to try to get the family out of Berlin, by pulling a few strings. That's what he had called it."

Diedre was startled by this announcement and sat up straighter in her chair, pressing the receiver closer to her ear. "What strings does he intend to pull?" she asked curiously, her voice rising slightly. "He's an academic with no political connections."

"Yes, I know, and I think perhaps he was just making that statement in order to give the professor a bit of hope, don't you?"

When Diedre was silent, Cecily prodded her. "Well, don't you? After all, you said there were no more visas being issued, and that your contact's contacts had dried up, gone away, finally fled."

"I did say that, and it is true. But sometimes strange things happen in life. Perhaps he has a way of helping the professor, although I doubt it, to be honest. Look, I really appreciate having this information, Ceci, and I'm going to pass it on to my contact in Berlin. I think that this would be really wise. After all, we don't want Sir Anthony doing something…**silly.** Now do we?"

"That's right, Diedre, we don't, and you know what men are like, they think they can solve every problem in the world."

"I didn't know men thought that about themselves." Diedre chuckled, showing a little levity for once. "I thought it was women who believed that. And why not? Because we can."

Cecily laughed with her sister-in-law, and said, "Let me know if you hear anything at all. **Anything**."

Deep in thought, Diedre sat at her desk for a while after hanging up with Cecily, pondering several matters. Then she picked up the receiver once more and made four telephone calls.

The first was to Valiant. She used the admiral's private line, a safe line, at Abwehr, the headquarters of German military intelligence in Berlin. They spoke for four minutes only.

The second call was to Tony Jenkins at the British embassy in Berlin. They spoke for five minutes on Tony's private line, which he deemed to be safe.

The third call was to Lady Gwendolyn, her

great-aunt who lived at Little Skell Manor on the Cavendon estate. They spoke for ten minutes, because Diedre had to start out with a certain amount of small talk before getting to the point.

The fourth call was to Cecily, whom she reached at her office in the Burlington Arcade shop. They spoke for two minutes.

Once these calls had been completed, Diedre got up and went out into the hallway, followed the short corridor down to William Lawson's office. She spoke to his secretary, Lois Bedford, and confirmed that she was available to meet with him at five o'clock.

Love in Many Guises

But when sleep comes to close
each difficult day,
When night gives pause
to the long watch I keep,
And all my bonds I needs must loose apart,
Must doff my will as raiment laid away,
With the first dream that comes
with the first sleep
I run, I run, I am gathered to thy heart.

—Alice Meynell

Twenty-five

William Lawson was, in certain ways, somewhat similar to Admiral Wilhelm Canaris. Both were career naval officers who had bravely served their countries on ships in the Great War, were drawn to the clandestine work of naval intelligence, had proven to have a genuine talent for this, and had become brilliant spies.

Lawson, like Canaris, had moved from naval intelligence to military intelligence, when he joined MI6 in 1930. Honorable and compassionate, Lawson was a man of honesty and integrity, as was the admiral. And both men were gentlemen.

Now, as he walked back from 10 Downing Street to the War Office, William Lawson's thoughts were not on the talk he had just had with the prime minister. They were focused on Diedre, and the meeting they would have later that afternoon. He knew from Nevile Henderson, the British ambassador in Berlin, that Diedre and Canaris had chatted together at the embassy reception last week, and he was quite sure this was the reason she wanted to see him. To report in, as she usually put it.

He liked Canaris, admired him really. The German admiral was a man of principle and they shared the same code of honor peculiar to naval men all over the world. And that was why he wasn't duped by Hitler and was anti-Nazi. They had met twice—once in Portsmouth and once in Kiel— and they understood each other instantly, had bonded, in a sense.

Thoughts of Diedre pushed the admiral out of his mind. He couldn't help wondering what he was going to do about her. Nothing. He couldn't. She was his best, most clever operative, and he needed her as war loomed. And yet he had developed strong feelings for her, much to his surprise, and she rarely left his mind.

Who would have thought that he of all men would fall for a woman he worked with? Forbidden. Especially to a man like him, who was devoted to his work night and day, and who hardly noticed what a woman looked like. He was forty-seven, and had long given up thoughts of marrying again. His wife, Nora, had become an invalid in the last years of their marriage and had died fifteen years ago. It had never been a good relationship and his marriage had not been happy. On the other hand, he had found the greatest happiness and solace in his work, and still did.

He sighed under his breath as he strode on, not noticing the admiring glances thrown his way by women who walked past him. He was six feet three, masculine in build, with black hair brushed back from his handsome, rather rugged face.

As always, he was well dressed in a dark blue suit, white shirt, and striped blue-and-white tie. Like his father before him, William favored Savile Row suits, the finest shirts and ties, and fortunately his father had left him enough money to indulge himself.

Sir Roger Lawson had been the owner of a string of popular magazines which had been very successful. His mother had died some years before his father, and when he, too, had passed last year, William and his brother, Ambrose, had become quite wealthy men.

William was well aware he could no more give up on his work than he could stop breathing, and his brother, a neurological surgeon, felt the same way. The money was nice to have but neither would change their lives because of it.

He was curious about what Diedre wanted to tell him about Canaris, yet he also needed to talk to her about two new agents he had found. He hoped that Diedre would handle them, and supervise their special training.

He smiled inwardly when he went into the War Office building, deciding he was a fool for even thinking of inviting Diedre to have dinner with him. He was the last man she would ever look at, and anyway, he believed she was still grieving for Paul Drummond. Wasn't she? He didn't know the answer to that.

As he mounted the stairs to the offices within the Administration Bureau he shook his head, puzzled by himself. He might be one of the best spies in the business but he certainly didn't know much about women. Nothing at all, really.

It was Charles who reminded Charlotte that she had promised to go across the park to Little Skell Manor, to collect Lady Gwendolyn and bring her to tea.

"How on earth could I have forgotten that," she exclaimed, immediately standing up. "I must go at once, darling, and bring her over. It's easier if I talk her into using the wheelchair."

"It's easier if you have Goff drive you there and back," the earl shot back, smiling at his wife indulgently.

"I think she likes to get a bit of fresh air," Charlotte murmured, kissing Charles on his cheek, then moving down the terrace, as graceful as usual. "See you shortly."

"I'll be waiting," Charles answered, and picked

up the book he had been reading.

Walking down the stone steps of the terrace, Charlotte realized she had been so focused on Margaret Howell Johnson she had forgotten about her promise to Lady Gwendolyn, made earlier in the week. Now she understood what a great opportunity this was; she had a good reason to go over to the manor, and would find it easy to start talking about the past. Somehow she must bring the conversation around to the child Great-Aunt Gwendolyn had given birth to all those years ago. She needed to know exactly how old the girl would be today.

When Charlotte arrived at Little Skell Manor, she knocked on the door, opened it, and walked into the entrance hall. At the same moment, Mrs. Jasper, the housekeeper, came hurrying out of the drawing room.

"Oh there you are, my lady," Mrs. Jasper exclaimed, smiling. "Lady Gwendolyn is waiting for you."

"Good afternoon, Mrs. Jasper, and how is her ladyship?"

"Very well, quite spritely, and looking forward to tea with you..." Mrs. Jasper hesitated for a split second before adding, in a lower tone, "But there have been moments this week when I thought she seemed a little bit sad."

Frowning, Charlotte murmured, "I've noticed

that myself on occasion lately, but I think older people are often like that at times, perhaps remembering things long gone."

"Yes, Lady Mowbray," Mrs. Jasper agreed, and showed her into the drawing room.

Walking across the room, Charlotte said in a cheerful voice, "Hello, Great-Aunt Gwen," and went and joined her in a seating area near the bay window looking out into the garden. She was delighted to see how well Lady Gwendolyn looked, her white hair well coiffed and gleaming like silver in the sunlight coming through the window. And her face still retained much of its beauty. Now there was a big smile on it, and her blue eyes were as bright as ever, and twinkling.

"It's so kind of you to come and collect me, Charlotte, my dear, and don't you look splendid. Just wonderful today."

"I've never felt better," Charlotte answered, and sat down in the chair opposite, suddenly noticing that Lady Gwendolyn was clutching a book on her lap, but making no comment.

"Have you any news, Charlotte?"

"Well, yes, Cecily and Miles are back in London, as is Diedre. The others will all return by the weekend. Everyone will be joining us for tea on Sunday."

"It will be like old times. I knew Diedre was back. She telephoned me, to tell me she had run into Sir Anthony Parry, the husband of my good friend Regina."

Lady Gwendolyn stopped abruptly, reminding herself not to say another word about her conversation with Diedre. Glancing down at the object in her hands for a long moment, she then looked at Charlotte. "I'm so upset. I've lost the little key to this old diary and now I can't open it, and I did so want to read it."

Charlotte got up and went over to her. "Can I have a look at it? Perhaps I can get it open."

Passing the worn, tan leather diary to her, Lady Gwendolyn said, with a chuckle, "It's Daphne who knows how to pick locks, isn't it?"

Charlotte stared at her in surprise, amazed that she remembered that incident from years ago, when Daphne had wanted to retrieve the stolen jewels from her mother's safe.

"Where do you usually keep this book?" Charlotte now asked, turning it over in her hands, staring at the lock, which would not open because it had been locked with the missing key.

"In the oriental chest over there," Lady Gwendolyn answered, looking across the room. "There are a number of diaries and photograph albums in there, but no keys. I've had Mrs. Jasper look." She shook her head. "It's not like me to lose **anything,** and wouldn't you know it's the key that really matters."

"I could try to pick it with a bit of wire or maybe a hairpin."

"I've already tried that and I couldn't get the thing open."

After another close examination of the diary, Charlotte said, "The one thing I can do is to simply cut part of the lock off. That would be easy. But then you wouldn't be able to fasten the clasp at all, you know."

"I don't believe that matters, Charlotte dear. I can put it in my safe."

"Very well then. Excuse me for a moment, Great-Aunt Gwen, I'll go and get a pair of scissors from Mrs. Jasper." Placing the diary in Lady Gwendolyn's hands, she hurried out.

Within seconds she was back, and taking hold of the diary, she cut off the clasp and handed it back to Lady Gwendolyn.

Letting out a long, satisfied sigh, Lady Gwendolyn smiled at Charlotte, and said, "Thank you, my dear. It's nice to be able to read about the past. When you get really and truly old like me, you tend to live in your memories. It's such a funny thing, you know. I can remember, and very clearly, the things that happened thirty, forty, and fifty years ago, but I'm very forgetful at times about the present." A little smile played around her mouth as she said this, and then she began to turn the pages. "I'm looking for the twenty-ninth of August," she explained, peering at the pages as she flicked through them. After a moment, she stared at Charlotte.

"I need my spectacles, I can't really see without them. Would you find the page and read it for yourself?"

Leaning forward, she offered the old diary to Charlotte, and went on, "You know so much about my past, and about Mark Swann and our love for each other. August the twenty-ninth was a few days after our baby was born, the one that lived…" Her voice faltered and tears came into her eyes. "I've thought of her every day."

Holding the diary in her hands, Charlotte gazed at Lady Gwendolyn, her heart going out to this very old lady of ninety-eight, and for a moment she was choked, unable to speak. And she could not help thinking of the woman she had just met in Harrogate.

At last Charlotte asked, in the gentlest of voices, "What was the date Margaret was born, Great-Aunt Gwen?"

"August the twenty-sixth. An amazing event, actually, since I was forty-eight. If she is still alive she will be fifty this year."

"In about a week," Charlotte murmured, her mind suddenly racing with myriad thoughts, and a plan forming in her head.

The front page of the diary had the year imprinted

on it: **1888.** Charlotte flipped through to August 26, which was a Sunday. The page was empty. Three days later, on Wednesday, August 29, there was a short entry in Lady Gwendolyn's fine, rather neat handwriting.

Taking a deep breath, Charlotte plunged in, began to read: **"Our little daughter Margaret has been on this earth for only three days. She is beautiful. Today she has been in my arms once more. I am happy I have been allowed this special time with her. Tomorrow she will be taken away by her adoptive parents. Mark and I will never see our sweet Margaret again. We hope and pray to God that they will love and cherish her and give her a good life. I have come to understand that you have to love a child so much you are willing to let it go, if that is for the best. I will think of my Margaret every day of my life until I die. And she will be in my heart forever."**

Charlotte's eyes were brimming with tears and she tried to blink them away without success. Reaching for her handbag, she took out a handkerchief and dried her eyes, then looked across at Lady Gwendolyn. She was so choked up she could not speak, full of emotion, and heartache for Great-Aunt Gwen.

Lady Gwendolyn said, in a slightly quavering voice, "Not long after I'd written those words,

Mark came to the hospital with the photographer from the studio in Leeds. Margaret was brought to me again, wearing her lovely christening robes. Don't you remember, Charlotte, I showed you that photograph years ago?"

"Of course I remember." Rising, Charlotte walked over to the small antique desk at the other side of the room, where she had spotted Lady Gwendolyn's glasses with the morning post. Picking them up, she brought them over to her. Handing her the diary, and then the glasses, she said, "Now you can read it whenever you want, Great-Aunt Gwen."

"Thank you, Charlotte, I will. But later."

"Where shall I put the diary for safety?"

"The safe is in the library, you can tuck it in there before we leave, lock it up. In the meantime, I just want to tell you something else. Although I wasn't supposed to, I wrote a note to the adoptive parents, and put it inside the box of baby clothes I'd bought, along with the christening robe. It was on plain paper and unsigned, and it was only one line...**Her name is Margaret**. Was I wrong to do that?"

"Of course not, and I know why you did. Because she **was** Margaret to you, and you wanted to think of her as Margaret always. And I believe they would have understood that, somehow, and kept the name."

Lady Gwendolyn's face changed, the sadness flushed away by sudden smiles. "Oh do you think so, Charlotte? I do hope you're right. That makes me feel happy...are you sure?"

"I'm sure," Charlotte murmured. Her mind was racing; she couldn't wait to go back to Harrogate to see Margaret Howell Johnson, and hopefully get a few answers to some very important questions.

Twenty-six

When Diedre knocked on the door and then walked straight into William Lawson's office, he was standing by a window, looking down into the street.

He immediately swung around, walked over to greet her. "Welcome back," he said.

"Back where I belong," she answered.

For a moment, he wondered what she meant but was sure she had been referring to the office.

"Let's sit down here," he said, indicating the two comfortable chairs next to a low table.

As they settled in the chairs, he continued, "I'm sorry I couldn't see you yesterday. I was out on an errand." That word was common usage in their unit, code for "in a foreign place."

"I suspected that," she replied.

Like Diedre he was very direct, always got straight to the point. He asked, "Do you have an operation going in Berlin? One I should know about?"

"Sort of, but I had to see you at once for another reason. Valiant asked me to tell you certain things. Do you want to have his message first or last?"

"Is his message good news or bad?" William asked, a frown creasing his brow.

"In my opinion, it's not good, it's **great.**"

"Then let's keep the great news for last. I want to know about the operation, Diedre. I trust you were going to clue me in?" This sounded like a question, and he raised a dark brow.

"Don't I always!" she exclaimed, and shook her head slowly. "This one's complicated, so I would like to begin at the beginning, which is not really where the operation started. You have a need to know."

"Tell it the way you wish. You know very well I trust you implicitly. Anyway, your narratives are always very clear and to the point." He leaned back in the chair and crossed his long legs. "Commence please, Lady Diedre."

She smiled as she generally did when he used her title and gave great emphasis to it. It really didn't matter to her how he addressed her.

Taking a deep breath, she said, "It all started some few weeks ago, when my sister-in-law, Cecily Swann, told me that her assistant, Greta Chalmers, was worried because her father and his second wife and two children were trapped in Berlin, couldn't get out, and—"

"Are they Jewish?" he cut in. "Greta Chalmers doesn't sound like a Jewish name."

"They are all Jewish, yes. Let me fill you in quickly. A bit of background. Greta's late mother was English and Jewish by religion. She lived in London and Berlin after her marriage to Professor Steinbrenner. Greta was sent to school in England when she was eight. After her mother died in London, the professor decided to let Greta remain there with her grandmother, to finish her education. This she did. She also fell in love with an Englishman, Roy Chalmers, and they married. She's now widowed and—"

"Wants to get her father and his family out of Germany as quickly as possible. Correct?"

Diedre nodded, and then proceeded to tell him the entire story, starting with her own efforts with Tony Jenkins and their lack of success, and ending with Tony's connections leading him to Princess Irina. She then explained that they met the Russian woman at the British embassy.

"Nobody was more surprised than I was, when I suddenly saw the admiral walking toward me at the reception," Diedre announced. Pausing, she gave her boss a small, knowing smile. "But I'm sure the ambassador mentioned he saw me talking to Valiant, and at great length."

"He did, and I told him I wasn't surprised, since you were old friends, that you had known him through mutual friends. And since the early thirties."

"I bet that surprised **him,**" Diedre said, and laughed.

William couldn't suppress the smile that crossed his mouth. "Nobody ever fools you, do they? Of course Nevile was startled. He usually is when women have large roles to play in world events."

"I don't think he knows much about women. He's never been married. Anyway, to finish up this story. I was talking to the admiral when Cecily came over. She wanted to know if she and Miles could have lunch with the professor and Sir Anthony Parry. I hesitated."

"Because you thought something might come up about the professor going to England. That was it, wasn't it?"

Diedre nodded. "I knew Cecily would not say a word, but I had no idea what the professor or Sir Anthony might bring up. Maybe things which would create problems."

He nodded. "Continue, Diedre."

"Valiant said he admired Sir Anthony, that it would be interesting to lunch with him. Cecily invited the admiral but he declined. I had realized that Valiant didn't see anything wrong with the lunch. I suggested Cecily should check with

Daphne, but that I was busy on Friday. Once we were alone, Canaris asked me why I had been hesitating about the lunch."

"And you told him about the connection between Cecily and Greta, and an urgent need for exit papers."

"I did. He wanted to know why I hadn't approached him. I said he'd done so much for me already. I then indicated that Tony and the Russian princess were talking in the corner, that Tony was dealing with her. He told me she was good, that she would come to him anyway. And that I should consider the matter a done deal."

"And where do we stand today?" William asked.

"I spoke to Tony this morning. He said it was more or less ready to go. The four new passports and exit visas would be handed to the professor by next Tuesday, Wednesday at the latest."

"Well, that's a relief. Good work, Diedre."

"Thank you. But Tony's doing the work."

"Under your supervision."

She inclined her head. "We've got a problem, Will."

William Lawson sat up a little straighter in the chair, his dark intelligent eyes riveted on Diedre. "Can we solve it?"

"We have to. Immediately. Time is short. The

Steinbrenners must leave next week, and the tickets have been bought, the train seats booked. And there's going to be a crackdown in Berlin."

"Tell me the problem, Diedre."

"Tony indicated to me today that Mrs. Steinbrenner has cold feet. She's frozen in place. Won't go. She's afraid they'll be caught fleeing Berlin, and be shot."

William let out a long sigh, shaking his head. "Surely she understands the hideous situation in Germany...the methodical mass murder of Jews."

"I think I know what to do about her. But I'm afraid there's another problem to solve. Sir Anthony has now told the professor that he can get them out, that he knows important people, politicians, and can pull strings."

"Oh, Jaysus!" William exclaimed, adopting an Irish accent. After a moment's thought, he asked quickly, "Does he know anything at all about Tony's plans for the Steinbrenners?"

"No! No! Nobody knows. Tony drilled it into the four of them that it had to be a total secret, that no one could know, not even other family members."

"So presumably the professor remained silent when Sir Anthony came up with this new idea? Why am I asking you that? Of course he said nothing, he's too smart a man to confide that he had all the arrangements made to leave Germany."

"That's right. I did some checking...about Sir Anthony."

"How?" William gave her a puzzled look.

"I phoned Great-Aunt Gwendolyn this morning. She knows Sir Anthony's wife. Without giving her the real reason, I asked her to give me her opinion of Sir Anthony. She chuckled and said he was brilliant, a nice man, but that he was boastful, a braggart, always wanted to make himself look more important than he really was. She said he promised people things he could never fulfill...like get them asked to tea by the queen. Indeed, even get them an honor from the queen. Or have the prime minister make them an MP. As if that's the way it works."

Diedre began to laugh. "I must admit, for a ninety-eight-year-old, Great-Aunt Gwen's really on her toes. She asked me why I wanted to know things about him, an obvious question. I just whispered that it was top secret, that she must keep this to herself. Naturally she agreed. She thinks I'm a spy."

William was half laughing himself, when he said, "So now we know pulling strings was just an idle boast on the part of the academic. Thanks to Lady Gwendolyn."

"That's correct. I'm not worried too much

about Sir Anthony anymore. However, going back to Mrs. Steinbrenner. I did feel concerned enough to speak to Cecily. She'd called me earlier, and I found a reason to give her a ring later. I then asked her if I'd mistaken what she'd said about Mrs. Steinbrenner being a nervous, somewhat high-strung person. She said, no, that she had said that, and wanted to know why I was so interested in Greta's stepmother."

"I bet that was a tough one to answer," William murmured, his eyes narrowing as he focused intently on Diedre.

"I'd thought of the reason before I called," Diedre responded softly, eyeing him. "I explained that it was really for her sake, Cecily's sake, that I'd been thinking about Greta. I had been wondering how Greta would react when she realized her family were not able to leave. I told Cecily she needed a plan if she was going to help Greta get through the trauma that was bound to ensue."

"Did she believe you?"

"She did. She's a brilliant woman, very intuitive. She confided that she had also been wondering the same thing. I suggested going to a psychiatrist for advice. And to learn how to handle trauma of that nature. I volunteered to go with her, to help her with Greta if I was needed."

Diedre paused, cleared her throat, and went on. "Cecily thought the idea of a psychiatrist to guide us, and also help Greta, was the best solution. Later today, it suddenly struck me that insecure people only respond to authority and that we should get help from a psychiatrist when Mrs. Steinbrenner arrives in London. Cecily had pointed out to me earlier that nervous, insecure, highly strung people can be difficult. Greta's stepmother will be in a new country, a foreign country, where everything is different, including the language."

William had listened attentively. "Well, you do now have an important insight into Mrs. Steinbrenner, but how will this actually help you to defrost her? You say she's frozen in place and won't leave Berlin."

"Good question, Will. What Cecily's comments told me is that we can't simply hand the passports, exit visas, and the train tickets over to the professor and send him and them on their way. The Steinbrenners have to be taken out of Berlin, and Mrs. Steinbrenner **forcibly,** if necessary."

A look of genuine alarm spread across Will's face. "**Forcibly?** Who's going to do that? And wouldn't it draw attention to them?"

"I don't mean **forcibly** in the way you think. I shall have Tony inform the professor that he is going to accompany them on the train. Just to make sure all goes well. However, I fully intend to see Jerry Randell, my friend in intelligence at the American embassy. I'm going to ask him to arrange for Alexander Dubé to accompany them from Berlin to Paris." Pausing for a moment, Diedre then continued, "Tony, if he wants, can leave the train in Aachen. Once he's sure the Steinbrenners have crossed the border."

Taking a deep breath, Diedre finished, "Alexander Dubé will be nice, but authoritative, and Tony will behave the same way. The professor will be told in advance that he must support them in this, and he will. And that's it, boss."

William Lawson sat staring at her for a long moment thinking she was undoubtedly one of the smartest people he had ever worked with. "Well done, Diedre. Well done, indeed. Extremely cleverly thought out, and you've covered everything to get the Steinbrenners away safely. And I know for a fact that Valiant will have made sure that the documents are perfect, cannot be challenged. And speaking of the valiant admiral, don't you have a message for me from him?"

"I do, yes, Will. And what I'm thinking, now that it's six o'clock, is that we leave here and go for a drink somewhere. I for one could use a glass of water."

William grinned at her. "I think a glass of champagne might be more like it. You've talked yourself dry." He stood up, and walked over to his desk, locked several drawers, pocketed the keys. "Let us wander over to the Ritz Hotel. The walk will do us good, as will the fresh air."

"You've got a deal," Diedre said, and thought to add, "I know it's totally safe here, but even safer in a hotel bar. No eavesdroppers."

Once they made themselves comfortable in the bar of the Ritz Hotel on Piccadilly, and ordered two glasses of pink champagne, Diedre said, "I want you to know that I trust Wilhelm Canaris implicitly. I'd trust him with my life. Do you feel the same way?"

Although he was momentarily taken aback by the question, William did not hesitate. "Of course I do. **Absolutely.** He's true-blue, and we share the same code of honor. And he's proven himself to me in the past."

The champagne arrived, they clinked flutes and said cheers. After a few swallows, Diedre murmured, "Just before he left the party, our friend asked me if I could meet him for lunch the next day. We did meet at that restaurant near his office. We were joined by Hans Oster. After **he** left, our friend spoke to me about you."

Diedre sat back, sipping her drink, recouping a little after her long story recited to him in the office.

William understood this, and simply did the same thing. He sipped his champagne and relaxed, knowing she was pulling herself together, in a sense catching her breath and going through the knowledge implanted in her brain by Canaris.

Moving closer to William, Diedre spoke at last, her voice low but her diction so perfect she was audible. "The first thing he said was that he wanted you to know that he had been, and would be, true to his last words to you. He added that you should never doubt his honesty and integrity. He asked me to tell you he would always speak the truth to you, never mislead you."

Nodding, William also drew closer; their heads were together across the table. "Continue, Diedre, please."

"He had four things he wanted me to convey. The first is that when you receive information from **anyone** in the Vatican, you must understand that it will be from him especially if it has to do with our country. The second thing is similar. Any information emanating from Spain, again affecting our country, will be from him. The third is that he will often funnel information through me, and sometimes perhaps through Tony to me."

After a moment, William said quietly, "And

what is the fourth message, Diedre?"

"That he will do everything in his power to keep Spain neutral, that he will endeavor to prevent the Nazis from invading Spain. He said I should tell you that he wants to protect Gibraltar for us, and the Mediterranean. His last words to me were: **Franco is my friend. Make sure William knows this, believes it.**"

William gaped at her, stunned by this last statement. How on earth could one man, a German admiral, keep Spain neutral? He had no answer for himself at this precise moment.

After a short while, Diedre said, "You haven't said a word. What are you thinking?"

"That he's just handed us something so fantastic I can hardly believe it. A source of invaluable information. **He himself**. And I'm thrilled, of course I am, Diedre. I just don't understand why he thinks he can keep Spain free of Hitler's domination. How can he do that?"

Diedre stared back at him, frowning. "Because he's head of Abwehr, German military intelligence. If that's not immense power, I don't know what is."

William nodded. "You're absolutely right." He tossed back the last drops of champagne and studied her face. It was beautiful. "I need another drink. What about you?"

She began to laugh, "You're the one who cautioned me, and later Tony, about not drinking on the job."

"Tonight's an exception to the rule; we're off duty. And by the way, will you have dinner with me?" He couldn't believe he'd just said this, and he motioned to the waiter, wanted to hide his sudden confusion.

Once the waiter had gone off to get their refills, William turned to Diedre, and asked, "Well?"

"I'd love to have dinner with you, Will."

Twenty-seven

They went to a little restaurant in Chelsea called Le Chat Noir, which William knew well. It was tucked away in a cul-de-sac, off the beaten track, and was run by a French couple whom William had known for years.

After they were seated and given the menus, Diedre turned to him. "Isn't it strange that all the spies I know have funny little restaurants hidden away somewhere? And I don't."

"Then you must find one, and make it your own. Or you can use this one…black cats **are** lucky, aren't they?" he said in a teasing tone.

Shaking her head, she answered with a slight shrug, "I don't really know. But I'll ask Charlotte this weekend. She's a mine of information about such things, like odd sayings and ancient superstitions." There was a pause before Diedre added, "Do you think Sir Francis Walsingham had a favorite little spot tucked away somewhere?"

"More than likely, I should think. England's greatest spy, and spymaster, was something of a magician, in my opinion."

"And our Tudor queen also thought that, Will. She put all of her faith in Walsingham."

"Who helped her to run England along with William Cecil and Robert Dudley, in whom she also had great faith. Now, enough history, shall we order?" He opened his menu as he spoke and scanned the dishes which were listed.

Diedre did the same thing, and said, "I'll be guided by you, Will. What are your favorites?"

"They do a great entrecôte steak with green salad and chips, one of their best French dishes. I also like their rack of lamb, Provençal style. I'm so tired of eating fish, I think I'll go for the steak, actually."

"I will too, and for the same reason."

William waved to the owner, Jacques André, who was by their side in a minute. After ordering their food, and a bottle of his favorite red wine, William turned to Diedre and asked, "Would you like a glass of champagne while we wait for dinner?"

"If you're having a glass, I will too. Thank you."

"So be it, Jacques. You heard the lady."

With a smile and a nod, Jacques departed, and William said, "There's one important question I have to ask you, Diedre, before we discuss anything else."

She nodded. "Please ask it then."

"Earlier, when you mentioned you had telephoned Cecily to ask about Mrs. Steinbrenner's health, she apparently asked you why you wanted to know." William's brow knotted in a frown. "But you didn't answer her. Not according to the way you related the story to me."

"No, I didn't. And on purpose. I really had no reason to know, because she wasn't coming. That wasn't true of course; she **was** leaving Berlin. But it was a secret. However, I couldn't say that to Cecily. So I sort of fudged it. Ignored it, actually. I simply rushed on at top speed, explaining that I was worried about Greta, and how she would cope with the knowledge that her father and the family faced death in Germany. I've known Cecily all my life, and I realized that she would mostly be concerned about Greta, to whom she is devoted."

"And you were correct. She didn't press you. And by the way, I do think you came up with the right solution, regarding a psychiatrist. One should be on hand when Mrs. Steinbrenner does get here. She'll need a lot of help."

A waiter came with their glasses of champagne, and they toasted each other. And then, very quietly, William said, "And to the remarkable Valiant who truly deserves the code name you gave him, Diedre."

"He does indeed," Diedre murmured, and they

touched glasses.

"And we must always protect him as best we can," she added.

There was a small silence, and neither of them spoke for a moment or two. This was not unusual. They had worked closely together for three years, and they understood each other. Their silences were always compatible, just as their everyday dealings were.

William was the first to break the silence, when he asked, "What exactly do we know about Alexander Dubé?"

"That he's a close, old friend of Jerry Randell's. They went to college together. Alexander is an impresario in the music world, and is constantly in Berlin, because of the philharmonic orchestra. Apparently he's willing to do a favor now and then for Randell, who only occasionally asks him. And it must always be a favor that doesn't put Dubé in harm's way. Jerry insists on that."

William took a sip of the wine, then asked, "So your idea is to have him on the train out of Berlin to Paris? As a sort of **guard,** someone to protect the family should trouble erupt."

"The trains are full of German troops, foreigners, Gestapo, and God knows who else. And, since Mrs. Steinbrenner has a nervous disposition, who knows what she might do. Unexpectedly. I think that the professor might be a little naïve, not as worldly as we might imagine. Dubé and Tony would be able to control any kind of situation that might develop." Diedre eyed William intently.

"And when they get to Paris?" he asked quizzically.

"Tony will take them to the British embassy, where the family will be issued visas. It has been arranged already. Dubé will be with them, and he will accompany them to London."

When William was silent, sat looking into the distance with a reflective expression in his eyes, Diedre wondered if he did not like the plan she had created. She sat back in her chair and waited, not only puzzled but worried. She had never seen him like this...was it pre-occupation? She did not know. The thing she did know was that she enjoyed being with him out of the office. He touched her, and made her feel like a woman again. Suddenly, she realized how attracted she was to him.

Eventually, William said, "It all makes sense to me, Diedre. I might be falling into the pro-verbial trap, thinking that all professors are absentminded, but I believe it's better to be safe. The protection sounds good to me; let's hope Alexander Dubé will agree to do it."

"I think he will. It's not a difficult task, and he's not in harm's way, not by a long shot," she answered, still full of surprise that William

Lawson appealed to her.

"Agreed. Moving on, I had a meeting with the PM today," William confided. "I came away frustrated and baffled. Chamberlain just doesn't get it, doesn't understand that appeasement is like…well, whistling in the dark. Lord Halifax doesn't help, goading him on." William shook his head, and there was a troubled look in his dark intelligent eyes. "Why won't they understand that Hitler's a killer, a proven mass murderer intent on world domination? They can't be that stupid. Or can they?" A dark brow lifted as he stared at her.

"Maybe they are exactly that. Or perhaps it's wishful thinking on their part. Then again, there is a segment of the British establishment who actually believe Hitler is much more preferable to Stalin. They fear Communism."

"I think I'll go and buy them copies of **Mein Kampf**. And tell them to believe every word they read," he exclaimed.

"They just won't read it, Will, so save your money."

He chuckled. "Well, I wasn't really going to buy them Hitler's book, you know. I was being sarcastic."

"My father believes Churchill should be prime minister. He says he's the only one who has vision, and who can save us, save Europe, and ultimately save Western civilization."

"I totally agree with him, and speaking of your father, I suppose you're going to Cavendon this weekend?"

Diedre gave him a swift glance. "Well, yes, I was. I haven't seen Robin for almost two weeks, and anyway I do want to give my father the once-over, so to speak. Before I left for Geneva he wasn't looking his best. But if I have to work, I'll stay in London, of course. If you need me."

He didn't answer. He just sat there gazing at her in the candlelight.

There was something in his eyes, an expression she didn't quite understand, and his face, frequently so alive and animated, was perfectly still. In fact, he looked almost sorrowful, she thought. Even troubled.

Finally, she asked, "Is everything all right, Will?"

Rousing himself quickly from his thoughts about her, his feelings for her, his need of her, he nodded. "No problem. I was just thinking about two agents I've taken on," he improvised and then continued, "A man and a woman who know France inside out. Both are half French, half English, and want to be operatives over there. When the time comes. Which it will."

"Do you want me to meet them? Are they in London?"

"Oh yes, they live here. And I don't want you to meet them, I want you to run them," he replied. "I think you should supervise them, and their special training."

"Are they related? A married couple?" she asked.

"No, no. They don't even know each other yet. So, what do you say?"

"I'll handle them for you, Will. You know I'll do anything you want."

He was silent, and before he could think of anything to say, Jacques arrived with the food they had ordered. Much to his relief.

Diedre woke up in the middle of the night, and within seconds she was getting out of bed, going into the kitchen. She boiled a cup of milk for herself, and took it back to bed, lay in the darkened room, sipping the milk, and thinking about William Lawson.

It had been a nice evening. He had been charming, amusing at times, and very clever about their work. But then he was brilliant when it came to military intelligence, and they saw eye to eye on most things. They had touched on a few personal matters and that was it.

Naturally, he had been the perfect gentleman all evening, considerate and kind. He had hailed a cab after leaving the restaurant, brought her home, said good night, and gone on his way in the cab.

But she knew something strange had

happened to her tonight, even as she was putting her key in the front door. But what was it really? She had unexpectedly realized she found him attractive, and very appealing. But there was something more there, underneath the surface. A strong physical attraction.

This thought made her sit bolt upright in the bed, and she almost spilled the milk. **Sexual attraction**. How could that be? She had not thought of sex since Paul died. Oh my God, she muttered, and put the milk on the bedside table because she had suddenly started to shake. Turning on the bedside lamp, she got out of bed and went to find a dressing gown and a pair of slippers. She felt chilled right through to the bone.

Now wide awake, Diedre sat down at her favorite desk which stood under the bedroom window. Because it was a French **bureau plat,** designed like a table, it worked well with the bedroom décor. Paul had bought it for her in Paris because he knew how much she loved desks, and had since her childhood.

Paul. She looked to her left, and stared at his picture in the silver frame. Her eyes suddenly filled with tears, but she managed to blink them away. She had cried so much after his sudden and unexpected death she thought she had no tears left in her.

How she had grieved for him...for a whole

year. At one moment she thought she would never recover, she missed him so much…his humor, his quirky American slang, his love and desire for her…gone from her in an instant.

It was Daphne who had taken her down to the gazebo at Cavendon and lectured her, telling her a year was long enough for this intense grief, and that she should look after her young son, also stricken with sorrow. Daphne's tough words had pulled her up short, and made her understand she had neglected Robin in a certain sense. She knew she must change and make amends.

When Hugo came to talk to her, some weeks later, he had suggested that Robin should go to boarding school. For a few moments she had balked at the idea, but had then begun to see the sense of this.

Robin would be with boys of his own age, and there would be schoolmasters to guide him. He needed men in his life, that was true.

Hugo had suggested Colet Court, and had taken her to see the school. And then she had broached the idea to Robin. He had not been interested at all and wanted to stay at home with her. In an effort to persuade him, she had adopted his father's language, and said, "Let's make a deal, Robin."

He had looked at her, and retorted, "What's in it for me?" Her son was also using Paul's business language, and suddenly he had smiled for the first time in ages.

She remembered now how she had been thrilled by that smiling face, and had shot back, "One month at Colet Court. If you don't like it, you can leave, and decide where you want to be educated until you go to Eton when you're thirteen."

He had accepted the deal on a handshake, again following his father's rules by saying, "My handshake seals the contract."

Fortunately, Robin had loved Colet Court right from the beginning, and was genuinely happy there. And in the holidays and the summer months he stayed at Cavendon. During the week he had his cousins, and most especially Charlie, his grandfather, Miles, and Harry, who had taught him to be a fine horseman. And she went every weekend.

Once Robin had settled at school, she had suddenly realized the flat was empty; she had nothing to do. At once she had known she must go back to work. She had always loved being in intelligence, and when she had gone to see the new head of the unit, she had been pleasantly surprised.

William Lawson had welcomed her with enthusiasm and open arms, and appointed her to the top position. In fact, if he was ever ill or absent, she would take his place, as his second in command, and reporting only to the prime minister.

Will. She closed her eyes, picturing them together in the restaurant last night. Why had it been different? After all, she had had dinner with him before. But previously it had been much more businesslike, and, more often than not, there was someone with them.

We were alone, relaxed. He was pleased with everything I'd done about the Steinbrenners. Also delighted with the news I had brought from Valiant. We had champagne, and wine and a cozy supper.

He was who he is as a man and not my boss.

And he was interested in me as a woman. What I thought was a sad look in his eyes was actually tenderness. And at one moment it was a yearning…for companionship? For love? For me? She wasn't sure, but she suddenly understood that just as she had found **him** appealing, he had felt the same about **her**.

This sudden insight into William Lawson startled her. But it also frightened her. She could not let herself fall under his spell. They worked together. They could not become involved.

Opening her eyes, Diedre rose from the chair, slipped out of her dressing gown, and went to bed, hoping to sleep. But it eluded her. She lay there in the darkness, thinking about Paul. Being attracted to another man was not a betrayal of their love. Not in any way whatsoever. Paul had been dead almost five years now. And he wouldn't want her to be alone. He would say life was for the living.

But why Will? she asked herself. The world is full of men. Why him, someone she worked with? Nobody would ever be able to answer that question. But she guessed it was because she found herself drawn to him, wanted to know him better as a man. That had begun to happen in the little restaurant in Chelsea. And of course it had been sexual attraction. Why pretend otherwise? But what she would do about it was another thing entirely. And what would he do? She couldn't hazard a guess.

He had never told her much about himself, but Tony had. They were related by marriage; Tony's cousin Veronica was married to Ambrose Lawson, William's brother, and they considered themselves family.

Tony had told her Will's wife had been difficult, a jealous, neurotic woman, and that she had made his life hell. And so he had thrown himself into work, had taken every foreign assignment offered. His wife had become an invalid; and she had been dead for fifteen years. "They didn't have any children," Tony had added the night he had filled her in about her boss...

three years ago now.

She couldn't help wondering if there was a woman friend in the background. It would be quite normal for him to have a relationship. After all, he was a handsome, rather masculine man that made a woman feel safe.

Her thoughts ran on, became more complex and intimate, which alarmed her momentarily. And then she let her imagination run free, and lay awake until dawn, when she finally fell asleep with the image of William Lawson engraved on her brain.

Twenty-eight

Diedre was blessed with an extraordinary memory, could recall conversations with people from years ago, as well as details of meetings and other occasions. For this reason she never took notes or wrote anything down, which she considered a dangerous habit. Any small notation she might make was burned at the first opportunity.

Her method of conveying information was to relay it personally and as soon as possible. She would then store it away in the recesses of her mind, to draw on when needed.

The moment she arrived at her office on Thursday morning, she telephoned Tony Jenkins at the British embassy in Berlin.

"It's me, Daffy Dilly," she said when he answered his phone on the third ring.

"I hoped it would be you," Tony answered, relief echoing in his voice. "I went for caviar last night. Wish you'd been with me. The pot of gold will be in my hands next Wednesday, six days from now."

"Congratulations. I hope the caviar was good."

"Delicious. Have you any news about the bedsocks?"

"I have. I'll explain in a moment. I just want to say you've done an excellent job, Tony, and at top speed. Thank you. Now, regarding the bedsocks. They're going to be delivered by you and Alexander Dubé, whom you've heard about."

"Oh, I see."

"From what I've learned, the person needing the bedsocks is highly strung, nervous, and could be difficult. She might need **help** putting them on."

"We'll manage it," Tony replied. "But what if she wants to take them off on the train and freezes again?"

"You and Alexander Dubé will know how to handle it, if you get my drift. Am I safe to keep talking?"

"I checked this morning, as I do every day, and you're good to continue. This phone is safe."

"I will arrange for Dubé to meet you in Berlin. He'll be filled in, will understand everything. You and he will escort the travelers to Aachen and continue on to Belgium, and then to France."

"So I will stay on the train, right through to

Paris and make sure all is okay at the British embassy. Is that correct?"

"Yes. But I thought that the visa situation had been put in place already."

"It has. However, I'll get in touch with the visa division, just to make sure. Anything to report on our academic friend?"

"I spoke to my great-aunt, who knows his wife. She told me that he's a very nice man, kind, but loves to brag. He promises people the earth, then can't deliver."

"That's what I thought. How do we shut him up? He might blab all over the place, saying he can get the professor out. That would be dangerous talk, draw attention to the prof."

"We don't, we can't shut him up. He's not under our control. And we can't tell him the truth. However, you might want to let the professor know that everything is set for next week. Insist it must be kept secret. He should know that if he talks it could be fatal."

"I'll deal with it."

"I'll never understand why people don't comprehend the gravity of events taking place around them. The world is changing and they don't pay attention."

"They don't see the menace or the danger," Tony answered.

"Correct. How's the weather?"

"Not good. Storms. Thunder and lightning

imminent. I'm happy you're not here. I wouldn't want you to get your feet wet."

"I'll be seeing my contact regarding Mr. Dubé later today. I'll fill you in tomorrow. And please decide where you want to end up."

"I can tell you now. I'll stay in Paris with Mr. Dubé until they leave for London. Just to be sure all's well that ends well, to quote good old Will…Shakespeare, that is."

"I know who you meant."

They said good-bye and hung up. Leaning back in her chair, Diedre focused on Greta Chalmers, wondering what to tell her, if anything at all.

After some consideration, she decided not to say a word. I'll let it just happen, she thought. Greta doesn't have to know in advance. Something could go wrong on the way to the border. It has in the past.

There was a knock on the door, and Will walked in. "Am I interrupting? You look lost in thought."

"I was about to come and see you. I just spoke to Tony. The Steinbrenners will leave next Wednesday. The documents are ready."

Will sat down. "So, the die is cast. All I can say is thank God for Valiant."

Diedre nodded. She was shocked at Will's appearance. He looked exhausted and had dark rings under his eyes. She couldn't help wondering if he'd had a bad night like she had. Her chest tightened. Was he experiencing the same feelings as she?

He said, "You're staring at me, Diedre. Is something wrong?"

"No, no. You look rather tired, that's all."

"I did have a restless night, mostly because of Valiant, and your message from him. Did he want an answer? Am I to be in touch?"

"He never said anything about a response. I believe he thinks you'll want his information, which you will, won't you?"

"Of course. **Absolutely.** He's invaluable. When I met him in Kiel last year, he muttered something about Germany having to lose the war in order to regain its humanity. He spoke so low I wasn't sure I heard him correctly."

"You did. I can tell you right now, he's totally anti-Nazi, and quite a few people know this. That's the reason I worry about him. And there's another thing I want to point out to you. When he was serving in the navy, Canaris had a protégé by the name of Reinhard Heydrich. There is a strong possibility he might become a rival, seeking greater power for himself. In my opinion anyway. Let's keep that in mind, keep Heydrich in our line of vision. He could become a problem, a danger to Valiant."

William nodded. "I understand he's a glutton for power. I'll pass it on. Now, let's discuss

Tony Jenkins."

"What about him?"

"I think he has to come out. Menzies over at MI6 just told me earlier that the intelligence coming in from Berlin is really bad…Hitler's on some sort of rampage."

"Tony indicated that the mood in Berlin is growing more dangerous. He's going right through to Paris on this upcoming exit. Shall I tell him to keep going?"

"Let's bring him in now rather than later. Tell him to come home where he's safe."

Twenty-nine

Charlotte stood in her upstairs parlor at Cavendon Hall, staring out of the window, smiling with pleasure when she caught sight of the two snow-white swans gliding together across the lake. They looked so elegant, regal even, in the bright August sunlight. It touched her that swans mate for life.

In a very short time she would be going to Harrogate, to see Margaret Howell Johnson. The image of her had hardly left Charlotte's mind. The physical resemblance to Diedre had been so pronounced it had been unnerving. Once again, she asked herself if Mrs. Johnson could be Lady Gwendolyn's daughter. She was not certain, not without more information; on the other hand, there was a strong possibility she was indeed Great-Aunt Gwen's **Margaret**.

How odd that she had met Mrs. Johnson because of a canning machine for the Women's Institute, but then no one ever knew what was going to happen. Life makes its own rules, she thought. It was Alice Swann who had first said that to her, and she knew Alice was correct. She had her own favorite saying about life: What is meant to be is meant to be.

Slowly, the swans floated off around the corner of the lake, and disappeared from view. How empty that large sheet of glassy water suddenly looked. Charles had always said that Cavendon wouldn't be the same without those swans, and also **the** Swanns. He was right on both counts.

Turning away from the window, she sat down at her desk and checked the list for Sunday afternoon tea. It looked as if everyone would be coming, except for Dulcie and James, who were still in Los Angeles. She was happy Charles would be surrounded by his children and grandchildren; he had been looking forward to this Sunday gathering, and a mingling of Inghams and Swanns.

Her mind strayed to the family history, and she recalled how, over a hundred and eighty years ago, a man called James Swann had become the liegeman of Humphrey Ingham, a clever businessman and trader, who traveled the world buying and selling everything from exotic spices in the West Indies, to gold and diamonds in India. In the process he became immensely rich and powerful, dabbled in politics, and had given back generously to the country of his birth in many different ways. Finally he was honored with a peerage which was gifted by the king along with a tract of land called Mowbray, in his native Yorkshire.

Once he became the Earl of Mowbray, Humphrey had bought up thousands of acres adjoining Mowbray, including the verdant valley called Little Skell which stood on the banks of the river Skell. The valley also had a rich and fertile grouse moor, which Humphrey and James had religiously cultivated over the years. It still flourished today and yielded a selection of game annually.

With the help of his liegeman, James Swann, Humphrey had created three villages: Little Skell, Mowbray, and High Clough. He had built Cavendon Hall, a great stately home, on a hill above Little Skell village, and had thus brought security and a degree of prosperity to the local people living in the three villages.

What a lucky thing it was those two men met, became close friends and associates, Charlotte thought. **It was meant to be.**

Because of Humphrey Ingham, there would always be swans on the lake at Cavendon, in honor of his dearest friend, James Swann. It was a tradition she loved.

So be it, she murmured to herself. Rising, she picked up her handbag, and went downstairs.

Charles had gone with Harry to look at the two allotment fields which the women of the WI had created. They were so proud of them; Charles had deemed it necessary to show an interest. They had worked hard, no doubt about that, and Harry had volunteered to give the earl a guided tour.

Goff opened the car door for her, and she got inside, settled back, her mind centered on Margaret Howell Johnson. Filled with impatience to get to the bottom of it, and discover the truth, Charlotte had telephoned her yesterday to ask if they could borrow the canning machine earlier than arranged. Mrs. Johnson was out at the time, but an hour later one of the salesladies had returned her call. Mrs. Johnson would be happy to see her tomorrow, which was today, Friday, August 19.

If Mrs. Johnson was who Charlotte thought she was, her birthday would be in a week's time, on Friday, August 26. But it still might not prove to be anything, just a quirky look-alike, and the birth date a coincidence. I need much more information, Charlotte thought, in order to make a positive identification. How to get it? That was the problem.

The only decent idea she had been able to come up with was to invent someone, a woman who once knew Margaret when she was a child, and wanted to know how the lovely little girl had fared in the world. So she had created a person and made a plan. Some might think it a flimsy idea, but she believed it would work. Anyway, what did she have to lose? Also, she was picking up the canning machine for the WI. It wouldn't be a wasted trip.

But it was, according to Mrs. Johnson, who greeted Charlotte when she arrived at the shop. She was looking most apologetic when she said, "I'm so sorry, your ladyship, but I made an error. My WI ladies are going to be using the machine this weekend. You see, I didn't know that they had already prepared lots of fruit to can this weekend, and they can't let it go bad, obviously." She shook her head, and finished, "I'm afraid I've wasted your time, your ladyship." She liked Lady Mowbray, and meant it sincerely.

Although she was taken aback for a split second, Charlotte was determined to spend some time with Mrs. Johnson in order to do a little digging. And so she improvised, when she said, "It's not really a problem, because I also wanted to look at a cameo brooch I noticed in the window on my last visit. I rather liked it."

Much to Charlotte's relief, Mrs. Johnson smiled hugely, and exclaimed, "I'm so relieved you're not upset, m'lady. Please, come and sit down, and I'll bring out a selection of other pieces as well. Excuse me for a moment."

As she walked away, Charlotte thought what

a really nice woman she was. Pleasant, well-spoken, genteel, and not a bit pushy like some salespeople were. Margaret Johnson had a warm and welcoming personality, and impeccable manners.

A few minutes later Mrs. Johnson returned, carrying a flat, velvet-lined tray, which she placed on the round table.

"My husband and I found some really beautiful pieces in Italy earlier this year, as well as these brooches. Here they are, and the brooch you liked."

"Thank you, Mrs. Johnson," Charlotte said, and surveyed the pieces on the tray. She picked up the brooch, which she had intended to give to Diedre, but now she wasn't sure if it was right. Diedre liked dramatic or unusual jewels.

Margaret Johnson, who was clever and astute, saw her hesitation, and said quietly, "I'm not sure if you would be interested, Lady Mowbray, but I bought a wonderful cameo necklace in Paris a few weeks ago. It is an antique and very rare. There is only one of it."

"I don't believe I've ever seen a necklace made of cameos," Charlotte said, glad to drag out the time with Margaret Johnson, waiting for an opportunity to tell her invented tale. "I would like to see it, please."

Mrs. Johnson excused herself again, hurried off, and Charlotte sat back, glancing around the shop. It was tastefully designed and decorated, and Charlotte could see that enormous effort and a lot of money had been used to create a comfortable and elegant setting.

A few minutes later Mrs. Johnson returned carrying another flat, velvet-lined tray, which she placed next to the other one on the table.

"This is just beautiful!" Charlotte exclaimed when she saw the necklace. "May I pick it up? Look at it more closely?"

"Of course, Lady Mowbray. Perhaps you would like to try it on."

"Well, yes, I would, thank you very much."

"Here, let me put it around your neck and fasten it," Mrs. Johnson said, then led her over to a mirror.

Looking at herself, Charlotte realized how truly unusual the necklace was, although it wasn't for her. She was seeking a Christmas present for Diedre, and decided this might be the perfect thing to give her.

"I like it very much," Charlotte said. "Would you be kind enough to unclasp it for me, please, Mrs. Johnson."

Once this little task had been accomplished, Charlotte returned to the chair, and again looked at the other cameo pieces, still wondering how to launch into her tale.

She was saved the trouble when Gillian Hunter, the younger of the two saleswomen, came over carrying a photograph and an empty silver frame.

"Excuse me for interrupting, your ladyship, but I do need to speak to Mrs. Johnson for a moment," Gillian said.

Charlotte nodded, and smiled. "There's no problem."

"It's all right, Gillian, I see what you have in your hands. You're going to the frame shop, aren't you?"

"Yes, I am. I think you ought to buy a new frame, Mrs. Johnson, as well as new glass. The frame's badly dented." As she spoke, she showed the frame to Mrs. Johnson, and in doing so she dropped the picture.

It fell at Charlotte's feet, who bent over and picked it up, then exclaimed, "What a beautiful baby! And the christening robe is exquisite."

Margaret Johnson smiled. "They don't make christening robes like that anymore, I'm afraid."

Nodding in agreement, Charlotte asserted, "This is you, isn't it? And the lady holding you must be your mother."

"That's correct." Looking across at the saleswoman, Mrs. Johnson said, "I think you're right, Gillian. Please pick something in silver, similar to this." Turning to Charlotte she said, "May I have the photograph, please, Lady Mowbray? So Gillian can be on her way."

"Of course. Here I am, clinging to it for some

reason." Charlotte gave the photograph to Gillian.

The saleslady hurried away, and Mrs. Johnson explained, "I knocked it over the other day and broke the glass. Sorry for the interruption, m'lady."

"Seeing that photograph of you reminds me of something," Charlotte began. "I have a friend who used to live in Yorkshire many years ago. She seems to think she knew your mother, and **you,** when you were a baby. Your name happened to come up when I mentioned I had seen a rather unusual cameo in your shop. She's interested in jewelry."

Charlotte laughed. "Oddly enough, I was telling her about the canning machine, and then spoke about the shop. She said when she lived in Yorkshire she knew your mother who had a jewelry shop, and that you were the most beautiful baby. She even remembered the christening robe, and she told me she came to your first birthday party, when you were one year old."

"Goodness, who is she? Imagine someone remembering the robe, and my first birthday. It must have been a really good friend."

"She said your birthday is the twenty-sixth of August. Is she correct?" Charlotte asked.

"Indeed she is. Please tell me her name, m'lady. You've whetted my appetite, and sadly

I can't recall her."

"Audrey Finch. She was a fashion designer and very much involved in clothes and jewels. From what I understood, she knew you when you were a toddler. Don't you remember her? A lovely brunette with bright green eyes."

Margaret Johnson shook her head. "I don't, to be honest. But that doesn't mean anything, really. What child could remember so far back? I will be fifty next Friday. It was a long time ago."

"Indeed it was."

Margaret Johnson said, "We didn't live in Harrogate then. My parents had a jewelry shop in York, which is where we lived until I was twenty. They moved because they liked Harrogate, and thought it would be a good place to do business. And when they found this shop they bought it immediately. I met my first husband here, and we married when I was twenty-two. Sadly, he was killed in a car crash when I was twenty-four."

"I'm so sorry to hear that, you were very young to lose your husband," Charlotte said in a sympathetic voice.

Margaret Johnson simply nodded.

Charlotte went on, after a moment or two, "So Howell isn't your maiden name?"

Shaking her head, Mrs. Johnson explained, "No, it was Matheson."

"What a lovely ring that has to it...Margaret

Matheson. Your parents picked a lovely first name for you."

Mrs. Johnson half smiled, and asked, "What else did your friend tell you about me? And my mother?"

"Nothing, actually. She just thought it was such an odd coincidence that I had come to borrow a canning machine for the WI in Little Skell, and that I had met **you.** She was really positive you were the child she remembered as the most beautiful blond baby she had ever seen."

"Mrs. Finch could have known my mother in York, and also visited us here, when she still lived in Yorkshire."

"That's very possible. Anyway, I would like to buy the cameo necklace, Mrs. Johnson. It's most unusual."

"We thought it was. We bought it from an excellent jeweler in Paris, who had purchased it at an auction which featured some important pieces. The necklace belonged to Pauline, Napoleon's youngest sister, who was the closest to him, you know, very loyal and loving. He may have even given her this necklace, according to the French jeweler."

"It's probably rather expensive since it's such a special treasure," Charlotte murmured. "But I do love it."

Mrs. Johnson went over to the counter and

found her list of French and Italian purchases. She jotted down the price of the necklace on a piece of paper, went back and handed it to Charlotte.

After glancing at it, Charlotte said, "I'm still going to buy the necklace, Mrs. Johnson, because of its provenance, as well as its beauty. I'm assuming you have all the papers pertaining to the necklace?"

"I do, m'lady, and I will give them to you. It's most important to have proof of provenance." There was a moment's hesitation, before she added, "I'm really happy you're buying it, m'lady. It **is** unique, a treasure."

Charlotte watched Mrs. Johnson placing the necklace in a round worn leather box, and after a moment, she said offhandedly, "Is your mother still alive?"

"Oh goodness me, no," Mrs. Johnson replied, closing the case. "After my father died she lived for about five years. But she missed him greatly. They were wonderful parents, brought me up so well, with such love…"

Her voice trailed off, and she got up, carried the leather jewel case to the saleslady and asked her to wrap it.

When Mrs. Johnson returned to the table, she sat down, and, quite unexpectedly, picked up her conversation where she had left off. "I say that because I was adopted. Some adopted children fall into the wrong hands. I was lucky; my parents adored me, made me feel I was their own flesh and blood."

Charlotte held herself very still. There was a tightness in her chest, and she was unable to speak. Eventually, recouping slightly, she managed to say, "Did they know your birth mother? Did you ever meet her?"

"No, they didn't. And we never met her. However, what they did know they told me when I was old enough to understand. She was a young woman who became pregnant out of wedlock, and from an excellent family from the gentry, they told me. She was unable to marry my father. She had to give me up. I'm sure you know as well as I do what it was like in those days, the shame of it all."

"I'm afraid things haven't changed much," Charlotte murmured. "People are still extremely bigoted."

"I do know one thing," Mrs. Johnson murmured softly. "The young woman who was my birth mother must have loved me very much. The christening robe and other beautiful clothes were packed up in a box for me, came with me from the hospital in Leeds, where my parents went to get me, and took me home with them."

Charlotte swallowed, and clasped her hands to her lap. They were shaking. She was now quite certain this woman **was** Lady Gwendolyn's child.

Taking a deep breath, she said slowly, "And did you not ever wonder about your birth mother, Mrs. Johnson? Or want to meet her?"

"Oh yes, I did, and so did my parents, but by the time I was ten, when they first told me I was adopted, the two solicitors involved had died." She shook her head.

"My parents didn't know where to begin to look for her, and so we just let it go." Mrs. Johnson smiled, finished, "You can tell your friend Audrey Finch that the little blond child she knew fared well."

"I will indeed," Charlotte said, getting to her feet. "Please let me know about the canning machine. And when I come back to get it, I shall look again at the cameo brooches, Mrs. Johnson. You have beautiful things."

"Thank you, Lady Mowbray, thank you very much."

"I must pay you for the cameo necklace," Charlotte said, walking over to the counter. Opening her bag she took out her personal checkbook.

Later, on the way back to Cavendon, Charlotte wondered what to do. Should she keep this knowledge a secret? Or tell both women? She was floundering, on the horns of a dilemma.

That evening, during dinner, it occurred to Charlotte that perhaps she ought to talk to

Cecily about this unexpected situation. It was rather a momentous discovery. There was no doubt in her mind that Margaret Johnson was Great-Aunt Gwendolyn's daughter. There was the physical resemblance to Diedre Ingham, and those Swann eyes they all had. Then the box of clothes and the christening robe, the hospital in Leeds, the mention of two dead solicitors. There was too much evidence now. And yet she felt the decision about telling the two women was difficult to make by herself, without advice.

Cecily knew about the mysterious entry in the record book made so many years ago by Mark Swann. She had shown it to Cecily around the time she married Charles, just to prove something about the strong attraction the men and women of the two families had had for each other over the years.

Mark Swann had been Walter's father and Cecily's grandfather. He was also the father of Margaret Johnson. Mingled blood. Swann and Ingham. History had repeated itself so many times.

What was the best thing to do? Charlotte did not know. She would sleep on it. I'll decide tomorrow, she thought. And she prayed to God for guidance.

Thirty

Hanson was in his element, which made him happy. He sat at his desk in his comfortable chair in his office downstairs, a few steps along from the kitchen.

Spread out in front of him were the different lists for the weekend activities. He glanced at the calendar which stood next to the carriage clock. Today was Saturday, August 20...the summer was almost over.

By next month the leaves would be changing, and knowing the Yorkshire weather the way he did, he expected chill in the air by September.

Leaning back in his chair, Hanson thought about the conversation the earl had started with him yesterday, one which had taken him mightily by surprise.

Lord Mowbray had asked him if he would forgo his retirement at the end of the year and stay on at Cavendon as head butler. Taken aback though he was, Hanson had replied in the affirmative at once. "It will be my pleasure, your lordship," he had answered swiftly, afraid the earl might change his mind suddenly. He had then asked politely the reason behind this request.

His lordship had explained that war was inevitable. He said he supported Winston Churchill, who constantly shouted that appeasement wouldn't work, that Germany would invade the rest of Europe, and also had its sights set on Britain.

"All the young men will be called up, Hanson," his lordship had continued. "That's the way it always is. We lose the flower of our youth to war, because only young men are able to fight. The village will be made up of women, as will Cavendon Hall. I'm going to need you, Hanson, we all are." His face was grave, his voice low. They both had Guy in their minds, the earl's charismatic first son. Could war really be coming again for their boys and men?

And that was the end of that, Hanson now told himself, shaking his head, his thoughts focusing on Gordon Lane, who would not be eligible to fight. Neither would Eric Swann, who, with his sister Laura, ran the London house of Miles and Cecily. So there would be a few men in the employment of the Inghams, but, in Hanson's opinion, women were just as good, if not sometimes better.

He smiled to himself, thinking of the last nine years and how Cecily Swann had led the four daughters of the earl in the battle to save Cavendon. She had been a great leader, a born commander, in his opinion. The four sisters had been as hardworking, diligent, and focused as she had. The men had helped, but it was really their achievement, he thought, as he looked down at the lists in front of him.

The earl had selected the wine for the dinner tonight and on Sunday; the countess had written out the menus for both dinners, and for lunch today and tomorrow. Lady Charlotte usually left the planning of the afternoon tea menus to Cook and himself, and he understood it was a compliment of sorts. She had enough sense to trust them.

Charlotte Swann, great-aunt of Cecily Swann, now the Countess of Mowbray, wife of the sixth earl. **Cecily Swann,** the wife of Miles Ingham, heir to the earldom, daughter-in-law of the sixth earl, and the future countess. Their son, **David Swann Ingham,** heir in waiting who would succeed his father as the Eighth Earl of Mowbray one day. **Walter Swann,** valet to the earl, father of a future Countess of Mowbray, father-in-law and grandfather to future Earls of Mowbray.

A lot of Swanns about these days. Hanson smiled. He was overjoyed the Swanns were coming into their own. They deserved it. He had always had a lot of time for them; they were the mainstay of the great family they had been interlocked with for over a century and a half. Loyalty binds them, that was the truth.

The small carriage clock struck six, and Hanson stood up, left his office, headed in the direction of the kitchen with the menus in his hand.

Susie Jackson, who had been the cook for some years now, was already frying bacon. His nose twitched and his mouth watered, as he said, "Good morning, Susie. Thank you for putting the menus on my desk last night. Here they are." He placed them on the Welsh dresser.

She swung around, smiling, and said, "Oh good morning, Mr. Hanson. How about a bacon buttie? Or would you prefer bacon and eggs? Which do you fancy?"

"The bacon sandwich, please. And a nice cup of your strong builders' tea. That's the best way to start the day."

Hanson sat down at the kitchen table, knowing that in about forty minutes the young maids would appear, along with the footmen. Breakfast for the family was served at nine in the dining room.

Everyone had arrived last night, except for Lady Daphne, Mr. Hugo, and Mr. Charlie. They would be driving up from London this afternoon.

As she turned the bacon in the frying pan, Cook said, "Her ladyship seemed a bit off last evening, rather absentminded."

"I thought of it as preoccupation," Hanson answered, and got up, went and closed the kitchen door. "It struck me that she might be a bit worried about something, to be honest."

"I hope it's not his lordship's health that troubles her."

Hanson stared at Susie, and exclaimed, "But he's in good health! I had a long chat with him yesterday, and he was in tiptop condition. On the mark about politics, planning for the future when war comes." He shook his head and added somewhat vehemently, "No, no. It's not Lord Mowbray that's worrying her; it's something else."

"Whatever it is, Lady Charlotte will deal with it," Susie remarked. "She's a strong, resilient woman." Her admiration for Charlotte echoed in her voice.

"Yes she is, thank God."

Cook put down the bacon butties for Hanson and herself on two plates, poured large mugs of tea, added milk and sugar, then carried the tray to the table.

"Here you are, Mr. Hanson," she said, placing the bacon sandwich in front of him. "Enjoy."

"I once showed you a notation in one of the old

record books," Charlotte said. "Do you remember it, Cecily?"

"Of course I do. It was strange, a little mysterious, the way it was written. It spoke of a relationship between a Swann and an Ingham. And a baby born dead."

Charlotte leaned across the table in the gazebo in Cavendon Park, and said in a low voice, "That couple was very much in love. They had another child. Some years later. It lived."

"What?" Cecily gasped, staring at her. She was obviously thunderstruck. "How do you know this?"

"I found out. Or rather, I should say the mother of the child told me," Charlotte murmured. Reaching out, she took hold of Cecily's hand and held on to it. "I know this might come as a shock, but the mother of the child was Great-Aunt Gwendolyn."

Cecily was even more stunned, and she simply gaped at Charlotte, unable to speak, endeavoring to digest this information. Finally, she managed to say, "Have you just found this out?"

"No, Cecily. It was years ago. Around the time of Dulcie's marriage with James. Great-Aunt Gwen confided in me, and she made me promise to keep her secret. And I have. Until today."

"Why are you telling me now? You've broken

your promise to Great-Aunt Gwendolyn. So things have changed. What's happened?" Cecily gazed fixedly at Charlotte, and her eyes narrowed slightly. "Something's occurred, I just know it. You'd never break your oath to an Ingham."

"I certainly wouldn't." Charlotte sat back in the chair and fell silent, her thoughts whirling around in her head. At last she said, "Well, of course you're right, you're very quick, Cecily. Quite by accident I met someone. Someone I'm fairly certain is the child Lady Gwendolyn had to give up fifty years ago."

"Why are you telling **me**?" Cecily asked, her eyes still riveted on Charlotte.

"Because I don't know what to do. I need your advice, Cecily. I can't go to anyone else, only to a Swann." She smiled faintly, and added, "And we are also both Inghams now."

Cecily nodded. "You have my loyalty, just as I know I have yours. So tell me the whole story."

Charlotte did, beginning with the gift of the swan brooch years ago to yesterday morning when Margaret Howell Johnson had told her that she was adopted, and Charlotte had been convinced of her identity. Charlotte did not leave out one detail, wanting Cecily to have the full picture.

When she had finished her tale, she leaned closer to Cecily and asked, "So do I tell each woman? And which one first? Or do I let sleeping dogs lie, as your mother would insist?"

"I don't know," Cecily answered. "But what a story it is, and how weird that you of all people would discover this." There was a pause, and Cecily then asked, "Does she really look like Diedre?"

"There is a very good likeness, yes, although Margaret is not quite as beautiful as Diedre, nor as blond, nor as chic."

"Nobody's as chic as Diedre," Cecily remarked, and then said, "Let's weigh the odds. If you tell Great-Aunt Gwendolyn, I'm fairly certain she'll want to meet the daughter she has thought about for the last fifty years. But she'll be awfully upset if Margaret doesn't want to meet **her,** don't you think?" Cecily raised a dark brow, and thought to ask, "What about your eyes? Hasn't Margaret noticed they're the same peculiar color as hers?"

"No. I don't think people go around staring at the eyes of others. However, I believe you're correct. I can't say a word to Great-Aunt Gwendolyn until I've ascertained what Margaret feels about meeting her mother."

"There's another thing," Cecily warned. "You must not tell Margaret who her mother really is, not until you know what her feelings are. She mustn't have Great-Aunt Gwen's identity. No way."

"I agree with you again." A long sigh escaped, and Charlotte said, "And what about Margaret talking to others? Saying Lady Gwendolyn Ingham Baildon is her long-lost birth mother, that she had an affair with Mark Swann. You know it would be a local scandal of no mean proportions, even now in this day and age."

"And his lordship abhors scandals, Aunt Charlotte." Cecily sat pondering and suddenly exclaimed, "There would have to be an oath of loyalty taken...**loyalty binds me**...after all, if Margaret really is whom you believe she is, she's a Swann. And her father was my grandfather."

"But why would she take the oath? She hasn't been brought up like we have...loyalty to the Inghams is bred in the bone with us. It's second nature."

"What is she like as a person? I know you've only just met her, but you're shrewd. **Think,** Aunt Charlotte. Is she a decent woman? Would she protect the honor of a very old lady? Does she have honor and integrity? A kind heart?"

Charlotte sat shaking her head. "I just don't know, Ceci. How could I? She seems like a nice woman, and certainly she's got a genteel air about her, and I did notice her manners. They're impeccable."

"You make her sound nice, but we don't really

know people, do we? Not even those we love… there's always a little part we don't get to see. A hidden part in everyone."

"You amaze me, Cecily," Charlotte responded, studying her intently. "Because I've only just discovered that in the last few years, and I'm seventy years old."

"Would you like me to come with you when you go to Harrogate for the canning machine? I'm going to be in Yorkshire all week. I could make an assessment of her for you. What do you think?"

"I'm relieved, Ceci. Thank you. I would appreciate it if you meet Margaret before I say a word to her about Great-Aunt Gwen." Charlotte looked at her watch. "I think we'd better go up to the house. It's almost time for lunch."

Later that afternoon, Diedre was walking through the grand entrance hall when she noticed Hanson standing on the staircase, peering at some of the portraits of her ancestors which lined the long side wall.

"Is there something wrong with the paintings, Hanson?" she asked, walking over to the staircase.

"No, Lady Diedre, they're all in good condition. I was examining the frames. Some are very old. I think I will have to have the paintings well wrapped before they go into the storage crates." As he spoke, he walked down the stairs to join her.

"How are they being stored, just out of curiosity?" Diedre asked.

"Ted Swann is making wooden crates, which the paintings will be slipped into. But I think the frames need some sort of padding around them. For protection. The gold leaf easily chips."

"You think of everything, Hanson, and I agree with you. Mrs. Miles told me you have prepared the cellars here, and that we can go down there to live when the Nazis start bombing us."

"They will invade us, won't they, Lady Diedre?" Hanson trusted Diedre's judgment, and also, she worked at the War Office.

"Mr. Churchill thinks they will, and I tend to agree with him...I follow the leader, so to speak. His lordship is also a great supporter of Mr. Churchill, as you know, Hanson. Papa thinks he ought to be prime minister."

"Well said, Lady Diedre. I agree with his lordship."

"By the way, Hanson, I'm so happy you've agreed not to retire at the end of the year. Papa told me this morning that you're staying on. It's great news. Whatever would we do without you?"

Hanson beamed at her. "I feel the same. Well, what I mean, my lady, is what would I do without this family? I've been here at Cavendon most of my life...I wouldn't know what to do with myself, and I would miss you all..." He let out a sigh. "I would miss my work, that I would."

"I want to thank you for telling my son so much about our family history and the house, Hanson," Diedre said, sincerity ringing in her voice.

"It's my pleasure, Lady Diedre."

"Do you know where Mrs. Miles is? I've been looking for her all over."

"I think she went to the office annex to do some work. At least, that's what she said to me about ten minutes ago."

"I shall go over there. Thank you, Hanson."

He smiled and inclined his head. And he thought about this generation of Inghams and prayed they could get through what lay ahead.

Diedre found Cecily in her small office in the annex next to the stables. Her sister-in-law glanced up as she came in, and smiled warmly.

Smiling back, Diedre said, "I'd like to talk to you for a moment or two, Ceci. Is there anyone here other than you?"

"No. Harry doesn't work on Saturdays, and Miles is with the children." She frowned. "You have a very solemn look on your face, Diedre. There isn't anything wrong, is there?"

Diedre sat down opposite Cecily. "No. I have to explain something to you, though. And you cannot repeat what I'm now going to say. Not to anyone. Not even Miles."

Cecily nodded, a questioning look on her face.

In a low voice, Diedre said, "I've heard from another contact of mine that there might be a way to get the Steinbrenners out of Berlin after all. Moves are being made. I don't know anything more than that. And Greta cannot know in case the plan doesn't work. She would be devastated if it failed. Which it well might. I have to warn you of that."

Cecily nodded. "Thank you for telling me, Diedre, obviously I'll keep it to myself. But knowing something is in the works helps a bit, perks me up. I've been rather downhearted, to tell you the truth. Greta is somewhat troubled and naturally it affects me, makes me sad."

"Yes, I noticed that at dinner last night. You were quiet, seemed worried. That's why I'm telling you about the sudden new development. Let's keep our fingers crossed."

"Fingers crossed, legs crossed, and everything else crossed," Cecily replied. There was a moment's hesitation before she asked sotto voce, "When is it supposed to happen?"

"I don't know...I'll tell you, **when** and **if** I do acquire that information."

Thirty-one

What was it about **her**?

What was it that drew him to her like a magnet?

That she was good-looking was a given. Her coloring was dramatic, so vivid it was quite startling at first: glossy black hair, pale ivory complexion, and eyes of such a deep blue they were almost violet.

And she had inherited her famous father's finely sculpted, classical features that made him so photogenic and had turned him into a matinee idol and international film star.

However, Harry knew it was more than just her looks, the physical attraction she held for him. Paloma Glendenning had something else that would entice any man to her side. Part of this was her lovely personality, so warm and outgoing. There was nothing phony about her; she was natural, without tricks and artifice.

He had arrived at her apartment in Lennox Gardens ten minutes ago, and they now sat in the living room sipping white wine.

As he sat listening to her explaining about her father's broken shoulder, it suddenly hit him. Paloma had the same allure as her mother, and there was a calmness about her that was soothing. He had already noticed this when they had tea together at Burnside Manor. It's **everything** that she **is** that works, he thought suddenly. The whole feminine package; her looks, her intelligence and charm.

Realizing that she was waiting for him to respond to her last comment, he said swiftly, "I think your mother is right about newfangled ideas sometimes working. I've never heard of a soft cast, but seemingly it's done the trick."

"It has. It's virtually impossible to put a plaster of Paris cast around a shoulder. So the ortho-pedic surgeon used bandages, and then put my father's arm in a sling."

Paloma grimaced. "What hurts most now is his arm, having it bent all the time. Anyway, he's managing and he's lucky my mother sprang to his aid." A knowing smile slid onto her face. "She still loves him."

"So you said before." Harry paused, then added, "I'm certainly looking forward to having lunch with them tomorrow. I liked your mother the moment I met her at your uncle's house."

"She said to tell you she is going to make you the best Sunday lunch you've ever had. Leg of lamb, roasted potatoes, and even Yorkshire pudding...the whole enchilada."

Harry laughed. "That's a funny expression. I've never heard it before."

"It's one I picked up from my father, and he picked it up in Hollywood. An enchilada is a Mexican...sandwich...kind of, and he explained it means lots of good things all rolled into one..."

The ringing telephone cut across her words, and she went to answer it. "Oh hello, Mumma." She stood listening patiently to Adrianna, and this gave him a moment to study her.

She was wearing a navy-blue chiffon dress with long sleeves and a pleated skirt that floated around her as she moved. Her jewelery was minimal, a long strand of pearls and dangling pearl earrings. She has the same kind of glamour as Cecily, he thought, and then it struck him that Paloma was wearing one of his sister's dresses.

After saying a few words into the phone, Paloma came back to join him. "Mumma wanted you to know there'll only be us for lunch. And Phoebe. The other Bellamy children are spending the weekend with their Bellamy father, but Phoebe wouldn't go. She preferred to see you, Harry. I think she's got a crush on you."

He started to laugh, then stopped, exclaimed, "I smell burning."

"Oh! My pie!" Paloma jumped up and ran

toward the kitchen, still crying, "My pie! My pie!"

"Don't open the oven door! Just turn it off," Harry exclaimed, put down his drink and rushed after her.

She followed his instructions, and stood staring at him, an expression of dismay on her face. "I made you a cottage pie but I think it's burned to a crisp."

"More than likely, from the smell in here." He opened the window, and said, "Keep the oven door closed; otherwise the kitchen will be filled with smoke."

Paloma nodded, and turning around she took hold of his hand and led him back to the sitting room. "I did so want to make a lovely dinner for you, Harry. What a shame the pie is ruined."

"No need to apologize. Tell you what, let's go to the Savoy Hotel. We can have supper there. Do you like to dance?"

"I love dancing. What a grand idea. Gosh, the Savoy and Carroll Gibbons and his orchestra! What a treat!"

Harry smiled at her, enjoying her enthusiasm, and also the way she did not harp on about the burned pie, merely dismissed it. Picking up his glass, he had a sip of wine and said, "You look beautiful tonight, Paloma. And if I'm not mistaken, you're wearing one of my sister's frocks."

"I am. Mumma bought it for me at the Cecily Swann Boutique in Harte's department store. I love navy blue, and it's not as funereal as black."

"That's what Cecily always says. You'll like her, Paloma."

"I want to meet her, Harry, and your mother and father, and everyone in your family. Will they like me, do you think?"

"Of course they will. How could they not? You're a very special person."

"Am I really?"

She was looking at him in such an odd way, he frowned, put down his drink on the small table, went over to join her on the sofa. He stared at her intently and for the longest moment, finally said softly, "I came to London to see you, Paloma. Surely you realize I believe you're very special, indeed."

She nodded, took hold of his hand and placed it against her face. "And you are, too, Harry. The most special man I've ever met. I'm flushed with excitement that you're actually here."

He recognized the longing in her eyes, and he knew it was for him, and he felt the same about her. He leaned forward, taking her in his arms, and they kissed passionately. Instantly, he was aroused, but within seconds a warning signal went off in his head. **Stop. Hold back.** A small voice told him not to rush it, to go very slowly with her. Suddenly he understood he was playing for keeps.

Releasing her, he touched her face gently. "And I'm excited about being here with you, Paloma. I want us to get to know each other properly as we start our friendship. You see, I want it to last for a long time."

They took a taxi to the Savoy Hotel in the Strand, and Harry was warmly welcomed by the maître d' in the restaurant overlooking the river Thames. Once they were seated at a table near the window, Harry ordered champagne.

He could see that Paloma was pleased they had come here. She was looking around, taking everything in. Finally, she leaned closer and said to him, "I've only ever been in this room once before. With my father."

"It's my sister's favorite place, and she's here often. If she's in London next week, we'll all come together. Would you like that?"

"That would be lovely."

A moment later the champagne was served. As they sipped it, they began to talk, first about her siblings, and then he spoke about Cecily and Miles, and his life at Cavendon. They were enjoying being together in such a lovely room, and discovering things about each other.

Carroll Gibbons, the American bandleader, and his Savoy Orpheans, as his orchestra was called, played popular music in the background.

The lights were dim, candlelight flickered, couples danced together, and an atmosphere of pleasant relaxation prevailed.

Eventually they looked at the menu, ordered a light supper, and then Harry took Paloma out onto the dance floor. She fitted easily into his arms, and since she was wearing high heels they were almost face-to-face. She held onto him, drawing closer as the waltz turned into a slow foxtrot. Harry loved having his arms around her, swaying to the music, breathing in the smell of her hair, the fragrance of roses that clung to her skin. He felt lighter in spirit, happier, freer than he had in months, and he was glad they had met. And all because of a little girl on a bicycle.

They were halfway through their main course of Dover sole, when Paloma suddenly said, "You are totally free, aren't you, Harry? I mean, to start a relationship with me?"

Taken aback though he was, he showed no reaction when he answered, "I am, yes. What made you ask me that?"

"My sister Claudia told me about that lady in Harrogate." She half laughed, and went on, "The two oldest are very protective of me. Claudia told me to ask you that question straightaway. And so I did. But I felt, deep down inside, that you wouldn't be playing around with me…you're not the type."

He bit back a smile, and said, "No, I'm not. And I am no longer seeing that lady in Harrogate. Actually, she's left Harrogate for good."

And because he felt so at ease with Paloma, and relaxed in her company, he told her what had happened, and how the affair had finally ended.

"Thank you," she said when he had finished his story. "You didn't have to tell me, but I'm happy you did. And now you can ask me anything you want."

"Let's begin the same way, shall we? Are you free to start a relationship with me?" he asked in a warm, loving voice, knowing the answer instinctively.

"I am, Harry. I've not had many boyfriends, and my last relationship ended over a year ago. It was not very successful. We were poles apart." There was a small pause, a hesitation before she continued. "I felt drawn to you the first moment we met. And I was at ease with you. I wanted to get to know you better, spend time with you, become close to you."

Harry reached out and took hold of her hand, kissed her fingers. "And I shared those same feelings. You've been on my mind every day since then."

"And you've been in my head, too," Paloma confided. "It's a funny thing. I want to do things for you, look after you." She made a face. "That's why I made the fateful pie."

The way she said this brought a gust of laughter, and he murmured, "You'll get another chance to make me a cottage pie, I assure you of that. In the meantime, I'm enjoying myself just being here with you, Paloma. And you can tell Claudia I'm now taking over as your protector."

"Are you?" she asked in her straightforward manner, her eyes sparkling.

"I am indeed."

They had dessert and more champagne, and danced the night away. Finally, over coffee, Paloma asked him another unexpected question.

"Who is Eric?"

"Eric?" Harry repeated, frowning, and then realized she had heard him phoning the South Street house earlier tonight, asking Eric to make the reservation at the Savoy.

"Eric runs Cecily's South Street house, which is where I stay when I'm in London. He used to be the butler for Lord Mowbray, but the earl doesn't have a home in London any longer. He's a Swann like us, a cousin, actually."

"I see."

"Why did you ask?" Harry wondered aloud, looking at her keenly.

"Just being nosy, Harry. I suppose I want to know everything about you."

"That will take a little while, I think."

"Will you stay at the South Street house when you come to London again? Or will you stay with me?"

He did not answer. He stood up, drew her to her feet, and took her to the dance floor. Holding her tightly in his arms, he pressed her closer to him, and said against her hair, "No, not yet, my sweetest girl. I want everything to go slowly and go right. I'm playing for keeps, you see. I don't like games of chance. Far too dangerous."

Diedre went down the main staircase, and into the library at Cavendon. Picking up the phone she dialed the international operator and gave Toby Jung's number.

"Hey, Daffy Dilly, how're you doing?" he said on hearing her voice.

"I'm well. How's the weather there?" Diedre asked.

"Lousy. I'm glad I'm going to be trotting. Early next week. Change of climate. Are you with Robin Red Breast?"

"I am indeed. He's a happy little bird. What about you, Toby?"

"I'm happy. Caviar was good. Source even better than ever."

"Excellent news. Earlier than you thought?"

"Yep. I met our musical friend yesterday at the Adlon. We are of the same mind."

"Thank heavens," Diedre said softly. "Keep in touch."

"You'll hear from me when the **clochards** are in my sights."

"I'm glad to hear that," Diedre answered. "And you do find the quaintest ways to tell me where you'll be calling me from...now it's the bank of the river Seine where the tramps meet for tea."

Tony chuckled. "Got to admit I'm colorful."

Diedre said, "The instructions from Will are to come in. You must kiss Berlin good-bye."

"Every intention, Daffy Dilly."

They said good-bye. Diedre rose, left her father's library, and went upstairs as the clock in the grand entrance hall struck seven. It was far too early for breakfast, she decided. As she went back into her bedroom she experienced an enormous sense of relief. The Steinbrenners would be leaving Berlin, more than likely on Tuesday now, escorted by Tony Jenkins and Alexander Dubé.

Fingers crossed, she said to herself, as she climbed into bed and pulled the covers over her. **Fingers crossed.**

Thirty-two

Cecily was well aware that a war would have an enormous effect on her business. And, since she was positive war was coming in the immediate future, she was making her plans accordingly.

Now, on this cool Monday morning toward the end of August, she and Dorothy Pinkerton were walking down the main floor of a factory in Leeds. Aunt Dottie had spent the weekend with Cecily's parents in Little Skell; earlier today Goff had driven them over to the city.

This particular building was close to the center of Leeds and, in fact, overlooked the Leeds and Liverpool Canal. The main floor was unusually light with many tall windows, and of the five factories she had recently decided to purchase, it was in the best condition.

"This was a really good choice, Ceci," Aunt Dottie said, after they had walked the length of the room. "Lovely, clear light throughout, spacious and airy. A good place for the women to work."

Turning around to face Cecily, Dorothy continued, "I know you're going to be using three of the other factories for the servicemen's uniforms, when you get the government contract, but what about the fifth one? What have you planned for that?"

"Nothing yet, Dottie," Cecily answered, leaning against one of the long workbenches. "It's a good thing to have handy for an emergency, and if I don't have any use for it, I can always sell it. Or rent it out. It's a good investment in the long run. And, anyway, it belongs to the company that owns this one, and I have to buy both factories. That is mandatory."

"I think you could have this one up and running within a few months, don't you?" Dorothy asserted.

Cecily nodded. "All of the wood floors are strong, and the walls are in good condition. They need painting, but that's all. The windows are also in good shape, and new electrical wiring was put in recently. So, in a sense, we're all set to go. Well, almost." She gave Dottie a questioning look. "You do agree with me about the importance of ready-made clothes for women, don't you?"

"Absolutely. Haute couture is going to suffer when war comes, that's a given. And to stay in business, you must have product. Let's face it, you're certainly in the right city. The ready-made clothing industry was started here."

"Yes, I know. John Barran opened the first ready-made clothing factory after Singer invented the sewing machine, and then a Jewish tailor who had a small tailoring shop came up with the idea of 'piecework.' Herman Friend invented it, actually. Small tailoring shops like his, mostly in North Street, would make 'pieces' of a suit. In other words, one tailoring shop would create lapels and sleeves, another, the back of a jacket, yet another, the two front pieces. And all the pieces were sent to Barran's factory where the suit was put together. And off they went to the stores. It was brilliant."

"I remember reading about that years ago. It revolutionized the business and has made Leeds the greatest center of ready-made clothing in the world. But you're not going to use that method, are you, Cecily?"

"No, I'm not. The entire garment will be made here." Walking into the middle of the floor, she spread out her arms. "From the entrance door over there, right down to the exit door down there, we'll have long workbenches like that one where you're standing, and comfortable chairs at the sewing machines. I want working conditions to be the best. Up-to-date, very modern."

Dorothy nodded her understanding. "When are you going to start hiring people?"

"Once the factory is ready, I'll have the management team begin to hire women, and men, if they're available. You see, Dottie, I'm not going to wait for the war to start, which it will within the next eight or nine months or so. I'm going to start making the clothes as soon as we can. I want to have them on the market, get my customers used to them. My intention is to copy much of the couture line. It will be very fashionable."

Dorothy grinned. "Bravo, Cecily. That's the right attitude, and what will you call the ready-made clothes?"

"I haven't come up with a name yet, but I'm sure I will. For the moment I'm calling it Cecily Swann Ready. But hopefully I'll come up with something better. Please put your thinking cap on."

"I certainly will." Dorothy glanced at her watch. "We'd better go. I don't want to miss my train back to London."

"I'll drop you off at the railway station. And thanks for coming up this weekend."

"I've loved it, Ceci, and I'm really excited about the new project. I'm positive you'll have another winner."

On the drive to Cavendon, Cecily turned her

thoughts to Charlotte and her predicament about Margaret Howell Johnson. Cecily had carefully hidden her reaction to the news that Lady Gwendolyn had given birth to a child, and that the father was Mark Swann. But she had been startled, even shocked, there was no doubt about that, and also terribly saddened that Great-Aunt Gwen had had to live with that kind of heartache for years.

She also now understood what Genevra had meant when she had talked about Ingham and Swann blood mingled **again,** with the emphasis on the word "again." Genevra always got it right.

Cecily had agreed that they ought to go and see Mrs. Johnson as soon as possible, mainly because of Lady Gwen's great age. As Charlotte had pointed out, despite Lady Gwen's desire to live to be a hundred, she might easily expire at any moment. They both wanted her to meet her daughter before she died. Cecily had suggested that Charlotte should ask Mrs. Johnson to see them this afternoon, and she hoped that the appointment had been made in her absence.

When they finally arrived at Cavendon Hall, the chauffeur dropped her off at the office annex. When she went inside, Cecily found an envelope on her desk, and opened it quickly. It was a note from Charlotte with only a few words on it. **We're all set. 4 p.m. today. C.**

She pushed the note into her bag when the door suddenly opened and Miles came in, smiling broadly at the sight of her.

After bending over and kissing her cheek, he asked, "How did it go? Was Dottie impressed with the main factory?"

"She was, and I've asked her to try and think of a name for the clothing line."

"You know what?" Miles said, sitting down on the edge of her desk. "I like Cecily Swann Ready. And I think it would look elegant on a label if the word 'Ready' was underneath your name. Just visualize that. Go on, close your eyes like you always do, and see the label in your mind's eye."

She did as he suggested, and in a second exclaimed, "Miles, you're right. And the word 'Ready,' with the capital **R,** should be in gold thread, indicating it's a special garment."

He nodded, and then said, "The word 'special' might also work. Anyway, we've time to play around with it."

"Yes, we do." Leaning back in her chair, gazing up at him, she felt her love for him flooding through her. He was hers, her better half, her husband. She marveled that she could think that and say it. Because it was true now. How lucky they had been that life had worked for them, not against them, as it once had.

"You're staring at me with such intensity, Ceci,

what's going on in that brainy little head of yours?"

She stood up, and drew close to him, put her hands on his shoulders, continuing to gaze unwaveringly into his blue eyes. Then she leaned forward and kissed him on the mouth, and very passionately. He kissed her back, putting his arms around her. And they clung to each other for the longest moment.

Finally breaking apart, Miles laughed softly, and then gave her a speculative look when he saw the expression on her face. She had a glow about her. "What is it, darling?"

Bringing her face up to his, she whispered, "Let's make a baby. I want another child with you."

Again putting his arms around her, he held her close to him. "But you were so relieved when you discovered you weren't pregnant recently. Why this change of mind?"

"I want to feel part of you growing inside me. I love you so much. And we always said we'd have four children."

He stroked her hair, his love brimming over. "I know. And now a war is coming. You said you didn't want to bear a child, bring a new life into a war."

"I know. Suddenly I feel differently. And I'm not going to let the Nazis frighten me..." She sighed. "I'm totally defiant."

He held her away, and looked at her, a thoughtful expression in his eyes. "We've been lucky, you and I, Ceci. Many times blessed, and I have a grateful heart...for all that we have together. But I agree with you, let's have another baby." Then he added, with a wicked glint in his eyes, "And you know what they say. Practice makes perfect."

Cecily was so happy she hugged him tightly. When she finally let him go, she whispered, "It's a deal, and we don't have to shake hands. My word is my bond."

"As is mine. Come on, we'd better go to lunch with Papa and Charlotte."

Walking across the stable yard, hand in hand with him, she suddenly asked, "Have you heard from Harry? How was this weekend with Paloma?"

"He did phone. He told me he's going to stay on in London for a few days, if that was all right. I said I could manage. As a matter of fact, he sounded...**euphoric**. I think that's the best word to use."

"Aha! That is good news. Let's hope he's found his soul mate."

"Those are few and far between, Mrs. Ingham, and hard to find. I can only add that I'm thankful I have mine right next to me."

Thirty-three

If she was surprised to see the famous designer Cecily Swann walking into her shop, Margaret Howell Johnson did not display this.

Gliding forward in her usual sedate way, she greeted both women cordially and, after being introduced to Cecily, said, "It is a privilege to meet you, Miss Swann. You are tremendously talented and I have been a great fan of yours for years."

"Thank you, Mrs. Johnson," Cecily replied, trying not to stare too hard. In a sense, she didn't have to, because the resemblance to Diedre was quite striking, and she was tall like Diedre and Great-Aunt Gwen.

"You said you wanted to speak to me about something important, your ladyship, so I think it's a good idea to go into my office."

"It is, Mrs. Johnson," Charlotte answered. "Thank you."

Margaret Johnson's office was large with a

bay window facing the Parade. The Georgian desk stood in the bay, looking out into the room, and there was a seating arrangement composed of a sofa and chairs in front of the fireplace. Lovely paintings hung on the walls; the office looked more like a sitting room than a place of work, and was tastefully decorated.

Once they were seated, Mrs. Johnson said, "I suppose you want to speak about the person who will come to Cavendon to show your WI ladies how to handle the canning machine. It will be Iris Dowling, who's the treasurer of the Harrogate WI. She's very skilled with the machine, and very helpful. You will like her. I'm sure."

"Thank you for telling me. We're ready to welcome her any time this week, whenever it is convenient for her," Charlotte answered. "Perhaps on Friday."

"Are you going to take the canning machine with you today, Lady Mowbray?"

"If that's all right, yes. I have the car and driver today, and he can help us."

Mrs. Johnson nodded, looked from Charlotte to Cecily, suddenly at a loss for words. She couldn't help wondering what this was all about.

Highly sensitive to other people, Charlotte noticed the bewilderment in Margaret Johnson's eyes at once, and she said, "There is something else I must discuss. The other day, you spoke about your childhood. You also told me about your adoption. Later, because of the details you gave me, I realized that I knew your birth mother."

Instantly, shock registered on Mrs. Johnson's face, and her voice rose an octave when she repeated, "**My birth mother?**"

Charlotte nodded. "You have a look of her, and of someone else who is related to her."

Stunned though she was, Margaret Johnson exclaimed, "Then she's still alive? Is she?"

"Yes," Charlotte replied.

"And you're sure of this, Lady Mowbray?"

"I am positive."

Cecily cut in swiftly, "I have just met you today, Mrs. Johnson, but I do see the resemblance her ladyship is referring to. She has told me your story, and it certainly fits in with what Lady Mowbray also told me about the woman in question."

Margaret Howell Johnson was obviously still thunderstruck, and she sat staring at Charlotte and Cecily, without speaking. Many different emotions were flaring in her: shock, surprise, curiosity, and also a kind of fear.

It suddenly occurred to Charlotte that Margaret might wonder why Cecily had accompanied her and she leaned forward slightly. "I asked Cecily to come with me, because she also knows the woman I believe to be your birth mother. She has just verified that she agrees with me with her words to you." Charlotte glanced at Cecily and raised a brow.

"I have had the same reaction as you, yes," Cecily asserted.

There was a short silence. None of them spoke.

Cecily became aware that the only sounds were the ticking of the carriage clock on the mantelpiece and the ringing of a telephone in another room. She sat back in the chair, understanding that Margaret was endeavoring to come to terms with Charlotte's announcement. It was news that anyone would be floored by, especially at the age of fifty.

Charlotte finally broke the silence. In a soft, warm voice she asked, "Would you like to meet your mother, Mrs. Johnson?"

"M-m-meet my mother?" she stammered, suddenly starting to tremble. "Of course I want to meet her! I've always longed for that. To see her, to have her arms around me, to love her, to know she loved me. I've always felt that something was missing in my life…and it was **her**—" The flow of words stopped abruptly as tears rolled down Margaret's cheeks, and she began to sob.

Cecily took out a handkerchief, went and sat next to her on the sofa. After pressing the hanky into her trembling hands, Cecily said, "Lady Mowbray had to ask you that first, before she could mention this to your mother. You see, we know she will want to meet **you**. We didn't want her to be disappointed if you refused."

Margaret's head came up with a jerk, and she frowned, gaping at Cecily. "Why wouldn't I want to see the woman I've thought about all my life?" she asked in a choked and trembling voice.

"Some might not," Cecily murmured gently.

After drying her eyes, Margaret answered, "Yes, I suppose some might be angry. But I'm not. Will you tell her about me? Will you arrange a meeting, Lady Mowbray? **Please**." Tears welled up again, and Margaret patted her eyes, tried again to gain control of her roiling emotions.

"Yes, of course I will," Charlotte reassured her.

"Thank you," Margaret managed to say, and wiped her eyes again. She sat back, trying to breathe normally, her mind racing, full of questions. Suddenly she asked, "Does she live in Harrogate?"

"No, she doesn't," Charlotte replied.

"Where then?"

"Another part of Yorkshire. I'll take you to see her later this week, whenever you wish."

"Tomorrow? Could we go tomorrow?"

"It might have to be Wednesday, Mrs. Johnson. I must prepare her..." Charlotte paused, hesitated, looked across at Cecily, who nodded that she should continue.

Charlotte explained, "You see she's quite old, much older than you probably think. My news will be as big a shock to her as it was to you, I can assure you of that."

Margaret Johnson frowned, looked perplexed. "What do you mean by 'quite old'? She was a young woman, wasn't she? A young woman from the gentry, who couldn't marry my father?"

"No, she wasn't. She was a widow. And she wasn't from the gentry, she is from the aristocracy. And she was almost forty-eight when you were conceived."

Stunned once again, Mrs. Johnson began to shake her head, obviously in disbelief. "That can't be, it can't be."

Cecily said, "This is the truth, Mrs. Johnson. Your birth mother never expected to become pregnant at that age. But she did. And she wanted to keep you, please, please believe that."

"I do believe it," Margaret Johnson murmured. "Somehow, deep inside, I've always known that."

"I must be very discreet, Mrs. Johnson, in view of her great age. Let me tell her about you, and then when I come to pick you up on Wednesday, I promise I will tell you who she is."

"I understand," Margaret Howell Johnson said, still finding it hard to come to terms with this astonishing news.

Diedre was still at the office on Monday evening, studying a map of Europe, which she had spread out on top of her desk. She had a red pen in her hand, and she was searching for Aachen on the map. When she found it she circled the name in red ink. As her eyes moved on to Paris, her telephone rang and she picked it up immediately, glancing at her watch as she did. It was seven o'clock.

"Hello? Who is this?"

"It's me," Tony said, his voice normal for the first time in several days.

"Where are you?" she asked.

"At the British embassy, saying good-bye to my desk."

"So, you're all set finally?"

"I am. Scooting. Tomorrow."

"Earlier, then?"

"That's right, Daffy Dilly. Thanks to Monsieur D. What a wonder he is. Calming." Tony chuckled. "Good at defrosting."

"So all's well that ends well?" Diedre asked, also laughing for once.

"So far, yes. I'll be glad when I'm having tea with the **clochards**."

"You'll call me from there?"

"I will. So long, Daffy Dilly."

"I can't wait," Diedre answered, and hung up without saying good-bye. She felt a certain sense of relief that Tony, Dubé, and the Steinbrenners were now departing on Tuesday, because the papers had come in early from Valiant. The little group would leave Germany tomorrow morning, taking the nine o'clock Berlin–Paris train from the Schlesischer Bahnhof. They would travel through the heart of Germany, cross over into Belgium at Aachen, go on to France, and arrive in Paris at six-thirty on Wednesday morning. She knew one thing for sure: The trains in Germany always ran on time.

It was a long overnight trip, but the only really worrisome part was crossing the border. At Aachen there were a multitude of border guards, border police, and always Gestapo hovering. But then the secret police were everywhere these days. It was normal.

Her eyes went back to the map. She circled Paris, and then drew a long line which cut through from Berlin to Aachen, from Aachen to Liège, and ended in the City of Light.

As she sat back in her chair, her thoughts ran on. Tony would deal with the British embassy visa division in Paris on Wednesday, and with a little luck the Steinbrenners would take the boat train to London thereafter. Unless they stayed the night in Paris to rest. That was a possibility...the Steinbrenners might need it. Saturday, she decided. I'll aim for a Saturday arrival in London.

Reaching for the phone, deciding to inform Cecily, she suddenly hesitated, put the receiver back in the cradle. Always wary, and cautious, she unexpectedly changed her mind. Not until they were on the train to London would she feel truly secure about the Steinbrenners. Only then would she tell Cecily that they were on their way to Greta. Fingers crossed.

Thirty-four

Ever since she was a small child, Cecily had been brought up to understand the rules. The Inghams came first, and then the Swanns and their entire family. Everything else was secondary. Now, early on Tuesday morning, walking up to the office annex, she thought of the Inghams or, more precisely, of Lady Gwendolyn Ingham Baildon, the family matriarch, affectionately known as Great-Aunt Gwen.

Cecily had always known that she was an unusual woman, unique, in fact, and as Miles often said, "They threw the mold away after they'd made her." And he was right. She was a mixture of things: independent, strong, highly intelligent, tolerant, loving, and compassionate. Also, these traits aside, she was outspoken, had a clarity of speech that left no one in any doubt about what she meant. And she told everything the way it was, as she saw it anyway.

For all these reasons, Cecily believed that

Great-Aunt Gwendolyn would react appropriately when Charlotte told her about Margaret Howell Johnson. In other words, she would want to see the daughter she had given away at birth, and she would be happy about it. Of course there would be tears, but they would be tears of joy…and surprise, perhaps. It was bound to be a bit of a shock.

Yesterday, on the way back from Harrogate, Aunt Charlotte had worried aloud about Great-Aunt Gwen and her nervousness about Gwen's reaction to the news.

Fortunately, Cecily had managed to convince Charlotte they should go together to see Great-Aunt Gwen, thus giving each other support.

"But then she'll know I've broken my vow to keep her secret a secret," Charlotte had protested. Cecily had to explain that this didn't matter. "She'll understand that you did not want to make decisions about the matter alone, and, anyway, I'm a Swann, and took the oath, and she'll be perfectly comfortable with that."

Eventually, Charlotte had accepted this, and had agreed with Cecily that they should tell Great-Aunt Gwen about her daughter immediately, adding, "Let's not forget how old she is. I always think I'll be awakened one morning by Mrs. Jasper, to be told she expired in her sleep."

This had been said in a light tone; Charlotte had half smiled, and Cecily herself had laughed out loud. "That's the way I want to go when I'm an old woman…in my sleep," she had said.

Last night, after dinner, they'd had a moment to talk quietly, and had made the decision to visit Lady Gwendolyn this morning.

After unlocking the door of the annex, Cecily went inside, turned on all of the lights, and hurried into her own office.

The contracts for the sale of the five factories were on top of her desk, and she looked at these once again, studied a couple of added clauses; she initialed these, then signed each contract.

The deal was closed, and that made her feel comfortable; they were a safety net if war came. When it comes, she muttered to herself, dreading it.

And then she thought of Greta. Her heart ached for her. The poor woman lived on the edge at the moment, frustrated, anxious, and troubled, because she could do nothing to change the family situation. And I can't either, Cecily reminded herself. But maybe something good will happen through Diedre's contacts in Berlin. Fingers crossed.

Whenever she thought of their few days there, the admiral she had met with Diedre sprang into her mind. She was riddled with curiosity about how her sister-in-law knew him, but hadn't dared to ask too many questions. Diedre had repeated what the admiral had said, that she knew his family through Maxine Lowe, but had not elaborated further on that. Curious though, that obvious friendship with a German officer in the High Command.

Pushing aside these thoughts, Cecily took out the latest sketches she had done for the ready-made line, and studied them. She liked the clean-lined suits and dresses; they had a certain austerity to them which would suit the hard times which were coming. They could all be enlivened by fake jewels, such as brooches and ear clips, as well as her silk flower pins and colorful silk scarves. The dark colors worked with the tailored styles, deep burgundy, dark red, deep blue, royal purple, gray, and black...

Her telephone rang and she picked it up at once. "Hello?"

"It's Harry, Ceci," her brother said, sounding bright and cheerful. "I hope I'm not getting you at a bad time."

"No, and you sound good, Harry. You must be enjoying London. And Paloma."

He chuckled. "Mam's been talking to you, hasn't she?"

"A little bit, but she tends to be discreet. However, I gather that you and Miss Glendenning have hit it off well."

"A little bit more than that, Ceci. I'm rather smitten with her, as she is with me."

"That's wonderful news. You see, you never

know what's going to happen in life, do you?"

"Only too true. I've managed to erase Pauline Mallard from my mind. She's gone for good."

"Have you heard from her at all?"

"Not a word, and I'm rather glad about that. Quite by accident I've met a really lovely, straightforward young woman who attracts me, and who likes me in return. There's a future for us, I think."

"I'm sure there is, Harry. When are you coming back to Yorkshire?"

"I told Miles I'd like to have the rest of this week off, and he agreed. And that's really the reason I'm phoning you, Ceci. Are you going to be in London?"

"I don't think so. I have rather a lot of work here, and having been away myself I want to be with the children, spend time with them and see our parents. Why do you ask?"

"I want you and Miles to meet Paloma. And she wants to meet you, and Mam and Dad as well," Harry explained, sounding disappointed.

"I'd love that but I'm fairly certain we won't be up in town. Why doesn't she come to Yorkshire?" Cecily suggested.

There was a silence, and Harry then murmured, "But where would she stay?"

Cecily didn't answer immediately. After a moment, she exclaimed, "She can stay with her aunt, Mrs. Jollion, and come over and be with you and all of us during the day. Burnside Manor isn't so far away."

"I'll think about it," Harry answered, then added a little sheepishly, "I'd like her to see my house. She told me she enjoys decorating."

"And she can take photographs of the gardens as well," Cecily pointed out, laughing as she spoke. "Wasn't that **her** ploy to see you again?"

"She can see us now," Charlotte said from the doorway.

Startled, Cecily sat up with a jerk and exclaimed, "Gosh, you made me jump, Aunt Charlotte."

"Sorry, Ceci. I didn't mean to creep up on you like this. Can you come with me, to talk to Great-Aunt Gwen?"

"No problem," Cecily answered. She stood up and went on, "Let me put these contracts in my desk. Then I'm all yours."

Several seconds later the two women were walking across the stable yard, heading toward Cavendon Park, going in the direction of Little Skell Manor. It was a sunny morning with a few puffy white clouds skimming across the blue sky in the wind. But despite the sun there was a chill in the air. August was almost over; the autumn would soon be here.

"I didn't expect to see you so soon," Cecily

remarked, as they walked. "But then Aunt Gwen's always been an early riser. Old habits die hard, I suppose."

Charlotte nodded. "She was having her tea and toast when I phoned her at eight. I said we'd be there about nine. I explained that we had something special to tell her, and after that we wanted to take her out to lunch at the Spa Hotel in Harrogate. To celebrate."

This surprised Cecily, and she said, "Why did you say that…**something to celebrate**?"

"Because that's what I want to do, celebrate with her. I thought we would tell her about Margaret as soon as we get there, and then we can drive over to Harrogate. I think Great-Aunt Gwen should know about her daughter now. Not tomorrow, not next week. She's old, Ceci."

"I suppose you're right. But won't she be upset because I'm there? After all, she confided a secret to you."

"You convinced me otherwise. Anyway, you're a Swann, and she loves you, is proud of your success. And delighted that Miles was finally able to marry you. Can't you come to Harrogate with me? Are you too busy today?" Charlotte sounded worried. "I do need you with me, you know."

"There's nothing that can't wait, Aunt Charlotte. I've signed the contracts for the five factories. That was the most important thing

I had to do today. And you're right, let's do it."

Mrs. Jasper, the housekeeper, greeted them at the front door of Little Skell Manor, and then asked, "Is her ladyship going out to lunch with you today, Lady Mowbray?"

"Yes, she is, Mrs. Jasper. I know it's your afternoon off. Lady Gwendolyn already told me. So you've nothing to worry about. We'll look after her for the whole day. And she told me Sarah, the parlor maid, will be on duty until you return tonight."

"That's correct, Lady Mowbray."

Charlotte nodded. "However, her ladyship will have dinner with us this evening."

"Thank you, m'lady."

A moment later they were hurrying into the sitting room overlooking the garden, where Lady Gwendolyn was waiting for them.

"How smart you both look...lovely, the two of you," she remarked after they had both kissed her.

"So do you, Great-Aunt," Cecily replied. "And I'm glad I altered that blue suit for you. It looks very chic on you, and the delphinium-blue blouse matches your eyes."

Lady Gwendolyn laughed. "Oh I know what you're thinking, Ceci. I do tease the Ingham girls about wearing clothes to match their eyes..." She shook her head. "But you know very well I've always done that myself. Can't help it."

Charlotte and Cecily laughed.

Eyeing them both somewhat suspiciously, Lady Gwendolyn went on warily, "There are no flies on me, you know, and I believe you're up to something. And why are we having a celebration? Is it something new and special which you've created, Ceci? That's it, isn't it?"

Cecily shook her head, and lowered herself into a chair, facing Lady Gwendolyn; Charlotte joined Lady Gwen on the sofa.

"Here's the thing," Cecily said. "Quite by accident, something that was obviously **meant to be** finally happened the other day."

"And what was that?" Lady Gwendolyn asked, leaning forward, her face riddled with sudden curiosity, but a flicker of something else showing.

"Your wish has come true. Charlotte went on an errand for the Women's Institute, and she has something to tell you."

Charlotte took the older woman's hand. "Do you recall when you confided your greatest secret in me? About the child, the daughter you had to give up?" She paused. "I think I might have found her."

Lady Gwendolyn was so taken aback she gaped at them, frowning. Then she repeated wonderingly, "You have found my **daughter**?" Turning to Charlotte, she asked in a tremulous voice, "Is it true? Did you find...**Margaret**? It cannot be true. How can it be true after all these years?" She sounded puzzled.

"But it is, Great-Aunt Gwen," Charlotte eplied, her voice firm. She took hold of her hand. "And her name **is** Margaret. I asked Cecily to meet her, and she agrees with me that she's the genuine thing. She really and truly is your daughter. I have all the proof you'll ever need."

Lady Gwendolyn felt herself filling up with tears. Her eyes were moist and she was so choked with emotion she couldn't say a word. Many questions were running through her head. She wanted to know everything, to ask questions. But she still didn't speak. She couldn't.

Cecily and Charlotte waited patiently, giving her time, knowing she was shocked by their news.

Eventually, she said softly, "They kept my name for her...her adoptive parents called her **Margaret**." Tears rolled down her cheeks and fell onto her hands clasped in her lap. "Can you tell me about all this, please, Charlotte?"

"Yes, of course I will." As she spoke, Charlotte gave Lady Gwen a handkerchief to dry her eyes. And then she began, explaining about needing the canning machine for the jam making, and going to meet Mrs. Margaret Howell Johnson, who looked so like Diedre, and how, during their meeting, Mrs. Johnson had confided to Charlotte that she was adopted.

Charlotte continued the story, told her about the other visits and why she had gone back to see Margaret.

Once she had finished, Charlotte added, "Mrs. Johnson was very moved when I told her that I thought I knew her birth mother. She wept, and she was sincere when she asked if I could arrange for you both to meet."

Lady Gwendolyn sat there staring at Charlotte, shaking her head, a look of disbelief lingering on her face. "Is it true? Is it really true?"

"I promise you it is, Great-Aunt. Can Ceci and I take you to meet her?"

"When?"

"Now. Today. If you're sure, and it isn't too much of a shock."

"Let us go," Lady Gwendolyn answered. "At once."

An hour later Cecily and Charlotte were escorting Lady Gwendolyn into Margaret Howell Johnson's jewelry shop on the Parade in Harrogate.

On the drive over from Cavendon, Lady Gwendolyn had been very quiet, lost in her thoughts and her memories. But she had managed to regain her composure, and was fully prepared to meet the daughter she had had to give up fifty years before.

Margaret was waiting in her office for them, having followed Cecily's suggestion, given over the phone, that their first sight of each other should be strictly private. Certainly away from the eyes of the salesladies.

Although she was ninety-eight, Lady Gwendolyn had good posture, and was well balanced. However, she walked slowly, and felt more secure when she was able to hold on to Charlotte's arm.

Margaret was standing near the fireplace. When she saw the regal and elegant old lady walking into the room, her eyes brimmed. And she couldn't help herself, she rushed over to meet her, anxious to know if this woman really was her mother.

They stood staring at each other for a split second, each one seeing a reflection of herself in the other. And then Margaret stepped closer and so did Lady Gwendolyn, and they embraced, held each other tightly; they were both crying. And they knew.

After a few seconds, Margaret stood slightly away, unable to take her eyes off Lady Gwendolyn. "I'm Margaret," she said in a low voice, and then she took an envelope out of her pocket.

It was yellowed with age around the edges, and as she handed it to Lady Gwendolyn, she said, "They kept this...it was in with the christening robe and the beautiful clothes. They gave it to me when I was ten. When they told me I was adopted."

Lady Gwendolyn opened it, took out the piece of paper inside, and recognized it from long ago. On it she had written: **Her name is Margaret**.

Tears trickled down Lady Gwen's wrinkled cheeks and she sighed deeply, remembering so much, and then she said, "I've thought of you every day of my life. And prayed you were safe, that they had been good to you."

"And I always knew there was something missing in my life...and it was you."

Stepping forward, Charlotte said, "Margaret, I would like to introduce you to your mother, Lady Gwendolyn Ingham Baildon, the matriarch of the Ingham family and the aunt of the Sixth Earl of Mowbray."

Margaret, now paler than ever, and obviously affected by the meeting, merely nodded. Suddenly, unexpectedly, she smiled and reached out to Lady Gwendolyn, took hold of her arm. "Please, come and sit down." Her voice was warm and filled with love.

Charlotte and Cecily followed the two women, and once they were settled, Lady Gwendolyn handed the piece of paper to Charlotte. "I wrote these words fifty years ago, and I believe I told you I had done this."

Taking it from her, Charlotte glanced at it, and nodded. "You did, Great-Aunt Gwen. And that's more proof for you. The final proof."

With a small smile, Lady Gwendolyn said, "I don't really need any proof." Studying Margaret, she murmured, "You look a little like I did when I was your age, and you have the Swann eyes…bluish-gray-lavender, just like your father had."

Margaret tried to return the smile, but she was still a little stunned by the grandeur and presence of this extraordinary woman who was still beautiful. And she was also so moved by the occasion her emotions were running high.

Understanding this, Lady Gwendolyn took Margaret's hand in hers. "I'm glad we're finally reunited…I could have been dead."

"Oh please don't say that, m'lady."

Lady Gwendolyn stared at her. "I am your mother, Margaret, and that is how I would like you to address me."

Margaret nodded, and unexpectedly began to talk, and Lady Gwendolyn listened and responded.

Charlotte and Cecily slipped out, leaving them alone, as they had prearranged to do. They walked through the town to give mother and daughter a chance to get to know each other. When they returned, to red eyes and faces lit by a new happiness, the four women went to lunch at the Spa Hotel and toasted each other with champagne. It was a grand day.

Thirty-five

Diedre sat at her desk at the War Office, staring at the small carriage clock facing her. It was almost twelve-thirty here in London. One-thirty in Paris. To her, the hands seemed to be moving slowly on this Wednesday morning. But it was always like that when you were waiting for an important phone call. Somehow the phone never rang when it was supposed to.

To distract herself, she clamped down on her worries about Tony and the Steinbrenners, and took out two folders containing information about the agents whom Will had recently taken on.

Opening the top folder, she began to scan it. As if on cue, the phone started to ring. She picked it up instantly. "Hello? Who is this?"

"It's me," Tony said.

"I've been on pins and needles, waiting for your call," she answered.

"Sorry. I'm afraid there was a delay—"

"Where are you?" she cut in peremptorily. "Your voice sounds strange, like you're in a tunnel."

"Actually, I'm standing in a telephone booth in the lobby of the Plaza Athénée on the Avenue Montaigne in Paris."

"Wow, very posh! And why there?" she asked, obviously surprised.

"I'm staying here. We all are, courtesy of Alexander Dubé."

"Good heavens, what next! How did that come about?"

"None of us slept very well on the train, which was jam-packed, by the way. When we arrived in Paris this morning Mr. Dubé decided we all needed some sleep. He was right."

"Am I to understand that Alexander Dubé is paying the hotel bills?" Puzzlement echoed in her voice. "You did say courtesy of Mr. Dubé, didn't you?"

"I did. He's not paying mine. I've already straightened that out. The professor has also insisted on paying his own bill. What I meant is that we went to the Plaza Athénée because Mr. Dubé has connections there, plus an old friend who is head of reservations. That's how we managed to get five rooms straightaway. It was obviously better to go to a hotel Mr. Dubé uses, than trying to find one."

"I understand. It was a good idea. What about

the visas?"

"I've been to the British embassy with their passports. I can collect the documents at four today," Tony replied.

Diedre sat back in her chair, relaxing, filling with relief. "Thank goodness everything has gone without a hitch, now—"

"Well, not exactly," Tony interrupted, his voice suddenly tense. "We've got a problem, boss."

"What kind of problem?" Diedre asked, sitting up in her chair, gripping the receiver tighter. "Not with Mrs. Steinbrenner? Oh God, I hope not!"

"I'm afraid it is. She's disappeared."

Diedre felt a cold chill sweep through her, and she held herself still, focused on what he had just said. "What do you mean by disappeared, Tony? As in **vanished**?"

"Yes."

"Tell me." As she spoke she pulled a notebook toward her.

"She was last seen in their bedroom," Tony began. "Apparently the professor went down to have breakfast with Elise and Kurt. When they returned to the suite an hour later she was gone."

"But she must be somewhere in the hotel," Diedre muttered, alarmed by this news, wondering how they would handle it.

"She's not in the hotel. The manager had

some of the staff do a full search." Tony sighed heavily. "She's bloody well scarpered and I don't know what to do, Diedre. Tell me what to do."

"Tony, I honestly don't know. Actually, there isn't anything you **can** do...where would you go? Where would you look? Wait a minute, does she know Paris? Does she have friends there?"

"Not to my knowledge. The professor says she's never been to Paris before."

"So she's not gone to a favorite store, or to see friends?"

"I'm sure she hasn't, Diedre. Believe me, the professor is as baffled as I am. And so is Alexander."

"This is the most preposterous behavior!" Diedre exclaimed, sounding even more exasperated. "A disappearing act like this is unconscionable. After everything that's been done to get them out of Berlin, the people involved, who were committed to help them." Diedre took a deep breath, endeavoring to curb her rising anger. "Doesn't she have any sense?"

"Listen, I agree with you. It's unbelievable. I was flabbergasted. As for sense, I don't know."

"What's she really like?" Diedre asked. "Tell me about her."

"Nervous disposition, very taut, I would say.

Introverted, wrapped up in herself. She's hard to explain, Diedre. However, I don't like her. And Alexander Dubé has some reservations about her as well."

"She was odd before they left, let's not forget that," Diedre pointed out. "She didn't want to leave. Anyway, what you're saying is she just left the suite, walked out of the hotel, and disappeared into thin air. And nobody knows anything. Is that it?" Diedre was fuming inside.

"You've got it," Tony replied. "Look, she could be anywhere...even on her way to another city, for instance. Fortunately, not to another country. Her passport is at the British embassy."

Diedre, listening carefully, suddenly exclaimed, "Tony, you're suggesting she's run away...do you really think that?"

"Not sure. But why did she leave the hotel? Where the hell is this woman? She knew all of the plans we'd made."

Diedre was silent for a moment, thinking hard, and then she said, "What is the time frame, Tony? Take me through it slowly."

"We arrived at the Gare du Nord railway station at six-thirty this morning. We took taxis to the Plaza Athénée Hotel. Alexander arranged for the rooms. And we all registered. We then went to our rooms. Obviously I had their travel documents, because I was going immediately to the British embassy. Which I did. I told the professor to make sure his family relaxed, rested, went to bed. They were exhausted, especially the children."

"I understand. And when you returned to the hotel she had gone. What time was that, Tony?"

"About eleven-fifteen, eleven-thirty. I was in the lobby buying a newspaper when Alexander saw me. He'd been waiting for me to return. He told me what had happened. I was stunned. And so was he, a bit shaken, in fact."

"I bet he was. Did he have any comments?"

"Not really. He just muttered that she was the oddest woman he'd ever met."

"I see. Let's move on for a moment. I assume you are booked on the boat train for tomorrow?" Diedre said.

"That's right. I stayed with our plan. We must rest tonight in Paris. Depart for London tomorrow—" Tony stopped abruptly, then exclaimed, "What the hell should I do, Diedre? Do you have any ideas?"

"Yes, a few. First, the professor should report his wife missing to the French police, and then he should check the hospitals. Just in case she simply went out for a walk and had an accident of some sort—"

"I already told him to do all that. I discussed the situation with Dubé before I phoned you, and he thinks we should keep going, take the children to Greta in London tomorrow."

"And you? What are your thoughts, Tony?"

"I agree. And I would go a step further. I believe the professor should also leave and come with us."

"Good God, Tony, you want him to abandon his wife? Very cut-and-dried you are. But practical."

"In my opinion, she's abandoned him. She's the one who's gone floating off. He could be sitting here for weeks, waiting for her. Listen to me, Daffy Dilly, there's something wrong with that marriage. They seem disconnected as a couple. They're friendly; there's no animosity, but somehow there's nothing else there."

Diedre said, "I think the marriage might be over. But why would she just walk off like that? It's very puzzling."

"We have to make a decision, boss. Right now!" he exclaimed, his exhaustion surfacing, making him impatient.

"We do, yes, Tony. You'd better give the professor his options. And, actually, I do agree with you, he ought to go to London with his children, not linger in Paris waiting for his missing wife to reappear. It's Elise and Kurt who matter, and he should be with them at Greta's house."

"Thanks, Diedre, we're on the same page. Talk to you later."

"Please get some rest," she said, but he had hung up.

After a few moments of thought, Diedre stood up, walked over to the window, and looked out, her mind racing. She had come up with a number of scenarios she could write about the strange disappearance of Frau Steinbrenner. However, none of them seemed quite right. But the woman **was** a problem, there was no doubt in her mind about that.

Turning on her heel, Diedre smoothed her hands over her skirt, straightened the neckline of her white silk blouse, put on her burgundy jacket which matched the skirt, and went out into the corridor.

A split second later she knocked on the door of William Lawson's office, and walked straight in.

He looked up and a wide smile spread across his face. "You read my mind. I was just about to come and see you."

"Here I am," she murmured, and sat down in the chair facing his desk.

"You've brought me bad news," he said, leaning over his desk, focusing his attention on her.

"How do you know that?"

"Dismay is written all over your face," he replied.

"You read me too well. I'd better get my act together. Find an obtuse expression and wear it."

A faint smile appeared in his eyes, then slid away. "Give it to me," he said.

Diedre did not respond. She simply sat staring at him thinking how tired he looked, worn out. And she couldn't help wondering why it was that single men didn't look after themselves. They don't know how, she decided. Because they've been used to their mothers coddling them. They all need a wife. Tony does, and certainly Will does—

"Something's gone wrong with the Berlin exit," William announced, cutting into her thoughts. "And shall we speculate? It's Mrs. Steinbrenner, I'll bet my last tanner on that."

Despite the seriousness of the moment, a smile flashed across Diedre's face, and she even laughed. "You're good, Will. We can all learn from you. And we've a lot to learn."

"I'm just good at reading expressions. So come on, let's have it. You've heard from Tony."

"I just hung up with him. Here's the thing, Will." She began to speak in a slow and precise manner, and recounted her phone call with Tony Jenkins, not missing out one detail, or nuance on Tony's part.

When she had finished Will was silent for a few seconds. "So you've told Tony to bring Elise and Kurt to Greta, and you've agreed that the professor should accompany them. Correct?"

"Yes, I did."

"To stay permanently?" His eyes narrowed slightly.

"Of course. The children need him to be there with them."

"So he shouldn't go back to Paris to look for his wife?" Will leaned back in his chair, still regarding her intently.

"No. That would be crazy. She's gone. There's no real way to find her, Will. Personally, I don't believe he can afford to live at the Plaza Athénée Hotel in the hopes she'll come back there looking for him. It's very expensive."

"I know it is." He fell silent for a moment or two, and then said in a low voice, "I don't suppose the professor has much of an alternative. Anyway, under the present circumstances, I think it's for the best." After a moment's pause, he asked, "Are you going to tell Greta Chalmers they are on their way?"

"No, I'm not," she responded instantly. "And I'm not going to tell Cecily, either. I can't guarantee anything, not until the professor and the children have their feet on English soil. That's when Greta will know. And only then."

William frowned when he said, "You're being extremely cautious. You don't think something else can go wrong, do you?"

"I don't know. It might."

His frown lingered. He studied her for a long moment, then finally asked, "Do you have any thoughts about this strange disappearance, any theories? What do **you** make of it?"

"Something's rotten in the state of Denmark," she announced.

"And the rotten apple is Mrs. Steinbrenner. Is that what you think, Diedre?"

"I do. My brother-in-law Hugo Stanton lived in New York for many years and picked up a number of expressions. If I told Hugo this tale, he would immediately say, **There's something not quite kosher about this.** Believe me, he would."

"Not kosher, eh? That's some statement. What brings you to that conclusion?"

"Mrs. Steinbrenner's behavior. She gets cold feet in Berlin, doesn't want to leave, is afraid they'd be caught and killed. Tony and Alexander Dubé manage to calm her down, and almost, but not quite, **forcibly** get her onto the train to Paris. The moment she is left alone in Paris she flees. Where to?"

Diedre gave William Lawson a long, penetrating stare. "Or perhaps we should say: **to whom**?"

Comprehension flooded William's dark eyes, and he exclaimed, "You think there's another man in her life?"

Diedre shrugged. "Another man, a beloved

relative, a child? Another woman? I don't know. I can hardly hazard a guess. But it's the only thing I can come up with, because certainly this behavior speaks of genuine emotion running very high. Just think about it…a Jewess wanting to remain in Nazi Germany, a woman who can't speak French or English leaves her hotel in Paris, leaving behind her beloved husband and children. Except that perhaps none of them are beloved. And she just vanishes in the blink of an eye. Motivation is paramount."

William was silent, studying her intently, thinking how brilliant she was in so many different ways. But he needed to prod her a bit more, and said, "I must agree with you. However, there is one flaw in the theory of her running off to another **person,** shall we say? And it's this. How did she make the arrangements with the other person? What time did she have or opportunity to work out plans?"

Diedre nodded swiftly, and said, "I agree with you. There are indeed many flaws to my theory. But you'd be surprised how crafty and clever some women can be, especially when love is at the core of the matter."

Thirty-six

Her name was Laure de Bourgeval. William Lawson had given her the code name of Étoile, because as he said in his note to Diedre, she was a star. Born of a French father and an English mother, she was fluent in both languages, and could pass as English or French. She had been educated at the Sorbonne. Laure had been sent to see Will by a contact of his in Paris, who highly recommended her. She was twenty-seven and very athletic.

Diedre studied the rest of the note Will had written to her, and then opened the file on the second operative. Alain Gilliot, twenty-seven, had been born in Provence, and was also of English-French parentage. He, too, had been educated at the Sorbonne in Paris, and was, like Laure, quick, smart, and athletic.

Diedre knew this was important, since both of them might have to be parachuted into France, and certainly they would be very active physically.

They were going to come in to meet with her next week, and at the same time they would become acquainted with each other. They were not working as a team, but both Will and Diedre believed they must know each other. They would be secret agents working in the same country, and might have need of each other in an emergency. Her job would be to see them through their training, at a special center recently opened just outside London.

The ringing phone interrupted her concentration, and when she heard Tony's voice she knew at once they had a problem.

"Something's gone wrong again," she asserted, settled back in the chair, expecting the worst.

"Not exactly," Tony answered. "The professor doesn't want to leave just yet. He says his wife has only been missing since this morning, and he thinks we should stay on in Paris for a couple of days."

"Well, we can't exactly put a gun to his head," Diedre responded. "And perhaps you should stay on. Obviously, she's not returned or been found in a hospital, has she?"

"That's right. But I do have a bit more insight on the situation, Diedre. I spoke to Elise, who's a lovely young woman and extremely grown-up for seventeen. She confided in me. Apparently

Heddy Steinbrenner is a depressed person, and has often disappeared for a night. Even two. Then she's just come back with very little explanation about where she'd been. And resumes her life with them."

"With no explanation?"

"Not really. Elise said her mother might say she's stayed with a friend, or at a hotel, because she just needed to be alone. Rightly or wrongly, they've all accepted this over the years apparently."

"But you indicated that the professor had been as baffled as you and Alexander Dubé."

"That's the way it seemed. I did question Elise about that, and she said her father never seemed to worry about the disappearing acts. Anyway, the point is she believes her mother will show up."

"I'll go with the girl's opinion, Tony. She has no reason to invent this story. Or lie. So stay on. I think that's the best course."

"I'll change the tickets for the boat train. Shall I book us for Friday or Saturday?"

"I'm afraid I have to throw the ball back to you, Tony. I have to admit I find this situation puzzling, even somewhat weird to say the least. But let's give the professor the time he needs."

"I knew you'd say that, and it is for the best."

"Keep in touch, Tony."

"I will. See you soon, Daffy Dilly."
"I'm counting on it, Toby Jung."

Diedre went back to the file on Alain Gilliot, reading the rest of the information about him, which was impressive. She noted that Will had given him the code name Émeraude, because his hobby was painting landscapes full of emerald-green trees which were uniquely beautiful.

But sudden thoughts of Heddy Steinbrenner began to intrude, and she closed the folder, and stared off into space, all manner of strange ideas running through her head. And eventually she came to some conclusions.

Picking up the telephone, she put through a call to Tony at the Plaza Athénée Hotel, and within a few minutes he was greeting her.

Having instantly noticed the worry in his voice, she said, "I've given the problem you're coping with a lot of thought, and I want you to be prepared. I don't believe the frau will return. I think she's flown the coop."

"Do you know something I don't?" he exclaimed, wondering where her information had come from.

"Not **actually,** no. But I have come to realize a few things. Obviously, we're seeing a pattern here, because of the information Elise gave you. According to her, the frau has always returned after a day and night away. I am certain that there is another person in her life and that she's now with that person. Be it a man or a woman."

"How can you be sure, Diedre?"

"Well, I'm not absolutely positive, but from what I know about her, she's a troubled woman, and has the need to escape her family. However, I think there's a lot more going on than meets the eye. Whatever that is, she won't go to London. She needs to stay in Paris. You'll see, she won't show up for tea tomorrow as you think."

"I hope to God she will. So shall Alexander Dubé and I stay with our plan to take the boat train on Friday or Saturday?" Tony asked.

"You can't leave tomorrow. Better stay on schedule, perhaps think about even going on Sunday."

"Good idea. It gives me a bit of leeway," Tony replied, his tension running high.

"I am now passing this problem over to you, Tony," Diedre announced. "It's your deal and I want you to handle everything. I need to move on. I have a ton of work piling up. So what do you say?"

"Of course I'll handle it. Who's going to let Greta Chalmers know they're coming? With or without the frau?"

"Why don't you have the professor phone

Greta tomorrow when the frau is either back at the hotel, or not. That way Greta can meet you at the railway station in London, and take them to her house." There was a moment's pause, and Diedre let out a weary sigh. She said, "And hopefully you and Mr. Dubé will be free of them finally. All's well that ends well, as Shakespeare so aptly put it."

Tony fully understood why she had passed this over to him now; he would never let her down. "I hope you and I can have lunch next week, Diedre. And you do expect me to report for duty, don't you?"

"I do, and Will has assigned you an office next to mine. Where will you stay?"

"At my mother's flat in South Audley Street, for the moment. She's mostly in Gloucestershire, as you well know, and I'll soon find a place of my own. Will you be around this weekend?"

"No, I won't, Tony. As a matter of fact, I'm leaving for Cavendon tomorrow. It'll be my last weekend with Robin before he goes back to boarding school. But we can speak whenever you want. And please keep me posted on developments."

"I will."

The following morning at six o'clock London time, Diedre's phone began to ring. Almost before she picked up the receiver she knew what the call was about and who was calling her.

"Good morning, Tony."

"How did you know it was me, Diedre?"

"I just did...mental telepathy, something like that. I assume it's not good news since you're ringing me at such an early hour."

"You were right. The frau didn't get back to the hotel yesterday. Now the professor seems quite determined to leave. He's worried about the safety of the children, wants them out of Europe. He's truly longing to get them to Greta's house in London."

"So he doesn't want to wait any longer for his wife?" Diedre asked, sitting up in bed.

"He says he can't be sure when she will come back. And that she might not. Ever. He suddenly became quite open with me and Alexander Dubé. The marriage is one in name only, that was the way he politely put it. He seems certain she's staying with someone in Paris. And as we know from Elise, Heddy has done these weird disappearing acts before. And the girl wouldn't lie. Also, the professor says he can't afford the expense of the hotel any longer. Certainly he can't stay indefinitely hoping his wife will show up in the not too distant future."

"I understand. But don't you have her travel documents?"

"I do, and when I gave them to the professor

he said he thought they should be held at the British embassy for her. He said he would write a note to her, put in some money, and he suggested that I add in the train ticket, which is valid for a while. Along with the passport and visa, of course."

"I suggest he writes a letter to his wife, explaining where her passport is, and gives it to the hotel manager for when she returns. Her suitcase will also be held for her, I assume?"

"Yes. We'd thought of all those things."

There was a silence, and then Tony said, "My God, how right you were! I honestly thought she would be going with us to London."

"I'm sorry I was right, but there you are. What have the children said? How have they reacted?"

"Elise seems to have taken it in stride. Actually, so has Kurt. I think they depend entirely on Professor Steinbrenner, and I must say he **is** a warm and loving father, and concerned totally for their welfare. The two of them seem to think that Heddy will just show up in London one day."

"I very much doubt that. Times are changing at a rapid pace. Don't think the Führer doesn't have his sights set on France. Is the professor going to phone Greta?"

"Yes, but only to tell her they're coming and to meet us at the railway station."

"I see."

"It's better that way, Diedre," Tony murmured.

"Probably. Thanks for letting me know, and give me a ring on Sunday. I just want to know that you are safely back in London."

"I will," he said, and hung up.

Diedre stared at the phone and a long sigh escaped her. What an odd thing for a woman to do, abandon her husband and children and just disappear into oblivion. Well, some might do that to a husband. But to children? She couldn't help thinking this was such a callous act on Heddy Steinbrenner's part. Then again, as Aunt Charlotte was always saying, it takes all sorts to make a world.

Thirty-seven

Lady DeLacy Ingham was happy to be sitting in the main dining room at the Dorchester Hotel, sipping a lemonade while waiting for Diedre, and relaxing. Unexpectedly, it had become quite a busy morning at the art gallery, and she was thrilled to have made two very good sales. Important sales, in fact.

Glancing around, she saw that the restaurant was rapidly filling up, and she was glad she had made the reservation earlier in the week. But they would always find a table for her, no matter what.

Before Dulcie had moved to Hollywood with James, she and Dulcie had made the Grill Room their "canteen," as Dulcie called it. They loved the food and the ambience, and the Dorchester Hotel was only a couple of minutes' walk from the gallery in Mount Street and therefore convenient. She missed her baby sister, the most irreverent and funny of them all.

She smiled to herself, thinking of the way Cecily and Diedre always used the Ritz for the same reasons, while Daphne favored Brown's Hotel for lunch and afternoon tea, as did Aunt Charlotte. Not that they worked and needed a nice place nearby, but they both liked the quiet, rather private atmosphere at Brown's.

Lost as she was in her thoughts, DeLacy was startled when she heard a familiar voice saying, "Hello, darling! Mind if I sit down for a moment?"

Instantly focusing her eyes on her current boyfriend, Peter Musgrove, who was suddenly standing there, she exclaimed, "Peter! I thought you were going to Paris early this morning."

"Well, can I sit down or not?" he asked, sounding suddenly terse.

"Of course you can," she answered, and beckoned to the nearest waiter. To Peter she said, "What would you like to drink?"

"Pink champagne," he said to the waiter now standing at the table, and then he sat down next to her.

"My client changed the time of the meeting. We're now having dinner tonight. So I'm going on a later train. I'm en route to the station now, actually."

"I see," she murmured.

"I know your sister is joining you, so I won't be staying long. I just wanted to ask you something, and it's very important," Peter announced.

DeLacy was relieved he sounded more like himself. She had come to realize in the last few months that he had something of a temper, and was an impatient man, a trait she disliked. So far she had managed to cope with these little frissons of anger but they were irritating. "I'm all ears." She pushed a huge smile onto her face, and took a sip of lemonade.

"There's a house in Cirencester I've been told about, a rather lovely house, actually, and I want you to come down and see it. Next weekend. Do say yes, DeLacy."

"I'll be happy to come and see it; however, I'm afraid I'm not available for the next few weekends. Daphne and I are working on a special project and that has to take precedence."

The smile slipped off his face, and he said peevishly, "Why is it you're never free on weekends? To be with me?"

"Because I go to Cavendon, and you know why. My father hasn't quite been himself in the last few months, and he likes me to be there," she said, realizing it was the umpteenth time she'd explained this. "I also do have that project with my sister."

He was about to start a row with her, which he loved doing because he enjoyed ruffling her cool demeanor. Then he instantly changed his mind when he saw the tight set of her jaw, and the steel in those baby-blue eyes. She could be tough. Better not push her too much, or she might cut him off without a shilling, and so he flashed her his warmest smile, and reached out, clasped her hand for a moment.

He said, "Never mind. Perhaps we can go down and see it during the coming week?"

"I think that will be all right," she replied, and sat back, looking at him carefully.

Vain and self-involved, puffed up with arrogance, he did not notice the appraising glint in her eyes, nor the way she had angled her body away from him. "As you know, I've been longing to find a place of my own, and I think this might be it," he told her, adopting a level tone.

DeLacy simply nodded, and couldn't help wishing that Diedre would arrive. "You'll know if it is," she said noncommittally, and went on, "Is your client interested in the Renoir you have? Or the Sisley?"

Peter Musgrove lifted the flute of champagne which had appeared in front of him. "Here's to you, sweetheart."

Silently, DeLacy lifted her glass of lemonade, then sat back, listened to him explaining the importance of the Impressionist paintings, and boasting that he would sell both to his client, one of the richest men in France. Because, after all, as she well knew, no one got higher prices than he did, or was as successful in the international art world.

Several minutes later, while he was still in the middle of his rant, Diedre arrived.

Peter had the good sense, and enough manners, to jump up at once. Smiling at Diedre, he said, "Please, sit here on the banquette next to DeLacy, Lady Diedre."

"Thank you," Diedre replied and did just that. After kissing her sister on the cheek, she stared at him intently as he lowered himself into the chair opposite DeLacy.

Knowing that Diedre wasn't exactly pleased to see Peter, DeLacy gave her a long, knowing stare and explained his presence by saying, "Peter just stopped by for a moment. He's actually on his way to Paris." She glanced at her watch, then at him, and said pointedly, "I think you'd better be going, Peter. You don't want to miss your train."

Turning to Diedre, DeLacy added, "Peter is the best in the business when it comes to selling art, you know. He's about to make a huge sale. A Renoir and a Sisley, no less."

Peter beamed at her, always thrilled by flattery. He also knew when to scarper off while the going was good. He didn't want to lose DeLacy, a hot little number whom he could so easily seduce into his bed at the flick of a finger. He guzzled down the rest of his champagne and stood up. "What would I do without you, DeLacy?" His eyes lingered on her suggestively.

"You're always looking after me…in one way or another, aren't you now?"

DeLacy winced inside and merely inclined her head.

"Have a nice trip, Mr. Musgrove," Diedre said in a cold voice, leaving no one in doubt that she longed for him to leave at once.

"Thank you, Lady Diedre." He brought his head close to DeLacy's cheek, murmured, "Can't wait for next week. We'll stay the night. Oh yes." And then he was gone, fully aware he was not welcome.

Once they were alone, Diedre stared at DeLacy and said in a low voice, "I can't believe he's still hanging around. I thought you were going to get rid of him."

"I was. I am. Frankly, I haven't seen much of him recently. But, to be honest, he can be quite charming and entertaining, and he has sent me a lot of clients. I haven't had the heart to be harsh. Or boot him out just yet, but I will."

Diedre sighed. "I know he's good-looking, film-star good-looking at that. And yet he's just so…**awful**. I know he went to Eton and all that stuff, but he's, well, he's sort of common, Lacy."

"He is, yes," DeLacy answered, and then thought, he's also quite extraordinary in bed. She said, "I am going to get rid of him, I promise."

"I don't want to deprive you of male company, Lacy darling. God knows, you've not had an easy time of it." She shook her head. "Oh well, you'll know what to do and when to do it. Because you're smart. I shall have a drink, I think."

"You look as if you need one, Diedre. You must have had a hard week. You're terribly tired, I think." DeLacy sounded suddenly concerned.

"I am weary. That's why I'm glad I'm going to Cavendon with you on the train this afternoon. I can't wait." Spotting a waiter, she waved him over and ordered a vodka and tonic.

DeLacy said, "Everyone's going to be there this weekend—" She stopped, made a face. "Well, not everyone. I do miss Dulcie and James. But I hear they're going to win their battle with Mr. Louis B. Mayer."

Diedre couldn't help laughing, as she always did, when DeLacy used this man's full name. "I miss her and James too, and I can't wait for them to get back to London. I simply ache to see them."

"I know that feeling." Leaning closer, DeLacy went on, "I made some rather good sales today, and there'll be quite a nice chunk for the Cavendon Restoration Fund. Papa is worried about all the broken walls and fencing. He and Miles have been wittering on about it for months."

Diedre looked at her younger sister and thought: How hardworking, uncomplaining, and wonderful she's been all these years. Nine years, in fact. She exclaimed, "What a success you've made of the gallery, Lacy darling, and you've worked like a Trojan. What you've done to help Cavendon has been tremendous. You really do deserve to have anything you want, including..." She let her voice drop an octave, and finished, "The awful Mr. Musgrove, who's no doubt a champion...in some ways."

Although she felt herself flushing, DeLacy started to laugh.

DeLacy sat watching her sister sleeping on the train. Her face was pale, and DeLacy could see now how weary Diedre was. She also had seemed far away, rather troubled during lunch.

When the steward peered in the carriage, wanting to offer them afternoon tea, DeLacy just waved him away, and smiled warmly, then looked at her sister, so that he understood.

The man smiled back, nodded knowingly, and went on his way.

DeLacy drifted with her thoughts; she could not go to sleep. And eventually her mind focused on Peter Musgrove again. There **was** a bit more to him than met the eye. He **was** matinee-idol handsome, although not as tall as he ought to be in order to be really dashing. And his eyes were a bit small. But he did have considerable charm, and he was well educated, and from a good family. Also, he was a successful art dealer. On the other hand, he had a strange side to him, and it struck DeLacy now that Diedre had been right. He was a little common.

I'm not going to Cirencester with him, she decided. He said we would stay the night. That's because he wants to lure me into bed. I must cut this off with him. The affair is going nowhere and I'm not in love with him. In lust though, she suddenly thought, remembering her brother saying that about Harry. Yes, that was it. Peter knew how to sexually arouse her, inflame and excite her as no other man ever had, not even her darling Travers...

She let all of these thoughts go, sat up straighter on the train seat, and took out a magazine determinedly. She wasn't going to think about Peter Musgrove. She would deal with that matter next week. For all of her resolution, deep inside she knew she **would** go to Cirencester with him. She wouldn't be able to resist him. Just one more time in his bed, she decided, and then I **will** break it off with him. I must.

Cecily was surprised when she saw Diedre standing in the doorway of her office in the annex, and she realized immediately how white she was and tired. She didn't look well last night. This morning she appeared done in to the point of exhaustion.

Getting up, going around the desk, Cecily said, "Diedre, are you all right? You look so tired."

"Hello, Ceci, and I am a bit. I need to talk to you. Just for a few minutes. Let's go to the gazebo. Can we?"

"Yes. Come on, let's go." Cecily took hold of her sister-in-law's arm and led her out of the annex, wondering if something terrible had happened.

Neither of them spoke as they walked through the park to the gazebo. It was a pleasant morning, rather cool, but the sun was out and the sky was periwinkle blue without a cloud.

Diedre relaxed as the peacefulness of Cavendon enveloped her, and she breathed deeply, enjoying the fresh air. Her family home always had a soothing effect on her.

Once they were seated in the gazebo, Cecily said, "I have a dreadful feeling you're going to tell me something really bad. You are, aren't you?" Cecily's eyes did not leave Diedre's face.

Diedre said, "The reason I look so done in is because I'm not sleeping well at the moment. We've an awful lot on at work. And yes, what I have to tell you is not all **good** news, I'm afraid."

Cecily was silent, waiting for Diedre to speak.

Pausing for a moment, looking reflective, Diedre finally said, "I want to explain several things, and I would prefer it if you would just let me do the talking, get it all out. When I've finished, I'll answer any questions. Is that all right with you?"

"It is. I'll just sit and listen," Cecily promised.

"As you know, Tony Jenkins came across a contact in Berlin, one involved with people helping Jews and dissidents to escape Berlin. I thought nothing had come of it, because he never mentioned it again to me. On Monday, Tony telephoned me. He wanted me to know he was leaving Berlin for Paris on Tuesday, because he was finishing his tour of duty earlier than expected. The next day, Wednesday, he phoned again, this time from the Plaza Athénée Hotel. He explained that he had escorted Professor Steinbrenner and the children out of Berlin with a friend of his. They are safe in Paris and will travel to London tomorrow. Greta will meet the boat train, and take them back to her house in Phene Street." Diedre let out a small sigh, and said, "But I'm afraid Mrs. Steinbrenner is not coming at the moment." Diedre sat back and eyed Cecily.

Startled though she was on hearing this unexpected good news, Cecily's face filled with happiness. "How wonderful! Thank you so much, Diedre."

"I didn't have anything to do with it, Ceci, neither did Tony really. The Steinbrenners' exit was accomplished by an anti-Nazi group of young internationals, who obtained the proper travel documents, made the arrangements."

"I understand. Greta must be thrilled...I can't quite believe it...that her family are going to be safely here with her on Sunday. She's been sick with worry about them. And why is her stepmother not coming with them?" Cecily asked this last question carefully.

"I really don't know the answer to that."

Cecily hesitated, before saying, "Is there some sort of problem hovering?"

Diedre did not answer this question. Instead, she said, "I think it's better if outsiders don't get entangled in someone else's family affairs."

Cecily stared at Diedre, and said in a low, concerned voice, "There's something you're not telling me, Diedre. I've known you all my life, and I can read you so easily. What are you holding back?"

Taking a deep breath, Diedre jumped in. "In my opinion there's some sort of trouble in the Steinbrenners' marriage." Swiftly, she told Cecily about Heddy Steinbrenner's reluctance to leave Berlin, how she'd been forced onto the train, her disappearance on Wednesday, Elise's confidences to Tony, and how Heddy had just disappeared into thin air.

"But how odd," Cecily cried. "Her behavior is weird, unbelievable."

"Better believe it, because it happened," Diedre replied succinctly.

"Is that all you know?" Cecily stared at her sister-in-law.

"How could I know anything else?" Diedre added, "I can conjecture, make assumptions, but what help is that?"

"It isn't," Cecily muttered, frowning to herself. Suddenly she said, "Could she have done these disappearing acts to go and meet someone? What do you think, Diedre?"

"That you're much too clever for your own good, Mrs. Miles Ingham!" Diedre let out a hollow laugh. "I have to admit, I came to the same conclusion. On the other hand, I have no explanation for this disappearing act."

Cecily shook her head. "Like you, I'm baffled but suspicious. Let's say there is another person. Someone she didn't want to leave behind. How could that person suddenly be in Paris?"

Diedre frowned and said in a stern, warning voice, "What I believe is that Heddy Steinbrenner is a problem, the professor's problem. Not yours or mine. You must not get involved, Cecily. Promise me you won't."

"I promise."

"Who can guess why she's vanished, or why she would risk staying in Europe instead of coming to England with her husband and children. And who knows what it might cost her." Diedre shook her head, her expression unreadable.

Cecily said in a low voice, "I bet you anything it's a man. Women do strange and crazy things because of men." Sitting forward, gazing at Diedre, she went on, "Now will you please tell me why you can't sleep? Is there something else really troubling you?"

"Many things, Ceci. Work, the coming war, bringing up Robin, lots of things which seem to have become enormous in my mind."

"I'm going to make sure you have a lovely, really restful, happy weekend, Diedre. Cavendon will cheer you up." Cecily stood. "Come on. Let's go and have a cup of tea and find the children. Oh, and by the way, can I tell Miles the news about the Steinbrenners?"

Diedre noddeed, and forced a smile onto her face. "It's a good idea to go and look for our children, and being home with the family is always lovely. I'll be able to relax." But would she? If the Steinbrenner problem was partially solved, certainly her concern about Will Lawson had not gone away. She had come to understand she was in love with him. But there was nothing she could do about that. Not ever. He was forbidden to her.

Thirty-eight

Charles Ingham climbed the moors to the enormous outcropping of giant-sized rocks, extraordinary monoliths that dated back through eons of time to the Ice Age when the whole of Yorkshire was covered with glaciers.

The great crags had been a favorite place of his since childhood, and he often went there when he needed to think clearly, or to sort out his troubled thoughts.

But today he was in search of Diedre. He knew she had come here earlier, because Hanson had seen her hiking up to High Skell, the name of this vast and empty moorland which stretched endlessly toward the North Sea.

That she was troubled was quite obvious to him, although perhaps not to others. He knew his eldest daughter so well, and she had inherited many of his traits. One was an inability to share worries with members of the family or friends. She carried her burdens alone, as he did.

When he arrived at the plateau of land under the shadow of the crags, he found her sitting on the ledge which had been used for centuries by Inghams long dead and gone.

She looked surprised to see him, but forced a smile as he walked toward her. He noticed at once that she had been crying.

"Papa!" she exclaimed. "I'm intruding on your private space up here, I'm afraid."

"No, you're not," he replied, sitting down. "I often brought you up here with me when you were a girl. Perhaps that's why you gravitate to it when you need to sort yourself out. None of your sisters ever come up here, nor Miles."

He took hold of her hand, and held it tightly in his. "I know you are tremendously disturbed about something, Diedre, so you mustn't deny it."

She nodded. "I am. But oddly enough, peace and quiet, and time to think does help. I've been so busy with a project lately, I've pushed private problems to one side."

"I know what you mean, and you take after me. I've done that for years. Somehow it's easier to cope with general matters than private concerns."

"Like you did when Mama was behaving badly. That's what you mean, isn't it?" Diedre remarked.

"Yes." He looked at her intently, searching her

face, staring deeply into her eyes, so very blue today they were almost startling. Slowly, he said, "Only one thing can make a strong woman like you truly vulnerable. And that has to be a man." He half smiled, shook his head as he continued, "Men. Women. How complicated we are. And yet we are so necessary to each other. We can't do without each other, actually. But we do cause each other so much pain and heartache."

Diedre nodded. "You always see through me, Papa, and get right to the heart of the matter."

"Shall we talk about it for a moment or two? **Please**."

"Yes, of course," Diedre said quietly. "I have discovered I'm in love with a man who is forbidden to me. But besides that, I'm not sure he shares my feelings. Certainly he's never made me aware of them."

"Forbidden? Is he a married man?" Charles raised a brow quizzically.

"Oh no, no, nothing like that. He was married; it wasn't a very happy union, I've been told. His wife died fifteen years ago. And he's never remarried."

"Perhaps he's involved with someone?"

"I don't know," Diedre murmured.

"So why is he forbidden to you? I don't quite understand."

When she remained silent, Charles said, "I

have a strange feeling you are in love with the man you work with. Your boss, as you call him. I am right, aren't I?"

"Yes," she said in the same quiet tone.

Charles stood up, offered her his hand. "Come on, Diedre. We must go back to the house. Now."

Frowning, she stood up, and hurried to keep up with her father as she strode across the flat bit of ground. "Why do we have to go to the house? You make it sound urgent."

"Not urgent, no, but important. William Lawson telephoned a short while ago. When Hanson told him you'd gone for a walk he asked to speak to me. He explained he was at Commander Jollion's and wondered if he couldn't stop by to see you. I invited him to lunch. I told him I would go and find you. And here I am. Come along, darling, hurry up. He's already waiting for you in the library."

For a moment, Diedre stood stock-still, truly shocked, gaping at her father, flabbergasted by his words. As he started walking rapidly again she hurried after him, crying, "I can't imagine why Will is here. It must be something really important. And why was he visiting Commander Jollion? He never told me he was coming to Yorkshire this weekend."

"None of that matters, Diedre. I'm sure he'll tell you everything. He did arrive with a suitcase, and I got the impression he is on his way back to London."

When they went into the front entrance hall, Diedre made for the main staircase, but her father held her back. "No, no, you don't need to go to your room. You look fine, Diedre, beautiful, in fact."

She stared at her father. "Aren't my eyes all red?"

"No, they're not. You've nothing to worry about. And if Mr. Lawson has to speak to you about something to do with your work, I suggest you walk him up to Skelldale House. Vanessa and Richard are not here this weekend, and you have great privacy there."

Diedre eyed her father appraisingly for a second, and then said, "I can assure you Will Lawson has come to talk to me about work, Papa. And perhaps we should do so in private. So many people are always in and out of the library."

"Quite," her father responded, squeezed her arm and headed for the staircase. "Lunch at one, as usual," he said over his shoulder, then mounted the stairs.

For a moment Diedre stood in the middle of the hall, watching her father leave, and then she took a deep breath, opened the library door, and went inside.

Will was standing with his back to the fire, and a smile slipped onto his face when he saw her. Immediately he hurried forward; they met in the middle of the floor.

"This is quite a surprise," she said, and was relieved her voice was steady. She was shaking inside and her legs felt weak.

"Sorry to barge in like this, Diedre," Will said. He took hold of her arm and led her over to the fireplace.

"I had to come to see Commander Jollion about something, which I'll explain later. After my chat with him last night, I had the urgent need to talk to you. I hope you're not angry, and—"

"No, no, I'm not. Just tremendously surprised. But pleasantly so. And I'm glad Papa invited you to stay for lunch," she managed to say.

"He's such a charming man and he made me feel welcome at once," William said.

"He's like that and very thoughtful. He suggested that we walk up to his sister's house. She's not here this weekend. He made the assumption that you might wish to speak to me in private."

"There's no problem here, Diedre, really—"

She cut him off. "The strange thing is that almost everyone in the family is always popping in here, for some reason or another." She gave him a small smile, explaining, "Skelldale

House is about ten seconds away. Come on, let's go."

"You told me it was always raining in Yorkshire," William said. "But it isn't today. It's lovely, almost like spring."

"September usually is nice, and sometimes so is October...that's when I say it's our Indian summer." Diedre lifted her head, looked up at the sky. "There are patches of blue, so we're safe for the moment. No downpours threatening."

William nodded, and glanced around as they walked through the park. After a while, he said, "I really do understand why you love to come here, it's so tranquil, and the park is truly magnificent. Especially these trees. They look ancient."

"They are, and date back to the first earl who planted them," Diedre explained. "And he also hired Capability Brown to do the landscaping."

She gave him a tentative smile. In the last ten minutes she had managed to recover from her shock at seeing William Lawson here at Cavendon, and was now able to speak in a normal way. At first, she had felt flustered. But years of continuous training in intelligence had kicked in, and she recouped very quickly, was able to put up a calm front.

Wanting to make small talk, she now said,

"My aunt Vanessa is married to a man called Richard Bowers. He's got some sort of management job at Scotland Yard. I don't know whether you've ever come across him?"

"I've heard the name, I think he's rather important, very high up. But I've never met him." William's voice was steady even though he was, as always, affected by her presence. It usually took him a while to get accustomed to her beauty and elegance.

A moment later, Diedre said, "Well, here we are at Skelldale House." She led the way up the stone-paved path, through a well-planted front garden. The manor house was set back from the main path in the park in front of a stand of tall trees which made a natural backdrop of verdant green for the gray stone house. High above the trees was a stretch of moorland, purple now as the heather was in full bloom.

Opening the door, Diedre ushered William inside. There was a small parlor just off the front hall. Diedre said, "Let's sit in here, it's a comfortable room, and near the door. Not that I think anyone will be coming in at this time of the day."

William threw her a curious look, frowned, "But who would come in when your aunt is away?"

Diedre shrugged. "One of the maids, the head housekeeper, or the butler, Hanson, from

Cavendon. Just to check things out. The door is opened in the morning, for an early check, and then it stays open until late afternoon."

Sitting down in one of the armchairs in front of the fireplace, Diedre indicated he should take the other one opposite her.

When he was seated, William sat thinking for a moment, wanting to focus entirely on business and not on her, which was proving difficult. Clearing his throat, taking hold of his flaring emotions, he finally said, "To get straight to the point, I know you have to be wondering why I came to see Commander Jollion."

"Actually, I am. You never mentioned it to me. Nor can I fathom out why you needed to see him," Diedre responded, betraying none of her sudden anxiety about William being at Cavendon. Everyone, and especially Cecily, had sharp eyes. And all were very curious about her life.

"Let me explain, you see—"

Cutting in she said, "Please do tell me."

"I wanted to pick his brains about Wilhelm Canaris, Diedre. Your friend Valiant has been puzzling to me. Not in terms of his dropping off messages for us to odd sources, like a contact in the Vatican, for instance. But his assessment of Spain's future." He paused and threw her a pointed look.

Before he could continue, she said, "You're

referring to his suggestion about Spain remaining neutral, aren't you?"

"I am. I wrestled with this for the past week and then I suddenly remembered that Commander Jollion was in the Great War, and served in the South Atlantic, during the Falklands War in 1914. I also knew that Valiant was a hero for the Germans in that war. He was the brilliant young intelligence officer on the **Dresden,** and drove the Royal Navy crazy with his hide-and-seek games."

"How extraordinary that you know the commander, our good neighbor," Diedre murmured, amazement echoing.

William nodded. "Yes, it is. We're not close friends or anything like that. I've met him socially. With my brother, Ambrose, who **is** a friend. To continue, I recalled that Edgar Jollion had once recounted a tale to us about the scuttling of the **Dresden,** and it struck me that he might know more about Canaris than either you or I do. This was my reason for coming to Yorkshire."

Diedre inclined her head, but remained silent. She couldn't help wondering why William hadn't confided in her; she could have so easily arranged the meeting. On the other hand, most likely he was protecting her cover.

"When I telephoned the commander earlier this week, he said the only time he had available was Friday evening because he was going to Portsmouth on Sunday. To take charge of his new ship. He insisted I come up yesterday for dinner and added I must stay the night. I didn't have any alternative."

"He must have wondered why **you** wanted to know what **he** knew about the head of Abwehr. Does he think you're with MI6?"

"No, he doesn't think I'm a spy. He's positive I'm in Administration at the War Office. My cover is as tight as a drum, Diedre, and so is yours. In fact, I'm sure he believes you and I are involved in moving troops around the world."

Diedre burst out laughing, shaking her head.

William laughed with her, and then went on. "When I asked him if he knew Canaris, he said he'd only ever met him once or twice and in a casual way, before the Great War. However, he was aware that Valiant had spent time in Chile as a naval cadet, spoke Spanish with a Chilean accent, and that over the years he had built important connections in Spain. Bankers, financiers."

"That in itself is very interesting," Diedre murmured, sounding reflective. "But don't let me interrupt you, Will. Please finish your story."

"I want you to understand how I explained my interest in the head of the German military intelligence," William announced. "I told him I'd heard on the grapevine that Hitler wasn't interested in Spain, had set his sights on Russia and on Great Britain. I hinted that this information had come from Canaris himself to MI6. And this was the point I made...I asked Jollion if he thought that Canaris would know the truth about Hitler's real intentions."

Diedre exclaimed, "He said **yes,** didn't he?"

"Indeed he did. Because everyone knows in Germany, and here at home, how powerful Canaris really is, that he has Hitler's total attention, and his ear. The commander told me something else...that Canaris does anything he wants, flies around Europe, sees whomever he wants, and visits certain countries all the time. He added that no one in the entire Nazi regime really knows how to run an intelligence organization. They're baffled. Only Canaris has the know-how and skill, plus experience. And that's why he gets to do anything he wants. They all genuinely believe he's the great expert. Which indeed he is."

"Did Commander Jollion go into any detail about Jollion's Spanish connections?"

"Not exactly. However, he did speculate a little. He told me that there was a rumor going around that the head of German military intelligence was a close friend of General Franco, and that he had been for some years. Very close, thick as thieves, was the way he put it."

"Well, there's the answer," Diedre murmured,

eyeing her colleague knowingly.

William gave her a long, questioning look in return. "Do you believe Franco will be in total power soon?"

"I do. By next year at this time. Just imagine having Franco's ear as well as Hitler's." She laughed out loud. "Bravo, Valiant, wouldn't you say?"

"I would." William glanced at his watch. "It's ten minutes to one. Perhaps we'd better go to lunch and finish this conversation later."

Thirty-nine

As they went into the main entrance hall at Cavendon, Diedre and William ran into Lady Gwendolyn, who was talking to DeLacy at the bottom of the wide staircase.

Lady Gwendolyn's face filled with smiles when she saw Diedre, who rushed over to her at once. After kissing her aunt's cheek, and greeting DeLacy, Diedre beckoned to William.

When he joined them he was given an unusually warm welcome by Lady Gwen, and Diedre smiled to herself. Her great-aunt had always had an eye for a handsome man.

After introducing him to DeLacy, Diedre swung around at the sound of footsteps.

Suddenly they were surrounded by the rest of the family. Her father and Charlotte, Cecily and Miles, and Daphne and Hugo were following on behind them. Once William had met everyone, they trooped into the dining room en masse.

Although their faces were calm and smiling,

Diedre knew that her sisters were all agog about William Lawson being at Cavendon. Because they were Inghams they wore neutral expressions and were welcoming. And so was Cecily.

However, it was Cecily who threw her a knowing glance, when no one was looking, and raised a brow. Diedre kept a straight face and shook her head in a denying way.

Charlotte, as usual the charming hostess, led William down the dining room. Diedre lagged behind; Cecily moved closer and took her arm, held her back. "What a good-looking man...so personable. It must be hard working with him." She gave Diedre a wicked smile.

"No, it isn't," Diedre said, her tone low. "And he travels a lot. But we'd better go in, Ceci."

Diedre took her usual place on her father's left. He was pulling out the chair for Great-Aunt Gwen, who sat on his right. She noticed that Charlotte had placed William on her right; DeLacy sat on his other side. Glancing down the table, Diedre offered him a faint smile, and settled back in her chair, deciding to keep a low profile during lunch.

Her thoughts focused on William. He had intruded into her private world unexpectedly, albeit by invitation, and he didn't know what he was in for. The Inghams and the Swanns could be relentless at times. They were nosy, curious about family members and their relationships, and probed. Still, she wasn't worried about him. He was a grown man and could defend himself. And he was a spy, to boot, who had certainly faced situations much worse.

Her thoughts about him ran on. She wondered why he had telephoned her this morning. Reviewing what he had recently told her about Valiant, and his Spanish connections, the matter didn't seem particularly urgent, nor did he really need her advice. Also there were no decisions to be made.

He had gathered some important information from Commander Jollion, there was no doubt about that. Jollion's opinion about Valiant and his influence with Hitler was important for them to know. Nonetheless, she was still puzzled.

Miles, sitting next to her, broke into her thoughts. "Why didn't you tell me your boss was coming to lunch?"

"I didn't know. Apparently he had arranged a meeting with Commander Jollion and phoned to say hello to me, according to Papa. I had gone for a walk, so Papa invited him to join us for lunch. Seemingly, he is going back to London later today."

"He looks like a nice chap. Why did he come to see Jollion?"

"I'm not really sure. But I think it's something to do with the commander's new battleship and his crew. William deals with troop movements. Soldiers, sailors, and airmen, and where they're sent. Not that we have much of an air force at the moment. That's what Winston Churchill's endeavoring to build."

Miles nodded, but she noticed the skeptical look in his eyes.

He leaned closer to his sister. His voice was quiet. "I gather from Ceci that Professor Steinbrenner and his children have been able to get out after all. But is it true the frau stayed behind?"

"That's what I've heard." Diedre was vague. "I don't know any more, only what Greta knows. She's expecting to go and meet them tomorrow, when they arrive from Paris."

"She's lucky. I can't imagine many Jews being able to get out these days, after what we saw and heard in Berlin."

Diedre responded noncommittally, not at all surprised by her brother's comments. "I'm happy for her and for those children."

A moment later Hanson came into the dining room, followed by two footmen and two maids. The first course, smoked salmon, was served, water and the white wine were poured, and lunch began.

Diedre, always the observer, saw that William was kept busy by Charlotte and DeLacy, who were both obviously plying him with questions as they ate.

Diedre was very conscious of Will being here, but then he was a man with enormous presence and charisma. She noticed how he seemed to suck up every bit of oxygen in a room and without any apparent effort. It was not only his good looks and easy charm that captivated but something else. He was well bred, mannerly, loaded with self-confidence, sure footed. He had once said to her that when a spy was a gentleman it didn't seem like such a shabby business after all.

Great-Aunt Gwendolyn caught her eye, and asked, "I hope that bit of information I gave you recently was helpful, Diedre?"

"It was, yes. And thank you very much."

"I'm always happy when I can be useful."

Diedre smiled at her, thinking how well she looked, positively blooming. Perhaps her aunt would make her hundredth birthday party after all. She hoped so. Lady Gwendolyn was a special favorite of hers.

The earl, turning to his daughter, said, "I think you're very lucky to work with a man like William Lawson, Diedre. He's first-rate."

"He is," Diedre answered. "And I learn a lot from him every day."

Gordon Lane and the two maids came and removed their plates, and within minutes the main course was being served. Today Charlotte had ordered a rack of lamb with roasted potatoes and mixed vegetables, a favorite of the entire family.

Sneaking a look down the table, Diedre saw that William seemed totally at ease, and was no doubt charming Aunt Charlotte and DeLacy, who was actually gazing at him with rapt attention. Oh my, Diedre thought, is he a secret lady killer? This thought amused her. She wanted to laugh, but swallowed the laughter, and cut into the lamb.

There was a lot of chatter and laughter around the table. Everyone seemed to be enjoying themselves. Diedre realized she was the quietest of all, but she was too caught up in her ruminations about Will to jump into the various conversations.

Seeing that he was holding his own, that in fact he had conquered them all in the shortest time, Diedre relaxed at last. What she was feeling surprised her. It was a kind of pride in him, for who he was, what he was. But then she had never doubted that he would fit in with her family.

During her many sleepless nights, when she had pondered about him, wanted him physically by her side, she had known deep down that he would measure up in any situation anywhere. There was no longer any doubt in her mind that she was in love with Will. The problem was she had no idea what he felt about her.

Rejection, she thought. Nobody wants to be rejected. Dare I make a move? Take the first step? Another thought struck her. Why had he telephoned her at Cavendon this morning? Because he was so close, only twenty minutes away? Had he actually hoped to be invited to lunch? She, who was so clever at her job, had no idea.

Her father startled her when he addressed Will at the other end of the table. The earl said, "I hope this question isn't out of turn, Lawson. But what do you think about the latest rumbles surrounding Sudetenland, and the way the Sudeten Germans have broken off talks with the Czech government? And what about all the public disorder there? Isn't it worrying?"

"The question's not out of turn, your lordship, and yes, the situation is volatile. In fact, the press will be running more and more stories about the problems over there. I'm certain Chamberlain will try to appease Hitler yet again, but eventually appeasement's not going to work." Will paused, then added slowly, "In my opinion, the Führer will take all the surrounding countries, including Poland. It's only a question of time, really."

There was a silence at the table. The entire room went quiet. Everyone appeared slightly stunned, Diedre thought, and leaned forward, looked at Will.

He stared back at her, raised a brow. She nodded. After a moment, Will continued. "The rumors of war are really not rumors at all, but predictions. I don't wish to frighten any of you, but you must be prepared. By next September or October Britain will be at war with Nazi Germany."

Diedre said, "Papa, you believe in Winston Churchill, we all know that and we believe in him, too. Pity is, he's on the backbenches at the moment. But at least he sees the world with clear eyes. He's not living in fantasyland. That's why he's busy building battleships and trying to create an air force."

Lord Mowbray nodded, his face set in grim lines. "You are correct, Lawson, we must be ready to fight. What was it that Nelson said at Trafalgar? I'm afraid I've forgotten."

" 'England expects that every man will do his duty,' " Miles said. "And indeed we shall."

A few minutes after dessert was finished, Charlotte rose and asked everyone to come to the yellow drawing room for coffee.

As they all stood up and began to walk out, Diedre noticed that her father had gone directly to William, spoken to him quietly. The two of them left together. She saw them walk into the library, and the door closed behind them.

She couldn't help wondering what this was all about, then decided her father wanted to talk a little more about conscription. She was well aware how much this worried him, because of Charlie and the twins. Basically, he was concerned they would all enlist the moment they could. Certainly Noel Jollion had been talking about doing that, and he was very chummy with the three Stanton boys, might influence them.

Diedre walked into the drawing room with Cecily. They sat down together on the sofa near the window, and within minutes Hanson was organizing the two maids, who brought around cups of coffee, milk, and sugar.

Not long after this Diedre was surprised to see her father coming into the room with William. Obviously, whatever he had wanted to talk to Will about hadn't taken very long. Her father ushered William over to the fireplace to sit with Charlotte and Great-Aunt Gwen. Instantly, Diedre had another sudden thought. Why was her father being so caring with William Lawson? He was always a good host, but today he was especially attentive to their guest. Perhaps because Will was her boss?

Daphne, DeLacy, and Hugo came and sat with them, and then Miles arrived. "Mind if I join you?" He sat next to Cecily and took hold of her hand, but looked at Diedre. "I think your boss is very nice, and well informed. We all hope war isn't **really** coming, and try to push it to one side. But he just spit it right out today. I for one am glad he did. We can't pretend it won't happen. It will. Harry's been saying that all along. The young men from the three villages will go, you know. They'll join up immediately, they won't even wait to get their papers." Miles let out a long sigh, a resigned look on his face.

Hugo said, "You're correct, Miles. War is a young man's game, I'm afraid."

"Fodder," Diedre said in a low voice. "Fodder for the guns of war. So many millions died twenty years ago, I can't bear to think about it."

Miles and Hugo continued to talk about what they were now suddenly referring to as the Second World War, and after a while, Diedre stood up, excused herself.

Walking across the room, she addressed Charlotte, "It was a lovely lunch. And thank you so much for including William. But now we have to go. We have work to do. I know you'll excuse us, Aunt Charlotte, Papa."

"Go and do what you must, Diedre," the earl said, smiling at his eldest daughter, whom he genuinely admired and loved very much.

William rose. He gave his thanks, said his good-byes with great courtesy, and he and

Diedre left the yellow drawing room together. They crossed the entrance hall and went outside. As they walked toward Skelldale House, he said only one thing: "I need to talk to you about an important matter."

Forty

The door of Skelldale House was still not locked. William opened it, ushered Diedre inside. She went straight into the small parlor, and stood near the window.

For a moment William hovered in the doorway, leaning against the doorjamb.

They stared at each other without saying a word.

Finally William said, "Do you mind if I take my jacket off? I'm very warm."

"No, I don't mind." She watched him as he slipped out of it, placed it folded on a chair. She noticed the muscles in his arms and across his back rippling as he moved, and she saw him properly for once. Usually she tried not to see him as he actually was, a powerfully attractive man, instead looked at him as if through a mesh screen.

But her eyes were wide open this afternoon. She admitted to herself that he was indeed

unusually good-looking. There was a masculinity about him that appeared to jump out
at her at this moment. He had a strong, even
tough look, and it suddenly struck her that
he was a lot like that actor James raved about,
who had become his best friend since he and
Dulcie had lived in Hollywood. **Clark Gable.**
Yes, that was whom Will resembled. The world's
greatest movie star.

Will had the same thick black hair, slicked
back above rugged features, and shining
white teeth. He was tall, about six-feet-three,
slender but broad chested. Yet there was a
gracefulness about his movements. She had
spotted that the first day they had met in his
office.

Unexpectedly, he walked out of the parlor.
Diedre stood perfectly still. She heard him
turning the door key, then shooting the bolt.

When he returned to the parlor his blue tie
was undone, hung loose around his neck, and
he walked toward the fireplace undoing the top
buttons of his white shirt.

She stared at him, surprise flashing across
her face. But she did not say anything. He had
told her he was warm, hadn't he? And it was
certainly not unusual for either of them to lock
doors. It was part of their trade.

He leaned against the mantelpiece, studying
her with such intensity she felt herself flushing.

Clearing her throat, she said, "What did my father wish to discuss with you?"

William did not answer. He wanted to say: **You. He wanted to talk about you,** but he didn't dare. In some ways she intimidated him. Not because of who she was, an earl's daughter. It was her enormous beauty that frightened him, actually overwhelmed him, and at times made him feel like a bumbling fool.

Nonetheless, he did want her. He'd always wanted her, from the moment he'd first set eyes on her. But she was so gorgeous with her golden-blond hair, beautiful features, peaches-and-cream complexion, and vivid blue eyes, he was afraid to touch her, to even get near her sometimes.

Her clothes were glorious, gave her a special kind of elegance, and often gave **him** a sense of awe. She was quite different from other women he had known intimately, off and on over the years, and in every way. To him she was the perfect woman.

In his mind William had named her Miss Untouchable. Yet he ached to touch her. It took every ounce of his willpower to keep his hands off her. He was in love with her, always had been from that first day. He yearned to hold her in his arms, to possess her. In fact, he lusted after her, though he also loved her deeply and sincerely for everything she was as a woman. A most unique woman, with exceptional looks and style and grace, and a truly extraordinary mind. She had an understanding heart, he knew that, and was compassionate and caring. He wanted to be with her. If she ever succumbed to him, he would never be able to leave her...

"Why have you gone so quiet and thoughtful?" she asked.

He roused himself. "Sorry, I was sidetracked for a moment. Your father wanted to talk to me about conscription. He's worried about your nephews running off to war, the moment it's declared."

"That's what I thought."

"I have something important to tell you. I have to go away."

She frowned, peered at him. "What do you mean?"

"I have to go on an **errand**. Business."

Diedre stiffened immediately and a small gasp escaped. "Where are you going?"

"To Sudetenland and Czechoslovakia. I need to know what's going on **exactly**."

"No, no, you can't go! I won't let you!" she cried, the words coming out of her mouth involuntarily. "Something might happen to you. It's too dangerous and—" Diedre stopped with sudden abruptness, realizing that she was revealing her feelings. She clutched the back of a wing chair nearby to steady herself. She felt weak at the knees.

William's eyes never left her face. Gathering all of his courage, he said, "Your father had other things to say. Actually, he chastised me. He told me I was breaking your heart, because you were in love with me. And I was not treating you properly. He—"

"Papa said that! He was wrong to reveal a confidence to you!" She could have bitten off her tongue for saying this. She knew she was blushing, and chastised herself. Blushing at forty-five. How ridiculous that was. She was floundering, losing her composure.

William took several steps toward her. When he saw her move back against the window, he paused. A faint smile played around his generous mouth when he said, "Your father told me that although I was obviously a clever man, I was also stupid...because I didn't see what was staring me in the face. And he confided that he had once done the same thing years ago. Would you like to know what else he said?"

She could only nod.

"Your father mentioned Charlotte's name. He told me he had gone to her house, walked into her living room, and found her standing on top of a ladder. Startled by his arrival, she had slipped. He realized that and rushed forward,

managed to catch her in his arms. He confessed to me that only at that moment did he
understand he was in love with her, and had
been for years."

Diedre was so stunned her father had confided such a personal and private matter to
William she was rendered totally speechless.

He came closer. "Are you in love with me,
Diedre?"

She did not answer him.

"When your father asked me if I was in love
with you, I told him I was. When he then inquired
what my intentions were, I explained that was
up to you. I admitted I was serious, but I didn't
know what your feelings were for me."

Still she did not say a word. William walked
over to the window, took hold of her hand,
brought her forward. He drew the draperies
across the window, led her to the middle of the
room, and immediately let go of her hand.

They stood facing each other, almost eyeball
to eyeball. She was tall, but not quite as tall as
he was. Neither of them spoke.

Their eyes locked and held.

He said, "Say it, Diedre. Tell the truth for once.
Are you in love with me?"

Her chest tightened and she was shaking
inside. She took a deep breath. "Yes."

"Say it. Tell me. I want to hear you say the
words."

"I'm in love with you, Will." Tears filled her eyes, and she was trembling, overcome by the depth of her emotions.

He made his move. He reached for her swiftly, brought her into his arms and held her so tightly, so close to him, she could hardly breathe. Against her hair he said, very clearly, "And I'm in love with you, Diedre. I have been since the day I first saw you."

Diedre was flooded with love for him. She leaned against his body, hanging on to him, relieved to be here in his arms like this at last. She felt secure, safe with him.

His mouth came down on hers. He kissed her. She kissed him back. They stood like that for a long moment before they stumbled together toward the sofa, fell down on it. He stroked her face, kissed her brow, told her how much he loved her, wanted her to be his forever. They kissed again, more passionately, then he said, "I think we must find a bed."

They went upstairs together. She took him into a guest bedroom, switched on a bedside lamp, and turned to look at him. She caught him unawares and saw the love for her in his dark brown eyes, tenderness on his face. She walked over to him, touched his face gently. "I love you very much, William Lawson, and I'm thrilled your intentions are serious because I can't ever let you go."

They wrapped their arms around each other, and stood holding each other, their hearts racing; a moment later he was kissing her again at the same time fumbling with her silk jacket, trying to remove it, just as she attempted to unbutton his shirt.

Suddenly William stood away from her. "Take off your clothes."

He watched her as she did as he asked. And flung off his own clothes, followed her across the room to the bed. They lay there side by side under the covers not saying a word. After a while, he pushed himself up on an elbow and looked down at her. "I never believed this would happen."

"Neither did I. But I've thought about it constantly, wanted it every night."

A lopsided, slightly cheeky smile hovered around his mouth. "And so have I."

William gazed at her wonderingly, gently touching her body, marveling at the silkiness of her skin. She had long shapely legs, a slender torso, and beautiful breasts. Putting his arms around her, he brought her closer to him, breathing in the scent of her, listening to her heart clattering against his. Soon they would be joined, become one, but at this moment he wanted to savor everything about her, this woman he had so yearned for, and for such a long time.

Her voice was low when she said, "Touch me, Will. I want you to touch me everywhere; I need to feel your hands on me, learning me."

He did as she asked, stroking and caressing her, and a sense of joy ran through him. Miss Untouchable was his. To touch. To love. To make his own. He was thrilled when she smoothed her hands over his stomach and down between his legs. He let her continue for a few seconds, but stopped her suddenly, placing one hand over hers. He stilled her fingers. She was fueling his excitement, his raging desire for her, and instantly he knew it was right for both of them to be joined. It must be now.

Slipping onto her, he put his hands under her buttocks and brought her closer, slid into her so swiftly, and almost roughly. She cried out in surprise. Her long legs went around his back, and he was filled with ecstasy, just as he knew that she was, because she was begging him not to stop. He didn't.

As they moved in rhythmic unison, William felt as though he were suddenly pitching over a precipice, falling into space. She cried out in pleasure, repeated his name over and over. He let go of his control, and gave himself to her as she did to him.

It took him a while to recover. He lay on top of her without stirring. Eventually he spoke. "My

God, oh my God, what happened to me?" he mumbled, holding on to her tightly.

"You made love to me, and I made love to you back," Diedre said. "And wasn't it wonderful?"

He wrapped his arms around her, and they lay together enjoying their newfound intimacy and closeness. Diedre liked the feel of his skin against hers, the strength of his body, the joy of being together like this. She knew him well in so many ways, had long understood certain aspects of him. But now she appreciated him for the man he was in his private life—who he really was as a human being.

As for Will, he could not believe that he now had his perfect woman. She belonged to him. He belonged to her. She had been worth the wait. He hoped she felt the same about him. At last he broke the long silence between them.

"Will you marry me, Diedre?"

"Yes, I want nothing less."

He felt her smile against his chest as she said this. "Can we do it soon? I want you as my wife."

"Yes. As soon as possible, Will. There's just one thing. I would like all my sisters to be present at our wedding. I know Dulcie and James will be back by December. She told me that James is completing negotiations about his contract with MGM. They're literally on their way home."

"That's something to look forward to in these dour times we're living in. A Christmas wedding."

"Do you really have to go to Czechoslovakia?"

"I should. But I'll send Gareth Jones. I'll pull him out of Paris for a week."

"You could send Tony," she suggested somewhat tentatively.

"He's not ready. Not quite experienced enough. You guessed correctly when you said it could be dangerous."

"What are we going to do about the office, Will?"

"I don't follow you." He appeared puzzled.

"I mean we are now having a love affair and we work together. Isn't that problematic?"

He couldn't help laughing out loud. "Don't be silly. That doesn't matter. I'm your superior, you know. The boss of the unit, as you keep calling me. I have no one to answer to, except the prime minister, of course."

She laughed with him, and it was the lighthearted laugh he had not heard for a very long time. "I don't think Neville Chamberlain will be interested in your love life," she said.

"Agreed. Nor anyone else for that matter."

"Do you think my father sent us to Vanessa's house so that we could make love?"

William began to laugh again. "I don't know for certain. But he did say I should take you to a private place to sort out the mess we'd made.

And that was the way he actually put it."

"I know he loves me very much, Will, as he loves all of his children and grandchildren. Perhaps he felt an intervention was necessary."

"It was. You know that. Haven't we been a couple of fools?"

"Yes, and we've wasted a lot of time. Oh, the train! What about your train back to London? I don't want you to leave."

"I'm not leaving. Your father invited me to stay tonight, for as long as I wanted. And when I said I was out of clean shirts, he told me that he was quite sure his shirts would fit me."

"Goodness me, you are obviously well liked by him. Just imagine, Will. You came, you saw, you conquered."

"Just so long as I conquered you, that's all that matters to me."

"I was the easiest conquest you ever had," she shot back, turning her head, looking up at him.

"That's not true, and you know it. Anyway, there haven't been that many conquests in my life."

She gave him a long, studied look but remained silent.

He said, "The past is dead and gone. We're starting a new life together. You and I and Robin. How is he going to feel? Will he accept me, Diedre?"

"Absolutely, I've no doubt at all about that. He has his uncles and my father, but I know that deep down he would love to have a man who was his own, a man to call **father**."

"And I shall be a good father to him, Diedre. I promise. And a good husband." He grinned a bit wolfishly, added, "And lover."

She smiled at him again, simply nodded.

William's face changed slightly, became sober. "Difficult times are coming, as you well know. A war will soon be upon us, and Hitler will attempt to invade us. I just want you to know that I'm happy and relieved we're together, Diedre. So that I can look after you and Robin. Protect you and keep you safe through the bad years that lie ahead."

NO GOOD-BYE

There are two days in the week upon
which and about which I never worry.
Two carefree days, kept sacredly free
from fear and apprehension.
One of these days is Yesterday…
And the other day I do not worry about
is Tomorrow.

—Robert Jones Burdette
Two Golden Days

Forty-one

Hollywood, California, USA. He loved it, and yet he was often perturbed and troubled by it. He wanted to stay. He wanted to leave. There was a certain dichotomy in him, an ambivalence of sorts. And yet deep inside he knew what he **must** do. He had no choice, really.

What James Brentwood disliked about Hollywood were the manifestly obvious things. The gossip, the backbiting, the boasting, the spite, the virulent envy. The fan magazines full of lies, innuendo, and wild assumptions. The titans of the industry who ran things the way they wanted in what was essentially a factory town. Men who could ruin a career, make or break a life with a snap of their fingers. And so many other things that bordered on the cheap, the sleazy, and the shoddy. And yet it was the most extraordinary place in the entire world, unique unto itself. Very simply, there was nowhere else like it.

What James Brentwood loved about Hollywood was the work; his fellow actors and actresses, those devoted folk who loved their profession, enthusiastically toiled with him every day, gave their all. He loved the talented screenwriters who put words in their mouths and without whom there would be no films, the brilliant directors who brought out the best in them, the producers who made it possible, the cinematographers who miraculously captured everything on film.

And then there were the makeup artists, the hairdressers, the costume and scenic design-ers, the film editors, the composers of the music that underscored the action. And countless technicians who made up a dedicated crew, pulled together to make everything work, to run smoothly without a hitch. The real pros, he called them.

Another thing he loved about Hollywood were those great empty spaces, the vast cavernous sound stages where filming took place. Klieg lights, cameras, sound recorders, the director and actors. All joined up to create a very special kind of magic which was captured on celluloid for all the world to see. Drama. Mystery. Romance. And musicals, a speciality of Hollywood.

James smiled to himself as he walked across the back lot of Metro-Goldwyn-Mayer in Culver

City, heading in the direction of one of those sound stages now. He wanted to take one last look at his favorite stage before he left.

Nineteen thirty-nine had just begun and, a week from now, he and Dulcie, and their little family, would be en route to New York where they would take a ship back to England. He would be leaving Hollywood, and there was much he would miss, not to mention the weather. But he was glad they were going to be in London soon. He worried about the war and all it would mean.

James glanced up into a clear blue sky filled with sunlight, and though there was a coolness in the air this morning it didn't matter, especially since the air was fragrant with the smell of the orange groves and the orchards that filled this area.

Felix Lambert had come back to Los Angeles last week, after his sojourn in August, to finally close the deal he had negotiated for him with Louis B. Mayer, the head of MGM. It was, finally, a compatible deal, one which L.B. liked. And so did they.

The final retakes of his current film were in the can. But it would not be his last Hollywood movie. He was once again under contract to MGM, and now owed Mr. Mayer four more to be produced in the future. Two could be made in England, but L.B. wanted him back here for the other two films. When the war was over. Mr. Mayer agreed to that. Whenever that would be. Nobody really knew the answer.

The war. There had been no declaration. **Yet.** James knew it was inevitable. It was whirling toward them like a tornado and would suck them into its vortex. That was why he could not stay here making movies. He had to go home to serve his country in its time of need. It was an imperative. He was far too patriotic to stay away.

As he drew closer to the sound stage he saw Patrick Kelly, the guard, who was always on duty here. A tall, genial man, unusually helpful at all times, he was a second-generation Irish-American who had migrated to Los Angeles from New York, where his father and brothers were all cops. "It's safer here," he had once told James.

Pat waved to him, gave him a cheery smile when he drew to a standstill. "Good morning, Sir James."

"Top of the morning to you," James answered, returning Pat's smile. "And what a beautiful day it is. Pat, I'd like to go in to take a last look at my favorite set, if I may?"

The guard nodded, unlocked the door, and ushered James inside. Pat flipped the switches in an electrical control box set in the wall, and instantly the giant sound stage was filled with brilliant light.

"What a wonderful sight that is," James murmured, walking forward, turning around, viewing the gargantuan space, a happy look on his face. "I shall miss this set, Pat, I really will."

"And I'll miss you, Sir James, all of us will. You're a real gent, if you don't mind my saying so. One of only a fine few who have passed through here recently. You, and Mr. Gable, of course."

"Thanks for those kind words. And I'll miss you too, and all my pals here. But I have to go home now. To fight a war, you know."

"It's really coming, then?" Pat asked, sounding suddenly worried.

"I'm afraid so," James answered, his voice solemn, his heart heavy. "And it will be worse than the last, a war like we've never seen before in the history of mankind, Pat. Take my word for it."

James drove out of the gates of MGM Studios, filled with good memories, and headed in the direction of Beverly Hills. He was meeting Felix at Chasen's for lunch, which would be another kind of farewell, in a way. Chasen's, once a chili place, was now a full-fledged restaurant, and the favorite spot in town. It was more like a club, in a sense, because all of the customers were friends of Dave Chasen's, the owner.

Frank Capra, the director, had put up money, and so had Harold Ross of **The New Yorker** magazine, who often came in from New York. It was Ross who had suggested Dave buy the lot behind the chili joint in order to expand. "And so I did as I was told," Dave had once confided when he was recounting the history of the place.

After parking his car, James walked into Chasen's, realizing he was early. But Felix was already seated and waiting for him.

"So, how did it feel, Jamie? Saying good-bye?" Felix asked after greeting him.

James laughed as he sat down on the red leather banquette next to Felix. "I didn't say good-bye. Because I know I'll be back one day, Felix."

"That you will, my lad. I can guarantee it. The contract's in the bag. And by the way, they'll never let you go and fight, you know, the British army. You'll get a desk job, or be induced to make publicity films for them."

"Don't say that!" James exclaimed sharply, and stared hard at his best friend, agent, and manager, frowning. "I want to join up."

"I know you don't want to hear this. But you're too old to be on the front line. You're forty-five, James, let's not forget that. It's the eighteen-year-olds they want in the trenches, not the likes of you, or me, for that matter."

James let out a sigh. "I know, I know. What you say is true. But Dulcie told me the other day that Cecily's worried Miles will get his papers, and perhaps even Harry. She's concerned on various levels. If the earl has to run the estate she thinks it might be too big a job for him."

Felix pursed his lips, nodded. "I can quite understand her feelings, Jamie. But somehow the Cavendon girls always seem to cope, don't they? The Inghams have not only been known for the loveliness of their women over the years, but for the **fortitude** of those women, who have apparently always stood up to be counted."

A small knowing smile slipped onto James's face. "I won't argue with you there, Felix. My Dulcie is the living proof...beautiful, strong, inventive, loving. And formidable. Just like her sisters and her sister-in-law."

"Only too true, and by the way, you haven't mentioned Cecily's brother since I arrived. I'm assuming all is well with the newlyweds, and that they're properly ensconced at Cavendon by now?"

"More or less. Paloma, despite being very pregnant, is in the midst of redecorating Charlotte's House, as everyone still calls it. Seemingly she's clever, a good designer. The Swanns are delighted, very happy those two met, married, and are about to produce the much-longed-for child Harry has craved for years."

"What is Dulcie going to do about the gallery in London? Constance seems to have the idea she intends to close it down. Is that true?" Felix wondered out loud.

"I don't think she has any choice in a war, Felix. The paintings would be in danger. From bombing raids. Dulcie mentioned that Hanson has saved a large vault for her in the basement of Cavendon, where everything from the gallery can be stored for the duration."

Their conversation instantly stopped when Dave Chasen strolled over to greet them. A warm, affable man, he was the perfect host. Since he knew everyone present the atmosphere was what James termed "old home week all the time." After exchanging pleasantries, Dave moved on to speak to Nigel Bruce and Ronald Colman, two of the English contingent, who were lunching at the other end of the dining room with David Niven, another Englishman soon leaving for home, to serve his country.

"Shall we order? I know I'm going to have one of those juicy steaks while I still have the chance."

"So will I," James said, and beckoned to a waiter.

Forty-two

Felix settled himself comfortably in the pass-
enger seat, relaxing after an excellent lunch
at Chasen's. As James drove them through
Beverly Hills, heading for Bel Air, he glanced out
of the car window.

He liked this place. It had a country-village
feeling to it, set among orange groves, orchards,
and pepper trees. The neat, tree-lined streets
with lovely houses and well-tended gardens
added to the special flavor of bucolic living at
its best. And yet it **was** a factory town. And its
product was much in demand the world
over: **Movies. With a capital** M. The public
couldn't get enough of them these days, were
addicted to films. And they turned many actors
into stars overnight, those devoted and often
frenetic fans who adored their favorites.

Felix was fully aware that the business was
now booming. He knew it would continue.
Nothing would hold it back. The amazing thing

was that the industry had been created by only a handful of young Jewish émigrés from Europe. Some had been brought to America at the beginning of the twentieth century by their parents, when they were small children. Or they had immigrated on their own when they were in their teens and twenties.

Felix suddenly thought of Louis B. Mayer, head of MGM, today the biggest and most powerful of all the tycoons. He had arrived with his parents from Russia at the age of three. These émigré Jews had started in the picture business mostly as owners of movie houses or as distributors of movies. Although Mayer had operated a movie emporium, as he called it, in New York, he soon began to realize it would be more profitable if he made his own movies. He set his sights on film production and headed to Hollywood.

Over the years this handful of brilliant young Jewish men created an empire of their own. They built the studios, controlled everyone and everything, and were the moguls of an industry which belonged entirely to them: MGM, Paramount, Universal, and Warner Brothers to name several.

Funny how life works, Felix thought, glancing at James. Thirty years ago he and Constance had gone to a children's theater performance and discovered a fifteen-year-old boy called

Jimmy Wood, the son of a docker from the East End. But on that stage, in a concert put on by Madame Adelia Foster's Drama School for Children, they had witnessed pure genius at work.

Little Jimmy Wood was not only loaded with talent, he had unique good looks and charisma, even at that tender age. Jimmy had become, under their tutelage and care, and that of his three sisters, James Brentwood, one of the greatest actors on the English-speaking stage today. He was Sir James now, having been knighted by the king, and also a world-famous movie star.

James Brentwood walked onto a set and underplayed everything. In a sense he was, very simply, just himself. His voice and his looks were the greatest of assets, and women the world over were his greatest fans.

"You're very quiet, Felix," James said, without taking his eyes off the road.

"I was just thinking about Hollywood, how it all runs. You've enjoyed being here, haven't you, Jamie?"

"I have. My fellow actors and actresses have been wonderful. Also I've learned a lot about making movies. It's a special craft; I'd even call it an art."

"So you're saying that they do it the best here...making movies?" Felix asked.

"Not only the best, but better than the best. There's so much creative talent and efficiency at the studios, and drive, ambition, enthusiasm, and more determination than I've ever seen. It's remarkable."

"Let's not forget the money you've made, either," Felix remarked. "These few years have been really good for your bank balance."

A few minutes later they were turning onto Bel Air Road where James and Dulcie lived with their three children.

It was Annie Farrell, James's assistant and secretary, who greeted them in the entrance hall, and James could tell at once that Annie was flustered, not quite her usual contained self.

"What's happened?" James asked, peering at her intently. "Is there something the matter? Something wrong?"

"No, no, not wrong. Sort of...unexpected, I'd say. An unexpected visitor, as a matter of fact."

Studying her acutely for a split second, noting her flushed face and the sparkle in her eyes, James thought he knew who had dropped in to see him. But he merely said, "Go on then, tell me who the visitor is, for heaven's sake. You look as if you're about to explode with excitement."

"Mr. Gable," she said at last in an awed voice.

"Clark Gable, I mean."

"Is there another Mr. Gable?" Felix asked in a teasing tone.

Annie shook her head.

James said, "Well, there is his father, Will Gable." Grinning at them both, James asked, "Now then, Annie, come along, tell me where you put him for safety?"

Felix laughed heartily.

Annie frowned at him. "He's sitting on the terrace, talking to Lady Dulcie," she answered. "Mamie brought them iced tea."

Nodding, now hurrying across the foyer, James said, "I'd better go and see him. How long has he been waiting?"

"Fifteen minutes, not much longer," Annie replied. "He did say he was quite happy to wait for you."

Forty-three

Go on, go and see Clark," Felix said, "I'll go upstairs and have a nap."

"Don't be silly. He'll be hurt if you don't come out to the terrace to say hello," James exclaimed. "He liked you so much when you met him last year."

"All right, but just for a few minutes. He obviously wants to talk to you about something important."

"He does, Felix, and I'm quite certain it's to do with **Gone with the Wind**. I know he's supposed to start shooting soon, and he's troubled by that."

Looking surprised, Felix asked, "Why? Every woman in the world insists he play Rhett Butler. No one else will do. He's a shoo-in."

"He doesn't think that. He knows he's **got** to do it, so as not to disappoint the public, the fans, or create problems for the studio. But he thinks he can't live up to their expectations, which are unbelievably enormous. Frankly, I understand how he feels. I'd be nervous about the role myself."

"Louis B. told me that to his knowledge this is the first time in the history of motion pictures that the public have played such an intense and integral part in the casting of a character in a movie. They just won't accept anyone but Clark Gable."

"They see him as Rhett Butler of course…and he certainly has all the assets. He's tall, dark, and as handsome as hell," James replied. "He's all masculinity. On top of that, he has a sort of cheekiness, a wicked glint in his eye, an audacity that thrills women."

Felix nodded. "There's no doubt about it, he's the greatest movie star in the world today. Male or female. And box office magic." Taking hold of James's arm, Felix led him across the entrance hall to the sitting room, adding, "Let's go and cheer him up, shall we?"

"I think a pep talk would be more help, Felix. Give him a boost," James suggested as they walked through the sitting room and out onto the terrace. This portico ran the length of the back of the house and faced the lavish garden, swimming pool, and grounds.

Dulcie was sitting with Clark and the moment she saw James walking onto the terrace she stood up, and hurried over to him, her face full of smiles.

She was wearing a peach-colored dress, his favorite color on her, and as she floated toward him James felt his heart tighten, as it always did when he had been absent for only a few hours, and saw her again. At eighteen, when they had first met, she had been a beautiful girl. Now, at thirty, she was the most gorgeous woman, the light of his life. He thought of her as the brightest star in the heavens above, or indeed on any sound stage in this town. She outshone and outdid every actress in the movie firmament, as far as he was concerned, and, if anything, he loved her more than ever after eleven years of marriage. There was no one like her, and thankfully she was his.

Dulcie came to a stop, stood on tiptoe, and kissed his cheek. "Felix and I will leave after a few minutes. Clark really needs to talk to you."

"I realize that," James murmured against her hair.

Felix said, "No kiss for me, then, missy?"

Dulcie stepped away from James, laughing as she did so, and went to Felix, hugged him tightly. She kissed his cheek, and said, "A few minutes and then we leave them alone, okay?"

"Okay, okay," Felix whispered back.

All three of them walked down the terrace to Clark Gable, who had risen and was waiting for them with a huge smile on his face. After shaking

Felix's outstretched hand, and greeting him, he turned to James and they embraced, gave each other a few huge bear hugs.

"I know I've made a habit of this, dropping in on you unannounced," Clark said. "But your beautiful wife says you don't mind, Jamie."

"No, I don't. But surely you want something better than iced tea, Clark? Champagne, wine, Scotch?"

"Thanks, this is just fine."

Smiling at Clark, Dulcie announced, "I have to go now. I have a few things to do, but I'll be back before you leave."

"I hope so," Clark answered and continued to puff on his cigarette.

"I'll be back later, too," Felix interjected. "I have to make a phone call to London, before it gets too late over there." Felix and Dulcie walked down the terrace and disappeared through the French doors into the sitting room.

James and Clark were of the same height and build, and the two of them stood side by side, shoulder to shoulder, smoking together on the terrace, staring out at the grounds without saying a word, both lost in their thoughts for a short while. Two handsome movie stars at a loss for words.

Clark suddenly said, "I really do need your help. I need to talk to you yet again about this

Rhett Butler dilemma."

"Let's sit down and attempt to figure it out," James suggested, and the two of them walked over to the grouping of chairs around a low table.

They sat opposite each other, and James said, "I know you've never wanted to star in **Gone with the Wind**, and the reason why. Millions of women have said they don't want anyone else but you to play Rhett. Correct? And you're afraid of failing them."

"You've hit it right on the nose. I'm bound to disappoint somebody somewhere, and I haven't figured out the right way to depict him."

James nodded, but remained silent. He knew Clark well by now, and while he was not an intellectual he was an extremely intelligent man, and well read. James was aware that Clark had read Margaret Mitchell's book many times and was puzzled by Rhett Butler and how to interpret him on the screen. And then it unexpectedly came to him.

Stubbing out the cigarette in an ashtray, James leaned forward and said with some intensity, "I think I have the best suggestion for you, Clark. And it is this. You should walk out onto that set and just be **yourself**. Those women who have written to the studio say that they want **Clark Gable**. YOU. Yes, they do want YOU to play Rhett Butler. But who is **he** actually? This Rhett? He's a man on paper, in a book, and the way Margaret Mitchell described him in words kind of resembles you, as you are right now sitting here opposite me. All man, very masculine, virile, sexually potent. But you're also a man's man. Just look back over the past two years.

"Since 1937 you've been a kind of national mania, so very popular. And men like you, too. You're the people's choice, also public affection for you is given unconditionally. You're their hero, Clark. I've seen you at public appearances and the public are euphoric with love for YOU. Not Rhett Butler. Go and be—"

James cut himself off, and chuckled before saying, "Be Blackie Norton in **San Francisco**, if I can put it that way. You wowed them in that movie and you were playing yourself then."

Clark was astounded, sat staring at James, looking somewhat bemused. And then he threw back his head and roared with laughter. A moment later, he said, still sounding amused, "So that's it? That's all I have to do? Be myself?"

"Exactly."

Chuckling again, Gable said, "I've told David Selznick I won't be able to fake a Southern accent. I could never master that. I'd make a fool of myself."

"I agree. Just be you. Tell Carole what I've said, get her take on it."

"I think she'll agree with you," Clark answered. "Anyway, I do believe this sudden solution to my problem deserves a toast. Shall we go inside to that bar of yours and have a drink?"

James jumped up, looking pleased. "I think the occasion calls for champagne."

The two men strolled off the terrace into the house, making for the den. It was a room with strong masculine overtones, decorated in a mixture of rich cream tones, dark coral, and burgundy. There was a large Georgian desk, piled high with scripts, lots of family photographs, several bookcases, and many treasured mementos that signified this was James's private haven. A grouping of armchairs and a large sofa covered in cream fabric stood close to the fireplace; the bar was at the far end of the room.

Whenever James and Dulcie gave a party the men always gravitated to the bar, and James walked over to it now. Addressing Clark, he asked, "How about a glass of bubbly? Or do you want something stonger?"

"I think I'd prefer a Jack Daniel's, please," Clark replied.

"Good idea. I'll have the same."

Clark stepped over to the window and looked out at the grounds, and after a moment he remarked, "I'm glad you're not selling the house, James. This reassures me you're coming back to Hollywood."

Laughing, James said, "I have to come back, since I'm now under contract to MGM. **Again**."

"I know you are, but MGM's the biggest, the best, and the most powerful studio in town. It dominates the industry, and that's where you should be. There at Metro with me. Anyway, this house can only grow in value, because of the way the industry's booming."

Clark swung his head, glanced at James. "And Bel Air is a good place to live. I found it quiet and secluded when I rented that house here last year. Carole also rented one, as you well know, and we had total privacy."

Carrying the drinks over to the window, James handed one to Clark. The two men clinked glasses, and Clark said, "Here's to your ingenious idea, James. Rhett Butler played as myself."

James grinned. "Just think of the way you succeeded doing that in **San Francisco**. It's become one of the highest-grossing movies in history, and you were wonderful...as yourself being Blackie Norton."

"Thanks for that, but Spence took the movie. It was **his** all the way. He was great; he's the best."

"You and Tracy work very well together, you're a terrific team. But I couldn't help wondering why Jeanette MacDonald was cast in it. A strange choice."

Clark groaned, and then grimaced. "I wasn't crazy about her. Never mind, Spence was wonderful. All he has to do is just stand there, doing nothing, saying nothing. It's the emotion he manages to convey just with his eyes, the expressions on his face."

"I know what you mean." James moved toward the armchairs, and lowered himself into one. Clark followed suit, placed his glass on a side table, took out a gold cigarette case and then a cigarette, and lit it.

James sat studying him for a moment, thinking what an unusual man Clark Gable was. Women all over the world worshipped him. Men admired him. He was a man's man, a woman's man. And everyone respected him, treated him like a king, and that was how they referred to him: the King. What was phenomenal was the adulation the public showed for him; it had never been at this level for any movie star ever, or anyone else for that matter, be it sportsman or politician. And yet despite this, and his overwhelming fame, James knew very well what a shy man Clark was, and a worrier. He was also down to earth, thoughtful of people and kind to them. Crews loved him; he was the ultimate professional. He was always on time, had never been late on a set in his life; he knew his lines and put everything into his performance. Clark was totally lacking in temperament, never showed impatience, unless an actor or actress was perpetually late, or constantly fluffed their lines.

Clark had suddenly become aware of James's fixed scrutiny. "You're really giving me the once-over, James. I wish I knew what you were thinking. Hey, old buddy, what gives?" Clark's light gray eyes were riveted on James.

"I was thinking that you are one of the most decent men I've ever met. We have a saying in England. When we genuinely admire someone for his standards, we call him 'true-blue.' And that's what you are, Clark. **True-blue**. I'm so glad we met, became good friends."

"Well, thank you for those kind words." Unexpectedly, Clark began to chuckle, and hilariously so. Once he'd managed to curb his buoyant laughter, he said, "I think **met** is an odd word to use, under the circumstances. You literally stumbled over me."

James also laughed. "Oh God, yes! I'll never forget that Saturday afternoon in Rory Gallagher's garage in Santa Monica. There I was, standing in his body shop, going on about the pinging noises in my Jaguar, and becoming more and more impressed with his knowledge of engines. Then he asked me to come to the back of the shop with him...he wanted to show me something. And clumsy fool that I am,

I tripped over two long legs in blue jeans and highly polished Texas boots sticking out from under a car, and fell flat on my face. And then I heard one of the most famous voices in Hollywood exclaiming, 'What the hell's going on here?' And Clark Gable was helping me up off the floor, worrying aloud about the gash on my forehead, all the blood flowing. You were very concerned."

"I recognized you; I knew you were in the middle of a movie. Of course, I was worried. That's why I got you to my doctor immediately."

"And thanks again for that." James shook his head, a twinkle in his eye as he remarked, "Imagine **my** surprise to discover Clark Gable stretched out underneath a car, fiddling with its innards."

Clark had the good grace to chuckle. "Mechanics. A hobby of mine." He took a sip of his drink.

"You're one of us, Jamie, one of the good guys, without pretensions. You've touched the rainbow without selling your soul." Clark paused, swallowed some of the Jack Daniel's, and changed the subject. "If I had a script I'd feel better about playing Rhett."

"I understand. And I've heard there are dozens of scripts, various versions. It that true?"

"Not quite dozens, but a lot. I have a feeling the best one is the first one, written two years ago by Sidney Howard. But Selznick hasn't been happy with any of them. Still, I do trust his judgment. He's a good producer."

"Principal photography starts next week, doesn't it? Isn't there a shooting script **yet**?"

"Not that I know of," Clark answered. "But fortunately I don't go before the cameras until January the thirty-first. Perhaps a miracle will have happened by then. Right now I'm depending on the book. As I've said to you so many times, I don't want to disappoint the public, that's my main concern."

"Listen to me, Clark, you can't go wrong. I keep telling you, **you** are Rhett Butler to the public. Think of him this way...Captain Rhett Butler, caught in the midst of the Civil War. Courageous. Sententious. A gentleman, a charmer, an adventurer, a man who loves women, who love him in return. A man's man. If you regard him in terms of a dashing riverboat gambler of that period, you'll have it down pat."

"From your mouth to God's ears," Clark responded. "And thanks for your tips, they're much appreciated, James."

"You'll be fine, just try to be relaxed."

"I will. And to be honest, there was no way out for me. I was trapped because I'm a contract player at MGM, and I can be loaned out to another studio anytime MGM wants to do that. Selznick was bugging Louis B., his father-in-law, to loan me to Selznick International and finally MGM agreed. Because they longed to be part of **Gone with the Wind**. They also loaned David O. one and a quarter million dollars, half of the budget, which he badly needed, and managed to get distribution rights as well. L.B. did all right."

Clark paused, and then added quietly, "I won, too, in a sense, because L.B. and David O. helped me with my very worrying marital problems last year. They made an arrangement with my wife, Ria, to give me an amicable divorce."

A sudden smile swept across Gable's handsome face, which instantly dimpled. He leaned closer to James, and said, "Confidentially, just between us, I am going to marry Carole Lombard. **Soon**. You see, when I met Carole I fell in love for the first time in my life. And she fell in love with me, her Big Lug, she calls me."

Staring at James intently, Clark continued in a low voice, "We'll get married the moment there's a break for me in the filming. Maybe in March. A quiet wedding, just Carole, me, two witnesses, and a judge. Pity you and Dulcie won't be here, Jamie, you could have been our witnesses."

"It is indeed, but funnily enough, that's yet another reason we have to get back to London as soon as possible. We have a wedding to go to."

"Who's getting married?"

"Dulcie's sister Diedre, and she postponed it so we could be present."

"I can understand why." Clark gave James a wry smile. "You'll not only miss my wedding, but my birthday party as well. On February the first I'll be thirty-eight." He stood up. "Let's have one for the road, and then I must scram. Carole's waiting for me. And remember, no good-byes, James."

"No good-byes, Clark, just a fare-thee-well and a see you later."

"I'm sure you helped Clark," Dulcie said. "He left looking much less worried."

James nodded. "I told him to just be himself, because that's what his fans want. Just Clark Gable, plain and simple."

Dulcie smiled. "He's hardly that." She leaned against James and said softly, "I will miss this place in so many ways, but I can't tell you what a relief it is to be going home."

James put his arms around her and held her closer to him. The two of them were sitting on the terrace overlooking the garden after supper. It had grown cooler, and the light had faded long ago, but it was a lovely night; in the clear air the stars shone brightly in the deep-blue sky.

He knew exactly what Dulcie meant. He, too, would miss many things here in Beverly Hills.

But what was happening in Europe overrode everything else. A dictator called Adolf Hitler was raging war against neighboring countries, and soon his own country would be dragged into the fray. Neville Chamberlain was forever appeasing that vile man, and it would all go to waste in the long run. Hitler had his agenda.

"You're silent as the grave," Dulcie murmured, and then shuddered. "I hate thinking of death, but that's all we read about in the newspapers and hear on the news. Do you think we will be invaded, James?"

"There's no question in my mind about it. That's why I have to get back to London. I must join up, do my bit. I feel really rotten, tense at times, being here in this lovely paradise not doing anything to help."

There was a moment of silence, and Dulcie finally said, "Felix said you are too old to fight, and I'd worry if you were at the front."

"I know you would, and Felix is right, actually. I doubt they'll take me, but I must do something useful, I can't just stay here making movies while everyone else is part of the war effort."

"I know. And I think everyone in our families will feel better once we are back. I know many people would say the children are safer in California, but I know we'll both feel quite safe when we are in England. And the children will be fine."

"You miss your sisters and Charlotte and your father, just as I miss my darling Ruby and everyone else. Better now we're going. And if we decide never to come back after the war it'll be easy to sell this house. That doesn't bother me. I just want to go as fast as possible."

"Actually it was Diedre who said the other day that the children should all be at Cavendon. It'll be much better for them in the country than in London. Her Robin is there."

"That'll make your father happy," James answered, bending over her, kissing her cheek. "I feel sort of ridiculous being in California, especially since I'm so patriotic."

"You're an Englishman from the top of your head down to the tip of your toes, James Brentwood, and where you should be is in your country. You will be soon. So stop feeling that you're a coward for not leaving before now."

"You're right, I do worry too much. But the mess with Louis B. was something to contend with. I thought for a moment he was going to make me stay here to finish my contract."

"So did I, and then I put my faith in Felix and said a prayer."

He laughed, then said, "I noticed the suitcases, there are so many I couldn't believe it. What we've acquired here, I mean."

"Actually, I'm leaving a lot of the children's toys behind, things they've outgrown, and clothes that are getting too small. But yes, we did seem to buy a lot of things. I've boxed the books we both love and they are going back by freight. There aren't many more cases, James. I've finished packing."

"Have you enjoyed living here?" he asked unexpectedly, taking Dulcie by surprise.

After a moment of thought she said with a light laugh, "Once I got used to the women ogling you, and the men ogling me, and the producers offering me a screen test! So yes, **eventually**. And most of the time it's been nice. But I'm glad we're going home."

"So am I." He kissed her cheek, then her neck, and suddenly their passion flared. He extracted himself and stood up, gave her his hand. "Let's go upstairs to our room, shall we, darling? I want to be close to you. Very close."

"And so do I," she said.

James was wide awake, lay staring straight up at the ceiling in the dark, his mind whirling with thoughts. Dulcie had fallen into a deep sleep following their passionate lovemaking. He glanced at her, smiled to himself. What a joy she was in so many ways. A wonderful wife, a good mother, a great companion, and a good sport.

He knew how homesick she was at times, longing to be with her siblings, her father, and

Charlotte. And Cavendon, of course. But she put up a good front for him and everyone else. He was well aware there were many things that she liked about being in Hollywood. But the pull of home was enormous now, had grown stronger by the day, and especially since war had begun to loom over England.

Family, he thought. The most fundamental thing of all in life. The family must always come first, Ruby had told him years ago. The family unit must be protected. He had his own family unit now: Dulcie and their three children.

But then there was his extended family. Ruby and his other siblings, and their spouses, children, and grandchildren. And then there were the Inghams and the Swanns. He wanted, no needed, to be back there with them. And that's what his anxiety was all about. He was like them, shared the same values and principles.

Here in Hollywood the British actors were of the same mind; they, too, were planning to return home. But not everyone here understood this terrible threat of war, or that it could become a world war. The Americans had always been isolationists. They thought the war would stay in Europe. The truth was it might well not. Fortunately, President Roosevelt was behind Winston Churchill, as much as he could be, at any rate. They had started to send ammunitions and food to Britain, but whether any men would be coming over to fight was another thing altogether.

The one person who had a genuine comprehension about the war was Clark Gable. He had even said he would join up if America entered the conflict, and James knew he meant every word.

Suddenly he thought of Bow Common Lane, the East End, and the docks where his father and brother had worked; and the Old Vic, and the other theaters he had played in, and Rules and the Garrick Club. But mostly it was the family that mattered. He missed them and so did Dulcie. They couldn't wait to get home...to get back to where they belonged.

Forty-four

Cecily and Dorothy Pinkerton were sitting in Cecily's office at the shop in the Burlington Arcade. It was still her favorite place; she did most of her work here, and designed in the adjoining studio. What also made the office perfect for her was that Dorothy was down-stairs and always available to her, whatever she needed.

Dorothy knew that Cecily was genuinely upset on this cold February morning, and she was wondering how to comfort her when Cecily mumbled, "So sorry, Dot, really sorry."

"It's all right, Ceci." Rising, she went over to join her on the sofa, put her arms around her. "Just stop blaming yourself. You've not done anything wrong. Even doctors don't know why a woman can miscarry at two months."

Swallowing her tears, wiping her streaming eyes with her fingertips, Cecily leaned against Dorothy's shoulder. "I'm all right. I'm healthy.

My doctor says that I'll conceive again. It's just that I'm awfully disappointed, and so is Miles. We've wanted another baby for so long."

"I understand. On the other hand, Dr. Denton told you the truth, I'm sure," Dorothy replied.

"I worry a bit, Dotty, because of my age. I'll be thirty-eight this year. I'll soon be too old to have a baby."

The older woman put her hand under Cecily's chin and lifted her face, looked into her eyes. "You're not too old. And we must always remember that you're not childless. You and Miles have three beautiful, healthy children... David, Walter, and Venetia. Just in case you've forgotten. So let's look on the bright side, shall we?"

Dorothy had said this in such a stern way, and there was such a serious look on her face, Cecily suddenly felt rather silly. "Yes," she nodded. "I do know I have a lot to be thankful for and so does Miles."

Pulling herself together, filled with irritation that she had been feeling sorry for herself, Cecily got up, went to her desk, and sat down.

She glanced at the carriage clock as she did, exclaimed, "Oh dear! I'll have to run in a few minutes. Dulcie invited me to lunch. Can we go over a few things quickly, Aunt Dottie?"

Nodding, Dorothy joined her, sat down in the chair opposite the desk, relieved she had managed to rouse Cecily out of her sadness. She opened her notebook. "One pressing thing. Joe Hardy in Leeds wants to know when he can get delivery of the white cotton for the white rose brooches. He's running low on stock."

"You can track that with the manufacturer in Manchester. If there's none available, we'll have to go to silk, but that makes the brooch more expensive, Dot."

"I know it does, so I'll get in touch with the mill immediately. Incidentally, I studied last month's sales over the weekend. Accessories and perfume are the top sellers. I'm afraid we're down on clothes."

"Do you mean couture?" Cecily asked, staring at Dorothy.

"No. I mean our ready-made clothes. The sales are really low. People are not spending …they're afraid of war, they know it's coming, and they don't know what to expect. They are saving their money."

"I agree with you. Everyone's being cautious. It also might be the winter blues, the weather's been awful. I'll try and do a revamp of the summer line, and get it going sooner. Women usually buy a few things for summer. I'll have a go at the designs this weekend."

"I don't think you will, Ceci. It's the wedding."

"What's wrong with me? I forgot for a moment.

Never mind, I'll get to the summer collection next week." The ringing phone interrupted their conversation. She picked it up. "Hello."

"Daphne, how are you?" Cecily said, listening for a few moments, her face changing radically, and she sat up alertly.

Dorothy, watching her, knew there was something wrong, but remained totally still and silent.

"So when did Charlotte break her leg?" As Cecily said this she stared across at Dorothy and grimaced. Then she continued, "So Goff drove her to the hospital in Harrogate with your father..." She listened for another few seconds, and then spoke again. "Yes, I do understand, Daphne. Just let me know what else I can do, and please do take it easy. Everything will be fine. Bye, darling."

Putting the receiver in the cradle, Cecily explained, "Charlotte tripped and fell this morning, poor thing; fortunately it was in the library which is carpeted. She broke her left leg, but otherwise she's all right, no other injuries. But, gosh, she **is** seventy now. Falls can be dangerous at that age. Daphne's taken on the running of Cavendon for the next few days. As you just reminded me, there's Diedre's wedding this weekend, and quite a lot of extra things to do. She wanted me to let Miles and Hugo know what's happened, since they're both here in town. She hasn't been able to reach them. I know Miles went to see his eye doctor for a checkup, and then he was going to look at a new tractor Harry's keen to buy. As for Hugo, I don't know where he is, if not at his office. Actually, he might have arranged to have lunch with Miles. They came to London together on the early train this morning. I'll call Miles's office before I go to meet Dulcie."

Cecily was wearing a navy-blue woolen topcoat and matching cashmere scarf, well bundled up against the icy-cold weather. Halfway down the Burlington Arcade she remembered she hadn't telephoned Miles, but kept on walking. He shared an office with Hugo and one of them would know by now about Charlotte's accident.

It was a grim day, windy, with an overcast sky the color of pewter. She felt the chill in her bones as she hurried out onto Piccadilly and crossed this main thoroughfare, heading for the Ritz Hotel.

The warmth of the hotel foyer was lovely after the bitter wind, and she slipped out of her coat and went to the ladies' cloakroom. A few minutes later she was walking through the beautiful dining room overlooking Green Park.

Three of the four Dees were already there waiting for her. Dulcie waved, and she waved back, a smile flashing across her face. Everyone in the family was thrilled to have Dulcie and James back home, along with their three children, Rosalind, Juliet, and Henry. In particular, they had all missed Dulcie's joie de vivre, her outgoing personality, and her quaint use of the language. Most appreciated in these dark times.

Once she had greeted everyone, Cecily sat down next to Diedre, and told them about Charlotte's fall, and shared her concern for Charlotte. They were sympathetic and promised to pitch in, even though they knew that Daphne ran Cavendon like Admiral Nelson had run the British fleet. Daphne's favorite motto was, "I want everything shipshape in ten minutes." How often they had teased her about this in the past, and would do so again.

"Now you're here, Ceci, we can make a toast to Diedre." As she spoke, Dulcie beckoned to a waiter, who came to the table and filled their crystal flutes with rose champagne.

Lifting her glass, Dulcie said, "Here's to you, our darling Diedre. We wish you much happiness and joy with William, who's the perfect match for you. And may you have a long life together."

They clinked glasses, and Diedre, flushed pink with happiness, took a sip of champagne, then thanked them for the gifts they had sent her last week, mostly treats of silky night-gowns and lingerie. "I can't wait to wear them,"

Diedre said.

"Oh but only for a few minutes, you know!" Dulcie exclaimed. "Then they have to come right off." As she said this, she winked at Diedre, who found herself actually blushing, and was mortified at herself.

The others also giggled, and then DeLacy looked across at Dulcie, and asked, "Is William really a look-alike for Clark Gable? If anyone should know, it's you."

"They're the same type, actually," Dulcie answered at once. "They're both over six feet tall, well built but slender. Certainly they have black hair and moustaches and are very masculine. But there is a difference in that Clark's eyes are a light gray, almost translucent, and William's are brown. Also, Clark has a cleft in his chin, and dimples. Those are most unique, and his cheeks actually **do** dimple when he smiles. To tell you the truth, I've only ever seen dimples like that on fat little babies," Dulcie finished, starting to laugh hilariously.

"Some baby, eh?" Cecily said. "Clark Gable or no Clark Gable, I think William is the most gorgeous thing on two manly legs. Except for Miles, of course."

There was more laughter and joking, and Diedre did not mind their teasing. She took it with amusement, joining in the fun. Later they ordered the same food, as they so often did.

Oysters, followed by grilled Dover sole, and only coffee for dessert. And Diedre couldn't quite believe that after her years of being widowed she had new happiness ahead.

After lunch Diedre took a taxi to the War Office, Dulcie and DeLacy went back to the art gallery in Mount Street, and Cecily returned to her shop in the arcade. The moment she entered the shop, Dorothy exclaimed, "Oh gosh, you've just missed Lady Gwendolyn. It's the second time she's phoned since you left for lunch."

Taking off her coat and scarf, Cecily asked, "Did she say why she was phoning me?"

"No, but she sounded like herself, normal, very together. I hope I'm like her, if I get to be her age. She's a wonder."

"I'll go up to the office and call her back now. Any other messages?"

"From Miles. He said he knew about Charlotte's accident from Hugo. They were having lunch together, and then Miles was going to look at the tractor. He said he'll see you at home tonight."

Cecily nodded, told Dorothy a few tidbits about the lunch, and then ran upstairs. Lowering herself into the chair, she picked up the phone and dialed Lady Gwendolyn.

Much to her surprise it was her mother who answered. "Mam, what are you doing there? Is everything all right?"

"Of course it is," Alice Swann said. "Charlotte had promised to come and look at various dresses Lady Gwendolyn had taken out of her wardrobe. For the wedding. His lordship's fussing around about Charlotte's broken leg, so I'm here instead."

"Oh good, I'm glad. I'm sure the best one for the wedding is the purple silk."

"It's the one we've settled on. I'm going to give the phone to Lady Gwendolyn now. I must rush, Ceci. I'm late for the meeting at the Women's Institute. See you tomorrow, love."

"You will indeed." A moment later Cecily was greeting Lady Gwendolyn. She then asked her, "Is there something special you want to discuss with me, Great-Aunt Gwen? About the dress, perhaps?"

"No, not about the dress, Cecily. I wanted to speak to you and Charlotte about my will. But Charles wouldn't allow Charlotte to come up to see me this afternoon, because of her leg. What I want to do is make an appointment to see my solicitor, and I do hope Charlotte and you can come with me. Well, maybe not Charlotte, not now."

"I will come with you. Next week?"

"Oh dear, why not sooner?" Lady Gwendolyn sounded dismayed.

"Because of the wedding. It's not **that** urgent,

is it?" Cecily asked.

"When you're my age, it is a bit. I could die in my sleep. Or at the dinner table."

"Oh you're not going to do that, Great-Aunt Gwen! You don't want to miss your big birthday party...when you're one hundred years old. You did tell me you have it planned to the last detail."

Lady Gwendolyn laughed, and went on briskly, "I shall write a codicil this afternoon, and tomorrow or on Thursday you can pop along to see me. I will sign it with you and Mrs. Alice as witnesses. Just in case I fade away before I see my solicitor."

Cecily picked up on the jocularity in Lady Gwendolyn's voice, and chuckled. "I don't think you'll fade away just yet. And I think that the codicil would be legal, but I'll check with Miles."

"Thank you very much, Ceci. I respect your judgment, you know, since **you** are the businesswoman in the family. I'm going to leave my house to Diedre. I was willing it to Hugo, but he told me recently he doesn't really want it. And it has to stay in the family. Also, I do wish to leave some of my good jewelry and various possessions to—" She broke off, lowered her voice and said softly, "Margaret, because she is my daughter. I want her to remember me and that I loved her all these years. She told me she doesn't want anything, just to know me. But I must give her certain things."

"Of course you should do that, I understand, Great-Aunt Gwen. I will make a point of coming up to see you tomorrow. Perhaps we can go to Little Skell Manor after tea."

"That is indeed an excellent idea, Cecily. I shall now go and write my codicil."

They said good-bye, and Cecily put the receiver in the cradle and sat back in her chair. She felt a sudden rush of pride in Lady Gwendolyn. What a truly wonderful woman she was and an example to them all. She certainly had her wits about her, there was no doubt about that, and was in good health. So far. Finding her long-lost daughter had been a miracle, to say the least, and Cecily knew this had given Lady Gwendolyn a new incentive to keep on living. At least for a little while. Since the introduction it had been touching to see their relationship develop.

Margaret had been very devoted to Great-Aunt Gwen, and came to see her regularly, but always escorted by Charlotte, so that the staff were not in any way suspicious.

From the moment she had met her, Cecily had liked Margaret, had believed her to be a nice woman, and decent; she had been proven right. And the one who had benefited the most was an old lady who had found peace of mind.

Forty-five

Miles Ingham thought his eldest sister Diedre had never looked more beautiful than she did tonight. She wore a red silk dress which made her look svelte and elegant, and the cameo necklace, which had once belonged to Napoleon's sister Pauline, sat perfectly on her neck.

They were all gathered in the yellow drawing room for a glass of champagne to toast Diedre and William. It was Friday, the night before the wedding. Diedre was standing near the fireplace with William, talking to Harry and Paloma, who was five months pregnant. How well suited they were and happy together, and like the Swanns, he was delighted that they had found each other. His old friend had never looked better in his life.

Cecily was standing slightly in front of Miles, and he drew closer, put his arm around her waist. She swiveled her head, looked up at him, and smiled. He bent down, kissed her cheek. "Well done, darling, Diedre looks amazing, and so do you." He increased the pressure of his arm against her body, and whispered, "Everything's going to be all right, I promise you."

Cecily nodded and leaned against his body, needing to be as close as possible to him. She had felt tired earlier, and slightly downhearted, obviously because of the miscarriage, but she had tried hard to put up a good front. She was aware that Miles believed they would have another child eventually; he had told her he felt it in his bones. God willing, she thought now, and smiled at him.

Looking down at his wife, seeing the shadows under her eyes, Miles thought about that awful night, so long ago now, when he had gone to her little hole-in-the-wall shop on South Audley Street. Knowing she wouldn't be there, he had walked over there, nonetheless, wishing to feel close to her.

The sign on the door had said SHOP TO RENT, and he had panicked, wondering where she had gone. He had come to realize that he would worry about her and love her for the rest of his life. This was when he had known that the die was cast, that there was no way out for him. He had to stay on the path which had been decided for him by others long before.

It was only recently that he had come to

understand that the die was cast long before then, when Cecily had been thirteen and he fifteen. They had become aware that they loved each other and were not simply platonic childhood friends anymore.

Years of heartache had followed, after his disastrous marriage to Clarissa; then Clarissa's tragic accidental death had brought him back to Cecily at last, the way it was meant to be. Forever.

Thoughts of his full and happy life with her and their three children filled him with a rush of pleasure, and helped to balance the massive worries that plagued him all the time these days. Cavendon, running the estate, the coming war and everything this meant. And the dismal future...what it held for them. I won't think about the future tonight, Miles decided. I want this to be a happy weekend for us all, and particularly for Diedre. It's probably the last one we'll have for a very long time.

Looking across at Diedre once again, he felt a rush of pride in her. She had been stoical for years, coping so well with her grief over Paul's unexpected death. Miles frequently wondered if the problems of Cavendon and the huge money losses had been responsible for that massive heart attack he had had.

Diedre had been brave, had pulled herself together, gone back to work at the War Office, brought up Robin. Finally she had allowed herself to open up her emotions, to fall in love, to start the relationship with William that had led to their marriage, to this very night.

Miles smiled inwardly, thinking about how Diedre had retained her independence, her need to be in control of her own destiny. As much as that was possible for anyone. He was amused that she had insisted on paying for this dinner party tonight, much to his father's irritation. But at least she had permitted her father to foot the bill for the wedding reception.

Glancing around the room, Miles noticed that everyone had now arrived. Aside from all the Inghams, and four of the Swanns, he spotted Edward Glendenning, Paloma's father, and her mother, Adrianna Bellamy, the Jollions with Noel, William's brother, Ambrose, and his wife, Veronica. Mark Stanton was also present, considered one of the family, and Tony Jenkins, Diedre's friend he had met in Berlin, was a guest along with another friend of hers, Alex Dubé. He was genuinely delighted that Felix and Constance Lambert had been included on Diedre's guest list.

"It's quite a crowd," he said to Cecily. "So much for Diedre's wish to have a really small wedding."

Cecily laughed. "Lists do seem to grow. Just look at Great-Aunt Gwen, she's positively regal in her royal purple, as she calls it. And she's really on form at the moment. She was full of beans when I saw her yesterday."

Miles nodded. "I bet she makes that hundredth birthday of hers, I really do."

"Oh she will. I've no doubt about that," Cecily replied.

A moment later, Constance and Felix came to join them, followed by Dulcie, who said, "James has found a friend. He and Edward Glendenning are off to it fast and furious, and Alicia's standing there with her mouth wide open, lapping it up. She can't believe it, being with two great actors."

"I didn't realize that this family had so many children," Constance commented, staring at Miles. "I've counted ten already."

"You're missing a few," Miles remarked. "Papa has twelve grandchildren altogether, and there are two more children here tonight, the niece and nephew of William."

"A potential army—" Cecily said, and stopped abruptly. Instantly her face changed as she caught Miles staring at her. She left the rest of her sentence unfinished, remembering that Charlie and the twins could easily be called up the moment war broke out.

Felix jumped into the awkward silence. "I'm so glad that Alex Dubé was invited. He's certainly going to make a star of Annabel. And my goodness, the girl's a genius at the piano."

A moment later Diedre came over to speak to them, immediately followed by William. Cecily was relieved that the conversation took yet another turn, went to a different subject.

It was not long after this that Hanson came to announce that dinner was served, and they all slowly trooped out to the blue sitting room. As usual, it was transformed into the blue ballroom for the wedding. There were two tables for the adults, two for the children, and they looked beautiful, filled with glittering silver and crystal. Yet again Harry and Charlotte had worked their magic with an array of flowers throughout, banked in the window area, and placed around the room. A fire blazed in the hearth and in a corner near the other window a trio played soft background music.

"How lovely," Constance murmured to Dulcie as they walked in together. "It's going to be a wonderful evening for Diedre and William."

After breakfast, Diedre's sisters and Cecily rushed her upstairs to her bedroom, where they followed the ancient tradition of giving the bride four tokens for good luck: **something old, something new, something borrowed, something blue.**

"Here is something **old**," Cecily said, presenting Diedre with a small box. Inside there was a lace handkerchief, with a tiny gold safety pin attached. "We'll pin it on the inside of your waistband," Cecily explained. "Nobody will see it. Also, it's not bulky."

"Thanks, Ceci," Diedre said, and accepted another box from Dulcie. Lifting the lid, she exclaimed, "Oh my goodness! Gorgeous stockings."

"I bought them in Beverly Hills," Dulcie told her. "And they're pure silk, perfect for a beautiful bride. Now you have something old from Ceci, something new from me."

"And now something **borrowed**," Daphne announced, handed her a velvet box. "Yours to wear today."

Diedre opened the box and was momentarily stunned. "Ruby-and-diamond earrings! They're spectacular, Daphne. Are they yours?"

"No, **ours**. Papa took me down to the big vault yesterday to look for something for you to wear at your wedding, and when I saw these I knew they were perfect for you. But they must go back into the vault tomorrow."

They all laughed, remembering the lost jewels years ago, and then DeLacy stepped forward and offered Diedre a small silk bag. "And finally something blue."

Opening the drawstring pouch, Diedre took out a blue silk garter trimmed with lace.

"Something blue to wear above the knee."

DeLacy grinned. "And unlike the rubies, you don't have to give it back to me. It's yours to keep."

"I shall treasure it."

There was more laughter, and then Diedre arranged the gifts neatly on the bottom of the bed. "Thank you. And I just want to add that you've been lovely to William, so thanks for that. Actually, I think he's fallen in love with all of you."

"But you're his one true love," Dulcie said, giving Diedre a hug. The others also hugged her, and moved toward the door.

There was a moment of silence before Diedre suddenly said, "I can't believe I'm getting married today. I never thought I would fall in love again."

"But you did. And it just goes to show that you never know what's going to happen. Life is just full of surprises," DeLacy remarked. "Of course, not all surprises are as nice as this one."

"Only too true," Daphne agreed. "Now we're going to leave you in peace for a while."

Cecily came back at one o'clock to help Diedre put on makeup and do her hair. And then she helped her to get dressed in her wedding outfit.

Because it was her second marriage, and also winter, Diedre decided she wanted to wear a suit with a long skirt rather than a dress, and Cecily had concurred. Avoiding white, cream, and the obvious blue, together they had settled on a deep rose pink, a color that was most flattering to Diedre with her creamy complexion and blond hair.

The fabric was a soft wool, and it fell beautifully because, as usual, the outfit was well cut and tailored. The long narrow skirt had a slight flare just below the knee and was ankle-length, topped with a short, cropped jacket which ended at the waist. It had a round neck, narrow long sleeves, and small buttons down the front.

Now as she stood in front of the cheval mirror in her bedroom, Diedre smiled and turned around to face Cecily. "I love the suit! Thank you, Ceci. It is so chic, and the color is marvelous. I don't often wear pink but it's going to be my favorite."

"It does suit you, Diedre, and so did the red dress. Another good color for you. I'll let you put on the Juliet cap yourself, but it must be right on top, on your crown and straight. Don't slant it."

Diedre did as she said, and nodded, liking the effect, and then she clipped on the ruby-and-diamond earrings. Her only other jewelery was her diamond engagement ring from William, and her own narrow diamond watch. She hated not knowing what time it was. My training, no doubt, she thought, and turned once again. "How do I look, Ceci?"

"Like a million dollars, as Dulcie would say."

A moment later Dulcie was rushing in, exclaiming, "Here I am for your inspection, Cecily. Oh my God! Diedre, you look like a million dollars!"

Cecily and Diedre couldn't help exchanging laughing glances, and Cecily said, "Come on then, Dulcie, I'd like to just check the back of your gown."

Moving forward, Dulcie glanced at herself in the cheval mirror, straightened a lock of hair, and then faced Cecily. "Do I pass muster?"

A faint smile flickered in Cecily's eyes, and she nodded. "You certainly do." She straightened the shoulders, and was satisfied.

She had designed a long tailored dress made of the palest of pinks for Dulcie. Like Diedre's skirt, it was ankle-length. The gown had long sleeves, and it was understated but elegant. Dulcie wore pearl earrings and no other jewelry except her engagement ring and wedding band. So that the matron of honor did not echo the bride, Cecily had made a headband of pale pink wool for Dulcie, rather than a Juliet cap.

"You'll both do," Cecily announced with a huge smile, went across the room and picked up her jacket. She was also in a long-skirted suit, which was made of silver-gray wool. She liked this look which she had just created. Quite aside from being stylish and elegant, the long skirts were warm in the winter weather.

"Shall we go?" Dulcie asked. "Papa is waiting in the library."

Cecily left Diedre and Dulcie in the entrance hall, and hurried off to the church. The two sisters went into the library, where their father was waiting for them.

Charles was standing near the fireplace. He was dressed in his morning suit with a white rosebud in his buttonhole, and at almost seventy he still looked handsome and in good health, which pleased the girls. They exchanged knowing smiles with each other.

After kissing Diedre and then Dulcie on the cheek, he said, "What a lucky man I am to have two beautiful daughters like you."

"You have a couple more," Dulcie said, laughing.

"Too true, and also Ceci, who has become my fifth daughter." His eyes swept over them, and he continued, "And she's certainly done you proud today. Your clothes are lovely, and I must admit, I do love this rose color on you, Diedre, and your pink gown, Dulcie. What a nice change after so many years of seeing you both in blue."

Dulcie chuckled. "Great-Aunt Gwendolyn won't be able to tease us today about wearing clothes to match our eyes."

Charles smiled, said, "We must go. We're

running a bit late."

Dulcie exclaimed, "I'll go on ahead, Papa. See you both in the church."

Charles and Diedre followed her, walking across the stable yard at a steady pace. "I'm very happy about this union, Diedre," Charles said, and patted her hand affectionately. "I liked William the moment I met him, and I knew he was interested in you as a woman and not just as a colleague. I'm rather pleased I decided to poke my nose in..." He let his sentence slide away, simply patted her hand resting on his arm.

"It was an intervention that proved to be most successful, Papa. And thank you for your little chats with Robin. He did like William the moment they met, but you've made him feel relaxed and very secure about trusting Will."

"He's a good boy, intelligent and sensible, a bit of an old soul, I think. He'll be right by your side today. As for William, he'll never let him down, or you either, for that matter."

They fell silent as they went up the hill, and a few seconds later they arrived at the little church. As they stepped into the porch they were greeted by the four ushers, who looked smart in their morning suits, each with a fresh white rosebud in their buttonholes.

Robin was in the forefront and came and kissed his mother. There was a wide smile on his face when he said, "You're a beautiful bride,

Mummy."

Charlie, and his twin brothers, Thomas and Andrew, were grinning from ear to ear, and they echoed Robin's sentiments when they complimented the bride.

The ushers led them into the church where Dulcie was waiting, standing next to a small table holding the bridal bouquets. She was matron of honor, the only attendant Diedre had wanted.

Dulcie handed Diedre her wedding bouquet, which was a mixture of deep pink roses and carnations of the same color; Dulcie's bouquet was a posy of pale pink rosebuds that matched her gown.

Charles led Diedre toward the nave where they stood waiting. She could smell the old familiar church fustiness, the dampness embedded in the ancient stone walls, but the mustiness was not too strong this afternoon, probably since Harry had filled the church with marvelous displays of flowers placed everywhere. Because it was a chilly winter's day, the freestanding heaters had been placed around the church, and the atmosphere was warm and welcoming.

Diedre was glad it was a clear, sunny day. Bright sunlight poured in through the many high, stained-glass windows, filling the church with shafts of rainbow hues. Her gaze rested for a moment on those windows, which depicted her ancestors in their armorial bearings, warriors all.

The church had been built at the same time as Cavendon Hall, and the first Inghams had worshipped here, just as she had as a child. Generations of us, she thought.

She was one of many Ingham brides who had gone before, and that was the reason she was glad to be having a small wedding so she could be married here. The church was much more intimate and meaningful than the larger village church in Little Skell. Here it reeked of family history, the past, their heritage...and the future.

Mrs. Parkington was still the organist, and she was playing "O Perfect Love," filling the church with music to the rafters. But Diedre could hear odd little noises around her... the rustling of clothes, coughs, whispers, shuffling of feet...she blocked everything out, her thoughts drifting.

Paul came into her mind, and for a moment she focused on him. He had a special place in her heart, would always be there deep inside her. She knew he would want this for her, and for Robin. Someone to love them, take care of them. A good man like William Lawson, who had already proved he would be a good husband, and a loving father to Robin.

The sudden loud commencement of the wedding march made Diedre jump, and she glanced at her father, looking startled. He whispered, "Mrs. P likes to do that…it shakes up the bride."

Patting her hand, her father stepped forward and so did she. They walked down the aisle, arm in arm and in step, staring straight ahead.

They came to a standstill at the altar, where William was waiting for them with his brother, Ambrose, who was his best man.

When her father handed her over to William and stepped back, she looked at her groom and smiled, and he smiled back, and Diedre felt a sudden sense of peace, of contentment.

Following local tradition, the villagers from Little Skell, High Clough, and Mowbray were gathered outside the church, cheering them, wishing them much happiness, a good life together, and showering them with confetti and rose petals. Diedre and William walked down the path, smiling, waving, thanking them, and a few moments later, they had crossed the stable block and were opening the door to Cavendon Hall.

The large entrance hall was still, the only sound the ticking of the grandfather clock. William put his arms around Diedre and held her close; they kissed, then stood apart.

He gazed at her. "You're my wife…that's so hard to believe."

"Believe it," she murmured. "You're stuck with

me now."

"With very strong glue, I can tell you that," he answered with a laugh.

"Come on. Miles told me we should go down to the pale green drawing room in the South Wing. He and Ceci will be meeting us there in a few minutes with the photographer."

"It's awfully quiet," William remarked as they went along the winding corridors.

"Because the entire staff attended the wedding. But they'll be back here soon, take my word for it."

The pale green sitting room was empty, and as they moved across the floor to the area where the chairs had been placed, William stopped suddenly, looked at Diedre.

"Are you sure you still want to go to Paris? Spend our honeymoon there?"

"I do, yes."

William nodded. "So be it, darling. Anyway, I love Paris. And this might be our very last chance to visit the City of Light. Before holy hell breaks out."

Miles and Cecily arrived with the photographer and his assistant, and a few moments after that the families came wandering in.

"I hope this won't be an endless session," Diedre said to Miles quietly.

"I'll make sure it isn't," her brother answered. "Leave it to me."

Part Two

**Women & War
1939–1945**

Against All Odds

We shall not flag or fail. We shall go on to the end, we shall fight in France, we shall fight on the seas and oceans, we shall fight with growing confidence and growing strength in the air, we shall defend our island, whatever the cost may be, we shall fight on the beaches, we shall fight on the landing grounds, we shall fight in the fields and in the streets, we shall fight in the hills; we shall never surrender.

—Winston Churchill
"Speech to the House of Commons,
June 4, 1940"

Forty-six

Alice Swann went down to the cellar to collect some of the jams and bottled fruit and vegetables stored on the shelves there. She went straight to the bottles which were labeled June 1939, and filled her basket with various items.

After returning to the kitchen, and lining them up, she shook her head in disbelief. How the year had flown. It was now May 1940, and she still had a bit of the old stock left. But like everyone else in the country she was very careful with food these days.

There were many shortages of produce because there were no imports coming in from abroad. They all had to live on what they could grow on the land and make here in Great Britain.

Alice sighed under her breath as she wiped the jars with a damp cloth. They had been at war with Germany since September 3, 1939, almost a year ago now, and nothing much had happened. They had gone on doggedly, doing their daily chores and countless other things as well, listening to the wireless and reading newspapers, exchanging information with each other. Now everyone was calling it the Phony War, and it seemed to be an apt name to Alice.

A week after war had been declared the government had issued ration books for food; they had been well prepared, had seen this coming for a long time. Everyone had a ration book, including children, and every type of food was rationed. Except for fish. Fortunately, they lived on an island, and fish was still being caught on a daily basis. For the moment. God forbid there was ever a shortage. It was their one true staple. The saying was there were nine ways to skin a cat; Alice had twelve ways to cook fish and make it taste different.

Clothes were rationed; they had coupon books to buy them; petrol was rationed, and coal, and just about everything else. Every woman in the three villages had more than one job. They ran their homes, looked after their children, cooked meals, and also made jam. Lady Denman and the National Federation of the WI in London had been well aware of trouble coming long before the declaration of war, as early as 1935, and so they were ahead of some of the other women's organizations in their planning.

So was Charlotte. It was she who made the production of jam in the villages much more professional. In the summer of 1939 there was a glut of fruit. She bought two canning machines, and Cecily bought two more, so that the women of their WI no longer needed to borrow the canning machine from the Harrogate WI.

Five women from Little Skell and High Clough were soon experts, and one of them even invented the best way to cool the hot cans. Gladys Miller had a large tin bathtub brought to the village hall, where the canning was done. It was filled with buckets of cold water; the hot cans were first laid on a large sheet, and then four women picked up the corners and placed the sheet holding the cans in the tub. Once cool, the cans were removed. Several days later they were labeled and sold.

Alice and Charlotte were very proud of their jam-making success, as were other women who were members of the WIs all over England. Eventually, Lord Woolton, the Minister of Food, told Lady Denman he was going to model a nationwide government-sponsored enterprise on the jam-making process created by the Women's Institutes. Because sugar was rationed by then, the government gave it to the WIs across the country for their national jam-making endeavors.

Placing the bottles of jam and bottled fruit and vegetables in her shopping basket again, Alice picked it up and left the house.

She crossed the main street in Little Skell, and a moment later she was knocking on the door of Charlotte's House and walking inside.

Paloma came hurrying to meet her, and embraced her, kissed her cheek. "Right on time," she whispered. She then indicated the cradle. Unable to resist, Alice put the shopping basket on the floor and went to look at her grandson. He was fast asleep, one fat little hand curled up against his pink cheek.

Alice smiled at Paloma and nodded, her love shining in her eyes. He was already one year old. Two weeks ago, on May 10, he had celebrated his first birthday. Alice would always think of that particular birthday as very auspicious, since it was the same day Winston Churchill had walked into 10 Downing Street as prime minister. She would never forget May 10, 1940, for that reason.

Paloma said softly, in a low tone, "I've made a pot of tea for you, and the tray's over there. With a little treat, some Cadbury's chocolate fingers, no less. Hard to get these days."

"Thank you, love," Alice said, and watched Paloma as she glided across the room, out through the French doors, and into the garden. She was going to the old hut at the far end of the lawn, which Harry had enlarged so that she could use it as a darkroom for developing her film. For the time being her favorite subject was a little boy: Edward Walter Swann, named for his two grandfathers.

Despite the war, the worry of it all, the hard work they were doing, and the dismal future ahead, Alice always felt a little rush of happiness when she came into this house. Paloma had made it beautiful, but that was not the reason her mood became lighthearted.

It was because of Paloma, who had changed Harry's life, and therefore hers and Walter's as well. They both loved his young wife. Not only because she was beautiful and wellborn, but because she was a sincere and genuine young woman, who adored their son and made him happy.

There was a calmness and serenity about Paloma. She was kind, and also clever and intelligent. Alice Swann knew deep down inside that she would always be true and loyal to Harry, a good wife, and a good mother.

Paloma was a blessing, and she had come into Harry's life at exactly the right moment. And the baby had been born at the right moment. Alice felt certain that there would be more children, and Harry would have the large family he had always longed for. Paloma would keep

Harry safe.

She sighed to herself, her mind suddenly going to the war. The British Expeditionary Force had gone to France, to help them fight the Germans, who were advancing rapidly across the country. All of the young men in the three villages had been called up. The ages of conscription for men were from eighteen to forty-one, married men exempt. For the moment. Alice knew only too well that as a war progressed more men were killed...and more men were wanted.

Charlie, Lady Daphne's son, had been called up and so had his best friend, Kenny Bourne, the son of Evelyne and Tommy. Kenny was one of Cecily's scholarship students, and had been at Oxford with Charlie. They were both twenty-two, just boys really.

Harry was forty-two and Miles was forty-one, and they wouldn't be going yet, if at all. They were married men, and also they ran an agricultural estate, and were exempt, had reserved occupations. Therefore they might not have to go and fight at all. She prayed that would be so.

A slight rustling noise made Alice turn her head. Much to her surprise she saw Evelyne standing in the doorway of the living room. She looked so upset, Alice immediately rose and went to her.

Taking hold of her arm, she said in a whisper, "The baby's sleeping, let's go outside." As she spoke she led Evelyne through the entrance foyer and into the small front garden.

"Whatever's wrong?" Alice asked. "You look as if you've had some sort of shock."

"I heard something. When I was in Harrogate earlier today…that all our boys are stranded on the beaches of France. And they're going to die there. They'll be killed by the Germans!"

"I think that's an exaggeration if ever there was one," Alice said in a soothing voice. "It's true the BEF has had a tough job of it, and they are retreating to the French coastline, but our boys will be rescued."

"But that's not what I heard," Evelyne mumbled, pushing back tears.

"I don't care what you've heard," Alice said in a confident voice. "Winston Churchill is now prime minister. He's not going to let any of us down. We are in safe hands. Have a bit of faith, love. He'll save our boys."

Evelyne leaned against the door. "I'm sorry, Alice, I don't mean to upset you. It's just that I'm so worried…I worry about Kenny and Charlie…Lady Daphne must be heartsick, too. Charlie's over there as you well know. In the midst of the fighting with my Kenny."

"They'll be brought home safe," Alice said in a strong voice, wishing to reassure her friend.

And in actual fact she did believe that…because long ago she had put her trust in Winston Churchill. She believed, and without the slightest doubt, that he was the leader they needed to win the war. The leader the world needed… to save civilization.

Forty-seven

Deep in the bowels of the earth, in the many secret tunnels beneath Dover Castle, there was always constant activity. Built into the white chalk of the famous White Cliffs of Dover, the tunnels were, in fact, bunkers to house officers and men who were there to defend Great Britain, the Straits of Dover, and the English Channel.

They had been carved out and constructed at the behest of Winston Churchill, and they housed gun battery teams to pound Nazi ships if they entered the Channel, sink submarines, and whatever other dangerous weapons came in sight.

Vice Admiral Bertram Ramsay, the flag officer in Dover, was in charge, and it was from there that he was currently directing the evacuation of French and English soldiers stranded on the beaches of Dunkirk. It was May 24, 1940.

One of the senior officers was Commodore

Edgar Jollion. He was there at the request of Vice Admiral Ramsay, who was well aware of his fine reputation. Plus his enormous knowledge of the French coastline, the ins and outs of it, and its peculiarities. Jollion also was an expert on the English Channel and the Atlantic Ocean in these areas.

Taking a sip of his tea, the commodore sat back, thinking about his luck at being where he was at this moment. He had arrived in March of 1940 to work with Ramsay in defending the English Channel. With his new position had come a promotion.

In 1938, when he had taken over his new ship, which was not a **new** ship except to him, he had been made a captain. But within a year the ship was sent back into dry dock to have its engines checked, among other things. No ship. No job. He had to be assigned to a new vessel, and was impatient to get one.

Not long after this, he was offered the job to work with the vice admiral, and unexpectedly, there was another promotion...**commodore**, just one step below rear admiral. And he loved the job he had now. When the disaster of Dunkirk occurred, Vice Admiral Ramsay was immediately put in charge of the evacuation. Its code name: Operation Dynamo. Commodore Jollion was a big part of it.

Edgar, a career naval officer, loved the sea

and being a sailor, but he was highly patriotic, and rescuing their soldiers, many of them the same age as his son, was a rewarding mission.

His son, Noel, was as patriotic as he was, all the Jollions were. Noel was now in the Royal Air Force, a fighter pilot flying Spitfires, bombing the advancing German army in France. His squadron was based at Biggin Hill, just outside London, and whenever he got a bit of leave he went to London to stay with Edgar's sister, Adrianna Bellamy. She had joined the Red Cross, and so had her daughter Claudia.

His wife had her hands full running Burnside Manor, especially since most of the younger men who worked on their land had gone off to fight, or had taken jobs in munitions factories. But their wives had helped to fill the gap, helped to work the allotments, the vegetable and herb gardens at Burnside. The latter had become important to the Ministry of Agriculture, who sought all manner of herbs for medicines. And the food they produced was vital. The shops were empty these days.

Phoebe came into his mind, and he suddenly realized he had forgotten to write to his sister about evacuating Phoebe and her siblings to Burnside. They would be much safer there, once the invasion started. And start it would.

Thousands of English children had already been evacuated, taken out of the towns and cities and relocated to rural areas. He knew from his niece Paloma that evacuees had started to arrive in Little Skell village, High Clough, and Mowbray, and had apparently settled in nicely. Although that wasn't always the case. Some were horribly homesick.

Lovely Paloma, who had given him his first great-nephew. Her marriage to Harry Swann had pleased him no end; Harry was the salt of the earth.

Edgar stood up, stretched his legs, and decided to take a walk around some of the tunnels. It was his way of keeping fit at the moment. Leaving his office, he strolled down a long corridor, which led to the wireless room. The interconnecting tunnels, all thirty-five hundred square feet of them, were reinforced with iron girders and metal sheeting. In a way, it was like a small town, with dormitories, bathrooms, kitchens, and mess rooms. Not too bad at all, under the circumstances. And the work they were doing was crucial. It was imperative that they rescue as many men as possible; soldiers were needed to protect the country. Edgar had been startled to discover what a small army the British had, and an even smaller air force. Only the Royal Navy was large, well equipped, and in total order. But then they were an island race, their navy had been their secret weapon for centuries. Not so secret, he thought, smiling to himself, and thinking of Horatio Nelson.

He was just about to turn around and go back to his office when he heard his name being called. He looked over his shoulder. It was one of the ensigns from the wireless room, who hurried toward him, explaining, "I was coming to see you, Commodore. This message has just come in."

Edgar nodded, took the paper from the young man. "Thank you, Judson."

The sailor nodded, saluted, and departed. Edgar returned to his office. He sat down at his desk and read the short message. Then he stared at it, frowning, and read it again.

"What the hell is this all about?" he said out loud to the empty room. The message did not make sense to him.

Suddenly it did. He jumped up, dashed out, and went two doors down to see Vice Admiral Ramsay. He knocked hard, and when Ramsay said, "Enter," Edgar did so.

Ramsay stared at him. "Something wrong, Jollion?"

"I'd use the word strange. I've just received this wireless message from headquarters in Dunkirk. General Rundstedt's just ordered General Kleist's Panzer division to halt at the front line. Not to go forward. Absolutely not to do that. Stay put, in other words."

Ramsay was flabbergasted. He exclaimed, "But they have us right in their sights. I've been worried they would move forward, capture our men in that pocket of land our boys have been maneuvered into by the Panzers." Ramsay shook his head. **"Strange indeed,** Jollion." There was a pause, and the vice admiral then said, "Are we sure of this information?"

"I would say so, sir. Yes. But to be safe, let's check with the source. Send a message back to headquarters in France."

"Do it at once. I'd like to know how we've suddenly found out about the plans of the Wehrmacht."

Within several hours Ramsay and Jollion had their answer from Lieutenant Colonel Lord Bridgeman of the Rifle Brigade on the Continent, who worked with Lord Gort, head of the British Expeditionary Force.

The message they had received **was** accurate.

General Kleist had remained on the heights above Flanders, which looked down on Dunkirk. Eventually his Panzer divisions had moved, but they had not gone down into Dunkirk to take it, or to attack and kill the British and French soldiers trapped in a pocket of land close by. Instead they had retreated.

It was Commodore Jollion who reasoned that perhaps the German general was leery of taking his tanks into the lower area of Flanders, which was full of canals, streams, and marshes. And there was another possibility he had pointed out to Ramsay. Maneuvering tanks in built-up areas such as villages and towns was usually difficult. Perhaps he had retreated for this reason as well.

But whatever had caused this sudden retreat of the Nazi tanks, Lord Gort, commander in chief of the BEF, Bridgeman, Ramsay, and Jollion grabbed the opportunity to start evacuating more troops from Dunkirk at once.

Thousands of British and French soldiers were soon scrambling onto the big British ships anchored off Dunkirk over a calm and sunny forty-eight-hour period.

Commodore Jollion considered this a God-given blessing. Because the attacks from Kleist's Panzer divisions soon started again and the Allied troops were mowed down relentlessly. Jollion was heartsick, knowing that almost the entire British army was over in France. There were not many soldiers left in Britain to defend it against the enemy. His country was vulnerable if the Germans decided to invade.

Forty-eight

Captain Charlie Stanton of the Coldstream Guards knew they had to leave the little town of Poperinghe as soon as possible. Right now, in fact.

They were on the southern perimeter of Dunkirk, and it was time to make the move back to the beaches. In the background, he could already hear the German guns, and he was certain they would soon be overrun by enemy troops. The British Expeditionary Force was surrounded. Doomed.

Last night he had been told by headquarters to take what was left of his platoon back to Dunkirk. There were now only twenty men but they were as ready and willing to leave as he was.

As he glanced around he saw Kenny Bourne walking over to him. They had left Oxford and gone through officer training at Sandhurst in 1939, and managed to stay together by joining the same regiment. They were lucky that the Coldstream Guards did most of their recruiting in the northeast of England. Kenny was a lieutenant, and the only other officer still alive in this troop.

"We're ready to go," Kenny said, and Charlie nodded. The plan was to get everyone into two trucks and a lorry and make a dash for it. This they did, and they were relieved to be heading to the coast of France where the rest of the regiment was, along with British battleships, destroyers, and hospital ships waiting offshore. It was going to be a huge rescue. Every regiment was being pulled out by the end of May.

Charlie's relief soon changed to impatience as he realized they might have been better off walking. The road was totally choked with fleeing soldiers, marching forward at a steady pace, and blocking their way at times.

Kenny, driving the Humber Snipe truck, kept his eyes on the busy road when he said, "Bugger! It's started to rain. That's going to slow us down even more."

"Maybe," Charlie answered, and then grinned. "But let's face it, rain keeps the Luftwaffe out of the air. If it was a sunny day we'd be sitting ducks."

"What a relief it's weather for ducks instead," Kenny shot back with a laugh.

The two men fell silent as they edged their way to Warhem, the next town on this route. It was filled with so many soldiers Charlie was astonished. There were thousands of men moving down this road, not only British but French and Dutch, as well. He was certain of that. None of them were defeated in spirit yet, but they had certainly been outnumbered. The Wehrmacht was massive, the greatest army in the world with the biggest supply of armaments and enormous fire power, not to mention those deadly Panzer tanks.

As they drew even closer to headquarters in Dunkirk, their trucks were brought to a sudden standstill by military police. Charlie rolled down the window to ask what was wrong.

"Sorry, Captain, but you must leave your trucks and the lorry behind. In that field over there, alongside the other abandoned vehicles. Set fire to them. Good thing it's stopped raining."

Charlie asked, "Why do we have to abandon them?"

"Orders, Captain. The top brass don't want traffic jams in Dunkirk. I'll instruct your men to follow you."

Charlie nodded his understanding and told Kenny to drive into the field. When they jumped out of the Humber they saw that many of the abandoned cars, trucks, and lorries were still burning, smoldering, or were totally burned out.

Charlie and Kenny looked at their possessions inside the Humber Snipe, and then stared at each other, grimacing. "I hate to leave my things behind, but we've no choice," Charlie muttered, and reached for his haversack.

"So do I, but we've got to travel light," Kenny replied, and also took only his haversack. "I'm leaving everything else."

Then the men followed suit. Once they had taken out their haversacks, Charlie told them to set light to the vehicles, which they did, if somewhat reluctantly.

Charlie turned away. Nonetheless, he could not resist going over to one of the trucks left behind earlier which had not been burned. And much to his surprise and pleasure he saw guns in the back, as well as food. Obviously it had been left hurriedly by other fleeing British troops.

He beckoned to Kenny and the men, and told them to take a rifle each and as much food as they could carry. They did so. Having a weapon in their hands again, as well as food, brought smiles to the faces of his men. And Charlie felt a lift in his spirits.

They were loyal and stalwart, and had obviously been relieved when he had taken charge of them after Major Barton had been killed in a heavy Luftwaffe attack. Charlie knew he could rely on them; these Coldstreamers were the salt of the earth. He also knew they were bone tired after three weeks of intense fighting in the fields of Flanders, protecting different perimeters. He was determined to find somewhere for them to sleep tonight. That was mandatory.

His men were standing waiting, looking at Charlie as if trying to read his mind. Most of them were wondering why they were lingering in the field filled with their burning vehicles.

Since they were staring at Charlie and had their backs to the main road, they could not see what he was gazing at across that road.

In fact it was smoke. Not drifting smoke from the burning trucks, but smoke of an entirely different kind. It was a spiral floating up into the sky, obviously from a chimney which Charlie could not see. But he thought that behind the stand of trees across the road there was probably a farmhouse.

That is what he told Kenny and the men, and added, "I don't want us to get caught up in those throngs pushing on to Dunkirk. We're going to go over to that field behind you and see what we can find."

Joe Wortley, the lance sergeant, understood at once. "You think there's a farmhouse back there, sir, don't you?"

"More than likely. Look, we all need a rest.

Food. And if possible some sleep. Before we tramp back to headquarters. Seeing hundreds of soldiers on this road tells me a vivid story. It's going to be very crowded in the port of Dunkirk tonight. I'd like us to get some of our strength back, leave for the port tomorrow morning."

The lance sergeant nodded. "A good plan, Captain. I assume you can speak French, so let's go and look for the farm."

Charlie laughed. "I learned it at school. So come on, let's walk across the road, calmly. No pushing and shoving through the marching soldiers."

The men did exactly as he instructed, crossing the busy road in twos and threes, not all at once and together. Charlie followed the men with Kenny, who said, "I'd give anything for a cig and a cold beer. But to tell you the truth, I'd prefer a kip. It would do me more good."

"Me, too. I wish I could lie down right here and go to sleep," Charlie answered. "Aha!" he then exclaimed, and waved back to the lance sergeant who was grinning ear to ear. Through the stand of trees a house was now visible.

Within minutes Charlie was leaning on a wooden gate, talking to the farmer who owned the property, which had not been visible from the road.

He looked wary when he first saw Charlie and

his troops, but Charlie started to speak French immediately. He said he was English and introduced himself, explained he was taking his men to Dunkirk. He asked the farmer if they could rest at the farm for the night if he had a barn. He added that his men were at the point of exhaustion after fighting the Germans in the trenches.

The farmer spit, and exclaimed angrily, **"Les boches! Merde!"** He opened the gate, welcomed Charlie and his men. Leading them around the back of the farmhouse, he showed them a big old barn. It was full of bales of hay, a water trough, and old harnesses hanging on a wall. **"Voilà!"** He grinned and told Charlie they were welcome, that he was going to bring them blankets, water, and bread.

Charlie thanked him profusely; he told his men to find a spot and settle down, explained they could rest here for the night. It was with relief that they slipped off their haversacks and sat down on the bales of hay; a couple of them fell asleep almost immediately.

The farmer was as good as his word. He soon returned with his wife and son. The farmer was carrying two large pitchers of water, and his wife and the boy were holding trays of assorted old mugs and glasses. The farmer's wife poured the water, and she and her son passed the mugs and glasses around. The farmer left, returning a few minutes later with several long baguettes, and large chunks of cheese on several platters.

Charles thanked the farmer and his family, and the men tucked into the cheese and bread, as well as some of the food they had brought from the abandoned truck.

"The farmer told me they hadn't seen any German troops. Yet," Charlie said. "But I promised him we'd be out of here tomorrow morning early. He was very understanding of our plight."

"I could tell," Kenny said. "He was charmed, no, perhaps 'flattered' is a better word... because you spoke French, Charlie. They like that, you know, the French."

"It helps to know French in France," Charlie said, and made a face. "Oh, you know what I mean."

"This bloody haversack is heavy," Kenny said the next moment. "I'm going to dump everything in it."

"But not here," Charlie warned swiftly. "We can't put the farmer at risk. The Jerries might arrive and find your stuff. They'd know at once it was English, and wonder about it."

Charlie lay awake on his bales of hay, listening to his men sleeping. They had pretty much all passed out from total exhaustion hours ago and were enjoying their first real sleep in several weeks. There were little noises, light snoring, and rustling, but for the most part the barn was quiet.

Moonlight filtered in through a small window set high on one of the barn walls, and pushing himself to his feet Charlie crept across the floor, opened the huge door carefully, and slipped out.

He took several deep breaths. The night air was cool on this May night, and refreshing. Glancing up at the full moon floating high in the dark sky, he realized what a lovely night it was. And the quietness was soothing. What a relief not to be pounded by the noise of gunfire, rifle shots, and bombs exploding.

Silence is golden, he thought, remembering an old saying his mother had used when they were growing up. **His mother.** His beautiful, adoring mother.

He knew he must keep himself safe so he could go home to her. If he didn't make it she would never forgive him. He smiled at the thought. Evelyne Bourne, Kenny's mother, wouldn't forgive **him**, if her son didn't make it, either. Maybe all mothers feel the same way, he decided.

He took a cigarette and lit it, inhaled deeply, sat down on a low stone wall to enjoy his smoke. The farmer had warned them not to even think of lighting a cigarette in the barn full of hay and they had abided by his rule.

Thoughts of his sister crept into his mind. Alicia had been gung ho for joining the ATS, but had suddenly changed her mind and enrolled with the Red Cross. She chose the division that served abroad, much to their parents' horror, who imagined her working in the trenches and getting killed. But she was apparently still in London, undergoing training. Charlie knew why she had chosen to help make the wounded well. She had always been a caring and compassionate child, worrying about their sick pets and any wild little thing that got caught in a trap. She would make a good nurse; she had an affinity for it…in a certain sense it was a calling.

He heard a noise and glanced across the yard. In the moonlight he saw Kenny slipping out of the barn; his best friend walked over to join him on the wall.

"I'm not used to sleeping this much," Kenny said in a low voice, and lit a cigarette. "I suppose because we've kept going on only a few hours in the last few weeks."

"I know what you mean. I feel the same, but I did have a deep sleep, and it's done me good," Charlie confided.

"What time do you plan to leave here?" Kenny now asked.

"I'd like to be on our way to Dunkirk by five or

six o'clock. The sooner we're back at head-quarters the better I'll feel."

"Do you think we'll be evacuated immed-iately? After all, the Coldstream Guards were the first regiment to arrive in France. We've been here the longest. By rights we should go out first."

Charlie chuckled quietly. "We'll probably be the last! But we'll soon know. If we start out early today we should be back on the coast by this afternoon."

"The men will make a big effort, Charlie."

Kenny sat smoking in silence for a short while, then said in a quiet but intense tone, "If anything happens to me and I don't make it, please tell my parents and my sister that I loved them very much."

"I promise. But don't think like that, Kenny. You're going to make it. You're a tough sod like me. And I'm **definitely** going to make it."

Kenny ignored this comment, and continued, "And I want you to thank Cecily, and tell her how much her support has meant to me over the years. Hiring that tutor for me and then giving me one of her scholarships so I could go to Oxford was the most wonderful thing that ever happened to me in my life."

"I will. But you'll be doing that yourself. We're going to be evacuated within the next forty-eight hours, Kenny."

"I believe that, too," Kenny answered. "But I just needed to get that off my chest, to say these words aloud."

Charlie nodded, and glanced up at the sky. Dawn was breaking, and it looked as if it was going to be a nice day. A nice day for walking back to Dunkirk, going to headquarters, and planning their evacuation. Which was more than likely planned already. We'll make it home, Charlie thought. **We must.**

Forty-nine

Their second in command, Major Tommy Riley, had sent them out on a recce, and Charlie was happy that he had. Like the major, he was all for checking and double-checking everything, and most especially things which were happening at the moment in Dunkirk.

There were thousands of troops everywhere: the British and the French, their ally; and the Germans, enemy of them both. And any situation at all could change in seconds. The Wehrmacht army was fast encroaching on Dunkirk, hitting all the different perimeters, and the Luftwaffe kept up constant attacks, bombing the town and the vessels anchored out at sea.

Kenny had been assigned to come with him and, at the last minute, the major had told Joe Wortley to accompany them.

The lance sergeant was in the Regular Army and had been in the Coldstream Guards since he was seventeen. An old hand, one of the best, just like most of the Regular soldiers who had made the army their career.

Charlie and Kenny had always paid strict attention to anything he had to say to them, and to anyone else, for that matter. Joe had taken to them the moment they had arrived for duty, and went out of his way to help them, teach them as much as he could. He knew good lads when he saw them.

Walking through the town, they had noticed that the beaches were a bit less crowded this afternoon, and out at sea, in the deep water, there was a big convoy of British battleships, destroyers, and other large vessels. They were reinforcements which had sailed in after the huge Royal Navy losses in the last couple of days.

The hospital ships were also floating out there, and were clearly marked with large red crosses. Not that this emblem prevented the Luftwaffe from bombing them on a regular basis. Most of the patients on board were killed along with doctors, nurses, and the crews. British casualties in all the services had been enormous. Such a lot of lives had been lost, it was heartbreaking.

Charlie was aware that the losses had been caused by torpedoes from U-boats and sub-marines, as well as the planes, and the fighting in the trenches. Unfortunately the Royal Air

Force had been badly decimated. After losing their last airbase at Merville in France, they now had to cross the Channel, which took much more flying time. But they were a good match for the Stukas.

This was a most deadly war, one being fought on the land, on the sea, and in the air, and against a vile and evil man and his violent regime, the Third Reich. Charlie understood they must win it at all costs.

"Let's walk down to the mole," Joe suggested, referring to the Dunkirk jetty. "I know someone who works for Vice Admiral William Wake-Walker, and he's often taking a stroll at this time. His name's Major Jack Remmington, and he's a mine of information."

"I know of the admiral but never met him," Charlie said. "He's in charge of directing shipping off Dunkirk, but I don't know of Major Remmington."

"I think we can pick up some bits and pieces, useful stuff, if he's around," Joe answered.

"Let's go and look for him," Kenny interjected. "I'd like to know if we're really leaving tonight. You never know, they might have got us mixed up with the Grenadier Guards—"

"Let's not forget our motto, **Nulli Secundus.** Second to None," Charlie said. "We'll be on a ship, you'll see...don't be such a doubting Thomas, Kenny. Be like me, an optimistic Oliver."

"I've never heard of that particular saying," Kenny said.

Charlie just laughed.

Joe Wortley had been right. Major Remmington was on the jetty, smoking a cigarette and gazing out to sea. He turned around when he heard the men walking along the mole, and his face lit up when he saw Joe.

After they had greeted each other warmly, Joe introduced his companions. "This is Captain Charlie Stanton and Lieutenant Kenny Bourne. Coldstreamers like me. We came out for a last look at Dunkirk. Hopefully we're leaving tonight."

Remmington nodded. "I believe you are—" He suddenly broke off, all of his attention directed at the sea.

"Well, I never thought I'd see this! I can hardly believe it!" Remmington exclaimed. "Oh my God, what a wonderful sight...for sore eyes. For any eyes. It's like a miracle."

"What are you talking about, sir?" Joe asked, sounding perplexed.

"Out there. Look out there, Sergeant."

Joe followed the major's gaze. So did Charlie and Kenny, and they all caught their breath and uttered exclamations of surprise and puzzlement.

"It's like a little armada," Kenny said, his surprise lingering.

"A little **mighty** armada, more like," Charlie

announced.

Major Remmington nodded, then smiled hugely. "They listened to Admiral Ramsay's appeal. He asked them to come. He said, **'Come and help our boys get off the beaches. Come and rescue them. They're stranded in Dunkirk.'** And they have come. To get the boys off the beaches...the citizens of England, civilians, ordinary men heard the admiral's call and responded."

The major straightened up. "It's **them**...they're the **great** in the name **Great Britain**...the people. **Our people**." He saluted the small craft coming toward them slowly, and so did the other three men.

Charlie said, "I can't believe the craft I'm seeing. Motor yachts, launches, fishing boats, pleasure steamers, canoes, ferries, barges from the canals, dinghies, even lifeboats. It truly **is** a mighty armada of little boats. What a beautiful sight."

"And they'll come to the mole. They can sail in easily, into the shallows. Whereas the big ships can't. And they'll soon be filled with our troops, and they'll be towed out by tugs...out to the ships that will carry them home to safety," Major Remmington said.

As the mighty little armada drew closer, Charlie was so moved by the sight, the meaning behind this extraordinary action, he choked up. Filled with emotion, he was unable to speak for a few moments.

Eventually, he said in a quiet tone, "These ordinary people left England immediately when they were called, and all they had were their mighty hearts and anything that sailed. And sail they did. Right into this hellfire that is Dunkirk. They **will** rescue us boys on the beaches, and they will be heroes, each and every one. But they'll brush off our accolades and our thanks. They'll simply smile modestly and say they just did the right thing."

Later that night, around seven o'clock, the First Battalion and Second Battalion of the Coldstream Guards marched to the mole, where they were to be ferried from the Dunkirk jetty out to the big ships.

As they passed one of the beaches, Charlie and Kenny were astounded by the number of soldiers from other regiments waiting there. Quiet, orderly, patient. Just standing in long lines. Waiting. Waiting. Waiting. For their turn. Exhausted, battle-scarred, and hopeful.

"That queue must be five miles long," Charlie muttered to Kenny, who did not reply. He could only wonder how the Royal Navy and the little boats would be able to move and save them all.

Major Remmington and a number of naval

officers were waiting on the mole, and quickly explained to the first troops to come up how they would commence the evacuation.

Already docked at the jetty was a whaler and one of the civilian armada boats, a motor launch manned by the owner, an accountant from Dover, and two of his sailing friends. The launch was named **The Flying Dutchman.**

"This is what's going to happen," Remmington announced in a clear, loud voice to the soldiers. "**The Flying Dutchman** launch will attach to a whaler and pull it in as close to the jetty as is safe. Men will get into the whaler and the launch, **The Flying Dutchman,** will then pull the whaler out to sea to the big ships. The launch will return to pick up more men. But in the meantime, as the first men are leaving, another armada boat will soon arrive attached to a whaler, and do the same thing. It's a kind of relay service, and it's worked well since we started at five."

Remmington grimaced. "Well, we did have one accident earlier, when a whaler overturned, because it was choppy and windy. But since then, it's been a smooth operation. The weather's improved. No wind and the sea is calm."

Group after group of Coldstream Guards went off in the whaler and launch, in an orderly manner, and after an hour Charlie's platoon, along with Charlie and Kenny, went down into the whaler and launch. Joe Wortley and another platoon would follow right behind in another whaler when it arrived.

Once they were away from the jetty and out to sea, Charlie looked back at Dunkirk and shook his head sadly. The town was fiercely burning, the air thick with acrid smoke; there was the smell of diesel oil, cordite, and another strange smell he couldn't quite define. When he asked Kenny, who was sitting next to him in the launch, what the weird smell was, Kenny whispered, "Blood. Gallons of it from the dead and the dying."

Kenny turned his head, looked over the edge of the launch. "All of them are floating around us. Look at the sea, it's red with blood."

Charlie did so and was stunned. He had been concentrating on Dunkirk going up in flames, looking ahead, not down into the water. A sense of immense anguish gripped him as he saw all these British soldiers floating every-where, and understood then why the launch was moving at a certain pace, not quite as fast as he had expected. The cries of the wounded and dying men made his heart clench with sorrow. **What a waste.**

A moment later he was ducking down as the Luftwaffe planes swept in, machine-gunning the little armada boats and in the distance the big ships.

As the planes drew closer to **The Flying Dutchman,** Charlie shouted to Kenny and his men, "Stay down! The bloody Jerries are bombing the destroyers. And our men climbing the nets on the sides of the ships. And us, too."

Several explosions rocked the whaler and the launch, but doggedly the three civilian men ploughed on undeterred, determined to carry out as many rescues as possible.

Charlie knew that earlier that week, on May 29, the Germans had targeted ten British ships, five in the harbor. Three big raids had put seven out of action. The damage and carnage were enormous.

The admirals in Dover and London decided the remaining ships had to be pulled out to protect them. But they were returned to action swiftly, in order to speed up the evacuation.

Today was May 31. Now he remembered that the rescue was supposed to end by June 1. **Tomorrow**. Would they all make it?

Unexpectedly the Luftwaffe raid ended and the planes flew off. **The Flying Dutchman** increased its speed at once and it pulled farther out to sea, away from all the dead bodies, the massive wreckage, and the sinking British ships.

Once **The Flying Dutchman** arrived at a destroyer with nets flung over the sides for the men to climb, Charlie felt a rush of relief. All of his platoon were in good shape physically, if somewhat tired. He knew they would make it up the nets without too much difficulty.

Charlie was pleased when he saw Kenny and his platoon scrambling up the sides of the destroyer. He went to join them. Charlie jumped forward, off the whaler, and landed on the nets, clung to them with both hands. Finding his balance, he began to climb up the side of the ship, going as fast as he could; he was in better shape than he thought.

Then it happened. Luftwaffe planes returned and were circling back in toward the destroyer and the machine guns started firing at the soldiers on the nets. Easy targets.

Charlie knew he had been hit in both legs. He felt the thud of the bullets penetrating them and then the pain. He pulled himself up the nets with his hands as best he could; his legs were now useless. At one moment, he stopped to catch his breath before moving on, and unexpectedly saw the face of a sailor looking down at him in concern.

"Having problems, mate?" the sailor shouted.

"It's my legs. They're wounded. Useless."

"Try to keep moving up. I'll get some help. We'll have to pull the nets up and you with them. Just hang on."

Most of the men who had been in front of Charlie were now off his section of the nets. He was alone. He made an effort to glance down, and did so with some difficulty. Thankfully there were no other soldiers below him, which meant the weight on the nets was lessened.

Suddenly the sailor was back with seven members of his crew. "Grip the nets hard," the sailor shouted. "We're going to drag up this section of the nets. They're heavy."

Charlie was beginning to feel weak; he knew he was in danger of falling off. Or bleeding to death. Nonetheless, he hung on, gripping the nets. He closed his eyes and prayed.

Eight strong sailors got the nets moving and slowly they pulled them up to the ship's rail. Finally two sailors were able to grab Charlie and get him onto the deck.

"We did it!" one of the sailors exclaimed.

"Thanks," Charlie muttered in a weak voice. "Captain Charlie Stanton, Coldstream Guards..." After uttering these few words he lost consciousness.

Within seconds medics were surrounding him, lifting him onto a stretcher. One of the doctors said, "His trousers are soaking wet with blood. Let's get him down to the operating room."

Land of Hope and Glory

Land of Hope and Glory,
Mother of the Free,
How shall we extol thee,
who are born of thee?
Wider still and wider shall thy
bounds be set;
God who made thee mighty,
make thee mightier yet,
God who made thee mighty,
make thee mightier yet.

—the Finale of Elgar's **Coronation Ode**
to music derived from the
Pomp and Circumstance March,
op. 39, No. 1 in D major

Fifty

Operation Dynamo, code name for the evacuation of Dunkirk, ended on June 4, 1940.

Almost four hundred thousand English and French soldiers had been rescued from the beaches in France. The success of the operation was mainly due to the Royal Navy and the 222 ships they had used, plus the daring little armada operated by brave civilians, which numbered over eight hundred vessels of all types. It was soon considered to be the greatest evacuation of troops in history.

That same day Winston Churchill spoke to the House of Commons and the nation. At first he told them they must be very careful not to assign to this deliverance the attributes of a victory. "Wars are not won by evacuation," he said.

Moments later his great gift of oratory flowed forth in full force, when he uttered the noblest words, perhaps his greatest, which would live on in history.

"We shall not flag or fail. We shall go on to the end, we shall fight in France, we shall fight on the seas and oceans, we shall fight with growing confidence and growing strength in the air, we shall defend our Island, whatever the cost may be, we shall fight on the beaches, we shall fight on the landing grounds, we shall fight in the fields and in the streets, we shall fight in the hills; we shall never surrender."

Churchill's words always inspired and reassured the British people. There might be naysayers in the establishment who did not like him, but the people loved him, had long put their faith in him. He gave them courage and reinforced their steadfastness with his mighty words.

An aristocrat, as the grandson of the Duke of Marlborough, he might be, but he had the common touch. And he understood that all-conquering spirit bred in the bone of the British, and he reached out to that, and encouraged it.

The Inghams and the Swanns had long understood that only Churchill could bring the country to victory. Knowing that he was at the helm of their government made them feel more secure than anyone else ever could.

Diedre, in particular, knew what a brilliant man he was, recognized that he had enormous vision. For years he had seen the threat of Hitler and the Third Reich, and nobody would listen.

Now they did. Only he could save Western civilization from the barbaric evil of the Nazis; William felt the same way as she did.

Her thoughts went to the prime minister now as she stared at the piece of paper Tony Jenkins had just handed her. It said: **Seelöwe also fly. In June**. And that was it. Staring at Tony, she said, "**Seelöwe** is the German word for sea lion. 'Sea lion also fly. In June.'" She frowned, then exclaimed, "'German will fly. In June.' It's a warning. We're going to be invaded anytime now." She glanced at the calendar on her desk. It was Thursday, June 6. "Where did this come from?"

"Our contact in the Vatican. I'm absolutely certain it's from Canaris."

"So am I." Diedre rose up, and walked across her office. "Let's go and see William."

A moment later William was reading the message and instantly agreed with them. "I'd better go right over to see the PM. He has to know about this. Although I do believe, with his enormous foresight, he's expecting the Wehrmacht to invade us at any moment. He's been pushing Lord Beaverbrook to improve the production of planes and ships, and working endlessly to prepare the country."

"Actually Beaverbrook's been rather good," Tony interjected. "Planes are being made faster."

"I'd better check that I can see the PM." William picked up the phone. Diedre sat down in a chair; Tony excused himself and disappeared.

After William had spoken to someone he knew in the prime minister's office, he stood up. "I am to go. **Now.**" He smiled at her. "Canaris will forever be **my** hero, and I know you'll agree with me that he is brave."

"I do indeed. He's been extraordinary. He's always endeavored to give us some time to properly prepare for bad events about to happen."

They left the room together. William kissed her on the cheek, and said, "See you shortly."

Returning to her own office, Diedre sat down at her desk and thought about Wilhelm Canaris, head of Abwehr, German military intelligence, his hatred of Hitler and the Third Reich. He was truly risking everything by helping the British, as were many of his colleagues and a number of German generals, those who also believed Hitler was ruining Germany beyond reparation.

She thought of the terrifying attack on Poland last September, almost a year ago now. The Polish people had been taken totally by surprise when their skies were blackened by the Luftwaffe planes, hundreds of them, and their streets demolished by the German Panzer divisions. Poland had been utterly destroyed in less than three weeks. Most of its citizens slaughtered, its Catholic Church crushed, and all of its clergy murdered in cold blood. There was no such thing as a Catholic priest left in Poland. When Hitler had declared, "We do not want any other God but Germany," he had meant it. Gone, too, were the aristocracy, intelligentsia, everyone of any talent in every field of endeavor, anyone of any caliber.

That's why we declared war on Germany, Diedre now thought. Some good it did. They would be next. She knew Canaris had been so stunned, horrified, and sickened by what he himself had witnessed in Poland, he had become physically ill. And his hatred of Hitler had grown and grown...

There was a light knock on the door, and Tony came in. "I've remembered something," he said. "Do you have a minute?"

She nodded. "I was just thinking about what happened in Poland last September, and the way Hitler had all of the Catholic priests killed and the Catholic Church totally destroyed. No wonder the Vatican is so anti-Nazi."

"I agree with you; not many people know that, though. When I was in Spain recently, Valiant made an offhand remark. He said that when the cardinals selected Pacelli to be pope, they had chosen the candidate who was the best politician, and a clever statesman. Because that was what they needed in this day and age."

"That doesn't surprise me, and there **is** a secret service within the Vatican. We know that because we deal with it."

There was a moment of silence, before Tony said, "Anyway, that comment went out of my head, and I only just remembered it. I thought I ought to tell you."

"I'm glad you did. It doesn't seem like an important comment from Canaris. But I think it is. He was telling us where we stand with Pope Pius XII...he's a fellow traveler. Of ours, shall we say?"

Tony smiled. "The pope will fight indirectly, but he will fight Hitler."

"That he will. He must if he's going to win. The Nazis want to destroy his church all over the world. He will defend it with all his might, whatever it takes."

"I have a feeling the Holy See is a hotbed of intrigue," Tony said. "But they certainly manage to be a good courier system for us."

"Indeed. Have you heard from Étoile? Did she get things right?"

"Funnily enough, I had a call about an hour ago. She's fully settled in Annecy, which is close enough to the border if she has to make a quick exit. All is A-okay with her."

Diedre was pleased to know that Étoile, her asset in France, was now in Annecy near the

Swiss border. On the other hand, she might
have to move to the south, the way the war in
France was going at this moment. She would
give some thought to that situation over the
weekend. The Wehrmacht were fighting the
French in the Dunkirk area, and the British had
left troops behind to assist their ally in the fight.
Provence was more than likely a good location
for Étoile.

Émeraude, her other asset, had remained in
Paris where he had family; she had no worries
about him. At the moment.

Unexpectedly, a totally different subject came
into her head. Did Canaris actually **know** Pope
Pius XII? Or had that remark he had made to
Tony really just been an offhand comment?
Earlier she had thought it was another message
to her, that the pope was one of them in principle. But how would Canaris know that, if he
was not personally acquainted with the pope?

She had a good memory; it had always served
her well, and now she looked back to last year,
to the spring of 1939. Unless she was wrong,
Cardinal Eugenio Pacelli had been consecrated
as the new pope in Rome around March or
April. He was a Roman, born and bred, that she
knew. And when he was made pope he had
been secretary of state of the Vatican.

That was about the extent of her knowledge.
She got up, went into Tony's office next door,

and asked, "Does Canaris know the pope personally?"

"I don't know. But I can find out. I can do a bit of digging," Tony answered, and gestured to a chair.

"Whose garden? We have to be careful," she said, sitting down.

"My cousin's. On my father's side. His mother is Catholic and he was brought up a Catholic, and, in fact, he's a Catholic priest."

"And here I was thinking all the Welsh were off to chapel every Sunday, singing their hearts out, a bell in every tooth."

Tony had the good grace to laugh. "I can phone him if you like."

"That's a good idea."

"What exactly do you want me to ask him? I can't very well bring up Canaris's name, now can I?"

"No, that would be unwise. Tell him you have to write something for your boss about the pope and what does he know that you might not. Something unusual perhaps. Or unique, special. Even a tidbit or two, to give some verve to the piece. Go on, pick up the phone. Do it now," Diedre said, sounding eager.

His curiosity aroused at her interest in this matter, Tony did as she suggested. He telephoned his cousin, and a moment later he was saying, "Oh hello, Ivor. It's Tony. How are you?"

After a little chitchat, Tony got to the point. "Listen, I could use your help, which is why I phoned you, actually. I've got to write something for my boss. About your boss. By that I mean Pope Pius XII. I need some background stuff, something unique, some sort of anecdote maybe, to spice up the piece."

He listened to his cousin, then began to laugh, "Well, I know you wouldn't know anything spicy about **him.** Perhaps unusual...a hobby? For instance, has he ever traveled abroad?"

At the other end of the phone in Cardiff, Ivor exclaimed, "Of course, yes. He's even been to America!"

"**America.** My goodness, how interesting, and has the pope been to any other countries?"

"To Germany, that I do know, because he was in positions there," Ivor explained with a hint of pride.

"Positions, **where** in Germany?" Tony asked, staring at Diedre.

Ivor again responded immediately. "He was in Munich, and it was official, if I remember right. He was also nuncio in Berlin in the late twenties, but listen, I don't know much else."

"Well, thanks, old chap. This is something to go on, and if you recollect anything else, give me a shout at home this weekend. And thanks again."

They said good-bye and hung up. Tony said,

"When he was Cardinal Pacelli, the pope was nuncio in Berlin in the twenties. That's what my cousin just told me, and that's interesting, isn't it?"

"Yes, and perhaps that's why he knows Valiant. From Berlin. From what I recall reading about him, I think Cardinal Pacelli was quite social earlier in his life, knew all kinds of fancy folk. You could do a bit more digging. With a very discreet spade."

"Can I ask why you're so interested in this matter?" Tony lifted a brow.

"I like to know about the relationships people have, who their friends are. It tells me a lot. Don't forget, Canaris knows Franco and very well from what we've discerned. Our friend seems to think he has so much influence with Franco, he can keep Spain neutral."

"You don't have to remind me. Now Valiant has the ear of **El Caudillo** and the pope..." He let the sentence slide away when there was a knock on the door. William Lawson walked in swiftly, and closed the door behind him.

"How was the PM?" Diedre asked.

"Fighting fit. He sends his thanks to my unit... that's you two. I showed him the paper, explained our theory, and he seemed to agree." William sat down in the chair next to Diedre.

"Did he ask how you came by the information?" Tony fixed his eyes on William, his scrutiny intent.

"Not exactly. He said, 'A good source?' and I answered, 'Yes.' I added it came from the Vatican, and he nodded...gave me a very pointed look, as if he knows all about Vatican spies. He wanted to know if he could pass it by C at MI6, and I obviously agreed."

"So did he call Menzies?" Tony said.

"He did indeed. In front of me. He told C I was there with him and explained why. MI6 had no information about sea lions. So C apparently said. But he added he would look into it. At once. Before I left, the prime minister thanked me again for everything we do, then announced that in his opinion the Germans would invade us in approximately a month. When I asked him if that date was official, he shook his head, and told me it was his gut instinct, adding that Hitler had to deal with France before he could invade us."

"That sounds about right, Will, because usually Valiant gives us a month's warning," Diedre said softly.

Fifty-one

Daphne sat at her desk in the conservatory, going over a list of things she had to do today. It was a sunny June morning and, as the sun filtered in, she felt a little frisson of something… **relief,** that was it. A good feeling to be here in this room she had made her own years ago. Because it was **normal,** an everyday thing, now that she was helping to run Cavendon again, from the desk she had always called her command post. Being busy helped to make her worries go away if only for a short while…

"Daphne!"

Hugo's voice startled her, made her jump, and she turned around in the chair. Her husband was hurrying across the floor and she stood up at once. He was as white as bleached bone and the shocked look on his face frightened her.

"Whatever is it?" she cried, running to him. "What's wrong? Oh my God! No, not Charlie! He's not dead, is he?" As she spoke the shaking began and she couldn't hold a limb still.

"No!" Hugo exclaimed. "No, not dead. But he's badly wounded. We just received this letter from the army." He showed her the envelope, and went on. "Charlie was rescued at Dunkirk, but he was shot in both legs. They were severely injured." Pausing, Hugo swallowed and said in a quavering voice, "They had to amputate his left leg."

"Oh God, no! No, not Charlie. Oh my God. It's ruined his life."

Hugo took hold of her, pulled her into his arms. "I know it's horrendous. But he still has one leg which they say will heal well. It hasn't ruined his life, I promise you. Knowing Charlie, he'll meet the challenge."

"But what will he do? How will he walk? He'll be on crutches, won't he?" She gazed at him through a blur of tears.

"Only at the beginning," Hugo answered, endeavoring to calm her, even though he was extremely shaken up himself. "Once the good leg heals he will be fitted for an artificial leg, and seemingly they are very good."

At this moment their daughter Annabel came into the conservatory looking for Daphne, and when she saw that her parents were upset, she rushed over to them, clutching at her mother's arm. "Is Charlie dead?" their youngest child asked tearfully, always expecting the worst in this war.

Hugo and Daphne looked at each other aghast, and pulled themselves together at once, because Hugo knew he could say emphatically, "No! No, he's not dead, Annabel, thank God. He's badly wounded but he is alive, and that's wonderful. **He's alive!**"

Hugo then explained to Annabel that his left leg had been amputated above the knee because gangrene had set in and it traveled fast. Fortunately the army surgeon had been able to save his right leg; he was recovering in a military hospital where he would have the proper medical care and attention.

Annabel had listened attentively, and asked, "When will he be able to come home?"

"Not for some months," Hugo answered. "The amputated leg has to heal, and then he will be fitted for an artificial leg. I've heard they are excellent."

"Knowing Charlie, he'll handle it well," Annabel said, smiling at her father and then her mother. "Shall I go and ask Lane to make us some tea?"

"Why not, darling," Daphne said, having managed to calm herself. Turning to Hugo she continued, "Let's go and sit on the sofa and talk about the future for Charlie. After all, he will be able to write, even work on a newspaper, perhaps, as he's always wanted to do."

Hugo looked at his wife, and nodded, his pride

in her enormous. Daphne could always cope, no matter what.

Since that day, at the beginning of June, Daphne had thanked God every night for protecting their eldest son, for letting him live. Charlie had finally written them a cheerful letter. In it he had explained that he would eventually be fitted with an artificial leg. These wonderfully made legs were lightweight, he had said, and he knew he would learn to walk properly, once it was strapped to him around his waist. He would be mobile again, he had promised them in his letter.

She and Hugo knew that the loss of a limb was a most horrendous thing for a young man to bear. But it had happened and Charlie was accepting of his fate. She and Hugo knew it would not change his positive personality or slow him down. They were certain of that, as was the entire family.

It was the middle of June and still they had not been invaded by the Nazis, but they would be soon. The country was well prepared. And so was Cavendon.

Six months ago Harry Swann had received his papers, and although he was now forty-two, he had chosen to enlist in the Royal Air Force. He was not flying planes, but manning the all-important radar at an airfield in the south, alongside the WAAFs. The Women's Auxiliary Air Force was not allowed to fly, although many of them wanted to be pilots. Too dangerous, they had been told by the top brass. And that was that.

Miles was exempt because he was running an agricultural estate; most of the young men at Cavendon had gone to war, but they had been replaced by the lovely Land Army girls. These young women were helping Miles and working hard; the women from the three villages were doing their bit as usual, and the Women's Institute was in full swing. They tended the allotments, bottled fruit and vegetables, made jam, knitted socks and balaclavas for the troops, and did their best to keep everyone cheerful.

We're lucky living in the country, Daphne suddenly thought. We have access to food more easily than people in the towns and cities what with the scarcities, ration books, and queues. The older men still working on the estate caught fish, shot birds and rabbits; others raised chickens. Mostly for the eggs and often for the pot. Her father had always insisted from the outset of the war that everyone in the three villages have their fair share of everything produced on their land, and it was distributed by Alice and Evelyne every week.

Papa. She thought of him now, still marveling at the way he had suddenly become himself again. It had happened after Charlotte had broken her leg and he felt the need to look after her. She remembered how he had bucked up at once, taking charge. He had been particularly thrilled to see Diedre married to William, as well. Those two were coming up from London tonight; DeLacy and Dulcie were already at Cavendon, checking the paintings in storage, and James would arrive tomorrow from Catterick Camp, where he was shooting a propaganda film for the army.

Daphne had been looking forward to this weekend. The sound of footsteps cut into her thoughts and she turned her head. Much to her pleasure she saw Mrs. Alice coming into the room, jumped up and went to greet her. They had been extremely close for years. Daphne would never forget that it was Alice Swann, Cecily's mother, who had saved her life and her sanity when she was seventeen.

After a warm embrace, Alice said, "I have wonderful news, Lady Daphne. Evelyne has just told me that Kenny is out of danger. The operation on his back was successful. I ran up here straightaway to tell you."

"This is wonderful news, Mrs. Alice, and I shall write to Charlie tonight. He'll be thrilled to know Kenny's going to get better. He's been worried."

Alice said, "Give Mr. Charlie my love, m'lady."

Daphne nodded, went and sat at her desk. She motioned for Alice to sit in the chair, which she did, and said, "There are a couple of other things I'd like to mention, Lady Daphne. The first is Lady Gwendolyn. To be honest, I don't think she likes the new housekeeper, Mrs. Raymond. That's the impression she gives me. So I was wondering if Peggy Swift might be interested. Oh dear, I should've said Peggy Lane."

Daphne laughed. "I make the same mistake all the time. I can ask Peggy, perhaps she would like to help out. But I do think it would depend on Gordon. Now that he's the head butler he might not want his wife to work."

"That's what Walter said," Alice confided. "But we can give it a try, can't we? And by the way, I just saw Hanson. He asked me to tell you he would be honored to help out with tea tomorrow." Alice smiled and shook her head. "He's bored to death, I should think, and wants to keep his hand in anyway."

"Fortunately, Gordon Lane doesn't mind. He loves Hanson. They've been working side by side for years and Hanson trained him."

"I keep an eye on Lady Gwendolyn, and she's doing quite well, especially since the weather's warm. But—" Alice broke off, hesitating.

"But what?" Daphne asked swiftly, frowning. "Isn't she all right?"

"She's pretty much the same, but I've noticed a change in her in the last week, m'lady. She does a lot of daydreaming, it seems to me. Sits in her chair, looking off into the distance... faraway, sort of. She really is old now."

"I know. And I appreciate that you go to see her every day. She told me how much she enjoys your visits."

"I want to tell you something else, Lady Daphne," Alice began and stopped abruptly, as if seeking words.

Daphne said, "Don't break off again. Please tell me what's wrong. I can see from your face that there's a problem."

"I'm not sure if it's a problem. As you know, a couple of days ago I was asked to look after a new evacuee. The girl who'd been staying with us went back to Liverpool, to move to America with her parents. The new girl is sweet. Her name is Victoria; she's shy, a bit tentative, rather quiet. Anyway, I saw her totally undressed for the first time last night, and I was shocked. She has a lot of fading bruises on her body. I think she's been physically abused, my lady, where she was before."

Daphne sat upright in the chair, and exclaimed, "Did you say anything to her?"

"No, I didn't. She suddenly realized I'd seen the bruises and put a towel around herself, looked at me in a peculiar way. As if she were embarrassed. She'd been taking a bath."

Daphne said, "Don't say anything to her, ignore it, and behave very normally. What you need to do is make her feel welcome and safe, put her at ease, and eventually she may confide in you. I honestly think that is the best thing. You mustn't mention the bruises."

"No, I won't," Alice assured her.

The arrival of Lord Mowbray ended Daphne's conversation with Mrs. Alice, who after wishing the earl good morning excused herself.

"I'll speak with you later, Mrs. Alice," Daphne murmured, and rose, went to embrace her father.

Standing away from him, a moment later, she said, "Good news, Papa. Kenny is going to be all right. The operation on his back was successful, and he will walk again. Eventually. Mrs. Alice just got the news from his mother."

"And good news it is indeed," Charles Ingham replied, and took hold of her arm. "Let's go for a walk. It's such a lovely day."

"Yes, of course, Papa." She looked at him surreptitiously, having detected an odd note in his voice. Sadness? Regret? Or disappointment? She wasn't sure.

Once they were outside, he said, "Let's head for the lake, Daphne. I feel the need to stretch my legs and breathe in some fresh air. English air. To me the rest of the world has a foul smell today."

Glancing up at him, she asked swiftly, "What's wrong? You sound disappointed, even a little...**bitter**." When he made no response, she said quietly, "That's not like you, Papa. 'Bitterness' is not a word I ever associate with you."

He stopped, turned to look at her. His beautiful Daphne who had always brought such joy to his life, had been his mainstay many times. Her great beauty was still there, appeared to some people to be almost delicate, fragile. Yet he knew that she had a will of iron and a spine of steel. Nothing would ever defeat her. And her stoicism and courage after she had learned of Charlie's badly damaged legs, and the amputation of one, had been quite remarkable.

He didn't actually address her remark, but went on, "The British fought so hard to help the French repel and beat the Germans when they invaded France, and Dunkirk was a magnificent evacuation. Thousands of French troops were rescued..." A long sigh escaped him, and he said, "And it's the French who have disappointed me..." He left his sentence unfinished.

His words startled her. Daphne exclaimed, "My God, don't tell me the French have surrendered? We have our troops over there, don't we?"

"Yes. The Second British Expeditionary Force went to help again. And, no, they haven't surrendered. But they have been grousing loudly about us, saying we retreated without telling them, that they went into the fray, that we left French troops behind on the beaches. We did, and some British troops as well. But we certainly didn't betray them, as they're suggesting."

"It's the pot calling the kettle black. Hugo told me that a lot of our troops coming off the beaches have been complaining about the way the French soldiers behaved."

He laughed quite unexpectedly, and drew her close. "My lovely, practical, down-to-earth daughter. What you're saying is forget it, Papa. It's just tit for tat."

Daphne joined in his laughter, and slipped her arm through his. "That's right. We've more important things to think about. Charlie, when he comes home, for one. He will need us to be there for him, and I know we will."

"The entire family will give him their support, have no fear. And by the way, who is coming here this weekend?"

"Diedre and William. Cecily. Everyone else is here. Not Alicia. She's working round the clock, taking a nursing course with the Red Cross, as you know. And some of your grandchildren are away at school."

He nodded. A smile flickered in his eyes. "I thought it had been a little quieter lately. With the boys off at Colet Court or Eton. Oh look, darling, at the swans. How beautiful they are, floating on the lake. They mate for life."

"I know. Like Hugo and me...we've been mates for life, thank goodness."

"I second that," her father said.

Later that day, just before dinner, Daphne went looking for her father. She had received a letter from Charlie in the afternoon post and wanted to share it with him.

She hurried along the corridor on the bedroom floor and knocked on his dressing room door. Charlotte opened it immediately and brought a finger to her lips.

Ushering her into the room, she pointed to Charles, who stood near the chest of drawers paying attention to the words the BBC announcer was saying as he listened to the six o'clock news.

"'Earlier this evening the German army entered Paris without a shot being fired. General Bogislav von Studnitz headed up the German Eighty-seventh Infantry Division, leading them through mostly deserted streets. Some citizens had stayed behind and were weeping, sorrowful witnesses to this tragic event. Others had fled along with Monsieur Paul

Reynaud's government.' "

Charles turned the wireless off. Both Charlotte and Daphne had noticed that angry look on his face.

Charlotte spoke first. "Does this mean the French have surrendered, Charles?"

"I don't think so. But they will. I've no doubt about that."

"So they've just run away?" Daphne asked, staring hard at her father. "Will the French now be considered cowards?"

"Some people may believe that, Daphne. Although I'm saddened, I don't actually think that personally. There is the probability that the government, as well as many of the Parisians, left in order to save Paris, their beautiful City of Light. By leaving the entire city empty for the Germans to take over, they have more than likely prevented shoot-ups, shelling, and general mayhem, and the destruction of some of the most beautiful buildings in the world."

"Do you really and truly believe that, darling?" Charlotte said, sitting down, looking at her husband thoughtfully, having noticed that look of anger earlier. His face was always so expressive.

There was a long silence before he finally said, "I want to think that…it's much more preferable than considering any other motive or reason for their sudden flight, their desertion, don't you think?"

Charlotte nodded in agreement. "I do. And I think we will know more when we listen to the nine o'clock news later. In the meantime we should go downstairs. I don't know about you, Daphne, but I would like a cocktail. For once in my life I actually need a drink."

After dinner, everyone went into the library to listen to the nine o'clock news, and the prime minister's speech. It had become a ritual, one none of them would ever miss. Hearing that inimitable booming voice with its unique cadences always cheered them up and reinforced their determination to win.

Not many nights later they gathered together again to hear the prime minister give a very special speech after France had surrendered to the Germans.

The room was eerily silent as they listened to Winston Churchill's words. As he was drawing toward the end of the speech, Charles moved closer to the radio, waiting for the last sentences to be spoken. He always found the final words to be the best, the most moving.

Churchill's voice deepened as he said, after a slight silence, "What General Weygand called the Battle of France is over. I expect that the Battle of Britain is about to begin. Upon this battle depends the survival of Christian civilization. Upon it depends our own British life, and the long continuity of our institutions and our Empire. The whole fury and might of the enemy must very soon be turned on us. Hitler knows that he will have to break us in this Island or lose the war. If we can stand up to him, all Europe may be free and the life of the world may move forward into broad, sunlit uplands. But if we fail, then the whole world, including the United States, including all that we have known and cared for, will sink into the abyss of a new Dark Age made more sinister, and perhaps more protracted, by the lights of perverted science. Let us therefore brace ourselves to our duties, and so bear ourselves that, if the British Empire and its Commonwealth last for a thousand years, men will still say, 'This was their finest hour.'"

Not one person spoke, and several Inghams and Swanns quietly wept, so touched were they by the words of their leader. And their belief and trust in him became deeply embedded in their psyches, and they understood that they would do their all to ensure the victory Churchill believed could be theirs.

Fifty-two

Sandbags around the front entrance of the Dorchester, Cecily thought, eyeing them as she walked into the hotel escorted by Hugo. Fancy that. Well, there's a war on.

As they walked across the large front hall of the hotel, Hugo exclaimed, "Gosh! What a lot of activity. And I always think everyone in London is hiding in a cellar. How wrong I am."

Cecily laughed. She loved Hugo; he was one of the best, and he had always been the one man in the family she relied on, other than Miles. Dear Miles. He hadn't wanted her to come to London this week because of the war, but he had relented when she had told him her secret. She was three months pregnant, and she had an appointment tomorrow morning with her doctor. "But please don't tell anyone in the family yet." He had understood and promised not to breathe a word. But once they were in bed he had held her close. And he had not been able to hide his own excitement and they had talked about it until they fell asleep. They had been trying for a long time to have another baby, after her miscarriage, and she knew he was as relieved as she was that she had conceived. She was now thirty-nine, and this was her last chance. At least that was what **she** thought. Miles reluctantly had agreed she could come up to London because Hugo would be traveling with her. He would also be staying at their house in South Street and they would both travel back to Cavendon for the weekend. Hugo had several important business meetings over the two days.

There were a lot of people milling around in the hotel's spacious front hall. Some were standing chatting, others moving toward the famous Grill Room. There were porters and bellboys busy with their duties, and concierges at the desk, handling ringing telephones. Busy the hotel might be but then so was London. Cecily had noticed that several weeks ago when she and Miles had been in the city. It was full of troops, enlisted men and officers, Royal Navy men, and many foreigners. Some chicly dressed, others who looked like refugees.

But no Royal Air Force pilots. They were up in the sky, fighting the Luftwaffe. The Battle of Britain had begun on July 10, and now it was the twenty-fourth, and they were well into two weeks of dogfights taking place high in the clouds. The Luftwaffe were targeting airfields, aircraft factories, and fighter bases. The central RAF airfields surrounding London had also become targets for enormous assaults. Dornier and Heinkel bombers swept over the airfields, while the fabulous little Spitfires, Britain's secret weapon, Noel Jollion called it, rose up to shoot them out of the "bright blue yonder," which was Noel's favorite phrase these days.

Sometimes Cecily felt afraid when she was here in London, because of the fighters in the sky. But somehow she managed to keep her fear in check.

The maître d' welcomed them warmly at the restaurant entrance, and escorted them to a lovely table in a quiet corner. Hugo told the maître d' that although they were waiting for guests, he would like to order a bottle of Dom Pérignon.

Once they were comfortably seated, Cecily leaned forward and said, "I'm so glad Daphne has managed to persuade Great-Aunt Gwendolyn to have a small birthday party. There's no reason for her to invite a hundred people because she's going to be a hundred in October."

Hugo couldn't help chuckling. "You're correct, but it wasn't that easy to get her to agree. She's still quite a tiger, good old Great-Aunt Gwendolyn. Typical Ingham, of course."

"So what did Daphne get it down to in the

end?" Cecily asked.

"About thirty nonfamily members, and all of us. The thing is, I doubt she has thirty friends left. She is very old. When you think about it, most of her friends are dead and gone...and have been for a long time. We, meaning the whole family and the Swanns, have been her entire life for many years now."

"I know. But let's face it, she is still a wonderful character. And our **matriarch**. I'm glad we're giving her this party, Hugo. She has so longed for it."

"She deserves it."

Hugo tasted the wine which had been poured in his flute and nodded. "You can pour us a glass now," he told the waiter, and looking at Cecily he went on, "She wished to leave her house to me, and was surprised I didn't want it. And then she asked if I minded if she left it to Diedre instead of one of my children. Naturally I said I didn't." For a moment Cecily made no response and Hugo eyed her curiously.

"Yes, I know about all that," Cecily finally said.

"You **do**?" Hugo looked truly taken aback, and he sat staring at her, a frown knotting his brows.

Cecily grinned at him. "Actually, she asked me to witness the codicil to her will, and Charlotte too, and we obliged her. She has a soft spot for the Swanns, Hugo, or hadn't you noticed?"

"Everybody's noticed, and for centuries! The Inghams are besotted with the Swanns, as the saying goes in the family."

He touched his glass to hers and said, "And may that lovely custom continue." After sipping the champagne, Hugo asked, "How's Harry doing?"

"Managing quite well, although he misses Paloma terribly. And why wouldn't he? He's very much in love with her...most of our men in uniform miss their sweethearts."

"But not always their wives," Hugo shot back, grinning at her. "I'm just joking, Ceci. I know I'd be lost without my darling Daphne."

A small silence fell between them as they sipped their glasses of champagne, but after a short while, Hugo said in a low voice, "She died, you know."

"Who?" Cecily sounded puzzled, and peered at him.

"Pauline Mallard."

"Hugo, you're joking! She's a young woman. Well, maybe not **young,** but certainly not old." Cecily shook her head. "Oh dear, I can see you do mean it."

"I do. I thought Daphne might have told you."

"I wish she had. When did Mrs. Mallard die?"

"January of this year. I subscribe to the **New York Times,** and I read her obituary. She had an inoperable brain tumor. That's what killed her."

Cecily opened her mouth to say something and then stopped abruptly. "Oh, here's Emma coming. With her very good friend, Blackie O'Neill. You're going to like them so much. And she, in particular, has become a very close friend of mine."

Hugo stood up to greet one of the most beautiful women he had ever seen. She had short auburn hair, and the greenest of eyes. Luminous eyes that matched the incredible emerald brooch and earrings she was wearing. What a stunning face, he thought.

The four of them got on well and had an enjoyable lunch together. Hugo was fascinated by Emma Harte, who was not only a beautiful woman, but the smartest he had ever met. No wonder Cecily was so impressed with her, enjoyed doing business with her, and viewed Emma as her hero.

However, Hugo knew Cecily had made her own career long before she had known Emma. It was not until the late 1920s that they had become involved. Cecily still had clothes boutiques at Harte's in Knightsbridge, and Emma was her partner in the Cavendon jewelry collection.

Quite unexpectedly, during their main course of chicken pot pie, Emma looked across the table at him, and said, "My brother, Winston, lost a leg in the Great War, and has worn an artificial one for over twenty years. If your son Charlie needs any help, please let me know. Winston will be happy to come and chat with him."

"Why, thank you, Mrs. Harte, that's so wonderful of you," Hugo answered. "Actually Charlie might need someone to talk to once he gets home. Someone who is not family member." He smiled. "He's very proud and independent."

"I understand," Emma said. "The artificial legs they are making today are far superior to the earlier models. For instance, they bend at the knee, because they're specially hinged, and also at the ankle. Quite remarkable objects. They are made of a very light material. But your son will have to learn how to wear it properly, use it to his advantage."

Blackie said, "When you meet Winston, you'll think that he's a man with a stiff leg who limps slightly, and that's all."

"Yes, it's true," Cecily said. "I know Winston and he walks very well."

"It hasn't stopped him living a good life," Emma added.

Hugo thanked her again, and then looked at Blackie. "Earlier you said the Dorch, as we all call it these days, was the safest hotel in London. Why is that?"

Blackie beamed at Hugo, happy to speak

about his favorite subject—building and construction. He said, "First of all, it's relatively new, built about 1931. And it is made entirely of reinforced concrete. Then last year, when they sandbagged the front entrance outside, shingles were added to the roof. They are extremely protective. I know the man who built it, Sir Malcolm MacAlpine, and he explained everything to me. I've used his ideas in some of my hotels and other buildings."

"Very interesting, and a good thing to know," Hugo remarked, thinking of Cavendon Hall, which still had parts in need of repair. Blackie O'Neill was a good man to know.

"What a fabulous woman Emma Harte is," Hugo said to Cecily as they walked down South Audley Street after lunch. "But I detect a certain sorrow in her."

Cecily glanced at him quickly and nodded. "Yes, you're correct, it is there. The man she loved died about a year ago, and she was broken by it for a while. But they have a daughter together, Daisy, and Emma pulled herself together for their child. However, I am certain she'll never get over Paul McGill's death. I know that for a certainty."

"Oh my God, of course! I remember reading the obituaries. He was a great tycoon, an Australian."

"But he lived here in London with Emma."

The wail of the air raid sirens cut into her words and Hugo got hold of her hand and said, "Hurry up, Ceci. We must get back to South Street."

"Please, please, Hugo. I can't run. They're not dropping bombs here. The Luftwaffe are heading to our airfields." As she spoke she glanced up and shuddered. The blue sky was darkening with hundreds and hundreds of German planes overhead flying in formations.

She tripped and fell. As she was going down, she twisted her body slightly and fell on her left side. She lay still, filled with fear. The baby. The baby. Dismay and anguish crushed her and she lay there not moving, silent.

Hugo was bending over her, looking worried, exclaiming, "Cecily, are you all right? Let me help you up."

"Give me a minute," she exclaimed sharply, and then started to take deep breaths.

Suddenly an ARP warden appeared from nowhere. "Can I help you up, Mrs. Ingham?" he asked, and she realized it was Mr. Clewes, who covered their area.

Before she could answer she heard the bright and beautiful voice of Alicia exclaiming, "Goodness me, Daddy, let me get to Ceci. I must help her up." Her niece bent over her, and said, "Just relax, take a moment, and then we'll get you to your feet. Mr. Clewes will take one arm and I'll take the other."

"Thank you," Cecily whispered, and shivered violently as the air raid sirens started wailing for the second time. How she dreaded that sound. It was like a death knell.

Eric and Laura Swann were standing on the doorstep of the house in South Street when they came down the street, obviously anxious about Cecily being outside. Eric ran to her at once to see if she needed help, but instantly saw she was being well looked after.

After thanking the ARP warden, they went inside, and Alicia led Cecily to a chair in the entrance hall.

"I so hope you're not hurt," Hugo said, looking worried and guilty. "I shouldn't have made you run like that."

"It's all right, Hugo," Cecily answered in a tight voice. "I'm fine. No broken bones." And no miscarriage, I hope, she thought. She was genuinely annoyed with him, but she had learned long ago that anger was a waste of time. It did nothing but upset her and interfered with her work.

Laura Swann, who was still the housekeeper at South Street, said she would go and make a cup of tea, and Eric, the butler, excused himself and followed his sister to the kitchen.

Taking charge in her firm and confident way,

Alicia said, "I'll help Cecily upstairs, Daddy. See you shortly."

Once they were in Cecily's bedroom, Alicia slipped off her Red Cross cape, and helped Cecily to get undressed. Earlier, when they were walking down the street, she had noticed that Cecily held her stomach protectively at one moment. Now she said, "You're pregnant, aren't you?"

"Nobody knows. Miles and I haven't mentioned it to the family yet. So keep it between us. I hope the baby hasn't been hurt."

"I'm sure the baby is safe. I noticed you had fallen on your side. By the way, you don't show at all. What are you? Three months?"

"Just over. Could you bring me a nightgown, please, Alicia? There are some hanging in the wardrobe over there."

Once she was in bed and feeling more relaxed, Cecily said, "Thank you, Alicia. You've helped me a lot and I can't tell you what a relief it was when I heard your voice."

"I'm glad I was on my way home. I can't imagine how Mr. Clewes and my father would've manhandled you. Men do mean well, but they're rather dumb about a lot of things."

Cecily couldn't help laughing and she reached out her arms to Alicia, who bent over the bed and held her close. "Don't worry about the baby. Everything's fine, I'm sure."

As it turned out, it was.

Diedre looked up as the door of her office opened and William walked in. Closing the door behind him, he leaned against it and said, **"Operation Sea Lion**. The Germans' code name for the invasion of Great Britain."

"How did you find that out?" she asked, sitting up alertly in the chair.

"I just hung up with C at MI6. He had the answer about a week ago, but he wanted to do some more checking to be certain. Now it's confirmed. The PM knows. And Menzies wanted us to know. Yep, Operation Sea Lion. Valiant was right; he **was** warning us."

"But the invasion's begun…we're in the middle of the Battle of Britain, aren't we?"

"Up in the skies, yes. It's air warfare. I think C believes Operation Sea Lion means an invasion by land. He thinks they'll start by bombing the hell out of us, our towns and cities, and not just airfields and munition factories as they are doing now. He's talking about the Wehrmacht crossing the Channel and conquering us on land. But I know we've really been at it on the coastlines. There are reinforcements every-where. And remember, we do have something called radar. The Germans don't have that, and, by God, radar does protect us, because it detects everything that's moving."

"I know Churchill's still on Beaverbrook's back about more planes, and on everyone else's about strengthening the coastlines." She smiled slowly, and said, "Remember that message you got last week?"

"No German boot will walk on English soil? Or something like that. That's surely the one you mean, isn't it?"

"Yes, it is, and it came from a contact in Spain."

"Via Spain. From Canaris," William corrected her and walked across the room. He sat down in the chair opposite her desk. "I trust him implicitly. He knows what he's doing to help us. He wants to do it."

When she was silent, he asked, "What is it? You looked troubled."

"I wish I knew that somebody had his back."

"I think C might have his back. Or let me put it this way, MI6 more than likely has his back."

"Your words make me feel better."

"Come on, let's go for a stroll in Green Park and have a bit of lunch. It's such a beautiful day. I can't believe the weather lately. Utterly perfect and the whole world in chaos, or about to be."

Fifty-three

The weather was incomparable. For several weeks now the sun had been shining all day, every day. The skies were a radiant blue and unblemished. Not a cloud. Not a drop of rain. Faultless, in a faulty world, Dulcie added to herself, as she walked out of her building, heading for Harte's department store in Knightsbridge.

They had a good food department, and still managed to stock quite a few staples, such as their famous pork and game pies, chicken pies, and various baked hams. But she had begun to notice they were now having shortages like most food shops. Because Rosalind, Juliet, and Henry were living at Cavendon for the duration of the war, she had their ration books, which meant extra coupons to use when she and James were in London.

Dulcie glanced around as she walked. She loved London, and couldn't help thinking how cheerful and positive the Londoners were.

Crossing Eaton Square, where they now lived, she nodded to one of the charladies she knew by sight, and waved to her window cleaner who covered the entire square, and cleaned their windows. He waved back, then dashed over to her. "Wot a day, m'lady," he said, grinning. "Wot a summer we're 'aving. Ain't seen a summer like this afore. If we dint 'ave Nazis in it, we'd be livin' in a perfect world."

Dulcie laughed. "You're absolutely right about that, Eddie. But we'll beat them, though, you'll see."

"I knows we will. They don't know wot they've bargained for, teking us on."

"I agree."

He saluted her as he always did, threw her his cheeky grin, and dashed back to his little van.

Eddie was a Cockney, born within the sound of Bow Bells, and as patriotic and cheerful as they come. But these Londoners she ran into every day were all made of the same good stuff. The postman, the ARP warden, the man who ran their local Home Guard, the bobbies on the beat, the newsboys with the papers—they just went on doggedly, laughing and joking, determined not to let anything or anyone get them down. It was the spirit of survival that kept them going...kept them all going. It was a British trait that nobody could knock out of them.

She finally reached Harte's, bought a game

pie and a pork pie, paid, gave her coupons, and left. Dulcie then went around the corner to her butcher, who smiled when he saw her come into his shop. For once there was no queue, and it was empty.

"Morning, Lady Brentwood," the butcher said. "I have something for you." He glanced at the door swiftly, disappeared into the back room, and came out with a wrapped package. "I kept these chops for you. I got a bit of lamb in yesterday, and I know Sir James likes his lamb."

"Why, thank you so much, Mr. Westin. That's so kind of you," Dulcie replied, and took out her ration books. "I hope I have enough coupons for lamb chops." She handed the two books to him.

The butcher nodded, smiled, and took out the coupons, handed her the package. After paying, she smiled and whispered, "Whenever my husband is in a new play, I'll be sure to have two tickets for you and Mrs. Westin. House seats."

A big smile settled on the butcher's face. "Are some theaters going to be opening up again soon?" he asked, sounding excited.

Dulcie grimaced. "Not to my knowledge. They're staying closed, and the cinemas, too, as you know. Everything is closed. Including my art gallery. Any public places where people gather."

"I suppose it's for our safety, but I gotta say London's a bit dreary at night, especially with the blackout. It's a dark city now."

"I know what you mean. However, blackout curtains are truly necessary. The prime minister doesn't want a chink of light to show through any window. Because of night bombing."

"Thank God Mr. Churchill's leading the country," the butcher exclaimed. And then he said good-bye to her as three customers came into the shop and he turned to greet the women holding their ration books.

On the way home to Eaton Square, Dulcie's thoughts went to the theater, and to James, who had been morose for months. Mostly because he had nothing to do. He had been making propaganda films for the government, the Ministry of Information, because there were no theatrical productions of any kind. Not on the stage or on the screen.

It was she who had come up with an idea that not only pleased him enormously, but actually worked. She had suggested he start a little group using actors and actresses he knew, and put on plays to entertain the troops.

"You could call it 'The Troupe for Troops,'" she had suggested, almost jokingly. But James had loved the name, and the idea, and when she had insisted he talk to Edward Glendenning, Paloma's father, he had gone to the phone at once.

Within a few weeks they had created the troupe and had decided to do variety shows rather than dramatic plays. And for two reasons: The first was the length of a play. The second, mentioned by Edward, was that the troops wanted to be entertained, wanted to laugh at comedians, hear popular singers like Vera Lynn.

Felix Lambert had helped, as had his wife, Constance, and in no time at all they would be ready to "go on the road," as James called it.

"Our little repertoire company will be going to Catterick Camp first," James had told her last week. "So I'll be at Cavendon with you for a few days, and Edward can stay with Paloma."

Dulcie hated it when James was discontented. They had the best relationship, a good marriage, and rarely bickered or quarreled. But there was nothing worse than a man with nothing to do, with time on his hands. Daphne and Cecily had been impressed that she had come up with the idea of the acting group.

As she approached Eaton Square the air raid sirens began to scream and she ran, although she was a bit impeded by the shopping bag. Dulcie made it to their flat in no time at all, and grabbed the ringing phone as she rushed into the hall.

It was James. "You made it home, darling."

"Yes, I'm fine. Where are you? At the rehearsal

hall?"

"Yes. But we're going to the basement. It's a proper air raid shelter down there. See you later. Oh, and do we have enough to eat if I bring Edward home with me?"

"Yes, of course. Guess what? The butcher got a bit of lamb in yesterday and he kept me some chops, because he knows you like them."

"All I can say is thank God Henry is at Cavendon. Because if he were at home, you'd have to give them away." He chuckled. "I love you. See you tonight."

"Love you, too," she said, and they hung up.

Dulcie carried the shopping bag to the kitchen where Mrs. Pearl was waiting for her. Dulcie handed her the bag and said, "Should we go down to the basement, do you think?"

The housekeeper shrugged and then chortled. "I don't think it's necessary, your ladyship. I mean, the Jerries are not going to drop bombs on London. They're going to do what they've been doing, hitting the munition factories. But if you want, I'll go with you."

"Oh let's forget it," Dulcie replied. "I agree with you. Oh and we'll be one extra for supper tonight, Mrs. P. Mr. Edward Glendenning will be joining us."

The post had arrived in her absence, and Dulcie went to open it in her small den. As she sat slitting envelopes with the silver paper knife, she suddenly began to laugh thinking of their son Henry. He was now eight and, although he looked a lot like his father, he had her personality and the same flair for the English language as she did.

She was laughing because James's comment had reminded her of Henry's confrontation with Miles earlier this year. One of their Land Army girls had persuaded Miles to buy a flock of sheep. The main point was that their lambs could feed them, and therefore save food coupons.

Miles had seen the sense of this, and one day the family was surprised to see sheep wandering around in two of the fields. Miles understood that the sheep could not go near the grouse moors; they had been penned in near the Romany wagons.

Unbeknown to anyone except Genevra, Henry loved one of the sheep, which she had helped to establish was "a girl sheep," as Henry called it. He had named her Ophelia and came to pet Ophelia every day. He had even tied a pink ribbon around the ewe's neck, although he did not need a ribbon to recognize her. She was the smallest of the flock.

Unfortunately, Henry had overheard a conversation between the Land Army girl and Miles, who were discussing where to have sheep slaughtered when that was necessary.

Later that day Henry had marched up to Miles and said it was wrong, a bad thing to do. He suggested that Miles should shoot his dog instead if he was hungry.

The boy had been so inflamed Miles had instantly given in. He promised that none of the sheep would be harmed.

To Dulcie he had said that Henry had inherited her volatility, and her outrageous tongue. She and James had laughed privately, but Henry was so attached to the animal James had made Miles promise not to harm Ophelia.

"I won't," Miles had promised. "I'll just keep killing off a sheep and replacing it with another one because Henry counts them every day. So he knows there are eight."

"And so does Genevra," Dulcie had reminded her brother. The ringing phone interrupted her thoughts. It was DeLacy, who said, "I want to tell you about my solution for the art. Oh dash, that's the all clear going off."

"I'll hang on," Dulcie answered.

In a short while the all clear ended and they were having their conversation. And they confirmed that they would both be at Cavendon for their usual Saturday morning meeting. "We've a lot of problems to solve," Dulcie added.

Fifty-four

For many years the Four Dees and Cecily had met in the conservatory every Saturday when they were at Cavendon. Since Harry's marriage to Paloma, they had become six, because she had accepted at once when they asked her if she would like to join their team.

On this particular Saturday in late July, they had gathered for coffee to review the situation on the estate and discuss any problems that might have developed.

Dulcie said that she and DeLacy had one major problem, although they felt they probably had the solution. She explained, "Before Hanson retired, he had wooden crates made in which to slide the family paintings. Ted Swann and his team made quite a few, and the paintings were put in them. About six months ago before war was declared. And then they went down to storage in the basement. The rest were wrapped in heavy quilted cloth sheets and also put in the vaults. DeLacy and I check the wooden crates all the time to make sure the art is in good shape. Recently, just two weeks ago, we decided to take the paintings out of the crates because they felt warm. One or two canvases even felt damp. So perhaps the crates are not needed."

Paloma was the first to comment, when she said, "The wooden crates might well have made the paintings sweat. Anyway, you did the right thing, in my opinion."

"I know you studied art history, as I did," DeLacy ventured. "So I wonder if you agree with me...I think the paintings should be simply stacked against the walls in the vaults. That would mean they are in similar conditions to those of the house itself up here."

"That's probably the best solution," Paloma agreed. "But you ought to compare the temperature in Cavendon Hall to the temperature in the vaults. Also, sometimes it is a good idea to install air-conditioning for coolness. Do you have electricity down there? I mean, can you plug in an air-conditioning unit?"

"Oh yes, we can," Daphne interjected. "I've always been glad electricity was put in years ago."

Dulcie said, "The paintings which belong to my art gallery were simply placed against walls, in one of the other vaults, and they are fine."

"Do let's double-check everything," DeLacy said to Paloma, who nodded her agreement.

Diedre looked over at Daphne and smiled. "I'm glad you agreed to let Susie Jackson go. There's no point trying to persuade someone to stay when they're itching to go off to fight in the war. You're bound to lose in the end."

"She was so gung ho about it," Daphne explained. "I finally gave in. I don't quite see Susie working in a munitions factory, but then it is her life. And anyway, Cecily found us a new cook within a couple of days."

"A lot of people want to get out of London, because they're fearful of being killed in the air raids," Cecily said. "Eric has a friend whose daughter is a chef. Her name is Meggie Trader, and she jumped at the job."

"Meggie came up to Yorkshire and cooked several meals for us," Daphne explained. "Last week. Papa and Charlotte enjoyed the things she made, so no problem there. Charlotte offered her the job the other day. She's here for the next few days to cook for us all. Then she'll go to London to get her things. She's on board."

"I'm looking forward to tasting her specialties," Diedre said, then changed the subject. "I would like to address something else. I think we should have an ARP warden in each of the villages. I know everyone knows what to do, go down into their cellars or into their air raid shelters. However, I think there should be a man in charge in each village, a person everyone can go to. The other point is, I'd like to see a first-aid station created, with someone trained in nursing in charge. For emergencies."

"Do you think we might be bombed?" Daphne asked, frowning. "Why would they bomb the country? Why kill cows?"

"I'm so happy you didn't mention lambs," Dulcie murmured, gazing at her sister, faking a look of sadness.

Daphne laughed. "Oh yes. Goodness me, Ophelia. I'd forgotten for a moment."

"So what about ARP wardens and a first-aid station?" Diedre reminded them.

"I like it," Paloma said.

"So do I," Cecily agreed.

"Then let's put it all in the works. I'll talk to Papa and Charlotte later, and Mrs. Alice. She—" Daphne paused, her eyes on the door, where Lane, the head butler, was standing.

"Yes, Lane?"

"Sorry to interrupt, your ladyship, but there is a telephone call for Mrs. Miles."

"Thank you, Lane," Daphne answered.

Cecily was on her feet immediately, and excused herself. She hurried out, hoping there wasn't something wrong at one of the clothing factories in Leeds. They were working overtime,

on weekends at the moment, producing over-
coats for the troops, proof to her the British
government expected it to be a long war.

When she went out into the entrance hall,
Charlotte was standing there. An anxious
expression had settled on her face.

"Whatever is it?" Cecily asked, hurrying over
to her.

"It's Great-Aunt Gwendolyn. Peggy just telephoned me. Apparently, Great-Aunt Gwen has
been asking for me and for you also. She hasn't
been herself for the last few days. I think we had
better go to her at once."

Cecily nodded, her face solemn. They walked
out of Cavendon and followed the path through
the park without speaking.

Peggy Swift, once Daphne's lady's maid, now
the wife of Gordon Lane, was devoted to the
entire family. She greeted them at the door of
Little Skell Manor.

"Your ladyship, Mrs. Miles, come in, please."
She opened the front door wider, and they went
into the house.

Charlotte asked, "Where is Lady Gwendolyn,
Peggy?"

"In the sitting room, m'lady. She insisted on
getting up this morning and getting dressed. I
did her hair, and she put on lipstick and rouge
like she always does. Herself. Then she asked

me to bring you to her. She needs to speak with you both, she told me."

Cecily glanced at Charlotte and touched her arm gently, so that she went in first. Cecily followed and closed the door behind her.

Lady Gwendolyn was sitting in her favorite chair. Cecily noticed at once that she was wearing one of her favorite Cecily Swann frocks. Purple silk with a frothy chiffon jabot at the front. She had also put on pearl earrings which they both knew had been given to her many years ago by Mark Swann.

When she saw them, she said in a clear, light voice, "How lovely to see my two very dearest Swanns. Whatever would the Inghams have done without the Swanns? Not been as happy, I suspect. Sit down here, next to me."

They did as she asked, taking a chair on either side of her.

Charlotte said, "How do you feel, Great-Aunt Gwendolyn?"

"I feel all right. But I also feel ready, if you know what I mean?"

Cecily gazed at her lovingly, reached out and took hold of her hand. "Ready to go? Is that what you mean? After all, you do look as if you're going somewhere, wearing your best purple dress, which I made especially for you."

"And Mark's pearl earrings." Lady Gwendolyn now stretched out her left hand, added, "And his wedding ring. We **felt** we were married though we weren't, you see. Don't let anyone take it off my finger, Charlotte, will you?"

"I won't," Charlotte promised, swallowing. She was endeavoring to contain her emotions; her throat was tight and she was choked up inside. Her admiration for Cecily knew no bounds. She was talking to Great-Aunt Gwen in a calm, untroubled voice, as if they were just having a little chat about not very important matters.

"The suitcases over there, Great-Aunt Gwen… are they going with you?" Cecily asked, trying to be a little lighthearted under difficult circum-stances.

"Don't be silly. They're labeled. There is one for Margaret." As she spoke she freed her hands, fumbled with her handbag on her lap. "These are the keys," she said, handing an envelope to Charlotte.

"So we're to give the suitcases to other people, as well as Margaret," Cecily asserted.

Lady Gwendolyn nodded. "There's one for you, and you, too, Charlotte." Leaning back in the chair, she closed her eyes for a few minutes. When she opened them she continued, "I'm sorry I won't make my birthday party. Celebrate anyway, won't you? I'd like that."

"Yes, we'll toast you to the heavens," Cecily promised, her voice suddenly wobbling.

"We'll sing for you," Charlotte managed to say, her own voice choked.

Lady Gwendolyn looked at Cecily, and then more intently at Charlotte. She smiled at her. "Thank you for so lovingly devoting your life to the Inghams." Turning to Cecily, she went on, "And you, too. You saved the family as only a Swann could. With immense cleverness." The smile lingered on her face. "You'll do, Ceci. No one better. And if that baby you're carrying is a girl, would you call her after me?"

"I will," Cecily said, her eyes filling with tears. She took hold of Lady Gwendolyn's hand and Charlotte reached for the other. They sat there for a while, filled with love for their matriarch, relieved they were with her at this time.

Quite unexpectedly, Lady Gwendolyn bestirred herself, sat up a little straighter. "I got dressed this morning so that you can say later that I died with my boots on."

Cecily said, "Oh, Great-Aunt Gwen, try to keep going, you sound so much better, stronger, almost like your old self. Please don't leave us yet. Stay a little longer. **Try.**"

Lady Gwendolyn's face was filled with sudden radiance, and her eyes were the most brilliant blue. "Mark is waiting for me..." She looked off into the distance as if she could see him and she smiled. There was a little guttural noise in her throat followed by a long sigh.

Cecily knew she had just heard the death rattle. "She's gone, Aunt Charlotte...gone to Mark, whom she really believes is waiting for her."

Charlotte did not respond for a moment; when she did her voice was quavering. "I expect he is. She's usually right." Rising, Charlotte bent over Lady Gwendolyn and smoothed back her silver hair, kissed her forehead.

Cecily did the same, and then gently closed each eyelid. As she did this, she murmured to Charlotte, "I've never seen her eyes so blue or her face as radiant."

"She was happy," Charlotte murmured in a voice so low Cecily could hardly hear it.

They left the sitting room and found Peggy waiting in the small library across the hall.

Cecily said, "Lady Gwendolyn has just passed away, and very peacefully, Peggy."

"I've been expecting it," Peggy answered, her face full of sadness, her eyes moist. Clearing her throat, Peggy said, "We can't leave her ladyship in the chair, Mrs. Miles. We have to carry her upstairs and lay her on the bed."

"Do you think you and I can manage that?" Cecily asked, giving Peggy a pointed look. "Can

we carry her?"

"I think so. I will go and get a sheet and we can put it around her." Peggy started to leave and paused. "I think you ought to call Mrs. Alice, ask her to come and help us."

"Good idea." Cecily reached for the phone and dialed her mother.

"It's me, Mam," Cecily said quietly, when Alice answered. "Aunt Charlotte and I are with Great-Aunt Gwen, she wanted to see us. I'm sorry to have to tell you this, but she just passed away. Can you come?"

"Immediately," her mother said, and the phone went dead.

"She's on her way," Cecily told Peggy. "She'll be here in a couple of minutes. Could you get the sheet please, Peggy?"

Peggy simply nodded and left.

Walking across the room, Cecily sat down next to Charlotte on the sofa. "Are you all right?" she asked, peering into her face. "Sorrowful, I know, as I am, though we did expect it."

"Yes, we did," Charlotte answered in a steadier voice. "But she's looked so well. And it's always a shock when a loved one dies, even when they're very old."

"Ninety-nine years old, just imagine that." Cecily then gave Charlotte a questioning look. "Whatever can those suitcases contain? It's a very weird thing for her to do."

Charlotte was silent for a moment, then explained. "She told me about them a few weeks ago. There's one for each of the Four Dees. And you and me, as she told you, and Margaret. There's also one for your father. They're small suitcases, Ceci. There can't be much in them."

"I suppose she's given us all the things she wanted us to have in memory of her."

"I agree and I must telephone Charles, ask him to come here."

"Yes, you must. And I have to speak to Miles. But first we have to carry Great-Aunt Gwendolyn's body upstairs. Make her look nice on the bed."

The front door opened and Cecily went out into the hall. Alice Swann was coming in, and she reached for her daughter immediately, held her close. "I knew it was going to be any day now," Alice said through her sudden tears. "I'm sure it was a peaceful passing, wasn't it?"

"Yes, Mam, it was…she was happy."

Peggy was running down the stairs carrying white linen sheets, and greeted Alice. "I thought we should wrap her in these clean sheets and take the body upstairs to her bedroom."

Alice agreed, then looked at Cecily. "Where is Lady Gwen? I would like to see her, say good-bye."

"In here." Cecily led her mother into the sitting room.

The members of the family who had come from London stayed on, did not return to the city. Trains ran late, were often jammed with troops, and petrol coupons were short. It was difficult to travel these days.

Daphne's twin sons, Thomas and Andrew, now twenty, did not come home from Sandhurst, where they were undergoing officer training. Nor did Alicia. She was working hard for the Red Cross in London.

Harry Swann could not get compassionate leave from the RAF in Manston, the southern airfield where he was stationed. Charlie was not allowed to travel because of his wounds.

Lady Gwendolyn Ingham Baildon, matriarch of the Ingham family, was beloved by everyone in the three villages. They were invited to attend her funeral alongside her family, which was to be held at the large church in Little Skell village. It was termed a private funeral, as she had so wished.

Charlotte and Daphne did the flower arrangements for the church and they were magnificent. On the day of the funeral service, three days after her death of heart failure, the sun was shining brightly in a pale blue sky.

The family arrived together and eight of the

earl's twelve grandchildren were present.

Lord Mowbray spoke first. He was then followed by Miles, his heir, and finally by his eldest daughter, Diedre, who said she spoke on behalf of her sisters as well as herself. After saying a few laudatory words, she recited the Twenty-third Psalm: **The Lord Is My Shepherd**.

By popular request within the family, it was James Brentwood who gave the eulogy. The church became very still when he spoke. No one wanted to miss a word, since it was England's greatest actor standing in their pulpit. His mellifluous voice rang out crystal clear and beautiful, reaching to the rafters. He spoke lovingly of the incomparable Lady Gwen, as she was so affectionately known by everyone. He spoke of her warmth, generosity, and kindness, and even touched on her spirited bluntness and frequently acerbic wit.

He ended his eulogy by asking for their indulgence, explaining that he wished to sing for them. "It was her most favorite song of all, and so patriotic. And therefore eminently suitable for the world we live in today. I will be accompanied on the piano by my niece, Lady Daphne's daughter Annabel."

He glanced over at the sixteen-year-old and nodded. She smiled at him, looked at the keys, and struck the first chord.

James had a marvelous voice. He was a tenor, and he sang with confidence.

> **Land of Hope and Glory,**
> **Mother of the Free,**
> **How shall we extol thee,**
> **who are born of thee?**
> **Wider still and wider**
> **shall thy bounds be set;**
> **God who made thee mighty,**
> **make thee mightier yet.**
> **God who made thee mighty,**
> **make thee mightier yet.**

Nothing stirred; there was not a single sound after James finished the song. It seemed to him that the congregation was frozen in place.

And he knew that Lady Gwen was surely looking down and smiling.

Fifty-five

Now, Victoria, let me look at you," Alice Swann said, smiling at the ten-year-old. "You're very bonny in that frock. It suits you. I'm glad I cut it down to your size."

A rare smile flickered on the child's face, and she said, "I like yellow. It's my favorite color."

Alice took the canvas bag off the kitchen table and put it on Victoria's shoulder, then pulled the strap across her body. "There we are, it's more comfortable like that."

Victoria looked at her warily, and asked, "Do I really have to take the gas mask with me, Mrs. Alice?"

"Yes, you do, and I have to take mine."

"Why?"

"Because it's the rule now, we can't go far without our gas masks. Everybody has one."

Victoria was thoughtful for a moment or two and then asked, "Do the king and queen have to take theirs when they go out? And Princess

Elizabeth and Princess Margaret Rose? Oh and Churchill?"

"Absolutely!" Alice exclaimed, smiling inwardly because Victoria had mentioned those people she was interested in the most, whom she only knew about through her frequent comments about them.

"It's for our safety, to protect us," Alice explained. "Just let me look in my handbag to make sure I have our identity cards, ration books, clothes coupon books, in case we can find a nice pair of shoes for you in Leeds. You do need some new shoes for the winter."

"Leeds!" Victoria cried, her voice rising shrilly. "No, no, no! I don't want to go to Leeds. I won't go."

Alice was so taken aback by this outburst, and the vehemence of it, she was startled. Victoria had never raised her voice before. The child's reaction had been so strong, and even fearful, that Alice now knew it was there she had been hurt. By someone.

Unexpectedly, Victoria began to weep. She just stood there in the middle of the kitchen, clutching the strap of the gas mask case and gazing at Alice helplessly, tears rolling down her cheeks.

Alice Swann had always been decisive, and she immediately went to the child, took off the gas mask, and gave her a handkerchief. "Stop crying, love, we don't have to go to Leeds. We can go to Harrogate. Next week."

Reaching for her, she drew the little girl into her arms and held her close, stroked her hair. "There, there, you mustn't be frightened, Victoria. I won't let anyone hurt you—" Alice stopped when she saw Paloma standing in the doorway, holding Edward in her arms.

Alice gave her a warning look, and said, "Hello, Paloma. Fancy that, I was just thinking of coming to see you. We were about to go shopping for a pair of shoes for Victoria. Winter shoes. And then I decided it was a silly idea since it's still summer."

Paloma picked up on the situation immed-iately. "That's a coincidence, Alice. I came over to invite you and Victoria to have lunch with me. I've made a cottage pie."

Smiling at her daughter-in-law, while smooth-ing her hand over Victoria's back soothingly, Alice said, "Victoria loves cottage pie, don't you?"

Moving slightly away from her, Alice added, "And we can take some pictures with the new camera Mr. Walter gave you."

"Oh yes," Victoria said, instantly cheering up, smiling at Paloma. "Can I take a picture of Edward?"

"That would be nice and I will send it to his father. What a kind thought, Victoria."

"Let's go then, shall we?" Alice murmured,

and putting her arm around her little evacuee, she ushered her outside.

Paloma said, "Harry phoned me this morning. He sends his love to you and his father. He's well. And enjoying learning so much about radar, too. What a godsend that is, the way it protects our coastline."

"Miles explained it to me. Oh and by the way, Miles told me we have to have two buckets in every household, to hold various things."

Throwing her a curious look, Paloma said, "What sort of things?"

"Metal. Most important. Tin cans that contained food, bottle caps, old nails, buckles cut off old belts, any old tools, hairpins, picture hooks, just about anything made of metal. Ted Swann will come and collect the metal once a week."

"What is all this metal for?" Paloma asked.

"The government needs it, and they will come and pick it up from the three villages. It's shipped to a factory and everything gets melted down. To make planes, guns, tanks, ships, and ammunition."

Alice laughed at the expression on Paloma's face as they crossed the village street to Charlotte's House. "Haven't you seen the posters in Harrogate? It's of three women holding a flag that says, 'Up Housewives and at 'em!' I laughed when I noticed it recently, but Miles says it's important. The government seriously needs our help."

"Then I'll do it. And what's the second bucket for?"

"Kitchen scraps of food. To feed the chickens and the pigs, and incidentally, Miles is going to buy some pigs." Alice added swiftly, "Don't ask about the pigs, please. We've had enough problems about lambs."

Once they were inside the house, Paloma put Edward in his cot, and insisted that Alice sit down in the chair. After she had done so, Paloma pushed the ottoman closer so that Alice could put her legs up.

"You're never off your feet," Paloma said. "I've never seen anyone work as hard as you."

Alice smiled. "Hard work never killed anyone, and I'm used to it, you know. Also, I've been running up and down through that park all of my life. My feet are used to it."

Paloma smiled. "I'd better put the pie in the oven. It's cooked but it needs warming up. And I'll open a jar of the peas you gave me." She glanced at Victoria, who was sitting on a chair near the cot, looking at Edward with great interest. "How does that sound to you?"

Turning her head, Victoria smiled. "I like cottage pie. I'd never had it before I came to live with Mrs. Alice and Mr. Walter. Oh, the camera!"

She looked across at Alice. "Shall I run and get it?"

"Yes, that's a good idea, before little Edward falls fast asleep. Otherwise you won't be able to photograph him."

Once they were alone, Alice said, "She's a lot better these days, Paloma, not so tense and shy. I did find out from the evacuee agency running Operation Pied Piper that she was not with another family as an evacuee, before she came here. She doesn't say much about her life, or anything else for that matter. But this is a child who hasn't had it easy in the past."

"She seems to have put a protective layer around herself. What I've also noticed is that she's become very attached to you. Also, she's lovely around Edward, and pays a lot of attention to him when she's with us. She's quite well spoken, Alice, and has good manners."

"That's true. Well brought up, I'd say. But I don't question her about anything. I was informed a while ago that family are allowed to visit their evacuated children now. But no one has requested to come to see her." Alice stopped speaking, and turned her attention to her baby grandson as Victoria came back with her Kodak camera.

Paloma lifted Edward up. "Now, where do you want to photograph us, Victoria? Here on the sofa? Or outside?"

"Here. Just near the vase of flowers, so they're in the picture, too."

Victoria snapped away for several minutes, then asked Alice to come and be in a photograph. Once this was accomplished, Paloma suggested Victoria should sit down holding the baby so that Paloma could photograph all of them together. By the time she finished, Paloma exclaimed, "Oh! The pie! I mustn't burn the pie!"

During lunch, Paloma told Alice and Victoria about her first date with Harry, and that she had wanted to make a special cottage pie for him and how it had burned to a cinder in the oven.

They all laughed, and Alice was glad to see that her ten-year-old evacuee was enjoying herself. As for Paloma, she was being adorable. But that was how she was. Loving, warm, capable, willing, and ready to please. She had joined the WI in Little Skell, had dug and planted her own allotment in the garden outside, learned to make jam and bottle fruit, and had become one of them. And everyone had welcomed her with open arms and loving hearts. They told Alice that Harry had found a very special wife, and she knew that was true.

Later that afternoon Alice and Victoria took their books and went to the lower moor. It was not far away from Cavendon Hall in the shadow of the North Wing. There was a sheltered spot where Alice had read her books since she was a young girl. Now it had become a special place for Victoria.

Alice had realized that this withdrawn little person liked being in quiet, protected areas. She wondered about that and this desire to be alone, away from crowds. And she still thought about those bruises. Alice had never mentioned them to her, having taken Lady Daphne's advice. One day she'll confide, tell me everything, Alice thought; unless anything untoward happened, Victoria would be with them until the end of the war, which Cecily and Miles insisted would be a long one. Then she would make sure Victoria was safe, would not come to any harm.

Alice glanced at Victoria and noticed that she hadn't opened her book. "Don't you feel like reading?"

"Oh yes. I was just wondering something. Where do we go when we die? I mean where is Lady Gwendolyn? Is she up there in the sky?" As she spoke, Victoria lifted her head, then cried, "Oh Mrs. Alice, look! Look, there's a plane coming right for us."

Following her glance, Alice saw a plane heading their way and jumped up, grabbed hold of Victoria's hand, and pulled her along, went higher up the moor. She had noticed the swastika, the Nazi insignia, on the plane, and realized it was actually moving toward the North Wing of Cavendon Hall. It was also dropping, losing height. Alice and Victoria stood watching as it sheared off two chimney pots and a large chunk of the roof. It plunged on, went beyond the house, and crashed onto the lower moor where they had been sitting a moment or two before.

Victoria was trembling, holding on to Alice very tightly, obviously afraid. Alice was shaken up herself, but she extracted herself. "Don't move. Stay right here. I'm just going to look at the plane."

Victoria nodded, stood perfectly still, wrapping her arms around herself protectively.

Alice edged closer to the plane until she was next to the cockpit. The pilot was crunched up in his seat, but he was alive. He stared at her, trying to speak. As Alice pulled away, stepped back, he said in English, "Please…help me… please."

She wanted to say, "Why should I? You're the enemy." And then she realized how young he was, just a boy. Twenty at the most. His eyes, pinned on hers pleadingly, were very blue.

"I'll get help," Alice said, and ran back to Victoria. Getting hold of her hand, she took her down the hill away from the plane. People were already coming. She spotted Miles and Lane, and behind them, the earl and Percy Swann, the head gamekeeper. And even Hanson was following on, lumbering up the hill, looking concerned.

Miles paused, asked swiftly, urgently, "Alice, did you see what happened?"

"Yes, I did. The plane was dropping lower and lower, falling really as if it were out of control. I suddenly realized it was heading straight for the North Wing. I was sitting with Victoria on the lower moor over there. It just missed us."

Suddenly Cecily arrived, out of breath and exclaiming, "Mother, whatever happened? Are you all right? How are you, Victoria?"

"I was afraid. Mrs. Alice grabbed my hand and we ran."

Cecily glanced at Miles anxiously. "Will the plane burst into flames, do you think?"

"I don't believe so. From what your mother has said, the pilot was probably out of fuel. And perhaps lost, off his course. But he's no doubt dead."

"He's alive," Alice said. "He needs help."

"I see my father is already up there with Lane and Percy," Miles said. "I'd better go and see what I can do to help. And, Ceci, you'd better ring up Topcliffe RAF station, tell them what's happened here, and ask them to send some officers and an ambulance for the pilot. I know they have a hospital unit there."

"I'll do that immediately," Cecily answered.

Alice said, "Oh here comes Alf Merton with his Home Guard."

Miles and Lane managed to get the Luftwaffe pilot out of the plane. As they waited for Percy and the two Home Guards to bring a stretcher from the cellar, Miles questioned the pilot, who was groggy, obviously wounded, but managed to speak fairly coherently. He told Miles he had suddenly realized he was off course and lost.

Miles couldn't help feeling sorry for the pilot. He was so young, couldn't be more than twenty, like their boys up in the air, fighting a war. Just a lad, really.

Known for his humanity and compassion, Miles knelt down on the moorland next to the pilot, touched his shoulder. "I believe you're wounded," he said. "Maybe something is broken?"

The pilot simply grimaced, then said, "My back. My leg. They hurt."

"Don't move, an ambulance is on its way."

"I did not want to crash. On land," the pilot stammered in his stilted English. "I was looking for the sea. Out of fuel. Losing altitude. No control."

"You weren't very far away from the sea, you might have even made it if you'd had only a quarter tank of fuel," Miles said.

The young pilot was silent, staring at Miles, his blue eyes suddenly filling with fear.

Miles told him, "Don't be afraid. We're not going to hurt you, even though you're in an enemy country. The ambulance will be here soon and your wounds will be properly treated. You will be going to a nearby RAF station, to their hospital. Some officers will come to help you, because you are now a prisoner of war."

Immediately the pilot appeared to be alarmed.

Miles continued in the same calm voice, "We treat our prisoners very well."

Unable to speak for a moment, the pilot simply nodded. Then he said in a choked voice, "**Danke schön** …thank you."

It was not long before a team of Royal Air Force officers arrived from Topcliffe. There were several senior men plus a medical team with an ambulance, and military police. Once the pilot had been carried on the stretcher into the ambulance by the medical team, the two military police officers went with them. The RAF technicians stayed behind to dismantle the German plane.

Percy and Ted were cleaning up the rubble around the North Wing when the earl arrived with Miles and Cecily. Lane had apparently hurried off to make sure the staff were calm and recovering from their fright. When the earl saw the damage he was stunned, and upset. The German plane had hit a tall chimney and had sheared off a portion of the roof. The wall below had collapsed from the force and weight of the plane pushing through the roof, and there was now a huge gaping hole. Three windows had been shattered and there was broken glass, bricks, and rubble everywhere on the back terrace.

To the earl's dismay he saw that some of the antique fine French furniture, which was of great value, had been smashed. "Thank God the paintings are in the vault," Lord Mowbray said to Miles, who noticed his father's face was deathly white, his expression grim.

Suddenly, Hanson hove into view, walking along the back terrace carrying a tray. On it was a bottle of excellent French cognac and shot glasses. Hanson said, "I thought a drop of our best Napoleon would do us good, your lordship. We've all had a bit of a shock."

"Well done, Hanson!" Charles exclaimed. "Pour us all a shot, and call Ted and Percy over, and the team. They need a good nip. And so do you, Hanson."

As they all lingered on the terrace, sipping the brandy, Cecily thought of Blackie O'Neill. It suddenly occurred to her that he might be of the greatest help to them. The damage was enormous and she had noticed that Percy and Ted looked worried and alarmed as they examined the ruined end of the North Wing.

She said to Miles, "I believe Emma Harte's friend Blackie O'Neill will be able to help us. He has a construction company. I was with him the other day, and I'm quite sure that he would be willing to come and look at the damage. I think I could make a decent deal with him. He'll be reasonable about the cost."

"Can you telephone him now?" the earl asked.

"Yes, and he lives in Harrogate. Perhaps he'll be able to come over later this afternoon."

"The sooner the better," Miles said.

Fifty-six

Daphne sat on the sofa in the little parlor next to the dining room, which Cecily used as an office. Her hands were clasped tightly together because she was shaking, devastated by the damage to the North Wing, which she had just seen.

Daphne and Charlotte had been in Harrogate that afternoon and had returned only a few moments before the RAF officers and their team left.

Cecily was seeing them off, and after parking her car, Daphne had walked over, followed by Charlotte, had raised a brow, asked why the RAF officers had been at Cavendon.

Cecily had explained there had been a plane crash on the moor and she had taken them to see the North Wing. Charlotte had been aghast and had hurried off to find Charles at once to commiserate with him. Daphne had simply stood there gaping at the ruined North Wing, and had then staggered toward a tree and leaned against it. Tears were rolling down her face.

When Cecily had spoken to her, she had not answered, and Cecily, believing her to be in shock, had taken hold of her arm, shepherded her into the parlor, and closed the door behind them.

After a moment or two, Daphne blinked several times, brushed her damp cheeks with her fingertips, and looked across at Cecily. They were still sitting there without speaking.

"It's funny, isn't it," Daphne suddenly began. "Everyone talks about the Cavendon luck and assumes it's only ever good luck. But I have never seen it in that way. Have you?"

"No, I haven't," Cecily answered. "I've always known this family would have bad luck as well as good."

"How did you know that?"

"I suppose because it's the way things are in the world we live in. But also because of Genevra. Since I was a child she has warned me to beware of the bad luck, because it would come. She never stopped saying that Cavendon would suffer, that the family would have deaths and chaos and troubles."

"And you believed her? Do you believe her now?"

"I did. I do. She has the sight, and I believe in

that, too."

Daphne let out a long sigh, and her voice suddenly shook when she said, "But **why** the North Wing? All those years I put into it, making it beautiful again."

"I've phoned Blackie O'Neill. He's coming to look at the damage later, give us an assessment. We'll get it rebuilt."

Daphne simply nodded, and the tears started again, but she managed to speak. "I have a son in hospital who has had his left leg amputated, high up, above the knee, who's waiting for the stump of his leg to heal, so he can start learning to walk again with an artificial leg. Great-Aunt Gwen, our matriarch, just died. My eldest daughter, now a Red Cross nurse, is about to rush into a dangerous war, and my twin boys will soon be soldiers fighting in the army. Besides all that, my youngest daughter is angry with me because I won't let her study at the Royal Academy of Music because the building is right in the middle of central London. And now the North Wing, which I put my heart and soul into restoring, has been destroyed by a plane with a swastika on it. I wonder what else is going to happen to me?"

Daphne had such a desperate look on her face, Cecily jumped up and went to sit next to her on the sofa. She put her arms around her sister-in-law and endeavored to soothe her, calm her; Daphne began to sob as if her heart were broken.

Cecily knew that her reaction to the damage done to the North Wing was genuine. Yet she also knew Daphne was tired out, bone weary. There had been the problems with Susie Jackson, the cook, who had been unusually terse about leaving and actually quite unpleasant in the end. This attitude had really annoyed Cecily. Now the housekeeper Mrs. Weir had gone, and a maid, Brenda Caine, was leaving. Both of them were going to work in the munitions factories.

And then there was Charlotte, who Cecily thought was showing her age. She was seventy-two, and ever since she had broken her leg last year, Charlotte hadn't been quite the same. The leg had healed, although for some reason, she had a slight limp. Cecily believed that Charlotte might have rheumatism, or perhaps another illness. Certainly she had lost some of that enormous energy, which had carried her through many years at Cavendon, doing so much for everyone. She's certainly served her time, Cecily thought, and so has Daphne. They both need a bit of relief. We need more staff here. If I can find a couple of people.

Unexpectedly, Daphne suddenly sat up, taking Cecily by surprise. Reaching for her handbag, Daphne took out a handkerchief, wiped her eyes and blew her nose.

After a moment, obviously endeavoring to restore her composure, Daphne said, "How terrible I am. **So selfish.** Thinking only of myself. What are my problems, really, in comparison to thousands of women in England? Many have lost their husbands and their sons in this hideous war, and don't have all the privileges we do. I'm ashamed of myself for being so weak."

"You don't have a selfish bone in your body, Daphne," Cecily exclaimed. "All you've ever done all your life is help others. Look, I've managed to find a new cook, and I'm now going to dig up a housekeeper. From somewhere."

"Don't worry about that, Ceci, thank you anyway, but I can manage."

"We'll see about that. Personally I think both Charlotte and you are exhausted. This is a huge place to run, with lots of children. Lane is good as head butler but not quite as good as Hanson. I think we should let Hanson help out more. He's fed up with being retired, and I for one would welcome his smiling face around here a bit more."

Daphne instantly saw the sense of it. "Yes, let's find a few tasks he can do. By the way, where is Hugo?"

"Oh gosh, I forgot for a moment, he's down in the bowels of the vaults, the very bottom one. He went down to remind DeLacy to come up for tea. You see, that vault is so deep she would not have heard the plane crashing. And maybe she's not aware of the time."

"They must be waiting for us in the yellow sitting room, don't you think? It's well after four," Daphne said.

Cecily nodded. "Probably. Are you ready to join them?"

"I am indeed. And I apologize for being so upset, Ceci. I'm an Ingham. And Ingham women are supposed to stand tall and take it on the shoulder. I'll redo the North Wing, and I'll make it even better than it was."

"With Blackie O'Neill's help," Cecily added, happy and relieved that Daphne was calm again and as stalwart as she had always been.

Cecily and Miles had long made a point of spending half an hour alone together in the sitting room adjoining their bedroom. They did this every night once they were ready for bed, to talk over things that mattered to them. It had become a ritual and they wouldn't miss it for the world.

Once they were settled on the sofa in front of the slowly dying fire, Miles said, "I don't know how you all do it, but the women of Britain are heroines. Once the war is over I think the government should give you all a medal. Or something."

Cecily laughed. "Well, at least you're one man who recognizes what we do. Some don't, you know. They tend to look down their noses at women in the war, which we **are** in actuality. I ran into Joyce Bourne the other day. She was on forty-eight hours' leave from the WAAFs, staying a few days with Evelyne. She was moaning that some of the enlisted men tend to mistrust them, treat them as imbeciles."

"They'll soon learn how fantastic those WAAFs are!" Miles exclaimed. "Harry's mentioned them to me. He couldn't do without them on the radar. They've become the real experts."

"I've been thinking about Daphne a lot tonight, Miles," Cecily said. "And I want to find a new housekeeper. She has a lot on her hands at the moment, and the plane crash today has really upset her."

Miles nodded. "I know that, but she certainly put up a good front both at tea, and dinner. In fact, I thought she was really quite magnificent. That's Daphne. She doesn't want to appear weak, doesn't want pity."

"I thought of asking Laura Swann to come up from London for a few weeks, until I find another housekeeper for Cavendon. Also, I told Daphne she should use Hanson more. He might be old, but he's rather fit, and he could do certain things for Daphne herself, so as not to step on Gordon Lane's feet, now **he's** head butler."

"I think bringing Laura in is an excellent idea. Eric always manages very well. He can run the South Street house easily, and there's Mrs. Wilkinson coming in every day to clean and do the ironing. Besides, we're not there that much at the moment."

"I'm glad you agree, Miles. There's another thing. I want to ask you..." Cecily paused, and said a little hesitantly, "I don't want to suggest that Aunt Charlotte is ill or anything serious like that, but she's slowed down, don't you think?"

"You're right, she has. However, as far as I know she doesn't have an illness. My father would have told me. Personally, I think it's her age. Look, Papa has slowed down as well." He frowned, moved closer to his wife, and put his arm around her shoulder. "Don't worry about Charlotte, I think she's doing fine."

Cecily nodded. "I want to do something to cheer everyone up, especially Daphne. I've had an idea which I want to pass by you."

He smiled. "You and your ideas. But they're usually good, so go ahead."

"Daphne and Hugo never went to the London opening of **Gone with the Wind** with us all this past April. Daphne was ill with the flu, if you recall. What I want to do is arrange for us to go and see it. Some of the cinemas have reopened again in Harrogate, and I noticed in the paper this morning that one of them is going to show **Gone with the Wind.** I thought of talking to the manager, trying to book a number of seats for us."

"I know she's longed to see it," Miles said. "And I have a better idea. Why don't you enlist Dulcie's help. James has the connections. Why not ask him to get a print of the film, if he can, and we can hire a projectionist up here, from one of the cinemas, and the equipment required. Let's show **Gone with the Wind** at Cavendon."

"And invite everyone?" Cecily exclaimed, sounding suddenly excited.

"What do you mean by everyone?"

"The entire family, not just Daphne and Hugo. If James can arrange it, we should play the film on a Saturday when everyone's up from London."

Hugging her to him, he kissed her cheek. "There's no one quite like you, Mrs. Ingham, and, by the way, I think Blackie O'Neill is our salvation. Not only for the North Wing, but other parts of the house which still need repairs."

"I'm happy you liked him, and thought his suggestion of tenting the North Wing with tarpaulins was a wonderful solution. That would isolate the wing and protect the rest of the house during the repairs."

"I was impressed with everything he suggested."

They both fell silent. Cecily leaned against Miles, enjoying those few moments alone. She was worried about so many things, yet happy inside. She put her right hand on her stomach protectively. **The baby was safe**. They would be all right. Somehow. They would get through this war no matter what it took. So would the rest of Britain. They were an indomitable race on this little island. Germany would never defeat them.

Fifty-seven

Noel Jollion sat on his bunk bed, reading the letter from his cousin Paloma, totally aghast that a German plane had plunged into Cavendon Hall. What a mess that must have been. Paloma wrote well, and she had described everything down to the last detail. Thankfully no one at Cavendon had been hurt.

Even the Luftwaffe pilot had lived. He must have been lost, off course, Noel thought, out of fuel, losing altitude fast.

Noel tore the letter up, tore it again into the tiniest pieces, and threw them in the waste-paper basket. He never kept anything written, especially family letters. He didn't want anything personal left behind, just in case he bought it, went down in the drink, never made it back to his station: Biggin Hill, just outside London.

Walking outside, Noel glanced up at the sky. Pale blue. No cloud cover. And for the moment no sign of the Luftwaffe. But they would be here soon and he would have to scramble. They all would. And they would then rise up into the air to fight the Heinkels, Stukas, and Messerschmitts sent to kill them.

It was a golden summer morning. The weather had been like this for days. He dropped down into the cool grass, leaned on his side, stretched out his legs, half dozing, as they tried to do as they waited for the alert to go off.

He was tired. Every fighter pilot was. But they could not give in to fatigue. Anyway, they were fit and young, and just over twenty; they were unmarried, and none of them had quite completed their formal education.

Instead they had become fighter pilots of the highest order. He had been one jump ahead of most, since he had learned to fly his own little plane in Yorkshire. The others were good, though, and the Fighter Command was the first line of defense in the Battle of Britain; it was under the command of Sir Hugh Dowding. Their commander in chief was nicknamed "Stuffy"; they were known as "Dowding's Chicks."

Like every flight lieutenant in the RAF, Noel loved airplanes, and the greatest thrill for the boys in blue was to soar up in their Spitfires and Hurricanes and defeat the Luftwaffe.

Noel flew a Spit, as they called it, and he loved her. She fit him like a glove, and he had named her Baby Doll, and that's exactly what she was:

his Baby Doll. Once he was in the cockpit, dressed in his flying suit, oxygen mask, Mae West vest, and parachute he felt truly secure, perfectly safe with Baby Doll. His right hand was close to the red button which controlled his eight machine guns mounted in the two wings. All he had to do was press it for firepower to start.

He had tried to explain these things to his mother, who worried about him constantly, had attempted to reassure her with good information. He had explained that he was flying a single-seater fighter that was so well designed the Germans coveted it. He said that to him it was a gorgeous thing, thirty feet of spectacular beauty. He added that it was powered by a Merlin engine of 1,030 horsepower, had a maximum speed of 360 miles per hour, plus a ceiling height of thirty-four thousand feet. He continued his little dissertation by pointing out that it was faster than its German counterpart at altitudes above fifteen thousand feet and that his Spitfire was highly maneuverable, could slip away from enemy planes with ease. He ended by saying, yet again, that he was in the best plane and she must not worry so much.

Sylvia Jollion's answer had been to announce she would always worry about him, but now needed him to write down all those statistics so that she could better understand what he had just told her. In fact, she learned everything by heart later, and never forgot them.

His father, the commodore, had reassured Sylvia that Noel was as safe as he could possibly be in the middle of a war, even when he was in his Spitfire.

Nonetheless, Noel understood, deep down inside, that his mother would worry. Every mother worried because sons at war were risking their lives every day. And hundreds of thousands of sons would never come back to hug their mothers again.

This morning Noel wore his flying overalls, and that all-essential white silk scarf. When in combat his neck swiveled a lot, and the scarf gave some comfort to him. All the flyers wore them. He reached down for his Mae West, his life jacket, and put it on. He and the other men in the Thirty-ninth Squadron were at Readiness; other pilots on Standby were already in their cockpits. Waiting.

When the alert bell rang, Noel jumped up. He heard his squadron leader's voice ringing out loud and clear. In the distance the sky was darkening. Hundreds of enemy planes were flying toward Biggin Hill.

He adjusted his scarf and scrambled to his Spitfire. He had joined forty or more fighter pilots sprinting to their planes. He was in the cockpit in seconds and his rigger was putting the parachute straps across his shoulders; the Sutton harness straps came next. Finally his oxygen mask was clipped across. Then the oxygen was switched on. He was ready for takeoff.

Noel turned on the engine, adjusted all the switches, and gave the sign to the mechanics on the ground. It was two thumbs up. Any minute now Noel knew the chocks would slip away and his Merlin engine, made by Rolls-Royce, would start to roar and lift his Spit up into the wild blue yonder.

Now his squadron rose. Up and up the planes went in formation. Suddenly the voice of Wing Commander Gerald Rayne was in his earphone, telling him what was happening out there. **Bandits approaching, angels one-eight.** Bandits were the enemy; angels meant height. He had his message loud and clear. He responded swiftly.

Suddenly he was in among the enemy planes. They were surrounding him. Stuka bombers and Messerschmitts fighters were out today. His head constantly moved from side to side, yet he had to keep his eyes peeled and on his front windshield as well. The scarf protected his neck, as he glanced every which way, and constantly so.

Noel saw two Stukas coming toward him, and

he handled his Spit adroitly, dropping down under their bellies. He swerved and he dodged and flew on. And he maneuvered his plane away; that was what he could do with a Spitfire. Then he pressed his thumb on the red firing button and his eight machine guns blazed on either side of him, hitting the oncoming planes.

He nodded. Then grinned, as he saw the Stukas disabled, losing altitude, spiraling into the space below him. Into thin air.

A good hit.

Suddenly, coming right toward him were a string of Messerschmitts and his maneuvering started all over again. His guns blazed, and then he flew higher, had to peel off into a steep climb. He went high up into the clouds for cover. But he knew he had hit one of the Messerschmitts.

Moments later he was plunging down, and a quick glance on both sides told him that all of the Spitfires were being beautifully handled by his brother fighter pilots. Huge damage had been done to the enemy planes.

And then, as sometimes happened lately, the Luftwaffe airplanes turned away, flew back toward the English Channel. Had they recognized that the RAF still had plenty of planes to fly and the guts to keep going, to attack and destroy them? Noel grinned. His squadron had gone up in the air today and other squadrons as well.

What a dogfight it had been. But they had not lost any planes. All flew back; some with damage. But there had been no crashes and not one pilot had bought it.

Noel made a lovely smooth landing at Biggin Hill. His Baby Doll had served him well.

For the past week Noel Jollion and his pal Victor "Tory" Yardley, another flight lieutenant, had often done two flights a day when the Luftwaffe frequently returned in the afternoon and evening. After their success that morning, their squadron leader told them to take a break. "Push off to Teddy Preston's pub, relax, have a drink. You're not flying tomorrow. You've earned it, and you both need a rest."

It was true they did. And they were soon piling into Tory's two-seater Austin Seven, and driving over to the White Hart in Brasted. If the car was a bit rackety it got them there nevertheless.

This pub was the favorite of all the Biggin Hill boys, and when they walked in they were greeted jovially by men from various squadrons based at their station.

Noel and Tory made for the bar, where they both ordered half pints of bitter. Tory said, "Do you have any Gold Flakes? I could do with a good smoke."

Taking out a packet of their favorite cigarettes, Noel offered it to Tory, and then took one himself. After lighting up, Noel glanced around.

It was softly lit, warm, smoky, and very welcoming. There was a piano in a corner where one of the local young women was playing a popular song, "Fools Rush In." Some of the boys in blue were crowded around the piano, singing along with her, letting themselves go.

Noel sighed with pleasure. How wonderful it felt to be here with the other lads, enjoying this much-needed break. The squadron leader had told him last week that he was soon due for a forty-eight-hour weekend pass, and Noel planned to go to London. He could always stay in Kensington with his aunt, Adrianna Bellamy, who was now with the Red Cross. And Cecily and Miles had offered him a room at their house in South Street. He quite liked that idea, because they had also extended the invitation to Tory. South Street was much closer to Shepherd's Market, where Shepherd's Club was located. Noel called it "the unofficial headquarters of Fighter Command." The pilots liked Oscar, the Swiss who managed the place. He knew the gossip, where every pilot was and what he was doing. He was a mine of information, and never failed to welcome them enthusiastically.

Tory turned to Noel and said, "Have you decided where we're going to park ourselves when we get our weekend passes?"

"You just read my mind. Hopefully with Miles and Cecily. I know my aunt would let you stay with her, she's bags of room. But South Street is in Mayfair."

"Aha! You're thinking of Shepherd's. But what about Quags? We could go there."

Noel nodded. "True. Still, I find Quaglino's a bit fancy. Anyway we've time to decide."

Tory nodded in agreement and ordered two more half pints. "I don't want to get sozzled tonight," he confided. "Although we're not going up tomorrow, I don't want to crash the Rolls. It's the only transport we have."

Noel burst out laughing. "If only it were a Rolls," he said, and swung around as two pals from their squadron joined them at the bar.

Burt Mayfield said, "Jesus, I couldn't believe it, Noel, when you pressed the tit and your guns started firing...it was great, and you brought down quite a few of the buggers."

"We all did," Noel answered. "It was a smashing dogfight today."

"And we'll have a lot more...we'll get those bastards in the end. We're going to win. Nothing will stop us," Burt said. "And that's a promise."

Fighter Command fought on courageously. The Luftwaffe continued to attack all of the airfields in England, and hit factories and ships at sea. They were tireless, ruthless, and relentless.

The boys in blue fought back, and in the summer of 1940 they fought the first great air battle ever seen. And, in fact, they thwarted the Nazis' preparations to invade Britain on land. Not one German ship had yet dared to cross the English Channel.

As the weeks wore on, Lord Beaverbrook managed to increase the output of airplanes, and repairs to damaged planes were done more swiftly. Thanks to Winston Churchill's efforts with President Roosevelt, ammunition was now coming from America; it was an immense amount.

At the same time local factories were stepping up on their deliveries of guns, machine guns, and shell.

Britain had never had armies such as those assembled in wartime. On August 15, all the resources of Fighter Command in the south were used as the most difficult period of the battle was approaching. The British government knew that the Germans were about to throw everything they had against their little island.

It was on August 20 that Winston Churchill spoke in the House of Commons. It was a long speech, one which informed the House, and later the people, when it was broadcast that night, just where the country stood at that moment in time. It was Churchill's last few sentences which were truly memorable and touched the hearts of everyone in the country, and indeed the world.

"The gratitude of every home in our island, in our Empire, and indeed throughout the world, except in the abodes of the guilty, goes out to the British airmen who, undaunted by odds, unwearied in their constant challenge and mortal danger, are turning the tide of the war by their prowess and by their devotion. Never in the field of human conflict was so much owed by so many to so few."

Blitz

This royal throne of kings,
this scepter'd isle,
This earth of majesty, this seat of Mars,
This other Eden, demi-paradise,
This fortress built by Nature for herself
Against infection and the hand of war,
This happy breed of men, this little world,
This precious stone set in the silver sea,
Which serves it in the office of a wall,
Or as a moat defensive to a house,
Against the envy of less happier lands,
This blessed plot, this earth, this realm,
this England.

—William Shakespeare **Richard II**

Fifty-eight

Diedre sat at her desk in the special office section at the War Office. As usual, there were no papers on it, only a small card. She picked this up, read it again, and then put it down; something of a puzzle, but she would figure it out.

It was a strange message. Yet her gut instinct told her it was from Valiant. It had not come from a known source, such as the Vatican or Madrid. It had emanated from Lisbon. **City of spies.** That's what she thought about Lisbon. It was a hotbed of intrigue.

Tony came into her office and Diedre picked up the white card. She read it aloud.

"Sea Lion drowned. Barbarossa floats."

Seating himself opposite her, Tony made a face. "From whence does that little epistle spring?"

"Lisbon. Early this morning. It smacks of Valiant, don't you think?"

"I do. Have you figured it out?"

"Some of it. 'Sea Lion drowned' obviously means that there's not going to be a land invasion, the Jerries are not going to cross the English Channel in ships. So therefore Operation Sea Lion is dead, not active any longer. But why Barbarossa?"

Tony frowned. "I'm not too sure who Barbarossa is or rather was. A tyrant of some kind?"

"You're correct. Actually he was King Frederick I of Germany, in 1160 or around that time, anyway in the period of the Holy Roman Empire."

William came into the office at this moment, and took a chair next to Tony. "Do we have a new message from Canaris?"

"I think it's from him." As she spoke, Diedre handed her husband the card.

William read it and said, "I think this means that there's something in the works, code name Operation Barbarossa, because we all know Operation Sea Lion is dead. It's a code name for an oncoming assault, in my opinion. Ahead of us. Valiant always gives us notice. Anyway, who is Barbarossa?" He looked at Diedre, his dark eyes questioning.

"A German king, Frederick I, from centuries ago."

"So why the reference to him? Any ideas?" William asked.

Tony said, "I know he was a tyrant, fought battles." He stood up. "I'm going to look in one of my encyclopedias. Back in a tick."

When they were alone, Diedre asked, "How was the PM, Will?"

"**Angry**. He doesn't believe that the bomb dropped on London on August twenty-third was an accident, which is what's coming from the Jerries. So he's retaliating. The RAF, which has been bombing other German cities, is going to shift to night raids. On Berlin."

For a moment Diedre was silent, her expression concerned. "So things are really stepping up."

"Only too true."

William paused when Tony came back and sat down. He said, "Barbarossa was a fighting man, a general. He died in battle; actually he drowned in a river. But here's the thing. He's a German hero, and local lore is that he is buried under the mountain range near Berchtesgaden, which is where Hitler's Alpine retreat, the Berghof, stands."

"So let's dissect for a minute. German king. A hero. Something of a tyrant. Buried close to Hitler's house. Several linkups there. Anything else about him, Tony?" William sat back, crossed his long legs.

"No. Only that he had a red beard," Tony replied.

"What does the beard signify? Nothing, I

suppose," William said with a slight shrug, looking as perplexed as Tony.

"Forget the beard," Diedre said. "Concentrate on its color. RED. What does that signify to you, Will? Tony?" She raised a brow. When neither of them responded, she said, "When I use the word 'red' I'm usually talking about a Communist."

"Russia!" William exclaimed. "Operation Barbarossa may well be the code name for Hitler's invasion of Russia."

"My God, he wouldn't do that, surely?" Diedre looked alarmed. "He can't possibly be that crazy. He'd be making the same mistake as Napoleon."

"That he would," William agreed. "But listen, nobody ever said the Führer was infallible. In fact, he's very often off the mark. And in my opinion he's a deranged man. I'm going to pass this on to C, find out what MI6 knows."

"Maybe more than we do," Diedre remarked, and stood up. "I'm sorry, but I now have to leave to meet Dulcie and Cecily, mainly to talk about the disposition of Great-Aunt Gwendolyn's property, as well as a few other bits of business."

Both men rose, and she kissed William on the cheek and said to Tony, "Don't forget, you're invited to James's concert on Thursday night."

"It's in my book, and I'd never miss something like that."

When she arrived at the Ritz Hotel and went into the restaurant, Diedre was relieved to see that Cecily was alone. Dulcie was often late these days. She always had a lot to do for James, and she was now a volunteer with the Red Cross doing office work several days a week. Like her sisters, she felt obliged to do her "bit," as she called it.

After kissing Cecily on the cheek, and sitting down, Diedre asked, "Are you still feeling all right? Baby is comfy, I hope."

Cecily laughed. "Baby is comfy and so is Mummy, thank you."

Diedre said, "This lunch is on me today. You're always picking up the bill. I know you think the Ritz is **your** canteen, but it's mine, too."

Shrugging, smiling, Cecily said, "That's fine. Anyway, it's a good idea to share. We should all take turns. DeLacy's not coming, by the way. She's still at Cavendon, sorting out the paintings at Great-Aunt Gwen's house. Making an inventory and cataloging every picture."

"That's a lot of work, Ceci. William and I could do it before we move in."

"You'll be too busy painting the house. Throughout. It needs it, although you might want to keep a few of the lovely old wallpapers on some of the bedroom walls. Now that the house belongs to you, there's no reason why you can't do whatever you want."

"I suppose the paintings are going to be put in the vaults?"

"Yes, for safety. Great-Aunt Gwen left the paintings to the Cavendon Restoration Fund. DeLacy and Dulcie will sell them after the war and the money will be useful. You can have your choice of her furnishings, though; the rest can be sold for the fund."

"I know. Her will was very clear. And incidentally I thought that was lovely of Great-Aunt Gwen to leave us each that little attaché case with some of her jewelry and one of her lovely shawls in it. What did she leave Walter?"

"She gave my father and Miles beautiful gold cuff links, and, like us, a framed photograph of herself, signed."

Diedre couldn't help laughing. "Like royalty. But I think she's been terribly generous to all of us and she cheered Papa up by gifting her art to the fund."

"I agree, and Daphne was elated, too. The destruction of the North Wing really hit home, upset her after the work she'd put in over the years."

"She's better though, isn't she?" Diedre asked, sounding worried.

"Like her old self. Oh here's Dulcie! Looking very glamorous indeed."

"You know she's defiant by nature, and once war was declared her defiance soared. She believes in getting made-up and dressed up every day, and is determined not to let the war get her down."

"Hello, you two," Dulcie said, and sat down at the table. "Gosh, I'd love a drink, a glass of champagne. It'll be a pick-me-up. I've had quite a morning with James and Sid at the theater."

"Oh Sid's back in the act, is he?" Diedre said.

"He has been for ages. He failed his medical for the army. He has flat feet. Can you believe anyone would be turned down for that reason? I thought we needed soldiers."

"Miles told me he'd heard we have an army of over two million men now. How about that! All of them in England."

Dulcie grinned. "I know we'll beat the 'Bloody Huns,' as Sid calls them. You're going to love the troupe and the show on Thursday. It's really funny. And it's been very successful traveling across the country, visiting airfields, military camps, and local theaters in the provinces. What a relief the West End is no longer dark, now that the government has allowed the theaters and cinemas to reopen. It's done everybody good, especially James, who's so busy acting he's no longer frustrated."

"The government began to realize the public needs to be distracted, to look forward to something, like going to see a film or a play. They want to take our minds off the war, keep us cheerful," Diedre remarked. "And I for one am glad. I've missed going to the pictures."

She now beckoned to a waiter and ordered a bottle of Pol Roger champagne.

Cecily, looking across at Dulcie, said, "How many are there in the cast of the show?"

"Six with James. Why do you ask?"

"I was thinking of giving a little supper after the show, at the South Street house. And I'm trying to figure out how many we would be."

Dulcie did a quick calculation and said, "Six of **us,** including James. Five in the cast. That's eleven. Oh, Felix and Constance, because James invited them to the show, make thirteen."

"And you said I could invite Tony," Diedre reminded Dulcie.

"The total comes to fourteen," Cecily announced. "I think I've enough food. I have bottled vegetables and fruit in the cellar at South Street, and I brought down two chickens from Cavendon last night. To be roasted. Oh, and a leg of lamb. And it's not one of Ophelia's limbs."

"That's a great idea, having the supper," Dulcie responded, her eyes twinkling. "But you don't have to invite all of the cast. Only Edward Glendenning. James wouldn't like to have him left out. He's James's partner in this endeavor."

"How will you manage with only Eric?" Diedre asked. "Laura's at Cavendon helping Daphne."

"There's my lovely char, Mrs. Wilkinson. And

she says she can bring her sisters Florrie and Gladys to help out. I'd do a buffet. Eric's good at that."

Dulcie said, "I can get my housekeeper, Mrs. Pearl, to make mashed potatoes, rice, and pasta. Eric would only have to heat them up. They'd work well with the chicken and the lamb."

"And I can go to my butcher," Diedre said. "I have a few food coupons left."

"Don't use coupons, either of you," Cecily said. "We've enough food, and of course all the cast must come. We haven't had much fun, any of us, for the longest time. Thursday will be a lovely get-together, and I think the cast deserves a treat, too."

The show starring James Brentwood and Edward Glendenning was sold out. There wasn't a seat left. And it was a hit from the moment the two actors walked on the stage dressed as the ugly sisters in Cinderella, with Marianne Taft as Cinderella. It was a skit and the audience roared and clapped and stamped their feet and wanted more.

Popular songs of the moment were sung, and the audience was invited to join in for a sing-song. The comedian told jokes, old and new, and had them in stitches. It was endless, simple fun that went down well.

Everyone enjoyed it because the audience needed a laugh, and laugh they did. Men dressed up as women hobbling in high heels always brought hilarity on any stage, and James and Edward were particularly good at camping it up even more, just to keep the laughter going.

Later, back at the South Street house, Miles and Cecily greeted the cast warmly, and within seconds wine they had found in the cellar and champagne were flowing. They were determined to make the evening as lavish and as successful as possible. Who knew when they would ever have a party like this again?

Fifty-nine

Finally the all-clear siren sounded. James and Dulcie left the air-raid shelter in the cellar of their building and went back to their flat.

The phone was ringing as they went inside, and James strode over to his desk and answered it.

"Brentwood here," he said.

"Hello, it's Miles, James. Just checking in to ask if you and Dulcie are all right?"

"We are, but it was a long raid this afternoon. I'm assuming you and Ceci are okay as well."

"Yes, we are, James. I'm phoning because I'm not sure whether you know this, but the East End has been gutted. They've taken a terrible beating and so have the docks, which are burning as we speak. A ball of fire, I hear."

James was silent for a moment, and then he exclaimed, "The docks are burning! The East End is gutted! Oh my God, I can't believe this. I come from there, that's where I grew up, and my father and brother worked on the docks. Oh my God, Sid still lives there." James suddenly realized he was shaking he was so shocked and undone.

"It's just horrendous, and we wanted you to know. We only found out because Emma Harte phoned Ceci a few minutes ago. Ceci wants to speak to you, Jamie, just a moment."

Dulcie had come into James's den at this moment and stood staring at him. She saw he was chalk white and trembling, and she stepped closer, endeavoring to understand.

"Yes, hello, Ceci," he said into the phone, turning away from the desk, sitting down before his legs gave way. That he was genuinely shocked was patently obvious to Dulcie, who took another chair, her eyes riveted on him.

"Yes, I know, Miles told me," James said. "I must go there immediately and find Sid. He's like family to me, Ceci."

"You can't go now, James," Cecily said at the other end of the line. "But you can tomorrow. That's why Emma phoned me a little while ago. She's looking for helpers for Sunday morning, to go and distribute food to the people who have been bombed out. She's trying to pull together a big team. Miles won't let me go, because I'm pregnant. But he's going and so are Diedre and William. What about you? And you might find Sid."

"Of course I'll go and help, and so will Dulcie, but I want to go **now**. To find Sid," he insisted, as if he'd not heard her a moment ago.

"You'll never find him, James, not tonight. Anyway the police won't let you get near the place. Right now they are escorting hundreds of people to the tube stations, so they can have shelter tonight, sleep there. The Red Cross is there and so is the St. John's Ambulance Brigade. Other agencies are also doing things to help."

"I just hope Sid is alive—" James could not finish his sentence, and his voice broke.

He beckoned to Dulcie and handed her the phone. Tears were running down his face; he groped in his jacket pocket for a handkerchief.

Dulcie said, "I sort of got the gist of it, Ceci. The East End has been bombed heavily, that's it, isn't it?"

"Yes, and we knew that James would want to know since he grew up there. And now he's worrying about Sid. I've no idea how he'd find him...I suppose James will have to just wait for Sid to contact him."

"Tell me about tomorrow, Cecily. What's that all about?"

"Emma Harte has a friend who's married to a government minister, who asked Emma if she could help with food from Harte's. Emma called to see if I would join a team of people going to the East End tomorrow to distribute food from her shop, hot drinks, blankets, that kind of thing. She wants people to take any food **they** can spare, and just go and be part of the rescue team. Miles, Diedre, and William are going, and Diedre's going to call Tony Jenkins. More hands, more food gets given away."

"You can count on us. Tell me where and what time."

"Nine tomorrow morning at the front entrance of Harte's store in Knightsbridge."

"We'll be there. Oh my God, the petrol. I wonder how many coupons I have?"

"Oh I forgot for a moment. Don't bring your own car. Emma has hired several buses to take the food and the people to the East End."

"That's a good idea. We're on board, Ceci. Tell Miles we'll see him tomorrow."

Once she had hung up, Dulcie went over to James and sat down on the arm of the chair. She repeated what Ceci had said, and he nodded, put his arms around her and pulled her onto his lap. He held her very close and wept quietly against her shoulder.

Eventually he took control of himself and wiped his eyes. "I can't bear the thought of the East End being wiped out, all those East Enders like me being robbed of their homes and their livelihoods. This bloody war is hideous."

The phone rang and Dulcie slipped out of her

husband's arms and answered it. It was James's sister, Ruby, at the other end of the phone.

"He's fine, Ruby, but rather upset. As I'm sure you are. Obviously. Let me put him on the phone."

"Hello, Ruby, darling," James said, "I just heard the news from Miles. The East End has been bombed to smithereens, and Docklands, too. All our memories are gone…Bow Common Lane gone and West India Docks close to Bow…"

"I'm glad you and Dulcie are all right, and also that you made us all move years ago."

"So am I, Ruby…the rest of the family are all right, aren't they?"

"Yes, Jamie, we're all alive and kicking. Now you take care of yourself, and Dulcie. I'm glad to know the children are in Yorkshire."

"Me, too, Ruby. I love you, and give our love to everyone else. By the way, we're going over there tomorrow to help distribute food. I'll put Dulcie on, she'll explain."

Dulcie did so and Ruby said she wanted to come and help; Dulcie told her she **should** join them and gave her instructions.

An hour later the phone rang once more, and James, who was still at his desk, picked it up.

"Brentwood, here."

"It's Sid."

"Oh thank God you're all right! I've been worried about you. Where are you?"

"I walked and walked until I found a phone booth that wasn't a bleedin' ruin. And I don't know where I am."

"Miles called and told me that the East End is wiped out and the docks. Were you there when it happened?"

"I was. I saw it all. Bleedin' bloody Huns, they bombed me 'ouse right out from under me. And the docks 'ave gone as well. Where yer dad used ter work, and yer bruvver David..." Sid started to snuffle and James knew he was crying.

After a moment James said, "Sid, where are you going to sleep tonight? Look, walk until you find a cabbie, get in and tell him to bring you here. I'll pay for the cab. You can stay here until Ruby finds a solution."

"Naw. Thanks, Jamie, but I'll kip down in the tube station wiv the others. Ta, anyway."

"Dulcie and I are going to the East End tomorrow, to help distribute food. We'll meet you."

"Where? It's bombed, every fing. It's a pile of rubble. Yer'll never find me. I don't even know where Bow Common Lane is, that's wot a bleedin' mess it is."

"Try and find me then. And if you don't I'll see you at the rehearsal hall on Monday. Take care of yourself, Sid."

"I don't aim to bloody well die 'cos of them bloody Huns," Sid muttered. "Not bloody likely."

Not one of them could believe the scenes of devastation they encountered on Sunday when they went to the bomb sites in the East End. They had been driven there on one of Emma's buses, and James, Dulcie, Ruby, Diedre, William, Miles, and Tony walked in a group, distributing food to the people who were working on the piles of rubble. It was rubble that had once been their homes.

But they were cheery and warm, polite and grateful. The men and women thanked them for bringing food and hot drinks; many of the men had quick retorts, always disparaging, about the Jerries. But the amazing thing was that they had ready smiles and easy laughter, and were obviously endeavoring to make the best of it. The attitude seemed to be: **What else can we do?**

As they walked carefully through the rubble, James said to Miles and the others, "By God, but they're strong and courageous. I don't mind telling you I'm proud to be English when I see this lot."

Suddenly, Ruby exclaimed, "Oh look, James …Dulcie. Over there. Isn't that Mr. Churchill? I recognize his big hat and his cigar."

"Indeed it is," James answered. People were cheering Winston, clapping, showing their appreciation. James said, "Let's go over and do a bit of cheering ourselves. That man needs our support today."

As they joined the throng, Diedre, sharp as always, noticed that Winston Churchill had tears in his eyes when he spoke to the crowds surrounding him. He spoke with a certain gentleness that was unique, and as always his words were inspiring. Diedre felt herself choking up. She knew he truly understood what this terrible devastation and destruction meant to these Londoners. And she believed he shared their hurt, suffered with them.

No wonder he was retaliating by bombing Berlin relentlessly. She recognized that it was nonstop warfare ahead of them and for a long time. But what else could Churchill do but defend his people? Not only with the RAF and their bombs, the Royal Navy and the army, but with his words as well. He gave them courage and hope with his uplifting speeches, and he did it better than anyone.

William put his arm around her and held her close. "He's the most amazing man, isn't he?" he whispered against her hair. Diedre could only nod.

Suddenly her head came up when she heard James bellowing, "Sid! Sid! We're over here!"

A moment or two later, James's dresser, a full-blown Cockney because he had been born within the sound of Bow Bells like James himself, was running across the rubble. He kept tripping, stumbling, and falling down, but he picked himself up again and again. And he ran on until James was hugging him close, flooded with relief.

"Thank goodness you're all right, Sid." James laughed, and added, with a wink, "You're very necessary in my life. I can't do without you."

"Yer dint 'ave ter tell me that. I knows it," Sid muttered, but he looked pleased.

Once the food had been distributed James's group began to slowly return to the buses. Unexpectedly, they were stopped by a line of policemen.

Within minutes they understood why. The police were making way for a large black car out of which stepped Queen Elizabeth and King George VI.

The crowds went mad, cheering them with all of their hearts.

Their king and queen walked among them, talking to them, showing their concern and their understanding of their terrible plight. And it was quite a sight to behold. The queen was dressed in one of her beautiful pastel outfits, the king in his Royal Navy uniform. These

Londoners stood taller, looked proud because they understood that they mattered to this royal couple, who walked in the rubble and dust to comfort them.

The Blitz had begun.

Everyone understood it would not end for some time. And it did not. The bombings went on for months and the British people realized that it would be their lot to live with the Luftwaffe raids. The casualties had been heavy already. Thousands and thousands died, both civilians and their fighting military. The Second World War would last longer than any of them had ever imagined.

Standing Tall

Bring me my bow of burning gold!
Bring me my arrows of desire!
Bring me my spear! O clouds, unfold!
Bring me my chariot of fire!
I will not cease from Mental Fight,
Nor shall my Sword sleep in my hand,
Till we have built Jerusalem,
In England's green and pleasant Land.

—William Blake, from the hymn "Jerusalem"

Sixty

The Cavendon Luck ebbs and flows. Cecily looked at the words she had just written in her private notebook, and nodded to herself. She liked the phrase. Genevra had said it to her yesterday, when she had dropped in to see her, after visiting her mother in Little Skell village.

"The little one is the luck," Genevra had then muttered. "She has all the luck in the world... treasure her. She's a blessed child...an old soul."

Cecily had always listened to Genevra, paid attention to everything the Romany woman had said to her over the years. And she had never found her to be wrong.

Turning her head slightly, Cecily looked at the child sitting at the small desk near the fireplace. Her burnished brown hair with its russet tints gleamed in the afternoon sunlight. Her head was bent as she concentrated on her drawing, her crayon held tightly in her hand. Not only did the child look like her, she had inherited her power of concentration and some of her other traits as well. But she was like Miles in certain ways, a little stubborn but as warm and loving as her father, and as good-natured as he was.

It was her birthday today. Later this afternoon she would have her party with her cousins in the yellow sitting room. It was January 24, 1944, and she was three years old.

How was that possible? The years had gone so swiftly. Good times, bad times; still, the family had survived. So far. And they had taken everything in their stride.

Only the other day, Dulcie had said they must be made of iron. Cecily had laughed, and retorted that she preferred to think of them as being cut from shining steel.

Turning the pages of her notebook bound in blue leather, Cecily searched for earlier years, her eyes lingering on them. The book was not a diary or an engagement book. It had plain white paper to be written on whenever she had something special she wanted to remember, things that were important to her. **Meaningful.**

Staring her in the face was the date she had written in on one very happy occasion. **Saturday, December 21, 1940.** She smiled when she saw the notation: **Charlie came home today with two legs.**

It was true, he had. No one had expected him.

It was a surprise for Daphne and Hugo. She and Miles had known because Charlie had phoned her at the shop in the Burlington Arcade. He had told her he was going to be at Chapel Allerton Hospital, just outside Leeds, for a week, then he would be released. The hospital was renowned for its work with disabled men, and especially amputees who had been wounded in the war. She and Miles had arranged with Winston Harte to go and pick up Charlie, because he was so well-known at the hospital. Also, Emma wanted Charlie to become acquainted with Winston. A clever woman, she foresaw that Charlie might need advice or help at some point in the next few months.

Sitting back in the chair, Cecily closed her eyes. She could recall that day easily. It had been a Saturday afternoon, just before Christmas, and she and Daphne had been hanging ornaments on the Christmas tree in the blue sitting room. They usually decorated the big fir tree over several days because it stood very high.

There had been a moment of quiet. They had both been concentrating on their selections of ornaments when a familiar voice said, "Hello, Mother. Here I am at last."

Daphne had instantly dropped the ornament she was holding, and swung around, a startled look of surprise on her face.

"Charlie!" She gasped when she saw him.

"Charlie, it's you." She was about to move toward him, but Cecily had held her back. "Let him come to you, so you can see him walk," Cecily had whispered.

Daphne had done exactly that, and they had stood together watching him walk forward, tall, straight as an arrow, with only the slightest limp visible. He was wearing the dress uniform of the Coldstream Guards and Cecily thought he looked astonishing. He was twenty-three and looked very young. His face showed no signs of damage or suffering. He was as handsome as he had always been. There was a dignity and an elegance about him as he walked toward his mother without faltering.

Miles walked in after him, grinning from ear to ear, and it had been quite a homecoming, and certainly it was the best Christmas they had had in a long time. Everyone in the family was very proud of Charlie, most especially his parents. He now had a job on the **Daily Mail,** where he edited one of the special sections on the continuing war. In her will, Great-Aunt Gwen had left her flat in London to her nephew, the earl, who had given it to his grandson Charlie. Charles and Charlotte rarely visited London these days, and it had been standing empty ever since Lady Gwendolyn's death.

Death. Too many deaths, Cecily thought, sitting up, leafing through the notebook. There had been several since their matriarch had passed. She flipped the pages.

She stared at the date she had written in after little Gwen's birth: **January 24, 1941.** A wonderful year in certain ways. The birth of their little girl, an easy birth, and the arrival of a most beautiful child.

Churchill had made a deal with President Roosevelt, and Lend-Lease had begun that year. The Americans had started to send food, ships, and ammunition to them, and were helping them to win the war.

Even though the bombs had continued to drop and had scarred London, smashed parts of it to smithereens, the public were in an upbeat mood. Cecily believed that this was because Churchill inspired them, kept them going with his patriotic speeches.

April 10, 1942, caught her eye. Elise Steinbrenner had been twenty-one that day. Cecily had given a champagne tea for her at the house in South Street. Tea sandwiches, scones and jam, and a sponge cake with a candle on it, the best they could do because of rationing. Elise was a beautiful girl and the professor was bursting with pride that day. **Heddy.** Suddenly Cecily thought of her, wondering if she was still alive. She had written to her family from Paris for quite a few months and then the letters had stopped abruptly. She was lost in the turmoil and chaos of war…

Her father-in-law, the Sixth Earl of Mowbray, had also died, but his had been a gentle death, and for that Cecily and Miles had been grateful. He had not been ill. Rather, he had been frail and absentminded in the summer of 1942. The day he had left them was imprinted on her mind, and would be forever.

It was Venetia, their nine-year-old daughter, who had run to Cecily in her office in the annex that fateful afternoon. Venetia had rushed in, looking worried, and explained that she had to come. Aunt Charlotte needed her. Grandpa was fast asleep and Aunt Charlotte couldn't awaken him.

That moment suddenly flashed through her mind and her eyes filled. Charles had been sitting with Charlotte after lunch, and he turned to her and said he was going to have a little doze. Charlotte had continued to read her book until she heard a rather strange gurgling sound. She had stood up, leaned over Charles, wondering if something was wrong. He had smiled at her, reached for her hand. And then he had died. Charlotte, who had run to the door of the library, searching for Lane, had seen Venetia going upstairs and sent her instead.

Three days later they had stood in the sunlight, all of them dressed in black, watching Charles Ingham's coffin being lowered into his grave in the cemetery near the church on the estate. The family was bereft, and let their grief and sorrow show. Why not? Cecily had thought that day, and she thought it again now. They had all loved him and he had been the most extraordinary man. It was only when the vicar had addressed her as "your ladyship" that she realized she was now the Seventh Countess of Mowbray and Miles the Seventh Earl.

There was a little rustling sound and suddenly a dainty three-year-old girl was standing next to her desk, holding out a handkerchief. "It's for you, Mummy. Why are you crying?"

As she took the handkerchief being offered by a small grubby hand, Cecily smiled. "I'm not crying, Gwen. I'm happy today because it's your birthday."

The child nodded and handed her the drawing she had just finished. "This is for you, Mummy."

"Thank you, darling, how sweet of you." Cecily took the drawing, stared at it, and smiled. It depicted a very wobbly-looking birthday cake with lots of wobbly candles on it.

Cecily bent forward and kissed the cheek of her daughter, who explained, "It's for **your** birthday."

"I'll keep it until then," Cecily said, and put her arms around Gwen and held her close. She adored all her children but somehow this child filled the sad little corners in her heart.

Sixty-one

Cecily was glad to be back in London, something that was harder to accomplish these days. She had come up to town from Yorkshire with Miles last night. He had an appointment to see his eye doctor, and she had jumped at the idea of accompanying him on the train.

It was a windy March morning, cold but sunny, and she enjoyed her walk from the South Street house to the Burlington Arcade. She was bundled up in a heavy overcoat and woolen scarf.

Cecily was meeting Dulcie there later as she wanted to buy one of her white silk scarves, a copy of those worn by the fighter pilots. Women loved them and she couldn't keep them in stock. She had also had good sales on her square scarves, which were bright and colorful. Women tied them in a turban around their heads. Even Clementine Churchill, Winston's wife, favored the scarf-into-turban look. All of

Cecily's accessories were selling well, but not couture. She hadn't expected it to be bought in wartime. Her ready-made line was breaking even, but she knew sales would probably pick up this summer.

Things were looking up for them, and there was a more positive feeling everywhere. This was due to America. On December 7, 1941, the Japanese had bombed Pearl Harbor. In an unprovoked attack, two hundred planes destroyed most of America's Pacific Fleet, killing thousands of troops and civilians. President Roosevelt immediately declared war on Japan; then Germany declared war on America. This prompted the president to declare war on Germany, and the United States entered the war. Fighter pilots, airmen, soldiers, and sailors had begun to arrive in 1942. Their presence had changed the face of London, if not indeed England.

It seemed to her that all of the Americans she and Miles had met were tall, good-looking, and full of natural charm, and she rather enjoyed being called "ma'am," quaint though it was.

She and her four sisters-in-law had mingled with quite a lot of American servicemen at Emma Harte's canteen on the Fulham Road. Emma was generous in every way, and with sons and a son-in-law in the war she had seen the need for a place where soldiers, sailors, and airmen could meet, relax, get to know local young women, and enjoy themselves in general.

To that end, she had bought a warehouse, fitted it out with several bars, kitchens, toilets, four comfortable sitting rooms, and even a dance floor. Which naturally needed a band, and eventually a singer, so that all of the favorites could be sung.

The canteen had become the talk of London, and young servicemen and women, and many local girls flocked to it. Emma had made it an international spot, and so every nationality could be found there. Poles, Czechs, and French men who had joined the RAF some years ago, as well as the Yanks, as Noel Jollion called them. There was a great spirit there, friendliness and warmth. It was not unusual to see Emma socializing several nights a week. Her daughters Daisy and Elizabeth often came and helped out, making sandwiches and coffee, pouring drinks and looking after the boys and girls of the armed forces.

It was their turn soon, and Cecily was looking forward to going to the canteen again. Usually Miles, James, and William tagged along, because they found Emma fascinating, and they enjoyed the buzz and the activity at the canteen and the company of the men.

Dulcie was waiting for her when she arrived at the shop, and Aunt Dottie was soon pressing a cup of hot tea in her hands.

"It's a stinker out there," Dulcie said, after giving her a hug. "And poor James is on location today. Shooting outside. I shouldn't say 'poor,' should I? He's a happy boy, now that he's making a film. For Sir Alexander Korda. In his element, he is. The good thing is Sir Alex is now running MGM in London for Louis B. so this film is part of James's contract."

"I've got to let Emma know when we'll go to the canteen. What about this Thursday? Miles and I are staying in London all week. Back to Cavendon on Friday."

"It's fine with me. Let's ask Diedre and DeLacy. I'll go with you, even if they can't."

After finishing their tea, they went upstairs to Cecily's office. Dulcie settled herself in a chair. "After the war, we might go back to Hollywood for a while," she confided. "James enjoys working there, and he misses Clark Gable. I think Clark might miss him, too. He was devastated when Carole Lombard was killed in that awful plane crash two years ago, and when he was here last year James thought he was a totally changed man. And I agreed. Clark has never gotten over her death. And he never will. James was a bit embarrassed not to be in uniform, when there was Clark, a captain in the American Air Corps and he'd been in combat too, a gunner. Flying over Germany."

"But didn't James tell him he had a problem with damage to a nerve in one of his ears?"

"Clark knew that already. But you know what men can be like. It's always irked James that he wasn't fighting in the trenches."

"Miles too, but he has problems with his eyes. That's why he's wearing glasses now. But let's face it, Miles is needed at Cavendon. Who'd run the estate without him?"

"Daphne of course!" Dulcie shot back. "You know she's ready to take on anything, especially if it has to do with Cavendon. We have to make her a halo soon. Or maybe even two."

"Don't be mean, Dulcie. You know she's a good person."

"I'm just teasing, Daphne's the best."

Noel Jollion made a beeline for the Four Dees and Cecily the moment he spotted them at Emma's canteen later that week.

After kissing each one of them on the cheek, he asked, "Where are your husbands?"

"In one of the sitting rooms, having a drink with Emma and Blackie. Why?" Dulcie said.

"Because I've brought some of my Yanks along, and they're itching to do a bit of jiving. Jitterbugging. What about it, girls?"

Cecily said, "I'm not the best person for jitter-bugging, Noel. However, I can do a foxtrot."

"I'd do a jitterbug," DeLacy said. "But I have a

friend coming and I'd better wait for him."

"Oh come on, give one of my great Yanks a chance, DeLacy. They're all wonderful guys. I love 'em all."

"I love their uniforms," Dulcie cut in, giving Noel a sly look and winking. "So I'll do a jitterbug with pleasure."

"Who's your Yank then?" Noel asked DeLacy.

"I thought you'd met him. Oh there he is now." As she spoke DeLacy excused herself and hurried over to a tall, good-looking colonel who was glancing around, seeking her out.

A moment later she was bringing him over to meet Noel. "This is Cameron...Cameron Daniels. Cameron, meet Noel Jollion. He's a fighter pilot from Biggin Hill and a neighbor from Yorkshire."

The two men shook hands and immediately started to talk about flying. DeLacy laughed, shrugged, and said to Cecily, "Let's go and get a glass of bubbly. Cameron's going to be at it for hours. He can't resist boy talk and being up there in the sky."

As she sat at the bar talking to DeLacy and listening to her comments about the world in general, Cecily was filled with admiration for her best friend, whom she had known since their childhood.

In the last ten years or so, DeLacy had changed,

had gained confidence in herself, and had become one of the great experts on art in London. Travers Merton, now long dead, had loved her deeply, as she had loved him, and his adoration of her had given her a sense of self, repaired the damage of her first marriage.

Cecily was relieved when DeLacy had given Peter Musgrove his marching orders and broken up with him a few years ago. He had been a bit of a pest at first, not leaving her alone, and then he had been called up. He'd gone off to war; Peter had been killed at Dunkirk. At least DeLacy assumed he was dead. His body had never been found. DeLacy had behaved like the lady she was and had gone to see his parents, to offer them her condolences.

"Do you like Cameron?" DeLacy suddenly asked, catching Cecily off guard, having been talking about art a moment ago.

"Yes, I do, and so does Miles," Cecily answered truthfully. "Why do you ask?"

DeLacy gave her a small, knowing smile. "He's very serious about me, Ceci. What do you think?"

"How do you feel about Cameron? That's what I want to know."

"Serious. But cautious. He's a really lovely man, a bit like Travers in certain ways, thoughtful, a gentleman, and he makes me laugh. By the way, he told me that Clark was stationed at

Polebrook, when he was in England in 1943. The other men had thought it was a big joke, a famous film star being in the air force. But Cameron had liked and admired him. He said he was a man's man, and the other pilots had eventually come around, had admired Clark, too. He's not a phony, that's what Cameron said."

"James swears by him, and I must admit I liked him myself. He's nice, not a show-off. Why did you bring up Clark?"

"Because he'd once said to Cameron that his own life had taught him to live each day as if it were his last."

"Perhaps that's because of the way his wife Carole died. Her body was...they didn't actually find her body, just parts," Cecily said. "Clark confided in Dulcie, told her that all he had left of her was a piece of a broken earring, a ruby-and-diamond earring. He had given them to her that Christmas. He wears that bit of earring in a locket around his neck."

DeLacy simply gazed at her, but her eyes had filled up. "How sad, how terribly sad that she died in that way."

A moment later Cameron came to ask DeLacy to dance and Cecily watched them on the floor together. DeLacy looked beautiful these days, better than she ever had. Tonight she was wearing a deep blue silk dress Cecily had made for her three years ago, and it swirled and floated around her as she danced. What gorgeous legs she has, Cecily thought. She is gorgeous. Any man would fall for her. She liked the look of them together...as if they were meant to be. Ginger Rogers and Fred Astaire, Cecily thought, smiling to herself. They did a very good foxtrot.

Later that evening, their little group gathered around the piano and joined in when some of the servicemen and women sang along with the pianist. All their favorites echoed on the warm air. "The White Cliffs of Dover," "I'll Be Seeing You," "Fools Rush In," and many other songs made popular by Vera Lynn, the Forces' Sweetheart, as she was called.

There was a moment, just before Cecily and Miles left, when she went over to DeLacy and drew her to one side. "Has Cameron asked you to marry him, DeLacy?"

"Not yet, but I think he will."

"And what answer will you give him?"

"I believe I'll say yes."

"You'll go away and leave us. We couldn't bear that," Cecily said, and then smiled. "But it's your life and you must find your own happiness."

Leaning forward, DeLacy kissed Cecily on the cheek. "Thank you, darling. I'll always be here for you."

Sixty-two

Almost five thousand ships. Over two hundred thousand soldiers, sailors, and coastguardsmen. An armada so massive none like it had ever been seen before in the history of mankind. Firepower beyond belief. And a will to win so deeply imbedded in the men, it had to succeed.

This vast armada stood just off the coast of Normandy. It was June 6, 1944, and at five minutes past the hour of midnight Operation Overlord would commence: the invasion of German-occupied France by the combined armies of the Allies.

The two supreme commanders were an American general, Dwight D. Eisenhower, and a British general, Sir Bernard Law Montgomery. Together they would lead their troops to victory by defeating Hitler and the Third Reich. They had vowed to aid their allies and so save civilization from an evil dictator who had sought to dominate the world.

Across the water, facing the armada, was the Normandy coastline, chosen because of its good beaches, favorable tides, and relatively weak coastal defenses. Five sections of the beaches were chosen by the commanders and they had been named Utah, Omaha, Gold, Juno, and Sword.

The Americans would land on Omaha and Utah, the Canadians on Juno, and the British on Sword and Gold. Their aim was to take the beaches, hold them, fight off the Germans, and push them into retreat.

After a massive naval and air bombardment, several thousand men waded through the shallow water to their given beaches. The invasion had begun at six-thirty A.M.

Among these first few thousand troops who went onshore were Thomas and Andrew Stanton, the twin sons of Lady Daphne and Hugo. They were in the Eighth Infantry Brigade, which they had joined once they had finished their military training course at Sandhurst, the military academy outside London.

They were typical Inghams—tall, fair-haired, blue-eyed, and identical twins. They found it difficult to be apart for long periods, but they knew that they might become separated in this huge battle about to begin.

To that end they had, a few days ago, spoken

to their parents, joking and laughing and mentioning nothing at all about their fighting lives as soldiers. Then they had gone out to dinner when they were up in London on a thirty-six-hour pass. They agreed that their responsibility was to themselves and the job they had to do. No looking out for each other, which would be distracting. They had to take their chances, and make it as best they could. "We've got the Ingham luck," Thomas had said.

At first, resistance on the beach was fairly strong. Casualties were mounting and some of the vehicles were wrecked. But most of their armored vehicles landed successfully, and the British troops were able to secure the area.

It was nine-thirty A.M. when the Royal Engineers had cleared seven of the eight exits from Sword, allowing the initial advance to begin. The troops flooded out, marched into the seaside town of Ouistreham, on Sword's eastern end. Again, there was a lot of tough resistance. But eventually soldiers were able to clear it of enemy strong points.

By nighttime, the Eighth Infantry had linked up with paratroopers of the Sixth Airborne Division, who were holding the bridges on the river Orne and Caen Canal. The paratroopers had earlier disabled gun batteries in a night-time battle at Merville. As it turned out the only major German attack in the area of Caen was launched by the Twenty-first Panzer Division.

Much later that evening, the Stanton twins found each other and smoked a cigarette together before preparing for the next day. And that was how it was going to be from now on, and they knew it.

Because the Germans had been caught off guard, not expecting an assault because of uncertain weather, they were not properly prepared. So the Allies on every beach mostly encountered poor resistance. They were able to push forward at a good pace. By June 11 the beaches Utah, Omaha, Gold, Juno, and Sword were linked by troops and armored vehicles in a continuous front. They had accomplished what they had set out to do. And they were closing in on the Third Reich.

Everyone in England was cheering this enormous Allied effort. It was not victory yet, but the newspapers and broadcasters were shouting out the good news constantly. It certainly helped to boost public morale.

Diedre celebrated along with the family, but in her heart she was deeply troubled. Her undercover asset, Étoile, had been missing for almost a week. Diedre had just been warned by a contact in the French underground that Étoile might have been captured. The Gestapo were now operating in the south of France.

She was well aware that the life expectancy for a member of the French Resistance was not much longer than six months. But Étoile wasn't a **maquisard** in the **maquis.** They were there to help her if she needed something, but that was all.

As she sat in her office on June 15, a few days after the success of D-day, she suddenly had a curious sense of foreboding. Something serious had happened to Étoile, and perhaps the worst thing of all. Earlier in the week, she had suggested to William that perhaps they should ask Émeraude to become involved. But William had dismissed this idea. He finally gave her the terrible news he had received several days earlier. Their other asset in France, Émeraude, had had a massive stroke and was paralyzed.

A moment later Tony knocked and came into her office, holding a piece of paper. "Where's William? Do you know, Diedre?"

"He went to see the PM, who's in one of his underground bunkers, no doubt. I think there's something Mr. Churchill wants to tell him, probably a bit of vital information coming from C at MI6. Do you need him?"

"Not really. I'm afraid I've got awful news."

"About Étoile?" Diedre asked quickly, sitting up. "Is she dead?"

"I don't know the answer to that, but Émeraude has died from his stroke. A message came through from our **maquis** contact in Paris. There's nothing at Émeraude's flat that would incriminate or endanger his wife. Our chap wiped it clean. Destroyed anything that needed to disappear into oblivion."

"Everything?"

"Everything."

"Good. I'm afraid we're in for a bad dose of trouble, Tony. With these flying bombs, they're lethal, and what's more, no one knows when one is about to hit a target. They are silent. They're rotten things."

Tony nodded. "The V-1 flying bomb is the Nazi revenge for D-day. There's no other way they can retaliate at the moment. They are not going to send the Luftwaffe. Most of their planes were destroyed in Operation Barbarossa... the battle of Stalingrad did Hitler in, that I do believe."

"That's true. They're not on the run yet but they know they've met their match with our Yankee friends. All I can say is thank God the Americans are our allies. Anyway, I suppose the buzz bomb, as some are calling it, is their secret weapon. The Germans have had it up their sleeve, haven't they?"

"I believe so. It was developed at Peenemünde, and, trust me, we haven't seen anything yet.

The Allied landings in France have got them going. I bet you they'll pepper us with the buzz bombs. They still want to whack us hard."

"I know. The war isn't over yet, not by a long shot."

Cecily was worried about Miles. He looked so tired, and he had for a long time now. As they sat having a cup of coffee in her office at the shop in the Burlington Arcade, she said, "Something's worrying you, Miles. Please tell me what it is, darling."

He let out a deep sigh. "Nothing you can help me with, so why discuss it?"

"Oh, Miles, don't be silly. Sometimes talking things out helps."

"I'm worried about the Land Girls," he began and stopped. "What I mean is, not having any Land Girls. After the war. They'll all go back to their civilian jobs and I won't have any help."

"You'll have Harry back, but I see what you mean. A lot of our young men have been killed in the war, more from High Clough and Mowbray than Little Skell, but I understand why you're worried."

"The Land Girls have been just marvelous and we've built up our agricultural output. But with no one to till the land, so to speak, I'll be up a creek without a paddle."

"Well, the war's not over yet. I was talking to

Uncle Howard the other day, and he said that despite the tremendous success of the D-day landings, we've quite a while to go. We've got to conquer Italy as well as Germany. He gives it another year."

Miles frowned. "So long?"

"He said thereabouts, but he doesn't make those sorts of comments lightly."

"Actually, he's usually right."

"I've made a date for supper with Dulcie and James tonight. She's going to cook a chicken pot pie."

"I'm glad to hear it's not lamb. She's given me something of a complex about those little woolly creatures, and all because of Ophelia and Henry."

Cecily began to laugh. "I know. You don't eat lamb anymore. Anyway, I'm finished here for the day. Shall we walk home? It's such a lovely June evening."

When Miles saw the fire engine, the police cars, policemen, and Home Guard on South Audley Street, very close to South Street, instinctively he knew something was terribly wrong. And so did Cecily. She stopped suddenly and grabbed his hand. "Something's happened on South Street."

"It looks like it." As he spoke he tightened his grip on her hand and they ran as fast as they could. When they came around the corner of the street where they lived, they saw the dying embers of a fire, charred wood, rubble, and broken glass. The acrid smell of burning and the smoke made them cough.

Cecily staggered slightly, leaned against him. In a choked voice, she managed to say, "Our house? Where is our house?"

Miles was speechless for a moment. His house, which he had left in good order this morning, was gone. It had been turned into a pile of rubble. "Oh my God!" he cried, looking around.

One of the policemen hurried toward him, and then Miles noticed Mr. Clewes, their air raid warden, and beckoned to him.

Taking control of himself as best he could, Miles asked in a shaky voice, "What happened, Mr. Clewes? Do you know?"

The air raid warden nodded. "I'm sorry, Lord Mowbray, but your house got hit. By a flying bomb. One of the buzz bombs."

Cecily was clinging to Miles. She was shaking so much he had to put his arm around her to prop her up. "DeLacy!" she said through her tears. "DeLacy was in the house, and Laura. And Mrs. Wilkinson—" She broke off, unable to say another word.

The policeman said, "We got here first, Lord Mowbray, and then the fire brigade came.

There **were** three people in the house, as Lady Mowbray just said. They were taken to Middlesex Hospital. That's the emergency hospital for Mayfair. On Mortimer Street. We'll run you and Lady Mowbray over there if you wish. I don't see any cabs around."

"Thank you, Officer. That's very kind of you," Miles answered. "I really would appreciate it."

Once they arrived at the hospital and spoke to a receptionist, they were immediately shown into a waiting room. "I'll be back in a moment, Lord Mowbray," the woman said and disappeared.

The moment they were alone, Miles wrapped his arms around Cecily and held her very close to him. She was crying quietly and so was he. They both knew that none of them had survived. The house had been smashed to smithereens. No one could have lived through such an explosion.

When a doctor came into the waiting room, they both sat up straighter and did their best to find some composure. Miles stood up and went to shake hands with him.

"The police told me that my sister Lady DeLacy Ingham was brought here a little earlier. With Miss Laura Swann and Mrs. Wilkinson. They were in our house on South Street—" Miles stopped abruptly. He knew from the expression on the doctor's face that they were all dead.

"They didn't make it, did they?" he asked, barely able to speak. His face was ashen.

"I'm sorry, Lord Mowbray. So very sorry."

Sixty-three

They took DeLacy's body back to Cavendon and Laura Swann's body as well. Her brother Eric was their head butler now, after Gordon Lane had suffered a heart attack a few months before. He had taken a leave of absence to recover.

They buried DeLacy next to her father, and Laura was placed on the other side of the family cemetery, where so many Swanns had lain for over a hundred years. They mourned Laura and tried to comfort her brother Eric.

It was a sorrowful day for everyone, and the entire family knew it would take them a long time to recover from the loss of their lovely DeLacy. If ever. Gone from them so unexpectedly, so suddenly, and in such a violent way. Charlotte, in particular, leaned heavily on Charles's sister, Vanessa, who came from London with her husband, Richard, for the funeral. They had been close friends since their younger years. But as the matriarch of the Inghams now, Charlotte did her best to be brave, and stand tall, and she succeeded albeit with a heavy heart.

DeLacy's three sisters and Cecily were inconsolable for months and months afterward. But the war was still on, the Allies fighting their way across Europe, and they accepted that they had their duties and went about their business.

Christmas that year was quiet. Everyone arrived at Cavendon and made their best efforts because of the children. Daphne was managing her worry about the twins battling away in the Eighth Infantry Brigade, and every day she was thankful they were still alive.

Alicia got leave from the Red Cross and helped her mother to make Christmas Day work, and most especially for the younger children. But there was a sadness at Cavendon that seemed to permeate the house with gloom.

Harry came home just after the holidays, invalided out of the RAF. His station had been badly damaged by a series of the pilotless flying bombs, and one side of his body was peppered with shrapnel. After months in a military hospital, being treated for his wounds, he was able to return home.

Miles as well as Paloma, Cecily, Alice, and Walter were thrilled to have him back, and soon he was working alongside Miles running the estate. He also helped to cheer them along. Harry had always been a favorite of Charlotte's, and he was often at her side, comforting her. DeLacy's death had taken its toll.

The Inghams and the Swanns clung together more than ever, protecting each other, making sure they were safe and well, had everything they needed.

January 1945 came, and then February and March, and the news grew better and better. The whole country knew that they had the winning hand because of the Allied advances. They expected the war would end sometime that year. Hope prevailed, fed their belief that they would come out on top.

Diedre was optimistic, pushing back her worry about Canaris, knowing how much he was at risk within the Third Reich. She and William, and Tony as well, were baffled about Étoile's disappearance. Her body had never been found. Both men endeavored to comfort Diedre, who had taken this matter to heart. She loathed mysteries she could not solve and wanted to know Étoile's fate.

One morning in April, Daphne went into the conservatory earlier than usual, because she wanted to catch up with paperwork and household bills. As usual she picked up some of the newspapers from the hall stand before she went to her command post, as she called it.

Seating herself at her desk, she opened the **Daily Mail,** wanting to read Charlie's column before anything else. But she did not get beyond the front page, her attention caught by the glaring headline. In large letters was the word GENOCIDE.

Horror swept across her face as she read the names…**Dachau, Belsen, Buchenwald, Ohrdruf.** Death camps all over Germany. Millions of Jews and others murdered in cold blood. Heinous crimes…unspeakable cruelty and brutality.

As she turned the pages and stared at the pictures, she could hardly bear to look at them, yet forced herself. Daphne began to shake uncontrollably as she read on. It was mass murder on a gigantic scale. Hardly believable. The photographs stunned her, brought tears to her eyes. Half-naked people, living skeletons, staring out through barbed-wire fences, hollow eyed. More and more photographs in the other papers, the **Daily Express,** the **Daily Telegraph.** Gas ovens, piles and piles of skeletal bodies thrown in a great heap, mass graves. Torture chambers, experimental hospitals. The Nazi death machine revealed at last.

As the pictures grew more graphic she thought she was going to vomit. **How had they dared to do this?** And she answered herself at once. They had dared because they believed they would never be found out.

Still shaking, Daphne put her head down on her desk and wept. Finally, she found a handkerchief and dried her eyes, and eventually the shaking stopped.

Turning to the **Daily Mail** again, she found Charlie's story. He had been given a full page and it was her son who had written the story of this horrendous discovery.

It had been the first British and American troops to enter the country who had found these camps in western and eastern Germany. The Allied soldiers had been shocked, sickened, and stunned when they had entered the camps, and all of them had been appalled at such an atrocity. Some had been nauseated, as she was now, and had vomited. Men, women, and even little children had been victims of this systematic torture and death. Millions and millions killed for no reason.

When Hugo came in to see her a little later, he stood at the door staring at her, aware of her face as white as chalk, her tears. "Whatever's happened?" he asked, hurrying across the room to her.

Daphne stood up and went to him, leaned against him, holding him close. "Read the papers and then you'll understand. Those Nazi monsters created a death machine..."

Hugo held her away and nodded. "I heard a

rumor of something recently…about gas ovens and mass murder in the camps."

"Read the papers," Daphne said. "Read Charlie's story."

He did so, and when he looked at her his shock and horror was apparent. "They've got to answer for this. Those bloody heathens have to be punished."

"How?"

"We'll do it. The Allies will. Have no worries about that. Whatever it takes, this genocide will be dealt with. In the meantime, the whole world will know and they will want the Nazis to pay with their lives."

On Monday, May 7, 1945, at 2:41 A.M. exactly, General Alfred Jodl, the representative of the German High Command, and Grand Admiral Doenitz signed the act of unconditional surrender of all German land, sea, and air forces in Europe. The war with Germany was over. The Allies had won, just as Winston Churchill had predicted they would.

It was May 8. Victory Day in Europe.

There had never been a celebration like it. So everybody said. But who knew if that was really true. And who cared? The whole of Great Britain was rejoicing, and they did it in the streets from Land's End to John o' Groat's.

The Union Jack hanging out of every window in the country, in every village, town, and city, church bells ringing. People singing, clapping, laughing, crying, releasing their emotions pent up for years. With their Allies they had won the war. They were free. Bonfires burned on every street corner, an antidote to years of the blackout. Effigies of Hitler were burned, and the cheering and dancing never stopped.

Street parties flourished. The pubs were filled to overflowing. What better way to celebrate with their fellow countrymen and women. It was a national holiday and would be forever after. It was the commemoration of the destruction of the Third Reich, the most evil regime in the history of the world.

Diedre's heart was heavy as she dressed to go to the supper Dulcie and James were giving to celebrate their victory. Her sorrow was two-fold. She grieved for DeLacy, so missed and loved, and also for Canaris, their brave Valiant. He had been arrested, put in Flossenbürg prison, and hanged in April. The Third Reich had called him a traitor. But he was not, in her opinion. He had never been a Nazi. He was a true German of the old school. He had been revolted by the war Hitler had waged, and horrified by the atrocities. Valiant had done his duty to suit his own conscience and that was good enough for her.

Winston Churchill had called him "a courageous man," and C of MI6, also known as SIS, the Secret Intelligence Service, had echoed those sentiments. She truly believed Admiral Wilhelm Canaris had helped to change the course of the war and in Britain's favor.

This thought cheered her as she finished her makeup and got up from the dressing table. She was wearing the red dress Cecily had made for her prewedding party, and when William walked into their bedroom, he told her she looked beautiful. And she did.

Then minutes later they left for Eaton Square where Cecily and Miles were waiting for them with Dulcie and James.

Cecily and Diedre laughed when they greeted each other. Cecily wore a bright blue cocktail suit and Dulcie was in her best white silk frock. Dulcie joined in the laughter and cried, "My God, we represent the Union Jack. Why didn't we check with each other about what we were going to wear? But then we've done it before."

James said, "But I like going out with the Union Jack. It's definitely my flag of choice."

After toasting each other and the entire family, those present and those gone, the six of them left and walked to Whitehall. The streets were so full of people it was impossible to take a cab.

They went to the House of Commons, waiting

with the crowds for the prime minister. He had spoken to the nation on the radio at three in the afternoon, but they craved to hear more from this great leader whom they loved and who had brought them to victory, hard-won but truly honorable.

They waited a long time but eventually he appeared on the balcony of a government building. It was ten-thirty at night and he was wearing his beloved "siren suit" and he gave his famous "V for Victory" sign.

The crowd fell silent and a hush of reverence descended on the streets around them, filled with people.

"My dear friends," Churchill began, **"this is your hour. This is not victory of a party or of any class. It's a victory of the great British nation as a whole. We were the first, in this ancient island, to draw the sword against tyranny. After a while we were left all alone against the most tremendous military power that has been seen. We were all alone for a whole year. There we stood, alone. Did anyone want to give in?"** Churchill paused and in answer to this question the crowd roared, "No!" **"Were we down-hearted?"** the prime minister demanded. "No!" responded the thousands in one voice.

The prime minister said, **"The lights went out and the bombs came down. But every man,** woman, and child in the country had no thought of quitting the struggle. London can take it. So we came back after long months from the jaws of death, out of the mouth of hell, while all the world wondered. When shall the reputation and faith of this generation of English men and women fail? I say that in the long years to come not only will the people of this island but of the world, wherever the bird of freedom chirps in human hearts, look back to what we've done and they will say, 'do not despair, do not yield to violence and tyranny, march straight forward and die if need be—unconquered.' Now we have emerged from one deadly struggle—a terrible foe has been cast on the ground and awaits our judgment and our mercy."

Once he had finished speaking the crowds didn't want to let him go. They cheered and clapped and called his name. They sang "For He's a Jolly Good Fellow," and "Land of Hope and Glory." The prime minister finally waved and went inside, and the people slowly left.

The six Inghams returned to the Eaton Square flat, where they had a late supper, and rejoiced quietly among themselves. The following morning they all took the train to Cavendon to celebrate VE Day with Charlotte, Cecily's parents, Harry and Paloma, Vanessa, Richard,

Daphne, Hugo, Charlie, and Alicia, and all the other children. They were going to give a party that night in the village hall, and everyone from the three villages was invited. Daphne would have the party catered so that all the staff could join in to celebrate.

Cecily wanted to look nice tonight not only for herself and Miles, but for the villagers as well. She wanted to set an example, to show that the Inghams were going to soldier on.

It was also for her beloved DeLacy, her best friend throughout her life, except for a short time when they had quarreled. She missed her so much it was unbearable at times and hard to believe it had happened. Gone like that in a flash, killed by a Nazi silent pilotless bomb.

There were days when Cecily slipped up to the cemetery and sat at her grave. She talked to her sweet DeLacy, telling her what was happening here at Cavendon, telling her how much they loved her, missed her. How they would remember her always. DeLacy...so lovely, fragile at times, but always strong, always an Ingham woman standing tall.

She brought a towel to her face to stop the flood of tears, and knew she must get ready for the evening. Suddenly she heard Miles walking across the bedroom floor. When he saw her, he said, "Oh darling, don't. Don't. I miss her, too, but we must be strong, and we must go on. We've so much to do here."

Gently he took the towel away from her and held her in his arms for a few moments, soothing her. When they stood apart he smiled. "You look beautiful no matter what."

She gazed at him. His was the face she had loved all her life. His hair was now streaked with gray, and he was older and still looked tired, but he was fit and well, and that was what mattered to her most of all.

A short while later, wearing her favorite summer dress made of purple chiffon and with amethysts around her neck, Cecily took hold of his hand, and together they went downstairs to the library.

Everyone else was still upstairs dressing, and she led him onto the terrace. Together they stood looking out across the park to the lake where the two swans floated.

Turning to him, Cecily said, "Once, long ago, when everything was crumbling around us, we vowed to build it again. And that's what we must do once more. If we did it once, we can do it again. We can repair the damages of this war."

He laughed. "That's right. My lovely warrior woman. Who's going to stop us?"

She laughed with him. "Nobody. Because nobody **can** stop us. We're the indomitable

Inghams, with a bit of Swann thrown in. We're going to win again."

"That deserves a toast." Miles went inside and returned a moment later with two flutes of champagne.

Passing one to his wife, he clinked his glass to hers. "Here's to Cavendon, Ceci. We'll bring it back to life because we don't know any other way."

"Yes, we will, Miles, as long as we have each other."

"And we do," Miles said. "Forever."

Acknowledgments

Some years ago when I was planning the Cavendon series, I was well aware that this third book would have to encompass the Second World War because of the time span.

I wasn't too worried about the research I would have to do because I was lucky in having had a World War Two historian as the mentor of my book writing career, the late journalist and war correspondent Cornelius Ryan. His book **The Last Battle,** about the fall of Berlin, served me well when I was writing **Letter from a Stranger**.

This time around I knew I must go back to Connie's book **The Longest Day** in order to fully understand D-day again. I immediately discovered that the book is as vivid and moving as it was when it was first published. My husband had recently bought me **The D-Day 70th Anniversary Collector's Edition,** a coffee-table book full of photographs as well as the text of the original book. Those photographs of

D-day boggle the mind, and the text is extra-ordinary in its detail. No wonder the French awarded Connie the Legion of Honor in 1970 for his books about the war.

Since **The Cavendon Luck** was covering the entire six years of the war, I needed to read many other books as well. I owe a debt of gratitude to those other authors who put pen to paper to tell various aspects of the conflict. Some of these are **The Storm of War** by Andrew Roberts, **Their Finest Hour: The Battle of Britain Remembered** by Richard Collier and Philip Kaplan, and **Dunkirk** by Hugh Sebag-Montefiore.

Of course, it is impossible to write about the Second World War without bringing to the fore Winston Churchill, and although I know a great deal about him, I did go back to certain books to refresh my memory. I gained new insight into this great man from rereading large chunks of **Churchill** by Roy Jenkins, and **The Churchill Factor** by Boris Johnson gave me a very modern look at him. **Blood, Toil, Tears and Sweat: The Great Speeches by Winston Churchill** edited by David Cannadine brought to life those extraordinary speeches and his gift for oratory that so moved and inspired people, as did **Never Give In**! edited by his grandson Winston S. Churchill.

I have always been fascinated by Admiral

Wilhelm Canaris, head of German military intelligence, and the role he played in helping Britain during those dangerous years. **Master Spy** by Ian Colvin, the first book written about Canaris, was helpful, and I gained new knowledge from **Hitler's Spy Chief** by Richard Bassett. Andrew Morton's book **17 Carnations** took me into the social world of Berlin in the late 1930s and revealed much about Hitler's attitude toward the British aristocracy and his admiration of MI6.

Now I must mention a most revealing book about the Vatican and Pope Pius the Twelfth. The author Mark Riebling, who wrote **Church of Spies,** informed me about the pope's secret war against Hitler, and how he saved the Jews of Rome. Fascinating reading for me since he mentions Canaris as well.

A Force to Be Reckoned With: **A History of the Women's Institute** by Jane Robinson and **Jambusters** by Julie Summers bring to life the enormous work the ordinary women of Britian did during the war. They practically fed the entire country, making millions of jars of jam, bottling fruit and vegetables, and tending to allotments where those vegetables were grown.

The government gave them sugar to make the jam, which went to the empty shops. They knitted scarves, balaclava helmets, and gloves for the troops and took in evacuee children in a scheme known as Pied Piper, providing them homes after theirs were destroyed by the bombing of our big cities. And working alongside these women from the WI were the energetic Land Army girls. I hope I have managed to bring all this to life in my own book.

Hollywood in the late thirties was very different from how it is today, and to get a sense of those years I spoke at length to my friend Anne Edwards, the biographer, novelist, and screenwriter. She grew up there and her uncle was Dave Chasen, the owner of the famous restaurant.

Anne's biography of Vivien Leigh took me into 1939, when **Gone with the Wind** was being made, as did **Long Live the King,** the biography of Clark Gable by Lyn Tornabene. **David O. Selznick's Hollywood** by Ronald Haver also gave me a wonderful view of those years, as did **An Empire of Their Own** by Neal Gabler. This author explains how the European Jews who emigrated to America created Hollywood, and it is full of wonderful stories.

From all this research has come the second half of **The Cavendon Luck,** in which I cover the evacuation of Dunkirk, when civilian men were called to rescue the British troops stranded on the beaches. They left in anything that sailed, armed only with their mighty hearts and great courage. There is the Battle of Britain, fought in the skies by young airmen no older than twenty, single, and not even finished with their formal education. Of them Churchill said, "Never have so many owed so much to so few." As I wrote about the Blitz of London and D-day I was constantly reminded how extraordinarily brave everyone was. Not only those in the armed services but civilians as well. Those horrific years demanded it, I believe, and everyone stood up to be counted.

After France surrendered, Britain stood alone for a year. And then, because of Winston Churchill's pleas to President Roosevelt, Lend-Lease was created, and America began to send food and ammunitions to Britain. After Japan attacked Pearl Harbor and destroyed three-quarters of America's Pacific Fleet, President Roosevelt declared war on Japan, and then on Germany. They had joined Britain in the fight, and if America had not become Britain's ally I'm not sure what would have happened. As we know we won the war together.

I owe thanks to a number of people who were involved in the writing of this book. Lonnie Ostrow of Bradford Enterprises helps in many different ways. Most especially, he is a whiz at the computer and somehow manages to get all of my changes and edits onto the manuscript with good humor and usually under a lot of pressure. I would like to thank Linda Sullivan of

WordSmart for producing a perfectly typed script, without typos!

My editor at St. Martin's Press, Sr. Vice President and Publisher Jennifer Enderlin, is a great sounding board, and I appreciate her ideas and her enormous enthusiasm for my books. Many thanks to Jennifer; her assistant, Caitlin Dareff; and the rest of Jennifer's team. Thanks are also due to Sally Richardson, President and Publisher of St. Martin's Press.

I am always thanking my husband last when really I should be thanking him first. Bob is the mainstay of my life and has never stopped encouraging me to write and given me the space to do so. He is wonderful the way he puts up with a wife constantly sitting alone in a room writing and he does so with humor and love. But when he feels it's necessary, he comes in and makes me close shop, and I do. I am lucky to have such an understanding husband.

My female friends are always telling me that, and I now realize I must thank all of them for being so nice when I won't make dates or cancel lunches and dinners because of my deadlines. You all know who you are and that I love you.